RUSHING PASSIONS

She's almost beautiful when she's angry . . . .
 Seated only inches away from Cynthia, Garrett couldn't control this strange attraction to her. And when the carriage made its swift turn, the momentum pulled him even closer. He reached out and touched her hand. She drew away. He put his arm about her. She shivered. Finally, he turned her towards him. Her eyes showed great anger, but before she could protest, his lips were upon hers.
 Cynthia was at once terrified and filled with wonder. Garrett, for all his brutal words, was suddenly gentle. Without conscious thought, she brought her arms about his neck—as the carriage continued in a rush . . . .

THE BEST IN HISTORICAL ROMANCE

PASSION'S RAPTURE (912, $3.50)
by Penelope Neri
Through a series of misfortunes, an English beauty becomes the captive of the very man who ruined her life. By day she rages against her imprisonment—but by night, she's in passion's thrall!

JASMINE PARADISE (1170, $3.75)
by Penelope Neri
When Heath sets his eyes on the lovely Sarah, the beauty of the tropics pales in comparison. And he's soon intoxicated with the honeyed nectar of her full lips. Together, they explore the paradise . . . of love.

SILKEN RAPTURE (1172, $3.50)
by Cassie Edwards
Young, sultry Glenda was innocent of love when she met handsome Read deBaulieu. For two days they revelled in fiery desire only to part—and then learn they were hopelessly bound in a web of SILKEN RAPTURE.

FORBIDDEN EMBRACE (1105, $3.50)
by Cassie Edwards
Serena was a Yankee nurse and Wesley was a Confederate soldier. And Serena knew it was wrong—but Wesley was a master of temptation. Tomorrow he would be gone and she would be left with only memories of their FORBIDDEN EMBRACE.

PORTRAIT OF DESIRE (1003, $3.50)
by Cassie Edwards
As Nicholas's brush stroked the lines of Jennifer's full, sensuous mouth and the curves of her soft, feminine shape, he came to feel that he was touching every part of her that he painted. Soon, lips sought lips, heart sought heart, and they came together in a wild storm of passion. . . .

Available wherever paperbacks are sold, or order direct from the Publisher. Send cover price plus 50¢ per copy for mailing and handling to Zebra Books, 475 Park Avenue South, New York, N.Y. 10016. DO NOT SEND CASH.

BY WANZA J. CAMPBELL

ZEBRA BOOKS
KENSINGTON PUBLISHING CORP.

ZEBRA BOOKS

are published by

KENSINGTON PUBLISHING CORP.
475 Park Avenue South
New York, N.Y. 10016

Copyright © 1983 by Wanza J. Campbell

All rights reserved. No part of this book may be reproduced in any form or by any means without the prior written consent of the publisher, excepting brief quotes used in reviews.

Printed in the United States of America

This book is dedicated to the members of the "5:30 Writers Group" and to my family, without any of whom it might never have been.

One

The coach clattered over the cobblestones, jostling its passengers. A cool summer breeze came through the open windows, gently raising tendrils of hair on the girl's temples. She dabbed at her neck with a handkerchief, then tucked the cloth into the sleeve of her gown and raised her chin a bit defiantly. I won't show him I'm afraid, she vowed.

"Where are we going?" she asked, wondering if her voice sounded a little too demanding.

Walter Fawley gazed at his wife sullenly, then looked out the window.

Cynthia suspected where they were going, but hoped it wasn't so. Does he really hate me so much? she asked herself.

Marriage to Walter Fawley had been a nightmare. She was only sixteen when her father literally sold her to Walter to pay off gambling debts and keep the family lands intact. But fate dealt a swift blow to her father. He was killed less than two hours after the wedding while celebrating in the streets of London. She always suspected Walter had a hand in his death, but there was no way of proving it.

Though Walter was near her father's age, there was nothing fatherly about him. She feared him from the very beginning. Their wedding night had been a night of horrors. She knew if she didn't submit physically Walter could do anything he wished to her. That was the law—not in so many words, she was sure, but still the law. Though he tried to be gentle, Walter's desires by far exceeded his ability and he forced her to demean herself. When she shrank from his touch he beat her, then slobbered kisses over her body whining how sorry he was. When his desire had been sated in the early dawn, she was finally left alone, but beating followed beating each time he approached her to satisfy himself until she felt like little more than an animal.

She shuddered as she thought about it. Had it really been only two years? She felt older. She kept trying to convince herself nothing could be worse than the hell she had lived in the past two years, yet she did not know what to expect from Walter. She was even learning there were times he could be avoided entirely.

She had little doubt of their destination. Fear gripped her. Tears stung the back of her eyes, but she was determined not to show any fear or softness to this man she called husband. She wished no further abuse at his hand.

He had left her entirely alone the past six weeks. There had been no beatings or degradations. She had begun to believe there was a God after all. Her bruises had healed. She had even gained weight which her figure needed. Cynthia knew she could not be considered a beauty and did not try to tell herself otherwise, but she had a pleasing figure and her recent weight gain had only rounded and softened it.

She had seen her girlish awkwardness leave with her bruises and in its place stood a lithe young woman who possessed a new self-awareness. Petite by most standards, sometimes called dainty, she barely came to the shoulders of many of the men she knew. She realized her long, blond hair and expressive, green eyes were her most attractive features and had often been complimented on both. She personally felt her eyes were set a little too far apart, and her father had always teased her about her too-short nose covered with a light spray of freckles, but her mouth, she thought, was just right and when she smiled, showing even white teeth, it brought a glow to her entire face. Smiling was something Cynthia had been doing more of these past weeks because the changes that had come about made her feel good about herself for the first time in a very long time.

Walter had seen the changes, too. She knew by the hungry look in his eyes, but he did not come near her. She wondered why, but decided he was trying to change—he wanted to make something of their marriage after all. During the last week, she had even stopped hating him a little and her revulsion of him was beginning to be replaced by pity. When he told her he had a surprise for her this evening and she was to dress in her finest gown, she obeyed, even became slightly exhilarated, but grew suspicious when he would tell her nothing of their destination. He grew surly when she asked again just as they were stepping into the coach.

The coach lurched suddenly and Cynthia was aware they had left the cobblestone streets behind. It can't be much further, she thought.

"Do you really hate me so much?"

"Hate you?" he asked as if surprised. "No, I don't hate you, my dear. I've never hated you." He paused a moment, then with a wistful look in his eyes continued. "I once thought I loved you. I considered you quite worthy to be the mother of my children." In an instant his mood changed. He glared at her. "But your utter revulsion to lovemaking and your pity for me of late makes life with you quite out of the question, Cynthia. Surely you can see that."

"Then we *are* going to the cattle market. You're going to sell me."

"Yes, my dear. Should you resist, I warn you, you will be sorry."

"I won't resist. Nothing could be worse than the last two years under your roof." She could see the remark stung. "But I don't think I need fear further abuse. It's taken far too much will for you to leave me alone these past weeks only to beat me now and lower your selling price."

"I admire your courage, my dear. I always have. There are ways, though, so the marks won't show." He paused and Cynthia decided he was trying to frighten her. She refused to let him. He continued. "You will one day be a beauty, but I pity the man who buys you to share his bed. The man who bids on you will do so because you look like a woman who enjoys life. I dare say he will find you as cold as the stones in the London Bridge."

"If I'm cold, it's your doing," she said, feeling braver.

Walter lapsed into silence but Cynthia could see the muscles working in his jaws. He never could hide his anger well, she thought.

She turned her attention out the window. Trying to imagine what lay ahead, she found her brain was numb with fear. She forced back tears and struggled for control. I will not become hysterical, she told herself. I must be strong.

Cynthia had learned strength in the years following her mother's untimely death. She had to contend with her father's frequent bouts with alcohol while his gambling stripped the home she loved of its finery. Now, because her father had thought by marrying her off to Walter he would not only cancel a gambling debt, but would also provide for her future, Walter had that home. Cynthia grimaced whenever she thought about the turn of events that put her and all her family's possessions into the hands of Walter Fawley.

Some time later she was aware of their arrival at the cattle market. Her nostrils were assailed by a terrible stench. She retrieved the handkerchief from her sleeve and pressed it to her nose. The coach stopped. Walter stepped down and walked away. Cynthia leaned her head against the smooth leather seat and closed her eyes. He's really going to do it. He really does hate me. Then she realized he didn't hate her—he had no feeling for her at all. She was simply a property to be used, then sold at the best price. She felt sure he had married her with this very purpose in mind. Over the past two years, he had only been waiting for her to develop from an awkward child into a woman. Hatred for him welled in her breast. She bit her lip to keep from crying. I will not show any weakness. I will not. It would only add to his delight.

She heard him returning. He opened the door and offered his hand as though they had just arrived at a grand ball.

"Keep your hands off me," she hissed through clenched teeth.

"As you wish, my dear." He stepped aside so she could alight.

She did so with considerable difficulty. Her knees were so weak she felt sure they would give way at any moment. Once on the ground, she held her head high and looked straight ahead. She found it hard to believe the sights in front of her. Everywhere, all she could see were cattle pens. And such a smell! She didn't know what she had expected to find at a cattle market, but it certainly hadn't been what she now looked upon. She pressed the handkerchief tighter to her face. It did no good.

She lowered her hand and looked at Walter in horror as he came toward her with a leather thong. Her instinct was to pull away but she stood very still and glared at him as he slipped it about her waist. She knew this was meant to debase her further as well as show legal possession.

"Really, Walter, that's not necessary. I'll come willingly."

"I'm sure you would, my dear, but afterwards, I won't have anyone saying the sale was not legal. I'm sure your buyer would have reason to want out of a badly made deal."

Cynthia raised her chin higher as tears formed in her eyes. Why did he feel the need to be cruel to her? She had never, never done anything to him. She choked back the tears. She would not cry in front of him.

"Come, my dear. We have to register for the sale," Walter said as he gave a tug on the leather thong.

Cynthia was only vaguely aware of her surroundings as Walter led her through a gate and spoke with a man she assumed to be the auctioneer. She was weighed and checked as to her general state of health and was even forced to open her mouth so they might check her teeth. She had heard of sales such as this—they weren't uncommon in London—but she had never, in her wildest imaginings, dreamed she would be a part of such a degrading experience. Had she believed such cruelty was in Walter, she would have killed herself long ago.

She began to talk to herself. Look on the bright side, she said. You might come out of this ahead. It's hard to believe there is another man as cruel and perverted as Walter. Surely, there is none worse.

Through the haze surrounding her brain, she could see other women who were brought here for the same reason. There were six of them altogether and a great crowd of men.

Walter pushed her in among the other women, but held tightly onto the thong. The women were talking excitedly among themselves as though they were embarking on some great adventure. As Cynthia sidled closer, the talking stopped and all eyes turned to her. She looked from one face to another, waiting for some sort of recognition. Finally, one of the older women spoke loudly.

"Well, now, looks as though her ladyship done got herself caught in the arms of her lover boy."

Cynthia didn't know what to make of this accusation. They surely couldn't mean her. She had never had an opportunity to be unfaithful to Walter, much less wanted to, and she knew none of these women. How could they accuse her of such a thing?

They started to circle around her, some fingering her gown.

"She'll bring a pretty penny, she will."

"Aye," agreed another. "She'll not be sold by weight. There'll be out an' out biddin' for this un."

"Don't know that there's many gentlemen in this crowd what can afford the likes of her, though."

"You don't understand. . . ." Cynthia cried.

"My, my, dresses like a lady, talks like a lady, but down underneath, nothin' but a 'ore," spat one as she made grotesque imitations of what she thought a lady to be.

"I . . . I'm not a . . . a . . . one of those," cried Cynthia, almost on the verge of tears. "Have you no sympathy? Aren't we all in this together?"

"Sure we is, dearie," said another. "Only me and my man agreed on this sale. I'd be wagerin' you and yours had no such agreement."

"Well, no, he only wants . . ."

"He wants a wife what'll be faithful to him," chortled another. "That's what he wants. Look at the nice gentleman over there now. Even had to tie you for fear you'd wander."

"Maybe she'll get a strong man what beats her when she strays. That's what some of these fine ladies need, it is. Let 'em know a man cares."

Cynthia shouldered her way out of the circle and went to stand closer to Walter. He had obviously heard the chiding of the women, for a smile played at the corners of his mouth.

"What, my dear? You don't find me as loathsome as usual this evening?"

"How can you enjoy such cruelty? You knew what it would be like for me. If you wanted to sell me, why couldn't you have made a private deal as I've heard others have done?"

"A private deal? Tut, tut, Cynthia. I should have missed the fun then. Besides, this way I will likely get more for you. Especially should you catch certain fancies."

Cynthia turned her back on him. She stood alone in her misery. Out of the corner of her eye she surveyed the sea of men. Many were leering at her. Some were poking their companions, laughing and pointing. She knew they were laughing at her. Good lord, did all these people believe the same of her? She knew instantly that they did. In their eyes, she was a faithless wife, a harlot, and poor, poor Walter was the cuckold. But why her? Why not the other women? Why were they jeering at her?

Then, for the first time, she noticed how the others were dressed and remembered the sounds of their voices. She was the only lady of class here—only no one believed she was a lady. Walter had meant it this way. How she hated him!

Finally the sale began. Cynthia watched with interest as the other women stood up on a platform one by one. The sales were swiftly made final. There was not the bidding she had expected. That was what the woman had been saying about the sales being agreed upon. Apparently, the buyer was a party to the agreement and all were happy with the outcome. Cynthia watched with amazement as the women went from old husbands to new ones as soon as the papers were signed and set with a seal. All seemed to be as excited as new brides, as indeed they were.

She was the last. When it came her turn, Cynthia turned pleading eyes to Walter. When she saw the sneer on his face, however, she squared her shoulders and walked to the platform. I won't beg, she told herself. I surely will come out of this for the better.

Once on the platform she could clearly see the faces of the men. At first, such close scrutiny caused her to be embarrassed. She could feel the blood rising in her cheeks. An instant later, she realized that within a short time she would be compelled to lie with one of these men as his wife . . . or worse, she could be sold to the owner of a . . . a . . . she couldn't think about it. All color drained from her face. Within seconds she felt as though the blood had rushed from her entire body. She began to tremble with fright. She looked to Walter who was standing below the platform holding onto the leather thong. The look of greed on his face astonished her. For a moment she imagined him to be an animal licking its chops hungrily just before devouring its prey.

Lost in disbelief, she raised her head again to the swarm in front of her. All the men seemed to be undressing her with their eyes. Some were old and dirty and toothless. Some were dressed in the finery of gentlemen, but she knew no real gentleman would be here. Judging from their clothing, the majority were workers and farmers. She prayed that she might be bought by one of the latter. Of all the participants at this spectacle, they looked to be the least horrifying. But she knew it wouldn't happen. She doubted those men had the money Walter was looking for. They were here only for the sport.

The bidding had just begun when all of a sudden there was a great commotion in the rear of the crowd. Cynthia's eyes were drawn to the sound. She couldn't believe what she was seeing. Coming through the crowd of men at great speed was a group of women slinging weighted socks. Men were falling before them like flies. Some fled only to be met and assaulted by other groups of women wielding clubs and stones.

She felt a tug at her waist. She was pulled from the platform by Walter and fell on all fours in the dirt.

"Get up, Cynthia. We'll return at a better time."

Cynthia arose and dusted herself off. She noticed the thong was held tightly in Walter's hand, but was not wrapped around it. "Oh, no, we won't!" she shouted as she jerked the thong free and ran towards the other women. When she felt it safe to stop, she removed the strip of leather from about her waist then reached down and picked up the biggest stone she could see. It wasn't very large, but nevertheless she felt armed. She glanced over her shoulder for Walter. When she saw no sign of him, she rushed headlong into the melee.

When the fight began, Garrett Carver and his companion parted company to make their own ways toward their separate coaches. It had never occurred to him that something of this sort took place at a cattle market. He had been totally unprepared for anything like a wife sale—a little aghast that men so unconcernedly sold their mates. He was painfully reminded of slave auctions he had attended.

He watched the first two women being auctioned off with some interest, then when he noted that it seemed to be an agreeable affair for all involved, he returned to the business at hand. He was relieved it was almost finished. He would soon head home. For the past few weeks he had traveled the length and breadth of England speaking privately, and for the most part surreptitiously, to knowledgeable men about the Stamp Act that had been imposed upon the American colonists. Last week he had traveled across the channel to meet with John Wilkes who was under self-imposed exile in France, and just yesterday he had been honored and awed by Benjamin Franklin, the American statesman.

The so-called Sugar Act, imposing a tax on molasses, had been bad enough, but when it was followed close behind by the proclamation prohibiting immigration west of the Alleghenies and then the Stamp Act, the roar heard in the colonies had been deafening. The colonists felt that Parliament had no right to impose such tariffs and regulations upon them since they were not represented and Garrett was trying to ascertain the support the colonists had among the English.

His companion today had obviously picked the meeting place because of the inconspicuousness of a crowd; just as obviously the warring women had not been expected. He silently sided with the fair gender, but had neither the intention nor the time to get involved.

He side-stepped two women slinging stockings with stones in them and tripped a third old biddy bearing down on him with a club. Then he saw her. She looked younger than the rest and she was trying to beat her way through the crowd with her bare hands. No, she held a stone in one hand. She's dressed quite prettily for such an adventure, he thought, and surmised she must be a prostitute. But she didn't have the look of a whore about her and he didn't think a professional would be liable to help wives—bad for their business. Most probably a young matron who had been convinced of the righteousness of the cause. He saw her go down and involuntarily moved through the crowd in her general direction.

Someone hit her on the side of the head and Cynthia buckled to her knees, tasting blood in her mouth. She sat there dazed for a moment, spitting blood. Then she realized her hand holding the stone was throbbing. She looked at it as though it belonged to someone else. It was badly bruised and bleeding. Remembering the handkerchief in her sleeve, she pulled it out, placed the stone in its center and gathered the four corners into her bruised hand. Then, shaking her head to clear it, she scrambled to her feet and rejoined the battle.

He saw her rise again a little to his left and unwittingly corrected his course. She now had something white in her hand. It looked even more menacing. He realized she had wrapped her stone in some sort of cloth.

The first blow she dealt with her improved weapon was staggering. A man collapsed at her feet. She knelt to hit him again. Her upraised arm was stopped in midair by a strong hand on her wrist. She looked up fully expecting to see Walter, but instead looked into the clearest blue eyes she had ever seen. An odd combination, she thought fleetingly—blue eyes with dark hair and complexion.

"Don't kill him," he said. "You don't want to be hanged as a murderess."

"Let me go," she sobbed, struggling in vain. "Let me go!"

"You are a little wildcat, aren't you?" He laughed, showing even white teeth, as he pulled her to her feet. "Come, the battle is fought. You'd best get out of here before the soldiers arrive."

The battle moved away from them. Cynthia was still struggling as he pulled her up. He now held fast to both wrists. She was momentarily surprised by his height, her head just came even with his broad chest. Still, she tried to kick him, but he held her at arms length and, throwing his dark head back, laughed again. She looked at him with fire in her eyes and, much to her own dismay, spat in his face.

"Why, you little . . ." he growled and hit her. Her head reeled and as she fell, he let go of her. She lay in a heap and could feel dirt and blood mingled at the corner of her mouth. She raised up to wipe it away. The world spun crazily around her. She could feel herself sinking into darkness.

He knelt in the dirt beside her to see how badly she was hurt. The man she had hit came to and scrambled away. "Damn," he quietly cursed himself for having hit her, even though he knew it had only been reaction. Seeing her lying so helpless, she looked like such a little mite of a thing.

Not knowing what else to do, he carefully picked her up and carried her across the now-deserted auction arena toward his coach. Past the open area, he looked back once, then increased his pace.

He found the coach where he had left it, behind one of the barns. The huge man standing by the horses visibly relaxed when he came into view.

"Well, now, lookey what you went and found."

"Get us out of here, Jacob," he snarled. "There are redcoats everywhere!"

The big man's expression quickly changed from one of taunting to one of fear and concern as he hastened to open the door so the other might climb in more easily with his burden. Garrett nestled her to his shoulder as the coach lumbered forward.

Two

Cynthia opened her eyes with a start. Where was she? How long had she been sleeping? She closed her eyes. She felt dazed. Where was Walter? She opened her eyes, more slowly this time, and found herself half-sitting, half-lying in the corner of a coach that wasn't Walter's. She tried to sit up and found her body would not cooperate. Her hand went to her pounding head. The movement caused it to throb. Raising her hand to faint light coming through the window from the side lamps, she looked at it. There was dirt and dried blood covering her hand and arm. The sleeve of her gown had been torn away. In the dim light she could see the white of her petticoats showing through rents in her gown.

She leaned her head back and remembered the events of the evening, recalling the sale and shuddering at the thought of it. She closed her eyes and once again could see the women storming through the sea of men. She remembered freeing herself and running to join the fight. Beyond that confusion reigned. How had she gotten into this coach? Whose coach was it? Where was she?

She looked out the window opposite her. All that could be seen were trees. With great effort, she raised herself to see out the window nearest her. The coach was stopped before some sort of inn. Two men were standing by the doorway talking. The shorter of the two was holding a torch. She sank back in the seat, her body feeling every move. She had no sooner settled, however, when she jerked upright again. She knew the taller of the men. She knew she knew him, but from where?

As she sat there staring, dumbfounded, the taller of the men turned toward the coach and, in the blaze of torchlight, she remembered where she had seen him. There was no mistaking that laughing face, that tall, lean frame, those broad shoulders. She shrank back into the corner hoping he hadn't seen her.

A moment later, she heard him giving directions to the driver. Then he was opening the door on her side of the coach.

"Well, I see you're awake. Come, let me help you out. We're staying here for the night."

"What do you mean staying here . . . for the night?" Having spoken for the first time, Cynthia was reminded of the cuts on her face. Her mouth felt sore and swollen. She remembered how he had struck her.

"Just what I said, but you needn't worry about your reputation or appearance. I told the innkeeper you're my cousin and we were accosted by road bandits. As you can see, I've ripped one of my best shirts and muddied my trousers to protect your reputation. Now, come before I drag you out."

"If you think for one minute I'm going to spend the night in your company, you're sadly mistaken, Mister . . . Mister . . . whatever your name is."

"My name isn't important, and to see that your reputation is fully protected, I have engaged two rooms for the night."

"Thank you for your concern, but I should be home. I . . . I . . ." Then Cynthia remembered she had no place to go. She could not and would not go back to Walter and if she went to any of their friends, he would be sure to find her. She held her hand out and tried to smile. "Very well, sir."

She let him help her down. He practically had to carry her into the inn. She hadn't realized how very tired and sore she really was. The innkeeper, the man she had seen earlier in the doorway, met them and showed them to their rooms. Once inside hers, Cynthia pushed the bolt, then sank onto the bed. Her eyes surveyed the room. Aside from the bed, there was a small table and two benches. She had only stayed in an inn once before. It had been decent enough—even charming—she recalled, but overall there were foul stories to be heard about inns. She decided the room looked clean and someone had had the foresight to open the window to the summer breeze. She lay back on the bed, found it to be slightly lumpy, but noticed the clean smell of the bedclothes. She was almost asleep when she heard a rap on her door. She bolted up.

"Who is it?"

"It's your dear cousin. Would your ladyship care for a bath?"

Cynthia couldn't believe it. A bath! She sprang for the door, then stopped. "Is anyone with you?"

"But of course, my dear. You don't think I could carry tub and water all by myself, do you?"

She stood in the middle of the room undecided if she should open the door. But he could get in anyway if he wanted, she reasoned, recalling the fury with which he had struck her. She didn't think he was the sort of man to be stopped by a bolted door. Still, he said he wasn't alone. Could he be trusted?

"Come, cousin, open the door unless, of course, you don't feel you need a bath."

Cynthia heard girlish giggles. So he wasn't alone.

But if she let him in, then what? She stood a moment longer, but the thought of a bath won her over. She opened the door a crack and peered out. He stood there smiling, a large wooden tub in tow. Behind him were two girls carrying buckets of steaming water. She stood aside to let them enter. He placed the tub in the middle of the room.

"Such a shame, the highwaymen and all," he tsked as the girls poured the water. "All your fine things taken. One of the girls here has a gown you can wear. About your size I would say." He held it up for inspection.

"Thank you," Cynthia said to the girls as they left for more water. Then she turned to her protector. "Where are we? What is this place? Who . . ."

"You mean you don't know where you are?" he asked, looking into the hallway.

"It's only that I fell asleep," she said, following his lead, but once the door was closed, she turned on him. "You know damned good and well I don't know where I am. I don't know who you are and I don't know why I'm here with you."

"Woking. You're just outside Woking. Close to London. And swearing doesn't become you, little one."

"But why? What's all this nonsense about road bandits? You surely don't expect these people to believe that bandits did this to me." She spread her hands and turned around so he could fully appreciate her dishevelment.

"People will believe anything if they are paid enough," he said languidly as he lounged on the bed.

Cynthia knew that was true. She had seen Walter maneuver people to his advantage with money.

"Why didn't you leave me in London? Why are we here?"

24

"I was on my way to Brighton."

"Brighton?"

"Perhaps you know it as Brightelmstone." He saw recognition in her eyes. "As I said, I was on my way to Brighton when I stopped at the cattle market to ... ah, for business reasons. I never dreamed I would get caught up in such a scrap. You women were surely steamed."

He doesn't recognize me, she thought fleetingly, then said, "It was a wife sale. Men were there to buy and sell wives. And just why were you there? I suppose you need a wife—or perhaps no longer need a wife."

"Sorry to disappoint you, but I was there neither to buy nor sell a wife. I had other business."

"Most women find it an abominable practice," she continued as though he hadn't spoken. "The law should be changed."

"Well, be that as it may, I couldn't very well let you kill that poor fellow you were beating on, now could I? Afterward, I couldn't just leave you there to be arrested. I doubt prison would suit you."

"Well, thank you for your concern, but if you hadn't knocked the daylights out of me, I should have been able to leave by myself."

"Possibly, but I think you would have killed that ..." There was a rap on the door.

Cynthia let the girls in. As they poured the water into the tub, she watched, thinking how delightful it was going to be to sink into the warm, steamy water.

"By the way," he said. "I've ordered food and drink for when you're more presentable. You must be starving."

"Yes, I am," Cynthia said as she held the door open for the girls. She stood waiting for him to also depart. He arose and walked toward her. He stopped at the doorway.

"What's your name, little one?" he asked softly.

"Cynthia, Cynthia Fa . . Faucieau," she lied, using her mother's maiden name.

"French?"

"Only part. And you, who are you?"

"I'll tell you later," he promised. Then he departed, leaving Cynthia feeling shaken. She bolted the door and stood trembling, wondering at the power she had just felt from this man whose name she didn't even know. Then she realized that with her silence she had just agreed to have dinner with him. The tete-a-tete was obviously to be in her room. She couldn't very well traverse the hallway in a nightgown. I just won't let him in, she decided. Having settled that, she turned to her bath. It beckoned and she longed for the feel of the clean gown against her skin.

When he heard the bolt slide into place, Garrett strode down the hall to his own room. Loud, boisterous noises filtered up the open stairway from the taproom below. He hoped the locals would make an early night of it. He knocked their signal on the door. It was opened slowly, then wider to admit him when he was recognized.

"Thanks, Jacob. Have you eaten yet?"

"Just finished. Who is she?" His friend was obviously much concerned.

"She says her name is Faucieau. I believe her. I also believe she's just what she appears to be—a young girl who got caught up in the ruckus."

"Then you don't think? . . ."

"No, but I'm having supper with her shortly. She's bathing just now. I'm going to change."

He walked across to his bag then turned to his friend. "Ease off, Jacob. You worry too much."

"But whatcha gonna do with her?"

"Send her back home, of course, first thing in the morning."

Cynthia eased herself into the large tub and let the warm water soothe her battered body. She lay her head back and thought of how often she had repeated this ritual in Walter's house. She recalled the number of times she had tried to scrub the feel of him from her body. The thought that she wasn't really so bad off now lifted her spirits. She examined her glistening body and found, aside from slight cuts on her hands and an overall soreness, she wasn't badly bruised. Not like when Walter . . . but she wouldn't think about that. She wanted to push such thoughts from her mind. If only he doesn't find me, she silently prayed. I won't think about that either, she told herself with determination.

She sat up. "But what am I going to do?" The sound of her own voice startled her. She glanced around, feeling foolish. She slid back under the water and gently scrubbed her face, arms and hands. She even gave in to impulse and washed her long, blond hair which was tangled and matted with dirt. At least I'm safe for the night, she told herself. I have a roof over my head. I'll think of the rest after a good night's sleep.

Her thoughts strayed until, disturbingly, she found she was thinking of him. He is quite the handsomest man I've ever seen, she thought. Scolding herself, she sat upright and scrubbed, but couldn't rid herself of his image. She could almost see those laughing, blue eyes and the dark hair just curling over his collar. The thought of his tall, muscular body made her tingle. She got out of the tub and furiously began to dry herself.

"Stupid," she said aloud. "Men want only one

thing from a woman and I've had my fill of such dirty, degrading animalism."

Only after she had toweled herself dry from head to foot and slipped into the lightweight summer gown did Cynthia feel human again. She wished she had a comb and looking glass. She could see a dim reflection of herself in the window, but was unable to see how badly her face was bruised and if it was cut. She knew the inside of her mouth was cut, but it was no longer bleeding. Her hand was still oozing in spots and she longed for something with which to bind it. She looked at her discarded petticoats, found some clean spots about halfway up the skirt of one and ripped it into strips which she bound around her injured hand. Next she examined the gown in which she had taken such care to dress only a few hours before. It was beyond redemption, she decided and dropped it in a corner. Then, remembering she had no other clothes, she reclaimed it and carried it to the light for closer inspection. Some of the rips were large. There were spatters of blood on it, but all the pieces were there. If only she had a needle and thread. She was sitting, wondering how she might make the necessary repairs when he knocked on the door. The knock set her to trembling.

"Yes?" She hoped he couldn't detect the fear in her voice.

"Dinner, m'lady. All the good and bountiful fruits of England."

"I . . . I'm not hungry," she lied.

"Come, come, dear cousin. You said you were famished."

"I . . . I was, but now I find I'm too tired."

"Very well. I shall dine in splendor on the meats, cheeses, breads and wines we have, but I assure you, it would be a happier meal should you join me."

Mention of the food made Cynthia painfully aware of the emptiness in her stomach. Her resistance failed her.

"Very well, cousin. I certainly can't let you dine alone after you so nobly protected my honor today." She crossed the room and opened the door. She noted he had also cleaned up and changed his clothing. At a glance from him, she tried to cover herself with the tattered dress.

He entered with the girls who had been there before. They did indeed carry platters of meats and cheeses and breads. He had a large bottle of wine, a basket of fruit, and goblets. As they set the food on the table, she looked around for something more suitable with which to cover herself. The only thing available was the coverlet on the bed. She pulled it off and wrapped it around her shoulders.

As the girls were leaving, Cynthia addressed herself to them. "Thank you again for the loan of the gown. Please leave the door open. It will give us more of a breeze through the window." When they were gone, she turned to him and saw laughter in his eyes. So he is amused, is he. Well, damn him anyway. It was all his fault she was here. She sat down opposite him and began to eat as though she hadn't eaten in days. It had, in fact, only been hours since her last meal but she couldn't remember ever feeling so hungry. Even the cuts in her mouth didn't stop her from enjoying the food. She glanced up to find him watching her across the table. He was fingering the wine goblet. A shiver ran through her.

"Aren't you hungry?" she asked.

"There are all types of hunger."

Cynthia glanced toward the door and pulled the coverlet tighter. Only then did it occur to her how ridiculous it was that she should be sitting in a room of a hostelry in a borrowed nightgown with a man she didn't even know. She fought back the terror that threatened.

"I need a needle and thread," she said as calmly as possible, "if I am to repair my gown to any semblance of what it once was. Perhaps the innkeeper has a wife or perhaps one of the girls . . ."

"As soon as we've eaten," he promised. "Or better still, in the morning. It's getting late."

"Very well, first thing in the morning."

There followed a long silence. Cynthia refrained from looking him directly in the face for fear she'd find him laughing at her. Why did he always find her so amusing? He broke the silence.

"Your face looks horrible."

"No thanks to you."

"I am sorry about that. But you see, I don't ever recall having been spit upon."

Cynthia didn't say anything.

"Does it hurt much—your face?"

Cynthia looked into his amused eyes. She was trying to decide whether or not he was genuinely concerned. His eyes held her in a trance. She felt a tightness between her legs and the color rise in her face. She forced herself to look away.

At length, he said, "I have an ointment that might help the scrape on your cheek."

"Then it's not badly cut?"

"No. Mostly bruised, I'd say. We'll be able to tell better in the daylight."

My God, her mind screamed. How can we sit here and talk like this when . . . when . . . I never should have let him come back. "What have you planned for me?" she blurted.

He exploded with laughter, throwing his head so far back Cynthia was afraid he and the bench were going over backwards.

"What *is* the matter?" she demanded as his laughter subsided. "Just what did I say that was so damned funny?"

"Nu . . . uh . . . uh . . . thing," he got out between peals of laughter. "It's . . . nothing . . . you said."

"Then what is it?" She was almost on the verge of laughter herself. Then the thought struck her. He's crazy. I'm in the hands of a crazy man. She pulled the coverlet closer and stood.

"Sit down." Laughter was still in his voice. "Sit down. It really was nothing you said. It's only the way you looked, as though you expected . . . as though you expected the worst. I assure you I have no designs on you."

Cynthia sat back down.

"As soon as you've mended your gown—or better yet, if we can buy a gown from one of the girls—I shall see that you have transportation to London. After all, I'm the—"

"No!"

"No? No what?"

"I don't want to go back to London. I mean . . . you said you were on your way to Brighthelmstone. I should like to continue on with you, if I may."

"Brighton," he corrected her, then added, "You do astound me. A moment ago you thought I was going to rape you and now you want to travel with me?"

Cynthia had no answer. He didn't seem to expect one. Perhaps he knew who she was after all, or perhaps he was running from something, too. He sat in thought for some time while Cynthia helped herself to more food. She watched him closely, wondering what thoughts were going on behind those blue eyes. Then she hated herself for her impulsiveness. She didn't know this man. Didn't even know his name. He seemed to be somewhat a gentleman, if he wasn't, as she suspected, slightly crazy. She consoled herself with the thought that short of killing her, no man could do worse to her than Walter had done in their two years of marriage.

Maybe Jacob's right, he was thinking. Maybe she is a spy, but who could have sent her? Who knew of his activities except those he had talked with and they were all in support of the colonies' plight. Jacob's fears are rubbing off on me, he decided, but better to keep her with me until I know for sure.

"All right," he finally said. "You can go as far as Brighton with me. Have you friends there?"

"Yes." I'm getting to be quite an accomplished liar, she thought. I don't know a soul in Brighthelmstone.

She had been there once as a child with her parents. It was the year before her mother had died. At that time, her father still had the means by which they could afford a few of the luxuries, and her mother had suggested the trip, on her doctor's advice, to escape the summer heat and disease of London. They had enjoyed the holiday immensely and all had agreed that in the future it would be a yearly sojourn, but her mother had died that winter and Cynthia had never been to Brighthelmstone again. Nevertheless, she could almost feel the sea breezes on her face and smell the peculiarly delightful scent of the ocean whenever she thought of the little village.

He interrupted her reverie. "Where are you?"

"I was thinking of Brighthelmstone . . . er, Brighton," she said honestly. "I was also wondering who you are. You said you would tell me. I suspect you're not English."

"And what makes you say that?"

"Well, your clothes and the way you wear your hair—shorter than most and loose with no binding or wig."

"A wig I find bothersome. I wear my hair the way it is most comfortable. But my clothing, is it not the height of fashion?"

"Well, yes. It's not so much the clothing, but . . . but the way you wear it." Cynthia blushed at being so personal.

He laughed. "You flatter me by taking notice, but as to your questions, I am an English subject. An American colonist to be more exact. My name is Garrett Carver from Georgia."

"America!" she exclaimed, forgetting her fears. "The colonies! I never should have thought of America. What are you doing in England? I've never known a colonist before. It must be exciting to live in a new land. Please tell me all about it."

Over their wine, she asked many questions about the New World and he laughed at her ignorance of the life led there. He also decided his first impression of her had been correct, but then he had already told her he'd take her to Brighton.

Much later, when Cynthia had grown quite tired, Garrett came around the table and lifted her to her feet. It's coming now, she thought, and tensed herself for battle.

She raised her fiery green eyes and found him smiling. His eyes were dancing. He bent and kissed her on the forehead.

"Sleep well, little one. Tomorrow's going to be a long day." He paused before going out. "Lock your door." Then he left, closing the door behind him.

Cynthia stood looking at the closed door for a

long time. She finally bolted it and turned to make ready for bed.

Garrett returned to his room and found Jacob waiting up for him.

"It's all right, Jacob. She's okay."

"And she's heading back to London tomorrow?"

"No, she's traveling to Brighton with us."

"She's what? Garrett, are you out of your mind—or have you just lost it?"

"It's nothing like that, Jacob. It's . . . well, she's afraid of something and she's young. I doubt if she's one and twenty."

"All the more reason to send her packin'," replied his friend.

"Jacob, Jacob have you so soon forgotten what it's like to be young and frightened?" He turned to make ready for bed. "Besides, she says she has friends in Brighton."

"No, suh, I ain't forgot, suh. Ya a'ways knows best, suh."

Garrett winced at the tone of Jacob's voice, turned and saw his friend's black face wrinkled in a huge grin.

"Just remember that," he said gruffly, then they fell into each other's arms in peals of laughter.

As tired as she was, Cynthia found sleep long in coming. Those laughing blue eyes had stirred her. This roguish American had touched something deep within her. She didn't understand. She was frightened.

Three

Cynthia looked at the countryside passing by. Here and there had been an occasional farm or inn, but they had traveled through dense forest most of the day. It was much cooler than London had been. She welcomed the change. She unfolded her hands for what must have been the thousandth time and smoothed the skirt of her dress. I look like a peasant, she thought but didn't care. She was decently dressed. She looked across at Garrett Carver who appeared to be asleep, and wondered how he had managed to procure her a dress, which almost fit, as well as a bonnet.

He had knocked softly on her door this morning just as the sky was turning pink. Forcing herself awake, Cynthia had wrapped herself in the coverlet and opened the door. She found Garrett standing there holding the garments.

"Here," he said, thrusting them toward her. "Dress. It's time to go." With that he turned and walked away, only to pause a few steps from her door. He returned, took a small tin from his pocket and handed it to her.

She closed the door, laid the clothing on the bed and opened the tin. It was the ointment he had promised for her cheek. She smeared some on her face which felt rough and abraded. She wondered if it was badly bruised and again wished she had a looking glass.

She then examined the plain brown dress and found it to be clean and free of holes, though the feel of the fabric told her it was not new. She slipped it on over her cleanest whole petticoat and found it fit well enough for traveling. Its only adornment was a row of tiny buttons down the front from neck to waist. Her biggest surprise was a bonnet which matched the dress. Like the dress, it was clean but had obviously been kept in some sort of covering to preserve it. There were folds of lace looking to be almost new on the underside of the brim. She swept her hair up under the bonnet as she placed it on her head, then smiled at her reflection in the window which told her it was becoming. She thought briefly that it must be one of the girl's best dresses and wondered what Garrett Carver had exchanged for it.

Just at that moment, he had knocked on the door. "Are you ready? It's time to leave."

"Coming." As she opened the door, he handed her a shawl.

"To ward off a chill."

"Thank you. But how, what?"

"Leave your old clothes," he said. "The girls may be able to repair them or use the material for something else."

She felt it a terrible loss, but deciding she had no use for a ripped and stained gown, followed him downstairs.

"I'm hungry," she complained as he handed her into the coach.

"Get in. You'll eat on the way. We haven't time for a leisurely breakfast."

Cynthia frowned at him, but soon enough she was eating in the coach. He had bought rolls and meat from the innkeeper which she washed down with water.

She fingered the buttons on the front of the dress. They hadn't traveled at a fast pace, but it had been steady. It was midafternoon now and their only stop had been at noontime. They had stopped for quite a long while, Cynthia thought, but Garrett said the horses needed the rest. Cynthia found out during their stop that their driver was no driver at all—at least he was not a servant or a hired man. He was a friend of Garrett Carver's. His name was Jacob Townsley and to her surprise he was a black man, the first she had ever seen up close. She knew the elite of London had black servants, kept them like pets she'd heard, and even though Walter was considered wealthy by most standards, he had never been one of the elite. Except for her surprise over Mr. Townsley, she had learned nothing of Garrett Carver or his friend or of what they were doing in England.

She thought of the towns they had come through and could remember little more than their names. After Woking, they had circumvented south London and in the course of the day they had passed through Guilford, Dorking, Reigate and Uckfield. She knew the next town was Lewes. She remembered it from when she'd been to Brighton before. She thought she remembered a very large, impressive castle sitting on one of its steep hills. She would have to look for it. Garrett had told her they would be in Brighton before dark. She looked forward to seeing the ocean again and feeling its cool breeze.

She looked at him now. He seemed to be sleeping quite soundly. The warm afternoon made her drowsy, but she fought sleep. She didn't know why, but she was afraid she would be at his mercy if she went to sleep. She chided herself for her fear. Mr. Carver had been nothing but kind to her except when he had struck her at the cattle market and she was beginning to think it was the best thing that could have happened. He had gotten her away from London and was now taking her farther away. She hoped it would be far enough so Walter would not find her.

She had had most of the day to her own thoughts. Garrett was not a curious man and would tell her little of himself, so after a while they had lapsed into silence. He had slept and she had begun to wonder what she was going to do once they got to Brighton. The thought of having to rely completely upon her own resources frightened her. What had she ever done besides care for a drunken father? Then she had decided: a governess. Certainly, this time of year, there would be well-to-do people in Brighton who would need a governess. With that settled, she rested a bit easier, thought she was still in a dither about tonight. What would she do if she didn't find employment right away? She certainly couldn't sleep in the streets and she had no money for lodging.

She finally pushed the thought from her mind. There was nothing she could do about it now. Things would somehow take care of themselves.

Garrett sat watching her through almost closed eyes. He knew she thought he was sleeping. He once again saw her fingering the buttons on the dress he had gotten for her. She glanced at him, then out the window. She's quite attractive, he thought, not beautiful, but attractive. She reminded him of someone—Priscilla, he thought, his first master's daughter. He hadn't thought of Prissy in years. The thought of her now warmed him and he knew how he had missed having a woman these past many weeks. But I'll not have this one, he thought. She's afraid of men. He briefly wondered why, then dismissed it from his mind, deciding that a tumble with her would be more work than pleasure.

He let his thoughts return to Prissy. Now there had been a girl! She introduced him to delights he had only heard about. She never demanded anything in return. He remembered hardly anything before Prissy, but he did have a dim recollection of meetings in dark corners in London with girls always older than himself. They had been hasty affairs, when he was barely more than a boy, with a lot of grunting, moaning and fumbling. But Prissy! Prissy had been a good teacher. He'd always wondered where she could have learned so much so well. Thinking of her again, he remembered how thankful he had been when he had been sold before her father found them out. He felt a tightening in his loins and shifted positions. Cynthia's attention focused on him. He stirred again as though waking and peered at her through dark lashes. He smiled. She returned his smile.

Quite handsome, she thought as his smile widened showing even white teeth. It then spread to a yawn.

"Terribly boring of me to fall asleep," he said. "Have we passed through Lewes yet?"

"Not yet, but Mr. Townsley just called back that we're almost there. That must be what woke you."

Not quite, he thought.

"It's certainly lovely country down here. I'd forgotten just how pleasant it was. It's been so long."

"You haven't been to Brighton for a long time?"

"No, not for a very long time."

"Yet you have friends there, you said."

"Yes, of course I do. I'm sure they're there, although I haven't heard from them in simply ages. They're always there this time of year. They'd be foolish to go anywhere else with the heat so unbearable inland."

Garrett frowned at her. He doesn't believe me, she thought.

"And what will you do if they're not there?"

"I'll manage," she said defiantly. "You needn't worry about me."

"Ah, but I would. You see, I'm growing quite fond of you. You're so unlike other women I know who prattle on about nothing and ask questions until your head spins. Yes, I'm growing quite fond of you."

Cynthia felt a knot of fear in her stomach and it must have shown on her face, for he began to laugh.

"Perhaps you don't talk much because you're afraid of me. Could that be it, little one?"

"If I were afraid of you, would I have asked to travel with you?"

He seemed to consider her question, then said, "You might, if there was something behind you of which you were more afraid."

"Of . . . of course not," Cynthia stammered. She knew her face was red.

"Do you want to tell me about it?"

"There's nothing to tell!" Cynthia stormed, then turned her head to look out the window. She knew he didn't believe her, but she didn't care. All she cared about was that in a short time they would be in Brighton and she would be free to do as she wished. She hated the way he was always laughing at her and he seemed to have a knack for putting her on the defensive. She decided she would be well rid of him.

She's almost beautiful when she's angry, he thought, as he moved to the other side of the coach.

Cynthia felt rather than saw him move to her side. In the closeness of the coach, she could detect his man smell. She shuddered and kept staring out the window trying to avoid him. I will show no fear, she told herself. He reached out and touched her hand. She drew away. He put his arm around her. She shivered. He turned her towards him. Her eyes were snapping but she choked back her angry words as his lips touched hers lightly. He pulled back to look at her for an instant and she realized she wanted him to kiss her. He did not repel her as Walter had, yet she was terrified of him. She wondered why even as he leaned forward and kissed her gently. Cynthia felt as though she were drowning in gentleness. Without conscious thought, her arms crept up around his neck and she leaned into him. When she felt his hand go to the curve of her breast, her eyes flew open and she stiffened. When she tried to push him away, his kiss became more fierce and he held her against him tightly. She was conscious of every part of him. She struggled to be free. She was like an animal in a trap, fighting for freedom. She felt as though she were suffocating.

Finally, he released her. She fell into the corner gasping.

"Is that how you always treat ladies?" she sobbed, not looking at him.

"But how do I know you're a lady?"

"Oh . . . you . . . you . . . you men are all the same, wanting only one thing. I was beginning to think that . . . that you were different, but I see I was mistaken."

Garrett threw his head back and laughed. "Come, little one. You think one kiss is some kind of ominous sign? Surely you've been kissed before. You don't mean to tell me you're . . . uh . . . inexperienced?"

Cynthia's mouth opened in amazement at his

frankness. She looked into his eyes and had an impulse to scratch them out. Only the memory of how he had struck her made her fight the impulse.

"You know, you're very attractive when you're angry. The color comes up in your cheeks and your eyes spit fire."

"Oh, you . . . how could you? I've done nothing to lead you on." Cynthia found herself crying for the first time in a long time.

Garrett, taken aback by the sudden change in her, pulled her to him. After her first resistance, she lay against his shoulder and cried into the handkerchief he handed her.

"I'm sorry, little one. I had no intention of . . ." He raised her chin and again gave way to the desire to kiss her. She tried to pull away, but when he continued to be gentle, her arms went up around his neck and she returned his kiss.

Cynthia couldn't understand what was happening to her. A moment ago, she wanted him dead and now . . .

Garrett held her tenderly against his shoulder. "What were you doing at the sale in London?"

Cynthia stiffened. Does he know? Perhaps he does, she thought, and only wants an admission. "Why do you ask?"

"You were the only one of the warring women I saw so prettily dressed. At first I thought . . . but that doesn't matter. Why were you there?"

Cynthia's mind whirled seeking an answer. "I abhor the practice of buying and selling women," she finally said, hoping he would draw his own conclusions.

When he said nothing she pulled away, then continued. "It . . . it puts us on the same level as slaves. Being married is slavery enough without the degradation of being put on a block and auctioned off . . . as some of those poor women are," she added hastily.

"So, you're married?"

"I . . . uh . . ." Why did he always seem to be trying to trap her? "I saw what marriage did to my mother. I've never wanted to be married."

That much was true, she told herself. She had never wanted to marry Walter. She could remember as a very young girl how she had dreamed of marriage, but after her mother's death, when she had finally seen her father for what he was, she had wondered how her mother had ever loved him. Then there had been Walter to whom, she told herself, she had been little more than a slave—a slave for him to use and discard as he wished. And now there was Garrett who was kind and gentle yet she sensed he could be brutal and demanding. Hadn't she seen some evidence of that?

Through her confusing thoughts she heard him.

"Let me tell you something about myself, Cynthia, then perhaps you will see that I really do understand what it is you're trying to say."

Cynthia looked up. His face was a study of concentration, his eyes clouded over with remembering. She felt as though they were suspended in time.

"As a young boy," he began, "I went to the colonies as an indentured servant. That, by the way, is a nicer way of saying slave. I was thirteen at the time, almost fourteen, but I was big for my age and was able to convince the ship's captain, without much difficulty, that I was sixteen, the age one had to be to sell their own head rights. My head rights were purchased by a gentleman and I was to work for him for a period of five years. In exchange for being his servant, at the end of my indenture I was to receive from him fifty acres of land and his help in getting started on my own."

Cynthia found herself listening in amazement. She had, of course, heard of indentured servitude, but it was something for the very poor or for those in debtors' prison. She had even heard of instances where murderers and rapists had been sent to the colonies as indentured servants. As he talked, she found herself wondering what kind of man Garrett Carver really was. He certainly showed no signs of poverty. Could it be there really was such freedom in the colonies? Was it possible for a man or a boy becoming a man to make something of himself in this new world? Could he have been some sort of criminal—surely not at such a young age, but then she had only his word for that.

As the thoughts raced through her mind, she found herself able to make the expected comments and ask the expected questions, but she didn't entirely believe him. Having lived in London all her life, she simply could not comprehend how a person—even a stubborn, single-minded person—could have done so much or come so far as Garret Carver professed he had.

"Do you really expect me to believe all that?" she asked as he completed his story.

"Believe what you like," he said. "I only wanted you to understand that I am in sympathy with those poor women who are sold against their will. In Georgia we prize our women. Many of them work side-by-side with their men. I know of no one who would think of selling his wife."

Cynthia sat in silence for a while wishing he would move back to the other side of the coach. She felt uneasy with him being so near. The silence lengthened. Finally, she asked, "Are you . . . are you actually as rich as you say?"

He threw his head back and laughed. "At least . . . maybe even richer."

"But you say you have all this land and . . . and you have slaves. How can you have slaves if you feel as you say you do about buying and selling humans? And what about Mr. Townsley? He's not a slave, is he?"

A frown wrinkled his brow. "No, Jacob is not a slave. He's a friend. I don't have slaves."

"But you said your land was worked by blacks."

"It is, but they're not slaves."

Cynthia bit her lower lip in perplexity. "But aren't all blacks in the colonies slaves?"

"Not all, most. There are some who think all blacks should be slaves. Jacob may very well stay in England when I return. I've certainly tried to persuade him to stay here."

"But why? I thought you said he was your friend."

"He is, but life is quite hazardous for free blacks in America."

"Isn't it just as hazardous for your other blacks?"

"They aren't my blacks. They only work for me." He sighed, then as though he were explaining it to a child, he said, "Legally, most of those on my property are slaves, so there's no great danger for them—at least not yet."

"You say you don't believe in slavery and yet you say you have slaves." Cynthia shook her head. "I just don't understand. How can you have slaves and not have slaves?"

"I buy them at the slave auctions, which are becoming all too frequent in the colonies." She heard a bitter tone creep into his voice. "Therefore, they are officially my property. I can't and never could afford to buy them and then give them their freedom immediately, so they work off whatever it is they cost me plus an additional five years service, then I give them their freedom."

"But where do they go? What do they do?"

"I'm not sure. I've never asked. Some, I believe, go to Savannah to find work. Most, I think, probably go into the wilderness and live off the land. I imagine a resourceful man could live in the wilderness indefinitely. It's incredible country. Most of the people work harder for me than they would for another master because they know there is freedom in their future. Believe it or not, this system has made me a rich man. I'll continue to be rich as long as the land produces and as long as the laws don't interfere with the freeing of slaves—but my neighbors think I'm crazy."

"Then that's how Jacob . . ."

"No, Jacob and I were indentured to the same man. He saved me from a beating once. I never forgot it. As soon as I could after I gained my freedom, I bought the remainder of his indenture. We've worked side-by-side for years like brothers."

"Then, why . . ."

"Enough of this. We must be nearing Brighton."

"If Jacob is such a good friend of yours, why are you letting him do all the driving?"

"Because, little one, he's afraid of you. He would rather drive than have to ride back here with you. He saw you knock that fellow down in the cattle market."

"But that's ridiculous. I only . . ." Cynthia could feel the color rising in her cheeks. She looked at Garrett. His eyes were twinkling.

He would be so easy to like, she thought, if only the circumstances were different. She turned, and looking out the window, saw Brighton in the distance. She thought she could smell the ocean even from here.

"I see Brighton," she said. "It's not at all far now." While they had been talking, they hadn't even noticed Lewes or how low the sun had gotten. It was just visible on the horizon. She shuddered with fear and anticipation, wondering what she would find in Brighton and how she would fare this night.

"By the time we get there, it will be getting late," he said, then as though he had read her mind he went on. "Would you care to have supper with me before looking for your friends? If you like, you could stay in an inn tonight and find them in the morning."

"I should like that," Cynthia said, "but I think I shouldn't like putting myself any further in your debt."

"But supper then? You will have supper with me, won't you?"

Cynthia looked at him and found he was smiling. "I will if you'll move to the other side of the coach. It really is warm yet."

As he moved, Cynthia noticed how very graceful he was. She marveled that such a large man could be so graceful.

"When are you going back to America?"

"Soon."

"How long will you be in Brighton?"

"I shall very likely leave tomorrow."

"But why? Where are you going? Brighton is such a lovely little town."

He began to laugh again. "I see I was wrong about you. You do talk as much as other women and ask just as many questions."

Cynthia blushed. "I'm sorry. I don't mean . . ."

"That's all right. You'll learn as you get older."

"But, I . . ." Cynthia exploded. She could think of nothing to say.

"Since we have at least a good half hour before we arrive, I think I shall rest." He closed his eyes.

Besides always laughing at me, Cynthia thought, you can be a very perplexing man, Garrett Carver. She then found herself thinking of all he had told her of the slaves who were not slaves who had helped to make him a wealthy man. He must be quite old, she thought, even though he doesn't look it. Then she thought of Jacob Townsley and wondered briefly if he would be staying in England. Oh, why bother thinking about them at all, she thought. After today it's not likely I'll ever be seeing either of them again. She dozed then without realizing it and awoke only when the coached slowed in Brighton.

Four

Cynthia felt a cleanness in Brighton she had forgotten existed. The ocean breeze refreshed and revitalized her. As they wove their way through the narrow streets, she could hear the gentle roar of the ocean and it seemed to mark time with the wheels of the coach. She hung to the window taking in all the sights as they passed. It seemed so much smaller than she had remembered. But I was only a child, she thought. Things always have a way of seeming to diminish as one grows older.

It appeared Jacob Townsley knew his way about the village. He didn't stop to ask directions but drove as though he belonged here. Cynthia wondered momentarily how colonists could know the town so well. She didn't dwell on it long for they pulled up before an inn. Her mouth opened in amazement. She felt certain this was the very inn she had stayed in as a child—The King's Head. She remembered how quaint it had been, so clean and well-kept, so unlike the inns she had heard about. The landlady had told her it was rumored that King Charles II had stayed in this very inn when he made a flight for his life during the Civil War.

"I think I've stayed at this inn before," she commented. "It was a very long time ago, when I was a child. The first time I ever came to Brighton. I remember I loved the garden. We could look out our window and see the ocean. It lulled me to sleep at night." She turned and looked at Garrett. "It is said King Charles II stayed here over a hundred years ago. Have you been here before?"

"Yes, a few weeks ago. But I'm afraid I didn't see the garden. I arrived late at night. Shall we go in and have some supper? I recall the food was quite good." He opened the door, stepped down then turned to help Cynthia.

"Do you think it's light enough so we could visit the garden before we eat? I would dearly love to see it again."

"As you wish, but aren't you tired? Wouldn't you like to freshen up first?"

"Oh, no. I'm fine. A little stiff perhaps from sitting all day. A stroll through the garden will do me a world of good."

He turned to Jacob. "Would you please see to our room? The lady desires a stroll through the garden."

Jacob nodded and disappeared through the doorway. Garrett put a hand under Cynthia's elbow and guided her to a gate at the side of the building.

"I thought you said you hadn't seen the garden."

"I haven't, but logic tells me it's through this gate."

"I believe you're right, though it's been a very long time."

There was just enough light for them to find their way. Cynthia discovered she had remembered well, although it again seemed much smaller. She felt as though the trees and shrubs had grown to be enormous. In the fading light she determined it was still lovely. She longed to be a child again and play as she had so long ago.

Garrett watched her in the fading twilight and thought again how very attractive she was. It was true, she had reminded him of Priscilla Dennison, the same coloring, the same facial shape, but Cynthia had none of the false beauty Prissy had had. Her attractiveness came from within. Neither did she seem to have the calculating coyness that he recognized in so many women and which had been so much a part of Prissy. She reminded him of a fawn he had once seen. Separated from its mother, it had been frightened and confused.

He knew she was frightened of something she had left behind in London and he sensed she had a fear of men. He wondered how one so young, who was obviously of class, had acquired such fears. He watched her as she leaned against a tree and looked up at the dark foliage. She looked so young and vulnerable. He felt an urge to reach out, enfold her in his arms and protect her.

Cynthia could barely see the lower leaves dancing in the breeze. As she stood looking up, she was carried back to a time in London as a child when her mother had kept a well-tended garden. It hadn't been as large as this one, but Cynthia loved it as her mother had. After her mother's death she had tried to keep the garden, but found how little she knew about the trees and plants. She begged her father to help or to hire a gardener, but he scoffed at her so the garden became overgrown, its beauty faded. As many of the plants died or were choked out, a little of Cynthia's childhood went with each one.

As she stood reflecting on the past, she realized that in that other garden she had been trying to hold onto a part of her life—that last summer so long ago when she, her mother, and her father had spent a few happy weeks at this very inn. Tears came to her eyes. She made a motion as though to pull a shawl about her and found she had forgotten it in the coach.

"Are you cold?"

The sound of his voice startled her. He had been so silent she had forgotten he was here.

"Not really." She brushed the tears aside, hoping that in the darkness he wouldn't notice. "It was just reaction. I'm afraid I've become very nostalgic. I was remembering the last time I was here. It was the summer before my mother died. We spent a very pleasant few weeks here at this inn, my parents and I. Standing in the garden like this rolled back the years for me, but it's silly. It was all so very long ago."

"It's not silly," he said with a tenderness that surprised her. "We all tend to remember the good times in our lives and have a desire to relive them."

"Yes, I suppose so, but I really shouldn't get so carried away with my dreams. My father always chided me for being a dreamer. Perhaps he was right. Shall we go in to supper now?"

"If you'd like." He led her back to the gate. "What of your father? Where is he now?"

"Dead. He was killed in an accident two years ago. It was on . . ." Cynthia caught herself. She had been about to say it was on her wedding day, but she wasn't sure she should confide so much in Garrett Carver. If he knew she were a runaway wife, he might return her to London. She couldn't bear the thought of being sent back to Walter and she didn't know what Garrett would think of her if she told him the entire story. Very likely, he would think what those at the cattle market had thought, that she was a faithless wife. No, she couldn't tell him more about herself.

"On what?" asked Garrett, obviously wondering at her abrupt silence.

"Well, it was ridiculous and so useless. He was

drunk at the time. He had been celebrating the marriage of a . . . a friend's daughter. He and this friend made a wager about jumping horses. Father lost. He fell and broke his neck."

"I'm sorry. I didn't mean for you to have to remember sadness in your past. Please forgive me."

"You're forgiven and I'm famished," Cynthia said as they entered the well-lit anteroom of The King's Head. She shielded her eyes from the light for a moment.

All through the meal, Cynthia kept thinking of what she could do now that she was in Brighton. She sampled the rich dishes set before her and drank too much of the heady wine served them. She discarded one idea after another, always coming back to the possibility of presenting herself as a governess. She knew little of children, but felt that somehow this was her only avenue. She had little formal schooling and knew she could never convince anyone she was a teacher, so a governess it had to be. But what about tonight? What would she do tonight? She was confident enough she could find employment tomorrow, but where would she stay tonight?

Garrett watched her from across the table and kept his silence even though he felt she was drinking far more than she should. Her face was a study of concentration. Even though he didn't know what she was thinking, he could see the change in her face as thoughts raced through her mind. Then her face changed to a definite worried expression.

"You looked troubled. Is something wrong?"

"No, no. I was only wondering about Mr. Townsley."

"He's probably eating in the room. I'm sure he's tired after such a long drive."

"Why did you let him drive all day? You said he

was your friend—and don't tell me he's afraid of me. I don't believe it.''

"He wanted it that way. Honestly. I wanted to relieve him, but Jacob wouldn't let me. He said it looks much better for him to drive and let people think he's my servant. I hate it, but I know he's right."

Not knowing what to say, Cynthia sipped more wine. She was feeling warm and knew she had drunk far too much. She wondered how she could convince Garrett Carver she didn't need an escort when she left the inn.

Suddenly there was a commotion across the room. Cynthia had been trying to ignore the group gathered there throughout the meal. She knew they were playing some sort of dice game, probably Hazard, and she knew, too, that dice games were illegal. As the evening progressed they had become increasingly rowdy. Now Cynthia looked up just in time to see a large, burly sailor flying through the air in her direction. When he landed at her feet and looked up with a "Beg pardon, ma'am," Cynthia burst into giggles. She knew it was the wine and there was absolutely nothing funny about the situation, but she couldn't seem to control her laughter.

Everyone looked at her as though they thought her quite mad. This sent her into new peals of laughter. The sailor backed away slowly, looking from her to Garrett.

"I think we'd best leave, Cynthia."

"Why, Mr. Carver, have you no sense of justice? That poor sailor is badly outnumbered."

"Yes, well, he was probably cheating. Come, this is no place for a lady."

"I don't remember The King's Head being such a rowdy place, I really don't."

"Things do change. Come now. Do you need help?"

"Of course not. I'm quite able to take care of myself." But when she stood her head reeled. She held onto the back of her chair to steady herself until the room stopped spinning then she took hold of Garrett's arm and let him lead her to the door.

In the entry, he paused. "Are you sure you're all right? You look quite pale."

"I'm fine. I'm fine. It was just the closeness of the room. Once I'm outside in the cool . . ." She paused. "No, Mr. Carver, I think I'm going to be quite ill."

Cynthia went running and stumbling out the front door and ran headlong into a hitching post. Garrett followed, tried to catch her when she stumbled on the stoop, then winced when she hit the post. He knelt beside her, realized she was unconscious but still retching. He lifted her head and held it to one side until her body relaxed. He turned her over, examined her head and found a small bump just below the hairline. He determined she had actually passed out and had only taken a glancing blow on the hitching post.

He lifted her and walked back into the inn bellowing for the landlord. A wiry little man with a beaklike nose came hurrying into the anteroom from a side door. "Yes, m'lord, you called?"

"My room? Which one is it?"

"Upstairs, m'lord, at the end of the hall, the door to the right."

"Have you a wife, man?" Garrett asked as he headed up the stairs.

"Y-yes, m'lord."

"Send her up quickly with extra towels and water." He yelled over his shoulder as he neared the top.

"R-right away, sir." The waspish little man hurried off, muttering to himself.

Garrett was at the room in a dozen strides and kicked on the door. Jacob answered his summons, then stood aside to admit him.

"Lordy, Garrett, what you doin' now?" he asked as he closed the door. "I thought she was goin' to stay with friends."

Garrett laid her gently on the bed. "She fell as she was going out the front door. I couldn't leave her lying in the street. Besides, she doesn't have any friends here, at least, I don't think she has."

"But you said that she said . . ."

"I know what I said, but I think she lied." He removed her slippers and tried to make her more comfortable.

"Jesus, she's a mess," Jacob offered. "Looks like she's been wallowing in a pig sty. Is she bad hurt?"

"I don't think so. She had a lot to drink and got sick. She fell in it. I shouldn't have let her drink so much."

There was a knock on the door. Jacob opened it to admit a thin, little woman with a pinched face. She carried a large pitcher of water and extra towels. When she saw Cynthia lying on the bed, white as the pillowcase beneath her head, she shooed Garrett and Jacob out of the room with, "I'll take care of her. Just be a trice."

In the hallway, Jacob asked in a subdued voice, "If she hasn't any friends here, why did she want to come? And what you gonna do with her?"

Garrett thought about it a minute as he leaned heavily against the wall. "I told you she was frightened of something. I don't know what, but something in London. Could be she's running from the law. As for what I'm going to do with her, I'll let her take the lead on that one. For tonight, she'll stay here. We'll see if we can't get another room for you."

Jacob shook his burly head. "In a place fancy as this, they'll likely frown on renting a room to a black servant."

Garrett ran his hand across his face. It had been a long and tiring day. He was beginning to feel it. "Maybe they'll be a bit understanding in this case. I'm sure they wouldn't want to be sued because someone fell over their doorstep. You wait here a minute. I'll talk to the woman inside." He rapped softly on the door, then heard a flurry inside before the woman admitted him.

"How is she?" he whispered.

"I think she'll be fine. A lovely young woman, your wife. Strong and healthy."

"Yes . . . yes, she is." He didn't try to correct her. "I . . . uh, I'll be needing another room so as not to disturb her." He decided it was best not to tell the woman it was for Jacob.

"Of course, sir. You can have the next one. It's a connecting room—right through there." She pointed to a door he had assumed to be a closet. "I'll get the key and return shortly."

"Thank you," Garrett said as she picked up her things to leave. At the door, she turned.

"I shouldn't worry about your wife, sir. Being with child often affects young women with fainting spells. Is she far advanced?"

"Being with? . . . Are you sure?"

"Oh, my, I see I've spoiled your wife's surprise. No, I'm not sure, just guessin'. Why else would a healthy, young woman pass out?"

"Yes, why indeed?" Garrett smiled. Better to let her think Cynthia was pregnant than to try to explain what had really happened.

"Now, don't you let on that you know. Women always have their own special way to tell their man. Wouldn't want to spoil it for her, now would you?"

"Of course not," Garrett agreed. "And thank you."

"Welcome, sir." She bobbed a little curtsey. "I'll be right back with that key."

"Thank you, again," Garrett said, smiling as she went out the door, stepping to one side so Jacob could enter.

"You'll be in the room next door," Garrett said when she had gone. He chuckled a bit. "The landlady thinks we're married and that Cynthia is with child."

"What's so funny about that? Are you sure she ain't?"

"Of course I'm not sure. How would I know? Do you think I greet attractive young women with, 'How do you do and are you pregnant?'"

"I don't think no such thing, but I know you, Garrett Carver. You already think she's in trouble of some sort. If it turns out she is with child and that's her trouble, you'll move heaven and hell to help her. Lord, man, did you ever stop to think she may have a husband or she may be a whore or somebody's mistress?"

"Not that one, Jacob. She's either afraid of men or terribly naive, or both."

"And how would you be knowin' that?"

Garrett yawned. "It's late, Jacob. I'm tired." There was a knock at the door. "And here's the key to your room." He opened the door and took the key, giving the landlady another smile and another thank you.

He closed the door and handed Jacob the key.

58

"You might as well come in the other room with me. There's no place for you in here," his friend said.

"I want to stay close to her, Jacob, in case she's hurt worse than we think."

"We can leave the door open."

"I'll stay in here, Jacob. I'm tired enough that if I laid down on a comfortable bed, I'd not hear her if she did need something. Having brought her here, I feel responsible. Good night, friend."

Jacob left, but Garrett knew he wouldn't let it rest as long as Cynthia was with them.

He walked to the settle on the other side of the room and tried to get comfortable on it. It was next to impossible, so he went to the bed to get the extra pillow. He stood looking at Cynthia. In the candlelight she looked like a child in slumber with her golden hair spread on the pillow about her. Lord, she is lovely, he thought, and his feelings were all mixed up with wanting to protect her, wanting to love her and wanting to make love to her. Fighting his desires and an impulse to lie beside her, he got the pillow, whirled around and went back to the settle.

He slept fitfully the rest of the night. His dreams were all confused with Prissy, of whom he hadn't thought in years, and Cynthia—golden hair and green eyes that teased one moment and spit fire the next.

He awoke before daybreak and dressed, then went into Jacob's room to wash and shave. He returned moments later to find Cynthia still sleeping, so he took her soiled clothing and left the room.

Five

Cynthia awoke in a very large bed in a very pleasant room. The sun was streaming through the window to her left and straight ahead she could see the ocean through gauzy curtains. She tried to sit up and found her head pounded with the effort. She sank back onto the soft pillow, then realized her clothes were missing. All she had on was her petticoat and stockings. The gown, shawl, and bonnet that Garrett had given her were nowhere in sight.

He's taken my clothes and locked me in, she thought. It's Walter all over again. Panic crept into her thinking. She jumped out of bed, wrapped the comforter around herself and immediately tried the door. It was locked. She began to pace back and forth. In a few moments she heard a key in the lock. She sat down on the edge of the bed, too frightened to be angry.

Garrett entered the room with her clothing in hand. "Ah, I see you're up. Did you sleep well?"

"Yes, thank you. Where have you been? What are you doing with my clothes? Why was I locked in?"

"You were locked in for your own protection. Sleeping behind an unlocked door in a public inn is not one of the safest practices, you know. Your clothes were downstairs being cleaned as best the landlady could do it. I just retrieved them when I finished breakfast."

Feeling more courageous, Cynthia flung her hair out of her face and raised her chin. "And please do tell me what I am doing at an inn with you again. I thought I was perfectly clear when I said I had no intention of putting myself further into your debt."

Cynthia saw a smile playing around his mouth and wondered what he found so damned funny this time.

"But, little one, don't you remember what happened last night?"

"I remember perfectly well. I supped with you, then there was a fight. Then . . . then I remember getting up to leave and find my friends, but I only remember getting as far as the anteroom. I was feeling dizzy and nauseous from the warmth of the room. Good Lord, did I faint?"

"No, you didn't. You were feeling dizzy and nauseous from too much wine, but when I tried to help you, you wouldn't let me. You went running pell mell out the door, stumbling on the way, and knocked yourself out on a hitching post out front. Not knowing what to do with you, or where to take you, I brought you here to my room."

"Your room! But . . . but where did you sleep?"

"Here, with you."

"Here . . . with . . . me?" Cynthia turned white, wishing she could think of something, anything, to say to that.

Garrett burst out laughing. "It was really all quite innocent, sweetheart. I slept on the settle."

"You . . . on . . . the . . ." Cynthia had been so self-concerned, she had hardly taken notice of the room's furnishings. Now, her eyes swept swiftly about. "But it hardly looks big enough for you," she finished slowly.

"And it's damned uncomfortable, I'll tell you."

"But why? Surely you could have stayed in Mr.

Townsley's room."

"And slept on the settle in there? What's the difference? One is undoubtedly as uncomfortable as another."

"But what will these people think?"

"I'm sure they could care less, but to ease your mind, the landlady thinks we're married and you're with child."

"She what? I'm what?" Cynthia stood and glared at him. "You told her a thing like that?"

Garrett backed up, smiling, hands held in front of him feigning fright. "No, I didn't. She decided that herself last night when she was helping me get you to bed. I saw no reason to tell her otherwise." He turned away. "Are you with child?" He tried to sound off-handed about it.

"Of course not, but what business is it of yours?"

He turned back to her. Those snappy green eyes again, he thought. "None," he said matter of factly. "Come now, get dressed. I'll wait for you downstairs. While you're having your breakfast, I'll find Jacob and we'll see that you get safely to your friends."

"Thank you, sir, but I can find my own way," Cynthia said as Garrett headed out the door. "And I'm really not very hungry."

Garrett turned and came back into the room. He closed the door behind him. "You know, little one, you really look fetching wrapped in that coverlet." Cynthia's eyes opened wide at his remark. "But what are we going to do with you? You haven't friends in Brighton. You've been lying from the first, haven't you?" He paused for a moment then went on. "You don't need to answer that. I can see it in your eyes. But why are you lying? Why did you want to come to Brighton? What's in London you're afraid of?

Are you running from the law?"

Cynthia lowered her head. "I didn't want to come to Brighton."

"Holy Jesus!"

"Let me finish, please." She looked at him. "What I meant was I didn't necessarily want to come to Brighton. I would have gone anyplace, anyplace at all away from London. And no, I don't have friends here. I did once, but that was a long time ago, when I was a child. I'm not running from the law—at least I don't think I am."

"What do you mean you don't think you are?"

"When I left London, I wasn't, but I may very well be by now." Cynthia looked up at him with tears in her eyes. When she saw the concern on his face, the whole story came tumbling out. She omitted some of the degradation Walter had put her through but otherwise she told Garrett the entire sordid story of the past two years of her life.

By the time she had finished, he was sitting on the bed with her beside him. He took her hand tenderly and spoke softly. "And now what are we going to do with you? Have you any plans? I know you have no money. How do you intend to get on by yourself?"

"I had thought of perhaps applying for a position as a governess. Surely the people who come here are wealthy enough to afford one."

"Of course they are, Cynthia, but if they had need of a governess, they would have brought one with them."

"Well, I'll find some kind of honest work. Never you fear."

"But aren't you afraid Walter might find you? You're not all that far from London, you know."

Cynthia bit her lower lip. "Yes, I've thought about that. He will very likely look for me, too. He doesn't want me any longer, but he does want the money I represent." All of a sudden, her face lit up. "Why don't you take me to America with you? He'd never think to look for me clear across an ocean."

"Come now, little one. You can't be serious. It's a hard enough life over there for a man, but a woman alone? I'm sorry, Cynthia, it just wouldn't work out. Besides, you've been trouble enough to me already."

"I'm sorry. Of course you're right. Besides, I have no money to pay my passage."

"It's not the money, Cynthia. I have the money. It's just that there's no place for a woman alone—except as a prostitute."

"Then, I'll go as an indentured servant. I'm old enough to sell my own head rights."

"Sorry, little one, but you're a woman, a young and not unattractive one. You would not be bought for general servitude, but for pleasure. You would still be no more than a prostitute."

"It could be no worse than living with Walter."

"My God, Cynthia! You want to go from one bad situation to another? You must be crazy."

"Funny you should say that. That first night I thought you must be a little crazy."

"I probably am or I wouldn't be here with a woman in tow. But listen to what I'm saying. In this day and age, few will pay for an indentured servant to have for a few years—not even one as pretty as you—when they can buy a slave for life."

"Do you really think I'm pretty, Garrett?"

"Yes, I . . . I think you're pretty and you're young and you can have a good life right here in England."

"Do you want to kiss me?" she asked, surprised at her own boldness.

64

He stood to leave. She grabbed his hand. He turned and looked at her. He ached for her. "Cynthia, do you know what you're doing?" His voice was husky with emotion.

"I . . . I'm not sure," she faltered.

They just looked at one another for a moment, then she was in his arms and could feel the warmth of him through her thin petticoat. He kissed her gently at first, then became more demanding. His tongue parted her lips. She met it with her own hesitantly. When he let the coverlet fall from her, she shuddered but made no move to withdraw from his embrace. His hands moved swiftly over her back then down to her buttocks and pressed her tightly to him. He could feel him hard against her stomach.

She gasped. It came out a low moan and he bent and picked her up with ease. "I'll be gentle," he murmured as he laid her on the bed. He quickly undressed and was beside her. Cynthia could not bring herself to look at him. She closed her eyes tighter as his hands began to caress her and she clenched her fists as he drew the petticoat over her head.

"Relax, little one. It can be lovely, this union between a man and a woman. We're not all animals."

She forced herself to relax, but when he began to remove her stockings, she bit into her lower lip. She could feel his nakedness beside her and she still could not bring herself to open her eyes. He gently caressed her breasts, then his hand slid down the curve of her body to her thigh.

"Beautiful," he murmured. "Just beautiful."

She opened her eyes and looked into his. He wasn't laughing at her. He wasn't mocking her. She couldn't believe the look of tenderness she saw on his face and in his eyes.

"Please don't look so frightened. I'm not going to hurt you."

She tried to smile. Tears came to her eyes. "I'm . . . I'm not frightened . . . at least not very much."

"Then why is your lip quivering?"

"It's only . . . oh, Garrett, I've never known any man to be so tender and so concerned for me." She broke into loud sobs.

He took her into his arms and rocked her gently back and forth. She felt his manhood hard against her and would have pulled away except for the strong, secure feeling she got from him. He continued to rock her gently, all the while caressing her back and buttocks. When her crying had subsided, he said, "God, what a lout your husband must be."

Hatred welled in Cynthia's breast as she thought of Walter. "Yes," was all she could say.

Garrett's hands roamed freely over her now and she felt a warm sensation creeping through her entire body. At first it frightened and surprised her, then she gave way to the feeling and found it enjoyable. She returned his kisses and slowly, to her astonishment, found she wanted to return his caresses. She hesitantly reached out to touch his chest. When he made no sound of protest, she let both hands run over his chest and back. His breath was hot on her breasts and she reached to press his head closer even as she felt his hand go between her legs. She stiffened momentarily then slowly relaxed and succumbed to the desires that had been dormant within her.

He raised himself over her and she could not bring herself to look directly at him. She was bewildered when she realized she wanted him—her body longed for him. She closed her eyes as he parted her legs with a knee and lowered himself onto her. She felt him enter. She was no longer frightened. Within seconds she was lost in a kind of bliss she had never dreamed existed. She clung to him and they moved together, at first a gentle, slow rocking motion, then as she sensed the urgency of his desire, she sped up her own movements to stay with him. Her passion mounted with his and they were lost to everything outside their own selves. When Cynthia reached the peak, it was like an explosion that slowly spread throughout her body. She was so entirely consumed by the most beautiful feeling she had ever experienced, she didn't realize she was moaning and thrashing about wildly.

Afterwards, they lay together and let the feelings subside. She clung to Garrett. She never wanted to let him go. He finally drew away from her, wiped his perspiring body with a sheet and began to dress.

"You were right," she said dreamily. "It is beautiful. I never imagined anything could be so . . . so . . ."

"Fulfilling?" he offered.

"Yes, that's the word, fulfilling."

He smiled down at her. "I'm glad you enjoyed it."

He sat down to pull on his boots. She rolled over and started tracing patterns on his back with her fingers. "You will take me with you now, won't you, Garrett?" It was out before she knew she had said it. She clapped her hand over her mouth.

His boots on, Garrett stood up brusquely and walked to the door. He turned to face her. "When you're dressed, I'll meet you downstairs. This doesn't change anything. Since I brought you to Brighton, I feel a sense of responsibility for you, but

America is out of the question." He walked out, closing the door.

Cynthia jumped up and began dressing. She pulled the clothes on roughly and muttered angrily to the empty room, "I will go to America, Garrett Carver. Somehow I will. Just you wait and see."

A few minutes later, Cynthia descended the stairs full of optimism. While dressing she had decided she would somehow convince Garrett to take her to America with him as his own indentured servant. He had said his blacks only worked for him a given number of years then he gave them their freedom, so they were really no more to him than indentured servants. She was sure she could convince him to take her.

Six

Garrett was shown to a table by the window when he entered the dining room. He ordered coffee for himself and breakfast for Cynthia, telling the serving girl his wife would be in shortly and to please watch for her.

He sat looking out on the expanse of ocean and wondered what he would do with Cynthia. He had to admit he had toyed with the idea of possibly taking her to the colonies until he found out she was married. Now it was out of the question. He knew there was a strong attraction between them and he might one day fall in love with her. Then their only option would be to live as man and wife and raise a passel of bastards. He was presupposing she would likewise love him, he told himself. He had never known his own father and had only a vague memory of his slattern mother. He wanted more for his children if there were any.

He had worked hard since his days of indenture to raise himself above his beginnings. He wouldn't let himself backslide now just because he felt sorry for a lonely, frightened girl—no matter how she might attract him.

His coffee came. He drank the first cup in hot, scalding gulps, angry with himself for having let her get so close to him.

She's just a . . a . . . But the thought was gone

before it was even completed. He felt she had been painfully honest with him upstairs. What she had blurted about him taking her to America had been done with no aforethought.

He thought about what had taken place between them and his thoughts warmed. He had been right. She did fear men and had every right to do so. He also realized just how naive she really was. He attributed it to her near seclusion the last few years. Years when she should have been enjoying herself as other young girls did—attending parties, flirting with admiring suitors—she had been looking after a drunken father, then married off to a beast.

In his mind, he explored the different ways he might help her. He was completely oblivious to Jacob's arrival until the black man spoke.

"You look mighty robust for a man who slept so little last night." He spoke quietly so only Garrett could hear.

Garrett glanced up at his friend to see if there was a double meaning to his words. He decided not.

"Come, Jacob, sit," he said, forgetting for the moment where they were.

"Thank you for the generous invitation, sir," Jacob said, bowing from the waist, "but I only came to see when you would be needing the coach."

Garrett glanced toward the doorway and saw Cynthia. "In about half an hour, I should say."

Upon entering the dining room, Cynthia saw Jacob Townsley waiting upon Garrett at one of the window tables. She wondered briefly if Garrett was telling him about her, but pushed the thought from her mind and moved across the room.

Garrett could see Cynthia approaching now after having paused in the doorway.

Jacob bowed again, his mouth close to Garrett's

ear. "Whatcha gonna do about her?"

"I hope to find her employment, Jacob, and a place to live. Perhaps after my meeting at the Castle. In the meantime, I'll be leaving her in your hands. I want you to know I was right about her. She is frightened and with just cause. Treat her with kindness as a favor to me."

Garrett stood up as Cynthia reached the table. She could see that while waiting for her, he had been drinking the now-fashionable coffee. Jacob bowed, held Cynthia's chair for her then left.

"He certainly takes his role as servant seriously," she said when he was out of earshot.

"Jacob understands his position," Garrett answered, with such sadness in his voice that Cynthia felt a stab of sympathy in her own chest. She looked quickly at Garrett and saw in his eyes the love and concern he felt for the black man. The moment passed quickly. He looked at her and smiled.

She swiftly cast her eyes downward. "I'm sorry about what I said upstairs. I really didn't mean to try to buy my passage to America—not that way. You must think horrible things of me."

"I don't think horrible things about you, Cynthia. It never occurred to me you were calculating enough to buy your passage with your body."

"I might have been once, but not with you." She looked up at him. "With you, it was different. It was just . . . just . . ."

"Spontaneous?"

"Yes. I don't know why I said what I did afterwards."

"We'll just forget it was ever spoken then, all right?"

"Thank you, Garrett, for understanding." Then, to change the subject, she said, "If it weren't for me, you'd be with Jacob instead of in this fine dining room with a bunch of stuffy people, wouldn't you?"

"Possibly, but just what makes you think people could understand a friendship between a black man and a white man? No, I must admit Jacob is right in this."

"You care for him a lot, don't you? It hurts when he has to be so subservient."

"Does it show so plainly? Yes, I care for Jacob. I love him like a brother."

"Have you family, Garrett?"

"A sister in London. I saw her when I was there."

"Oh." Not knowing what else to say, she made a face at the coffee as he took a drink. "Ooooh, how can you stand that bitter black stuff? I've never been able to develop a taste for it, and although it's not as expensive as it once was, it's still dear."

"I like it. It's about all we drink at home. I never developed much of a taste for tea myself. As an urchin in London, gin was easier come by than tea. When I arrived in the colonies, I was introduced to coffee."

"Garrett," Cynthia began, now that the somber mood had passed.

"Ah-h-h, here's your breakfast," he said as the serving girl approached with a heavily-laden tray. "I hope you don't mind. I took the liberty of having some prepared for you. We shall have to exchange your coffee for tea. I'm afraid I wasn't thinking when I ordered."

"No, that's all right. I'll try it again. It's been some time since I've had any." And I'm going to like it, she told herself, if that's what they drink in America.

Cynthia looked at the breakfast before her. There was hot porridge in thick cream, fresh coddled eggs, a slab of ham large enough to feed two grown men and, much to her surprise, a fresh orange. "An orange! Oh, Garrett, how ever did you know how much I love oranges?"

"I hoped you'd like it. I was surprised when I was told they had some, at a price, of course. In Georgia, when we're lucky enough to get oranges, even as expensive as they are, they sell like hotcakes."

"Garrett," Cynthia said again as she began to peel the orange, unconcernedly dropping the peel onto the floor. "Why don't you take me to Georgia with you as your indentured servant?" She didn't look at him for fear he was either laughing or would be angry with her.

"I won't do it, Cynthia."

"But why not?" she almost wailed, looking up now. His eyes looked stormy and a little frightening.

"What kind of servant would you make? Can you cook?"

"No."

"Would you know how to take care of my laundry?"

"Uh . . . no. But I could learn Garrett. I could learn."

"Be serious, Cynthia. Have you ever really done a day's work in your life? I can answer that for you. No. I'll be frank with you, Cynthia, in America you'd be suited for nothing better than a man's plaything. Those who survive over there are hearty, strong people—farmers and tradesmen—or they're the scum of the earth. It's no place for a young girl of gentility."

"You're only trying to frighten me."

"I'm not trying to frighten you. It's the truth. One day America will be a great nation. Perhaps even greater than England, but for now, just day to day living is a struggle. It's work, hard work, and I doubt it would suit you."

"But other women have gone as indentured servants."

"Yes, but they had no choice. For them, it was either transportation to the colonies or rotting in Newgate. You have a choice. You're a free woman, at least as long as Walter doesn't find you. It's best for you to stay right here in England. Make a new life for yourself. Change your name if you have to." He paused. "Now let's not talk of it any more. You're only spoiling your breakfast."

Cynthia forced back the tears that threatened, and struggled to finish eating. *You haven't frightened me, you know,* she silently told him. *I will go to America.*

"When you're finished," he said, "would you like to take a ride with me around the village?"

"If you wish."

"Come, cheer up. I have some business to conclude and I thought you might enjoy seeing the town again."

Once settled in the coach with Jacob up front, they turned east and drove along the shoreline some distance. Cynthia marveled at the way the little village had grown since her last visit. There were numerous inns along the waterfront she couldn't recall having seen there before. As they rode, her spirits lifted. She tried to take note of the buildings she remembered as a child.

"My goodness! I hardly recognize anything along here. It's grown so much. Brighthelmsto . . . er, Brighton was little more than a fishing village when I was here before. It must be the popularity of the cure."

"The cure?"

"Yes. When I was here as a child, there was a noted doctor, a Dr. Rushton . . . no, that isn't right . . . a Dr. Rush or Rus something—Russell, that's it. Dr. Richard Russell was advocating the sea cure. Oh, it helps all sorts of ills. One reason we came was so my mother could take the cure. She hadn't been well for some time and her physician had heard of the benefits of the cure—purging one's body with sea water and being submerged in sea water. I fear in my mother's case, it came too late to help her. She died that same year."

"And you have no other family?"

"None . . . except, of course, Walter."

Garrett could detect the cold hatred in her voice when she said her husband's name. "Then you really are all alone, aren't you?"

"That's what I've been trying to tell you. There's no reason at all for me to want to stay in England."

"Except, perhaps, to save your life."

Arguing got her nowhere with Garrett, so Cynthia changed the subject. "Where are we going?"

"I have an appointment to meet with some gentlemen at the Castle Tavern. I shan't be long, but while I'm there, I've instructed Jacob to take you to see the remains of the old fort. I thought you might enjoy it. I understand the East Gate is still standing."

"That does sound like an adventure. My father was always going to take me to see the old fort when we were here before, but for one reason or another, we never made it. I should like that very much. And when you're finished, what then?"

"Then, little one, we shall see what we can do about finding you proper lodgings and employment. I can't very well just leave you here."

"Leave me . . . but where are you going? Are you

sailing for America so soon?"

"I told you I would probably be leaving today. We're going to Worthing, a few miles west of here. We'll sail in a day or two."

A day or two, thought Cynthia. Then I'll never see you again. Oh, what do I care if I never see you again. I only want to go to America, to start over, to make something of my life.

It never occurred to her to question why she had never before entertained the idea of going halfway around the world to live her life.

They pulled up before an inn. The large sign hanging out over the street identified it as the Castle Tavern. Garrett turned to her and placed a number of coins in her hand. "In case you would like some refreshment before I'm finished. Trust Jacob. He'll look out for you."

"Why, do you think I need looking out for?" Cynthia asked with a note of laughter in her voice.

"It's possible. There are some rough-looking seamen about town, and there's always some rogue out to take advantage."

Garrett got out and gave instructions to Jacob about when to return, then he was gone. Cynthia was jostled about as the coach took off. She looked at the coins in her hand. She had no idea how much money he had given her. She had very seldom had the opportunity of having any money of her own, but she fancied the coins in her hand to be a large sum. She carefully placed them in the handkerchief Garrett had given her the day before, tied it, then slipped it into her bodice.

She hadn't noticed until now, but the Castle Tavern was almost on the edge of town. Within minutes they had left the village behind and were heading east and south, back toward the sea.

Cynthia looked out the window trying to see the ruins she had been told about. She knew they weren't far from town. Her father had told her the fort had been built a very long time ago, Cynthia couldn't remember how long, for the protection of the town. She recalled something about the town having, at one time, been almost totally destroyed by invading Frenchmen. The townspeople rebuilt and when the did, they petitioned the Crown for funds to build some type of defense. Their petition had been granted and the fort built. It had stood on a bit of land which jutted out into the sea.

Cynthia was trying hard to remember all her father had told her when the coach stopped. Jacob came to help her down. She smiled, then looked around. To her disappointment there was nothing much to see.

Oh, well, all the better, she thought. It will give me a chance to talk with Jacob.

Seven

Cynthia wandered over the ruins watching Jacob out of the corner of her eye. He was a tall man, almost as tall as Garrett, but broader built. Even at a distance she could tell he wasn't as black as some of the blackamoors she had seen in London and she wondered why. He seemed content to wait for her by the coach, so she walked over to what had to have been the East Gate. It was the only thing standing of what she surmised to have once been a substantial fortress. She continued on to the cliff's edge and felt as though she were on the edge of the world. She peered over to the beach below and could see more debris from the fort. She guessed correctly that through disuse the fort had been abandoned years before and over the passage of time storms, which often battered the coast, had taken their toll.

She turned back toward the coach, walking slowly. She enjoyed being out in the open and momentarily wished she were a child again. She longed to scamper down the cliff and play in the surf. As she came up to Jacob, she selected a large stone block near him and sat down.

"Does Madam wish to leave?" He startled her when he spoke.

"No. No, I don't wish to leave, Jacob. May I call you Jacob?"

He acknowledged with a bow of his head.

"Jacob, you needn't be so formal with me. I know you're not a servant. Garrett . . . uh, Mr. Carver told me you were his friend. I'm not sure I understand all of it, but I accept it. I like Garrett a great deal."

Jacob sat as though he hadn't heard her. The silence lengthened. Cynthia made a pretense of looking at and finding enjoyment in first one thing and then another. She kept watching Jacob. He seemed to be looking at nothing. Why doesn't he like me, she wondered. Why the formality? She glanced at him sideways and decided he probably didn't know how to act toward her. She wondered again why he appeared lighter in skin tone than other black men she had seen and wished she had the nerve to ask him about himself and Garrett. Then she remembered what Garrett had said about trusting Jacob. She turned to him again.

"Jacob, tell me about Garrett. What type of man is he?"

He turned and looked at her. Cynthia could tell he was trying to decide what it was she wanted to know. "I don't know what you mean. Mr. Carver is a gentleman, a fine gentleman."

"Yes, I'm sure he is, but tell me how he happened to go to the colonies."

"You'd better ask him."

"I did. He told me he went as an indentured servant when he was quite young."

"Then why are you asking me? I've never known Garrett Carver to lie."

"I'm sorry. It's just . . . well, was there more to it than that?"

"More to it?"

"Was he . . . was he running from the law?"

"I don't think so. I've never asked. He was quite

young, hardly more than a boy. I think he was running all right, but I don't believe it was from the law. I can only surmise that he envisioned a better life for himself than the one he had in London."

"You and he are great friends, aren't you?"

He seemed to consider her question, then spoke slowly and deliberately, "Considering all, I suppose we're as close as two men ever get."

"He says he has a great plantation in the colony of Georgia."

"He does."

"How did he acquire such holdings?"

Jacob studied her a long time before he spoke. Cynthia couldn't determine whether he was just thinking or was trying to decide how much he should tell her.

"When he was freed from bondage," he said, "he was given fifty acres of land wherever he chose. 'For having been a good and loyal servant for the Trustees,' that's what he was told, he was also given a substantial amount of money. With part of that, he bought the remainder of my indenture. The rest was used to purchase additional land and materials. Our first few crops were meager but we somehow managed to make profits those years. We saved the money in hopes of purchasing additional land. I don't think he started out with the idea of being a large landholder. We were both just looking for a way to get on and to be our own men. We'd worked long enough for other people."

"Then how . . . the plantation . . . he says he's wealthy."

"And that he is. Me, too." He smiled. "I'm probably the richest nigger in all of Georgia, if not the colonies."

"But how?"

"Just before Georgia reverted back to the Crown, he was given a sizable grant from the Trustees. Several notable grants were given at the time—few to former servants, however. Having gotten the land grant, we were able to use the money we'd saved for seeds and seedlings and equipment we needed. From there, it just flourished. We . . . er, Garrett owes all his present wealth to having serving faithfully so many years. Or perhaps it would be more correct to say he owes it to himself for having been what he was."

"But he could be wealthier if he kept the slaves he purchased, couldn't he?"

Jacob relaxed visibly. "He told you 'bout that, did he?"

"Yes, he told me." She was feeling quite a camaraderie with Jacob.

"He undoubtedly would be wealthier, but he doesn't feel the need. He told me once that his expectations for a new life in the colonies have been exceeded a thousand fold."

"But why does he let them go?"

"Partly because he hates slavery. He says slavery does more harm to the slaveholders than it can ever do to the black man."

"Do you believe that?"

"I'm not sure. I'd like to, but I'm just not sure. I've seen some good white men behave abominably when it comes to their slaves. They think nothing of beatings or of using chains and thumbscrews. These are men who, before slavery was allowed in the colony, preached against it, saying it would only do harm to the colony and would make the poor poorer. So, I guess in some ways I do believe it."

"Garrett told me you once saved him from a beating."

"I did. I would have spared him more if I had been able. He was young and headstrong. His first master in the colony and my only master was a ruthless man who used his servants badly and his slaves worse. Fortunately, for me, I was one of the former. Luckily, Garrett was saved from his harsh hand or he probably would have been killed."

"And you saved him."

"Not in the way you're thinkin'. I only saved his hide from the whip, and only that because the master had known me since boyhood and would listen to me when he was in a benevolent mood. If he had really wanted to whip Garrett, he would have, regardless of what I or anyone else said."

"Then how was Garrett saved?"

"He was noticed by a visitor one day. The master agreed to sell him since he was thought to be a troublemaker. He went for a high price. Young men always go high—and he was younger and stronger than most. The gentleman who bought him turned out to be an agent for the Trustees of the colony. I suppose he noticed Garrett's youth and felt something for him. Garrett told me he was always treated more like the man's son than a servant."

"You say Garrett frees his blacks partly because he hates slavery. What other reason is there?"

"Partly in deference to me. We've worked the land together but it's against the law for a black man to own land. So, in this way, he's paying me since everything is in his name. But he'd do it even if he didn't know me. He's that kind of man."

"But if you can't own property, how are you so wealthy?"

"Garrett's set aside for me all these years. I contribute a share to the running of the plantation. I reap a percentage of the profits."

"And you're free?"

"I'm free. Garrett gave me my papers when he paid out my indenture."

"Why did you stay with him?"

"He asked me to and I had nowhere else to go. He knew he needed help. I said he was young and headstrong, but he wasn't stupid. All the farming he'd ever done he'd done in those five years he was indentured. He had a lot to learn. I taught him. He learned quickly. He's very resourceful. I could have left any time after he got the land grant, but by then we were sort of like partners. It never occurred to me to leave. He's never suggested it."

"The slaves, do they mind your position? Do they ever object to helping make you wealthy?"

"Most don't. They respect it. They know we're helping them and others like them. Those who do mind, either my position or the fact that we're getting wealthy, are just given their freedom when Garrett feels they've paid for themselves. Come to think of it, most probably don't realize we make a profit. All they're interested in is their freedom."

"You mean once he frees them he continues to help them?"

"No, ma'am. We can't afford to do that. After they've worked their additional five years, we give them money to get them out of the colony if that's what they want, or to Savannah where they can find work. Of course, some choose to stay on. If there's a place for them, we pay them a fair wage."

"Isn't it dangerous, this freeing of slaves?"

"Not in Georgia, it's not, at least not yet. I hear that in other colonies it's against the law."

Cynthia stood. "Could we walk awhile, Jacob?"

"Of course, if that's what you wish."

"That's what I wish. That stone isn't getting any softer."

"Yes, ma'am."

They walked in silence for a few minutes. Cynthia wondered what people would say if they were seen walking side-by-side. She discovered she didn't care. She bent to examine a pebble that caught her eye. Jacob waited patiently. She stood, then turned to him.

"I don't mean to pry, Jacob, but aren't you well-spoken for a black man? I mean, even in London, servants, be they black or white, aren't given an education."

"I ain't no servant, miss," he said, then smiled. "I don't always talk this way, but I can manage in polite society thanks to Garrett. He was given some education under the gentleman I told you about. He passed on to me what he had learned. Since then, we read and study together whenever we can."

"Do you share everything?" She wondered what Garrett had told him about her.

He smiled again. "No, ma'am, though it might seem so. We share only what's important to the running of the plantation and, of course, things we both enjoy. Garrett's absent a great deal on business, especially now, so it's important I know what's going on."

"What do you mean especially now?"

"There's a big uproar in America right now. Garrett, being a big landowner, is in the thick of it. It hasn't anything to do with the land, but the landowners are the ones who run the colony. Garrett's not one to be left out and learn about things second hand. He's a doer."

"Garrett tells me he wants you to stay in England. Are you going to?"

"No, ma'am. My whole life's in America. I belong there."

"Your whole life? But . . ." Cynthia was somewhat confused.

Jacob continued, "I was born in the colonies. My mama was a freed indentured servant. My father a white man."

"Then that explains why you're so much lighter than other blacks I've seen," Cynthia blurted out without thinking.

He stopped walking and looked at her. "I suspect, Miss Cynthia, that I'm more white than black. I'm lighter still than other half-whites I've seen."

"But you're . . . then how can you be considered black?"

"It only takes a drop of black blood to be black, Miss Cynthia. Look at me. There's no way I could pass for anything other than a black man."

Cynthia hadn't considered it, but knew when he spoke he was right. She herself had seen few blacks in her lifetime and yet she had known instantly he was black. "Then, you're a . . ."

"A bastard," he said matter-of-factly.

"No, that isn't what I mean." She knew she was blushing. "You're a . . . a quadroon . . . or an octaroon . . . or something like that, right?"

Jacob threw back his head and laughed much as Garrett did. "I don't know about that, Miss Cynthia, I really don't but I do know I'm a bastard."

They continued to walk.

"What became of your mother?"

He turned serious again. "I don't know that, either. Once her indenture was up she could hardly keep herself together, let alone a child. She sold me into bondage when I was six years old. I've never seen her again."

"Your father? Couldn't he have helped?"

85

"Miss Cynthia, you just don't understand how things are."

"But how deplorable, to sell one's own child."

"It's done," was all he said.

Yes it is, thought Cynthia. Hadn't her own father sold her? It was different, of course, but still the same. After a long silence, Cynthia asked, "Did you ever look for your mother? Since you've been free, I mean?"

"I looked. I couldn't find her. No one seemed to know what had happened to her. Most likely, she's dead."

"Well, then, I don't see why you wouldn't want to stay in England."

"I've been here several weeks, Miss Cynthia. I haven't seen anything to make me want to stay."

"Oh . . . well." For some reason, she felt slightly offended. "If that's the case, when do you sail?"

"I don't know. Two or three days, I believe."

"Garrett told me you're going to be sailing from Worthing. Why? Why not from right here, or indeed, why not from London?"

Cynthia had hardly noticed they were back at the coach. He was opening the door for her.

"That you'll have to ask Garrett."

"Has it to do with the trouble in the colonies? Is he in danger?"

"I'm sure I've already talked more than I should have. Are you ready to leave? We must be returning shortly."

"Yes, I'm ready." She raised her foot to the step and let him take her elbow, then she turned to him. "Can you at least tell me what ship you're sailing on?"

"The only ship anchored off Worthing, the *Providence*."

Cynthia smiled to herself as he handed her into the coach. She liked Jacob. She had found him to be a fountain of information.

Eight

On the way back to the Castle Tavern, Cynthia thought about the plan that had begun to form in her mind. Garrett had said they were going to find her lodging and a place of employment before he left. Well, she would let him do whatever it was he had in mind, then once he had taken his leave, she would see what she could do about securing herself some clothes and tomorrow or the next day she would hire a coach to take her to Worthing. Once there, she would convince the ship's captain that it would be to his advantage to take her to the colonies and sell her into indentured servitude. She shuddered when she thought about being sold into bondage, but had decided it was the only way and it all sounded very simple to her.

The only part of the plan that worried her was the acquisition of clothing. She knew it often took days and sometimes weeks for a dressmaker to complete even a single gown. Yes, clothes might present a problem, but she would cross that bridge when she came to it.

Just as they pulled up in front of the tavern, Garrett came through the doorway. Cynthia once again marveled at the grace with which he carried himself. She wondered momentarily how he had acquired such an easy, natural elegance, then dismissed it from her mind as he stepped into the coach.

"And now, Madam Faucieau," he began once he had seated himself. "Where would you like to have dinner?"

She realized she had never told Garrett her married name, opened her mouth to correct the situation, then decided it made no difference what he called her.

"Dinner?" She flashed him what she considered to be a dazzling smile. "My goodness, is it that time already? I'm really not very hungry."

"Well, I am. I've just heard of a new inn not far from here. The cuisine is reported to be heavenly. Jacob," he raised his voice only slightly as he leaned out the window, "take us to the Fountain Inn. It's supposed to be somewhere close by."

"Yessir, Mr. Carver. I'll find it," came the muted reply as the coach began to move.

Garrett leaned back in the seat opposite her. "Did you enjoy the old fort?"

"Very much so. It was fascinating. I thoroughly enjoyed the entire morning. I even got to know Jacob a little better."

"I hope he didn't talk an arm and a leg off. He dearly loves to talk."

"Quite the contrary. I found him interesting and very informative. But I don't think he's going to stay in England as you'd like," she hastily added. "He talks of America with love."

"Well, I can't say I'm disappointed." She saw a frown crease his brow. "I wish he would stay, but I'd miss him."

Just then the coach stopped. Jacob jumped down to open the door. "The Fountain Inn, Mr. Carver, Madam," he said, a huge grin on his face.

All through the meal, Cynthia could think of nothing but her plans to get to Worthing and onto the ship Garrett would be sailing on within the next few days. She hardly noticed the succulent dishes set before them, although she tried hard to comment to Garrett upon each one. There was pea soup cooked with leeks, chopped bacon and small crusty meatballs to open the meal, and a main course consisting of roast duck stuffed with oysters, onions and walnuts, with side dishes of fried mushrooms and sweet biscuits. For dessert there was an orange pudding baked in a dish with a crisp, flaky crust. It was decorated with candied orange blossoms. This was served with coffee and Cynthia found that coffee combined with the sweet flavor of the pudding was delightful.

The next few hours seemed a blur to her when she later had time to think about it. She felt sure they traveled back and forth across Brighton repeatedly before Garrett found just what he was looking for in the way of lodgings for her. What he finally did secure was a rather pleasant room in a private home with breakfast and supper included in the price. He assured her it really wasn't what he had hoped to find—he thought she would want something more private—but he nevertheless paid for three months lodging without blinking an eye. Cynthia's eyes opened wide when she saw him drop the gold coins into the outstretched hands of her new landlord. Oh, if only I had that money, she thought.

Since she had no luggage, they simply walked into her room. Garrett explained that once the summer was over, he was sure she could find lodgings more to her liking, even though Cynthia thought what she now had would have been quite adequate had she intended to stay.

At Garrett's insistence, the landlord was prevailed upon to bring them a pot of ale—the only thing he had in the house, he said—and with this they celebrated Cynthia's new home.

Sometime later, Garrett asked her what type of employment she thought would suit her.

"I have given it quite a bit of thought," she said. "I think perhaps I could work as an assistant to a dressmaker. Every young girl is taught stitchery, you know, and it is decent work for a woman."

"A fine choice. Shall we go see what we can find?"

Cynthia leaned back in her chair. "I'm really very tired, Garrett. You've been running me all over the town this afternoon. I think it would be better if I were fresh and rested when I go to look for work."

"You're probably right in that," he admitted, "but I will be leaving shortly and I should like to leave knowing that you are employed and will be all right."

"Why are you treating me like such a child? Do you think I can't take care of myself?"

"Have you ever had to?"

"Well, no. But you can rest assured I won't give up easily. I'll find myself work, and I'll do it on my own, but I will do it tomorrow."

"If you're sure . . ." he began.

"I'm sure." She leaned forward, extending a hand to him across the table. "Besides, since you will be leaving in just a matter of hours, I would like to spend them with you."

"But I thought you said you were tired," he teased as he caressed her hand.

"Garrett, I didn't mean . . ." she was flustered and lowered her head.

"Of course you did. And I'm glad you did. Come now, there's no need to feel ashamed. I'm not."

She withdrew her hand and stood. "Of course

you're not. It's different for a man."

"So I've heard, but for the life of me I don't know why."

"It just is, that's all," she said stubbornly as she began to unbutton her dress.

Garrett moved around the table and behind her. "Here, let me do that."

Having him so near, tending to so intimate a task gave Cynthia a tingling sensation and when he pushed her hair aside and bent to kiss the nape of her neck she moaned and leaned against him. She worked the sleeves of the dress down as it fell to the floor at her feet Garrett encircled her with his arms cupping a breast in each hand, kissing her neck and shoulders. When she could stand it no longer she turned in his embrace. Tender blue eyes met soft green ones for an instant before their lips met hungrily and her hands began to work at the buttons on his shirt. He picked her up and moved to the bed. Setting her on her feet, he reached down and tossed the bedclothes back.

There was no hurry as each leisurely undressed the other. Every touch, every caress added fuel to the fire which had been kindled within Cynthia at his first kiss.

Though finding it somewhat difficult, Garrett held his own passions in control wanting, for a time, no more than to feast on her beauty. At one point he directed Cynthia's reluctant hand to him and she was amazed that she should enjoy touching a man there. When she raised her eyes once again to his she could read the desire written there and sensed the playfulness had come to an end. As their lips met in passion, she wanted nothing more than to love and be loved by this colonist.

As his hands roamed over her body a warm

sensation spread to her extremities. She felt as though she were wrapped in soft, silky velvet. She even closed her eyes momentarily and luxuriated in the gentle aura surrounding her. She felt Garrett's hand on her breast, warm and loving and arched up to meet the caresses. As he moved his hand down, she spread her legs invitingly but he stopped and began caressing her belly, prolonging the ecstasy. Her breasts were being fondled by another hand, the nipples softly teased.

She opened her eyes and found him smiling down at her. Instantly his mouth was on hers, his tongue probing deeply, enticing hers. She returned his kiss with all the passion she was feeling.

His hand slid from her belly to between her legs. She welcomed it and spread her legs even wider. Within moments she was aroused as she had never been before, and Garrett was lavishing kisses over every part of her body. She reached down to caress him and he pulled away.

"Ah, little one, I dare not let you touch me there."

Not understanding, but wanting to please, she turned her attention to other parts of his body. She relished the hard flatness of his belly and the broad strength of his shoulders. She returned caress for caress until Garrett, eyes burning with desire, lowered himself onto her and penetrated deeply. Cynthia instinctively arched up to meet his thrusts, riding the crest of one wave after another before he joined her in one final zenith.

They lay still then and Cynthia could feel his heartbeat against her naked breasts and hear his ragged breathing in her ear. Time seemed to stand still until Garrett raised his head and smiled. He saw a myriad of expressions on her face. Confusion, excitement, amazement and contentment. She smiled back dreamily then pulled his dark head down to where their lips could meet in a gentle kiss.

He pulled away and sat on the edge of the bed, a teasing look in his eyes. "You know, little one, I do believe you are becoming a wanton woman."

Cynthia picked up a pillow and threw it at him, then laughed. "I believe, Mr. Carver, that you may have ruined me for sure. Wherever else will I find a man who so enjoys the things you've taught me to enjoy?"

He lay down beside her again and ran his hand over her flat stomach. Neither said a word, but their eyes held a conversation all their own.

Suddenly Garrett was off the bed and moved toward the washbasin.

"I can't, Cynthia. I just can't."

"Can't what?"

"Take you with me."

"But I didn't ask you to."

He turned and in his eyes she saw—what? Not exactly anger, or maybe it was anger, but directed at himself and not at her. "No, you didn't, but you were trying to entice me with those devilish green eyes of yours."

Cynthia didn't know what to say. What had made him think such a thing?

"Garrett, I . . . I don't know what you're talking about. I was thinking no such thing. When we were looking so intently at each other a moment ago, I was only thinking how much you've come to mean to me."

He hung his head sheepishly. "I'm sorry. I guess I read more into it than that."

Cynthia lay watching as Garrett pulled on his clothes. Tears threatened, but she forced them back.

Won't you be surprised when you see me on the ship day after tomorrow, she told him silently, for she had definitely decided she would somehow crowd all she had to do into tomorrow and leave for Worthing early the following morning. She didn't want to take a chance on missing the ship and she wasn't exactly sure when it sailed. Garrett had said a day or two. Jacob had said two or three days. She certainly could not dally in Brighton.

"You surprise me," Garrett said as he stood to button his trousers.

"I do? How's that?"

"Well, I expected tears or attacks of recrimination or something—anything. But you seem perfectly willing for me to walk out of your life."

"Are you really walking out of my life, Mr. Carver? Won't you ever be back in England?"

"Yes, I suppose I will one day."

"Well, then, we will possibly meet again."

"Possibly." He turned his back and sat down to pull on his boots.

"Are you feeling guilty, Garrett?"

"Guilty? Not really . . . well, perhaps a little, but you do understand I have to leave?"

"I understand. One way or another, I've always lost anyone I ever cared for. My mother and father, a boy I once thought I loved. I think I'm destined to live a lonely life."

He turned and looked at her. "I'm sorry, Cynthia. I never thought . . ."

"Don't be. I'm not. It's just the way things are." Then a thought struck her. "Oh, God, you're not married are you, Garrett? You never mentioned a wife, not even when I asked you about family. That's not why you won't take me with you, is it?" She didn't know why she had never thought to question him about a wife before.

He threw his head back and laughed, the laugh she had come to love. "Good Lord, no, love. I haven't had time to think about getting married. I've been too busy with the land and the blacks and . . . well, I've just never thought about it. Like you, maybe I'm meant to be alone or maybe one day I'll marry. I don't know. But that isn't why I won't take you with me. The dangers I've told you about are very real. I wouldn't want to subject anyone I cared about to such dangers."

"Do you care about me, Garrett?"

He stood and pulled on his coat. "Of course I do."

"Do . . . do you love me—maybe just a little?"

He looked down at her and grinned. "May a littie—or maybe a lot. At least, as much as I've ever loved any other woman."

"Then we will meet again, Garrett. If it's in the stars, we will. I know it."

"Jesus, don't tell me you believe in astrology!"

"Well, not exactly, but if something is meant to happen, it will, don't you think?"

"Perhaps. Now be a good girl and get up here so I can kiss you goodbye."

Tears were brimming in Cynthia's eyes as she wrapped the sheet around herself and stood on tiptoe. "Do you really have to leave so soon? There's still plenty of time to get to Worthing before nightfall, isn't there?"

"I really must. Now don't disappoint me and start crying."

"I won't." She swallowed hard. "It's only . . ."

"Only what?" He smiled as he looked at her.

"Well, it's a little frightening to be entirely on my own with no one to call on for the first time in my life."

"You'll be fine, sweetheart, just fine. I left some money for you on the table."

"Oh, Garrett, don't spoil things. Don't . . . don't pay me."

"I'm not paying you, dear girl. I'm being practical. You'll need it to help you get on the next few days."

"But you gave me some this morning. I still have it."

"Do you?"

"Well, I never had an opportunity to spend any of it."

"I haven't left you much. It's just in case you need anything. It may be a few days before you find employment. Now, I really must go. Jacob will be wondering what happened to me. Take care of yourself, little one. Believe me when I say I'd like to stay."

"I do," she said as he bent and briefly brushed her lips again.

He smiled at her, then he was gone. She backed up to the bed and stared at the closed door. She sat down heavily and glanced around the empty room, then huddled herself in the middle of the bed, pulling the sheet closer around herself.

Suddenly she jumped up and threw off the sheet. What the hell am I doing? she thought. I've almost got myself believing I'll never see him again. Good Lord, I've got things to do if I'm leaving early day after tomorrow!

She hurried around the room gathering up her clothes and throwing them on. She completed a quick, but satisfactory, toilette at the washbasin then turned to make up the bed. Laughing, she dropped the bedclothes in a heap, scooped up the money Garrett had given her and left the room.

Garrett walked out into the sunlight and stood looking at the house for a moment. He had told Cynthia the truth when he'd said he wished he could stay, but he knew if he had, it would only have made their parting harder. He had known her only a few days and now he discovered he loved her. He didn't know if he loved her because he felt sorry for her or protective toward her, or if he loved her for herself, but he knew he had to leave when he began considering the possibility of taking her with him, husband or no husband. He had already decided that would be foolish.

He turned and walked up the street. The carriage was nowhere in sight, but he hadn't expected it to be. He had told Jacob he wouldn't be ready to leave until dusk, so Jacob had returned to the King's Head for their baggage. He inhaled deeply of the tangy sea air, then sighed. He was glad he would be heading home in another couple of days. He longed to be on his own land again, to feel the rich soil between his fingers. If only he could have taken Cynthia with him, he thought, they could have had a good life together.

He scuffed his boot at a rock in his path, turned for a last look at the house, then went on. It's better this way, he told himself. He sensed that Cynthia would be all right. She had a determination that would see her through. He considered briefly delaying his journey home and returning to London to find her scoundrel of a husband and have it out with him, but if what Cynthia said was true, he'd never let her go and if Garrett were to call him out . . well, he had no desire to become involved in any legal entanglements in England.

He was halfway across town when it came to him. He stopped in his tracks. "Jesus," he swore softly.

He turned and retraced his steps. Why hadn't he thought of this before? He could delay his trip a couple of days, return to London and pay the man whatever he asked for Cynthia. He had, after all, been going to sell her at the cattle market.

He paused momentarily to wonder how Cynthia would feel about such an arrangement, then went on. He would present the idea to her and let her make the decision. Whether she chose to go with him or not, and he felt she would, he could at least give her her freedom from the tyrant.

When he got to the house, he bounded up the walk and banged loudly on the door. He was greeted by a round little woman he hadn't seen before and assumed she was the landlord's wife.

"You have a boarder here, a Madam Faucieau."

"Aye."

"May I see her, please?"

"She's out."

"Out?" He couldn't believe it. "But when? Where? I only left her a few minutes ago."

"She left just after you did. I don't know where. Just went rushing out. I 'spect she'll be back shortly. All but the taverns will be closing soon. Ye can wait if ye like."

Garrett considered her invitation then changed his mind entirely. "No, I can't wait. It wasn't important. Just some instructions I failed to give her. I can post them and she'll have them on the morrow. Please, don't even tell her I returned." He pressed a shilling into the woman's hand.

"As you say, sir."

Garrett left, chuckling to himself as he went down the walk. It's probably for the better, he told himself. I can look her up on my next trip to England.

He admitted to himself he was disappointed. He had expected to return and find Cynthia miserable over their parting. He had envisioned her flying into his arms when she saw him, but he certainly hadn't counted on her being out. Just proves I'm no judge of females, he told himself.

Nine

Cynthia stood looking at the possessions she had acquired in the last twenty-four hours and felt very proud of herself. It was the first time she could remember having done so much on her own without some sort of help. She had on a new dress and on the bed before her lay an assortment of toilette articles, a nightgown, a complete set of underclothing, stockings, a shawl which had been given to her by her landlady, a not so pretty, but very serviceable, cloak, a small valise in which to carry her things and her most prized purchase, a lovely gown. On the floor beside the bed sat a sturdy pair of shoes which almost fit. The new dress and gown, the things she had thought would present the most trouble, had been almost the easiest to find.

After leaving her room the day before, her first purchases had been the necessary toilette articles: soap, a comb and brush, hairpins, bodkins, ornamented with tiny pieces of colored glass, for her long, blond hair, and on impulse she had gotten a small vial of scent. She had also gotten some lip rouge, a small amount of which she had learned to use to color her cheeks. She felt very wanton when she used it, but liked the effect it gave her glowing face.

She discovered the money Garrett had given her was more than she had thought and she felt very rich indeed. The toilette articles had cost her only a few of the small copper coins.

She had hurried back to her room with her purchases and found it was suppertime, so decided to leave off the rest of her shopping until morning. Before going into supper, Cynthia had spread her remaining coins out on the table to look at them. She still had several copper ones and she counted ten other coins of different denominations. One she recognized as a half-crown and there was one gold coin she decided must be a half-sovereign.

At a call from her landlady, she gathered the coins into Garrett's handkerchief, tucked them into her dress and went to eat.

At supper she told her landlady she wished to purchase some clothing as hers had been delayed in arriving. Madam Courtney replied that she had a friend who was a dressmaker and she would be happy to escort Cynthia to her house when they finished eating.

As they were leaving the house, Madam Courtney insisted Cynthia wear one of her shawls. It was an old one, she said, and on second thought, Cynthia could just keep it. Cynthia smiled her appreciation as they hurried off up the street. It would soon be dark and Madam Courtney admonished Cynthia about the dangers of being on the streets too late in a town like Brighthelmstone.

Cynthia smiled and thought of Garrett when she heard her landlady pronounce the name of the town. It will be a long time before this town is called Brighton, she thought.

The dressmaker, Madam Simpson, had been delighted to see Cynthia. No, she could never make a dress, not even one of the simplest pattern for Madam Faucieau so soon. She had too many commitments to other ladies, but it just so happened she had a very nice day dress and a gown she believed to be about Madam's size which a customer had neglected to pick up before leaving town. Would this be of some help?

Cynthia had silently thanked the stars for her good fortune when she was shown the dress, a simple cotton frock, and beamed her delight at the gown, one of the prettiest she had ever seen. It was of apricot-colored silk with lawn fichu and undersleeves. She immediately told Mrs. Simpson she would take them both, even though she felt the gown was far too dressy and probably not very practical for an ocean voyage. She couldn't help but think what Garrett's reaction would be when he saw her dressed in a pretty gown.

She had tried them both on and found they fit far better than the dress Garrett had gotten for her. The full-skirted gown enhanced her figure and she loved the effect given by the quilted petticoat, just a shade lighter than the gown, which peeked provocatively around the edges of a bibbed muslin apron stitched in front. Madam Simpson assured her they would take only the slightest of alterations and she could easily have the dresses ready for her the following morning. If Madam liked, she could alter the dress she wore at a later time.

Cynthia thanked her, but told her the dress she had on was an old one she had worn only for travel.

Before leaving the dressmaker's, she inquired where she could purchase the additional articles of clothing she felt she would need until her own arrived. Between the two ladies, she was told where to find all the necessary items.

She had been so excited she could hardly sleep and after an early breakfast had set out with a list of items she wished to buy and written directions on how to get about the town. She decided to walk, for even though she had more money than she had ever held at one time, she had a lot of purchases to make and didn't want to run so short that she couldn't afford a coach to take her to Worthing.

With the precise directions given her by Madams Courtney and Simpson, she easily found all she needed and more. The cloak had been an afterthought when she saw it in one of the shops. She had searched for shoes when she found how impractical her slippers were for walking about town.

After completing her shopping, she had stopped by Madam Simpson's, then hurried back to her own room. Once there, she asked Madam Courtney if she might have a bath. The landlady had complied, but mumbled something about the indecency of bathing in the middle of the day. Cynthia would not let it daunt her good mood, though, and told her she wished to bathe and dress in clean clothes as she had not had the opportunity to bathe or the means to put on clean clothes since her arrival in Brighton.

After her bath she scrubbed the clothes she had worn and hung them out to dry. She amazed herself that she knew just how to do the things that had to be done. She then rushed off, feeling clean and enthusiastic, in search of a coach to hire for the next day. She wanted to be sure it was there early in the morning.

After securing the promise of a coachman that he would indeed be at the Courtney's early the following morning, Cynthia turned her steps toward the seashore. She suddenly felt a need to walk and to gather her thoughts.

When she saw some young boys cooking fish over an open fire she realized she had not eaten since breakfast so walked over and asked if they would sell her a piece. They had at first been a little frightened of her and could hardly believe a lady wished to buy some of their fish. Once they decided she was harmless, however, they laughed among themselves, told her they wouldn't sell her fish, but she was welcome to help herself.

Finding it hard to believe such generosity, Cynthia questioned them and one, who was more outspoken than the rest, had finally told her, 'Well, Mum, it's poor boys, we be—there's no way we could explain ha'in a copper on us, and if we were to buy som'thin', the constable would likely think we stole it. We fish about every day when we have nothin' else to do and when our luck is good, we cook some of it here. Saves our folks ha'in to worry about feedin' us, and it's far better than the bread and mush we'd get to home.''

Cynthia had smiled and thanked them, then walked down the beach with the warm fish in hand. She sat on a large rock to eat it, watching the ocean and listening to the sounds. Afterwards, she rubbed her hands in the warm sand until they felt clean before going back to the Courtneys. She retrieved the garments she had washed and now she was looking over all she had in the world.

It should frighten me, she thought, having so little with which to start a new life, but it doesn't. She had decided that at supper she would ask the Courtneys to return the rent money Garrett had given them, or at least part of it. She hadn't decided how she would convince them to give it to her, but she felt it shouldn't be too difficult. Perhaps she could say she called at the inn where she stayed and had received word her mother was ill and needed her at home—or perhaps her guardian, who left her with them only the day before, sent word for her to join him in Worthing. At any rate, she would try to get the money back. She now had with her only two of the coppers, three coins she had learned were shillings and the half-sovereign.

She folded the things on the bed as neatly as possible and tucked them into the valise. Then she lay down on the bed to rest until suppertime. She must have fallen asleep, for she awoke to Madam Courtney calling her through the door.

"I'll be in shortly," she answered, as she sat up and rubbed her eyes. She looked around the room, but it was empty. Why, I must have been dreaming about Garrett, she thought. She hurriedly splashed water on her face, dried it, then went in to supper.

Unlike his robust little wife who was friendly enough to Cynthia, Mr. Courtney was thin, wiry and, Cynthia thought, weasel-eyed. There was something about him she didn't trust. He frightened her just a little, but it was to him she turned at the supper table. "Mr. Courtney, I've received word from my guardian. . . ."

"Your guardian?" he interrupted. "You mean the gentleman who was here yesterday? Is he your guardian?"

"Well, yes, in a way," Cynthia stammered. She knew he didn't believe her when she saw a sly look pass between husband and wife. She felt the color creep into her cheeks as the thought went through her mind that he had been spying on them the day before. But, of course, that wasn't possible. Mr. Courtney had left the house shortly after they had taken the room. Then, perhaps, Madam Courtney. She stole a glance toward the landlady, but could detect nothing in her small, round face but friendliness. "He's in Worthing now and I received a message from him this afternoon that my mother is ill. I'm needed."

"A message? My dear," he addressed himself to his wife, "was there any message for Madam Faucieau this afternoon?"

Cynthia spoke before the round, little woman could answer. "Of course, your wife wouldn't know of the message. I encountered the messenger in front of the house when I returned from a walk."

"Of course." He grinned placatingly. "And what has this to do with us?"

"I . . . I need to return to London. I want the money back that was paid to you for my rent and meals—minus, of course, for the last two days."

"I'd be glad to return the money, madam"—Cynthia couldn't believe her good luck—"if I had it," he finished, stuffing a huge roll into his mouth and smiling at his wife.

"If you had it!" stormed Cynthia. "But it was only given to you yesterday afternoon. Where could you have spent? . . ." Then she caught herself. "But, of course, it was yours to do with as you wished."

"That it was," he agreed. "And I'm sorry about your mother." He cast a look which told Cynthia he could care less. "Will you be leaving us anyway?"

"Yes, first thing in the morning," Cynthia said, feeling beaten. She had counted on that money to pay part of her passage. The rest would be worked into a deal with the captain of the ship. Garrett had told her that persons often paid part of their passage; the captain of the ship furnished the rest, then he would sell their head rights in the colonies for a return on his investment. She, of course, didn't believe she would ever be sold beyond the ship's captain, for once Garrett discovered she was on board, she felt certain he would pay her passage.

She excused herself from the table and as she was leaving the room she heard Mr. Courtney scoff, "Guardian! Is that what they're called nowadays?" The sound of his laughter followed Cynthia into her room.

It was still daylight outside, but she stripped and lay her clothes carefully on a chair. She debated about putting on her new nightgown, but since it was packed, decided to save it until she was with Garrett. She tucked the handkerchief with her few coins in it under her pillow and crawled into bed.

She lay for a long time before sleep overtook her. She was awakened some time later by the barking of a dog. The moon shone full in the window and cast eerie shadows about the room. She pulled the covers closer about herself and was almost asleep again when she was aware of someone in the room, very close to her, on the far side of the bed.

She lay very still hoping it was her imagination, but when she felt a pressure on the bed, she turned and opened her mouth to scream just as a hand came down over her face.

"Screaming won't help," he said. "If you promise not to, I'll take my hand away."

Cynthia stared in disbelief.

"Promise!" he snarled.

Cynthia nodded.

"Mr. Courtney," she got out when he had removed his hand. "What? . . . Why? . . . Where's Madam Courtney?"

"Asleep. Quite sound asleep. I gave her a little something. Poor woman sometimes has trouble sleeping. So, you see, screaming would do you no good." All the time he was talking, he was removing his clothes and Cynthia felt a sickening horror. She looked at the door.

"It's locked," he said, "and I have the keys."

"You planned this," she accused as she pulled the covers to her chin and edged to one corner of the bed. "You planned this!"

"But, of course. I had thought it might wait until you knew me better, but since you're leaving tomorrow, there'll be no time. Don't you see?"

"I see no such thing. You're sick. A sick, evil, *old* man," she lashed out while trying to make herself as small as possible.

He laughed. "Not sick. Not evil. I'm one who, shall we say, appreciates fine things and you're one of the finest I've seen hereabouts lately." He chortled, then taking hold of the bedding, pulled it from her hands in one swift motion. Cynthia gasped, tried to cover herself with her hands and inched off the bed.

"Don't touch me!" she yelled at him. "Don't touch me or I'll . . . I'll . . ."

He began to crawl across the bed. Cynthia grabbed the pillow nearest her and flung it at him. He pushed it aside.

"Ah-h! I like spirit," he said as he continued to stalk her.

She backed into the chair holding her clothes and, without looking, reached for her petticoat, quickly pulling it over her head as she continued to move toward the door.

He was off the bed now. "I told you it's locked. You have no escape."

Cynthia glanced around the room for something, anything, with which to defend herself. In the instant she had her eyes off him, he lunged for her, pinning her against the door. She tried to bring her knee up between his legs but found it impossible. He pressed closer. She could feel him against her through the petticoat and began to twist, first one way and then the other, trying to free herself.

He laughed gleefully as though it were a game, then said, "If you don't stop, you'll only make it more difficult on yourself."

Cynthia stood still for a moment. She was perspiring from her efforts, her muscles were beginning to feel weak, and his foul breath nauseated her.

"That's better," he cooed. "Besides, what difference could it make to you whether you're riding a young stud or someone who's older, more experienced?"

"You spied on us!"

"I did, but I didn't have to to know your sort."

"You worm," Cynthia snarled between clenched teeth as she pulled her arms free. "You low, sneaking little bastard." Her hands clawed out toward his face, but his movements were quick. He stepped back so she narrowly missed his eyes. Her nails encountered the flesh on his chest and they both looked at the wounds as blood began to ooze slowly.

She looked up, caught an evil glint in his eyes and was really frightened for the first time.

As he reached for her again, she braced herself against the door and, summoning strength she didn't know she possessed, pushed him backwards, sending him sprawling to the floor. As she raced past him toward the far side of the room where the chest holding the washbasin and pitcher stood, he grabbed for her petticoat. It halted her movement only an instant before the bottom flounce was ripped away. She stumbled slightly as she extricated herself from the torn fabric. Regaining her balance, she reached out for the heavy pitcher and turned to see Mr. Courtney on all fours in the process of getting to his feet. Sloshing the water, she raised the pitcher high as she moved toward him. On his knees now, he looked up and made a grab for her as she brought the pitcher down as hard as she could on the crown of his head.

He slumped against her and, still holding the pitcher, she stumbled backwards against the table. She set the pitcher down, moved away from the inert figure at her feet and sat on a chair. When the knowledge of what had almost occurred struck her, she began to shake. Then realizing her task was not yet finished, she took a deep breath to control herself and moved to where Mr. Courtney had dropped her bedclothes. She picked up the sheet and methodically began to tear it into strips.

A grayness was showing through the window as she bound Mr. Courtney's hands and feet, pulling the knots as tight as she could get them. Feeling safe and knowing the coach would be arriving soon, she rummaged through the pockets of Mr. Courtney's discarded clothing until she found the key, then moved to dress. Within minutes, her valise in hand and her money tucked securely in her bodice, she was closing the door behind her. Mr. Courtney hadn't moved and Cynthia hoped his wife would find him before he was able to free himself. She smiled when she thought of how he would explain his predicament to Madam Courtney.

Ten

The house was quiet as Cynthia made her way to the kitchen. She found leftover biscuits and stew from supper and helped herself to a generous portion. She figured the Courtneys owed her that and much more. While she was eating she was assailed with thoughts of what Mr. Courtney had tried and she began to cry. She could hardly choke the food down, but knew it might be a long time before she had the opportunity to eat again. She wasn't yet finished when she heard the coach pull up in front. She wrapped some biscuits in a napkin to take with her, but left everything else on the table just as it was and started for the front door. She paused in the entry and picked up what looked to be an expensive vase. She raised it high over her head and threw it as hard as she could toward the far end of the hall. Then she was out the door, laughing hysterically and feeling better for it.

The trip to Worthing was uneventful. Cynthia slept most of the way. She asked the coachman to drive her directly to the beach, which he did, then he helped her out of the coach. She paid him, leaving only the coppers, one shilling, and the gold coin. He drove away. Cynthia was left standing there quite alone. It was still early, but she hoped to find someone to row her out to the ship she could see clearly in the distance. She sat down on a huge tree that had washed ashore and waited.

After a while, when there was still no activity on the beach, she walked to the town and into a tavern. "Are there no fishermen in your town putting out today?" she inquired of the host.

"Some," he said, "but they left hours ago. Is there something I can do for your ladyship?"

"I'm not sure. I need to find someone who will row me out to the ship, the *Providence*. Might there be someone like that around?"

"Could be. What would you pay?"

"Tuppence."

"Come now, your ladyship, 'tis a long way for one to row for a mere tuppence."

"A shilling, then," she replied. She knew it was too much and rebuked herself when she realized she could have bought herself a pot of tea and paid less.

"Done," said the man, grinning broadly. "My eldest son will row you."

Cynthia thanked him grudgingly and told him she would wait on the beach.

"The shilling, your ladyship?" He held out his bearlike paw.

"I'll give it to your son when I reach the ship safely," she replied as she turned and walked out the door.

She hadn't long to wait. She had hardly reached the beach when she saw a barefoot, gangly youth, tucking in his shirt, running toward her from the tavern. When he came up to her she saw that he was older than she had supposed—close to her own age, perhaps a year or two more.

"You the lady what wants to be rowed to the ship?"

"Do you see anyone else about?" she asked flippantly, still smoldering over the shilling she had said she'd pay. "I'm sorry, you didn't deserve that. Yes, I'm the one."

"Come on, then. The boat's this way." He picked up her valise where she had set it on the rocks and led Cynthia down the beach to a number of boats. He set the valise in one of the smaller ones and started pushing it toward the water. Cynthia followed.

"Are you sure that little boat will get us there safely?" she asked.

"Yes'm," he grunted between pushes. "Me and . . . me . . . brothers . . . use it often. 'Twill get you there safely." He was at the edge of the water now and he offered Cynthia his hand to help her in. She smiled her thanks, hiked up her skirt and somehow managed to get into the boat.

"It's larger than I thought," she said, laughing a bit nervously.

"Yes'm. Now sit yourself down in the bow—there," he said pointing, "and I'll push off."

Cynthia did as she was told. When he had the little boat waist deep in water, he hoisted himself over the side. Cynthia grabbed hold and squealed. She had never been in a boat before. He grabbed up the oars and started rowing vigorously.

"Have to . . . get . . . beyond . . . the breakers," he called over his shoulder.

Even though he couldn't see her, Cynthia nodded and gripped the seat tighter as the little boat bounced on the waves.

Beyond the surf, the water was smooth and Cynthia quickly adjusted to the roll of the boat. She watched the muscles in the boy's back and arms as he pulled steadily on the oars, and noticed how he flipped his long hair from his eyes with each backward movement. It was a silent journey and longer than Cynthia had expected. She kept watching over her shoulder as they slowly inched toward the ship. He stopped once to rest for a few minutes and told her if she wanted she could turn around and face the ship. She assured him she was doing nicely where she was.

As they drew close to the ship, she could see figures lining the railing, watching them. Then they were quite close and the men on deck were laughing and joking among themselves, slapping one another on the back. She couldn't hear what they were saying, but felt sure it pertained to her. She lowered her head and hoped Garrett wasn't on board yet. He couldn't possibly ignore such goings on.

The boy stopped rowing and yelled up, "The lady wishes to board."

"Does she now?" yelled one of the men.

"Send her up," resounded another.

"Aye, we could use a woman, sure," came a third and they all laughed.

The group quietened. Cynthia looked up. A tall, good-looking young man had stepped to the railing. "State your business," he shouted.

Cynthia yelled, "I have business with your captain. May I come aboard, please?"

"What kind of business?"

"That, sir, is none of your business." Cynthia didn't believe this man to be the captain. He looked much too young.

The sailor turned from the railing and in a moment a rope ladder snaked its way down the side of the ship. The boy rowed the little boat deftly to within inches of the ladder. Cynthia reached for the ladder as the boy held it for her, then had the overwhelming thought that the Captain might turn down her proposal.

"Please wait for me. I may be going back to shore with you."

When he made no reply, Cynthia turned and looked at him. "Will you?"

"Yes'm, and your valise?"

"I'll send someone for it if I'm staying."

"And the shilling, mum?"

"Whoever comes for my valise will pay you."

Cynthia started up the ladder, but found her shoes were a hindrance. She stepped back into the little boat and removed them. She had no place to carry them on her person so she handed them to the boy. "Do you think you can throw these up once I've reached the deck?"

"Yes, ma'am," he said with a grin.

Cynthia smiled in return, then with him holding the bottom of the ladder taut, she slowly inched her way up it.

"Don't look down," the young sailor above warned, "and feel for the ropes with your feet."

Cynthia heeded his warning and thought how very practical it was for men to wear pants.

When she reached the top, the young sailor who had taken charge took her arm and helped her over the railing. "Mr. Mason. At your service, ma'am," he said as he bowed.

"Then you're not the captain," she said matter of factly.

"No, ma'am."

"I didn't think so. Would you please take me to see your captain?"

"And are you going to go barefoot?" He smirked as a sailor handed him her shoes.

"Why, no, I . . . Look, I'm terribly sorry. I seem to be getting off on the wrong foot, so to speak," she said as she put on her shoes. She straightened and looked at him. "I meant no disrespect. It's just that you look much too young to be the captain of a ship."

"I am," he said as he offered his arm and they walked away from the group at the rail. "I'm quite low on the totem pole. Just one step above that scruffy lot back there." He motioned toward the group they had left with a backward toss of his head.

"Totem pole? What's that?" she asked as he led her below deck down a narrow, dark stairway.

He laughed easily but ignored her question. "Is Captain Tarrillton expecting you, Miss . . . Miss? . . ."

"Fawley, Cynthia Fawley. No, I don't know the captain. I hope I won't be disturbing him."

He stopped a moment when they reached the bottom to let her eyes adjust. "You will, but I doubt he will mind such a lovely disturbance," he said gallantly as they traversed a narrow passageway.

They stopped before a heavy wooden door. Mr. Mason rapped lightly.

"Yes, yes, come in," came to them impatiently through the door.

Mr. Mason opened the door and stood aside for Cynthia to pass, then stood stiffly in the doorway. Cynthia's eyes scanned the cabin. It was smaller than she had expected. A large, gray-haired man sat bent over a desk.

Mr. Mason cleared his throat. "Um, a lady to see you, Captain."

The captain raised his head and Cynthia looked into the ugliest face she had ever seen. Bushy, gray eyebrows did little to camouflage the right eye that was askew and seemed to look at nothing. A large mole rested on his cheekbone just below the wandering eye, and huge jowls drooped on either side of a mouth which was pulled into a permanent snarl by an ugly scar zigzagging up and over his left cheek, almost to his ear. Another mole alongside his large, bulbous nose only added to the horror. Cynthia was taken aback and afraid it showed. She quickly tried to compose her features.

He looked at her for what seemed like an eternity, then turned his good eye to the young sailor. "That will be all, Mr. Mason."

The young man turned and left the cabin, closing the door behind him.

The captain's gaze returned to Cynthia. "You've gone to a lot of trouble to see me. Do I know you?"

"No." Cynthia's voice came out almost a whisper. She cleared her throat. "No, no you don't know me."

"Then how may I be of service to you?"

"I understand you will soon be sailing for the colonies."

"Yes." He waited for her to continue.

"I want to go with you."

"We have no accommodations on board for a lady, miss."

"Mrs." she said.

"Beg your pardon?"

"It's Mrs. Mrs. Walter Fawley. My given name is Cynthia."

"Well, Mrs. Walter Fawley, as I said, we have no accommodations for a lady."

He rose then and Cynthia could see he was a barrel-chested man very close to her own stature. He reminded her of a fat turtle, his head set on a very short neck. He came around the desk toward her. "Come. I'll escort you topside." He reached out to take her arm.

"Oh, please, you don't understand. I've come to

make you a . . . a . . . bargain."

"A bargain?"

Cynthia saw a greedy expression cross his face. But in no time, he regained his equanimity. "And what kind of bargain would a lovely lass like yourself have in mind?"

He was so close, Cynthia could smell the foulness of his breath. She backed up slightly. "As I said, I want to go to the colonies, but I have no money with which to pay my passage."

He scanned her clothing then gave her a look of disbelief.

"It's true. I haven't any money aside from a few coppers and a single shilling." She could feel the weight of the gold coin between her breasts, but continued. "The shilling I have promised to the young boatman who rowed me here."

"I don't tote charity cases."

"I don't expect you to. I have heard of ships' captains who will give passage to persons then sell their head rights on the other side."

"Aye, 'tis done. Done it meself, but not for some time. Indentured servants are hardly a profitable commodity nowadays, what with the blacks being brought in by shiploads."

"But it is still done?"

"Aye, by some." As they talked, he was closely inspecting Cynthia from head to toe—more closely than he had before. She had the same sickening feeling she had had on the auction block, that he was undressing her with his eyes.

"And what of your family?"

"Dead, all dead."

"Your husband, too?" he asked with one eyebrow raised.

"Yes," she lied.

"Left you penniless, did he?"

"Yes."

"Well, Mistress Fawley, I believe we can strike a bargain. Indeed, I do. Won't you sit down? I'll have to draw up some sort of legal form to make this binding, you understand."

Cynthia nodded and sat where he had indicated.

"In the meantime, I'll have one of the hands pay off your boatman."

Cynthia handed him the shilling. "He has what few belongings I possess. If someone could bring them to me, please."

"But, of course." He left and Cynthia watched the door close behind him. She wished she could run, but where to? She hadn't like the sudden change in the captain's attitude, nor the glint in his eye. Neither had she liked how he had put her under such close scrutiny. Well, she decided, if he gives me any real trouble, I will call Garrett—but please, not before we sail, she thought. Garrett mustn't know I'm on board before.

Captain Tarrillton returned momentarily. He strode across the cabin and sat behind his desk. Cynthia almost laughed when she realized he was strutting for her benefit. She decided she would have no real trouble from him.

He hastily scribbled a few lines on a piece of paper then handed it to her. "This should cover it, don't you think?"

Cynthia looked at the paper in her hand but could make out very little of the captain's scribbling. Not knowing what to look for in a legal agreement, she took the pen he held out to her and carefully signed her name below his.

"There now, 'tis done, lass."

Cynthia tried to smile, but couldn't. The realization had just crossed her mind that she had herself done what Walter had tried to do. She had sold herself. But it's not the same, she argued. This I did of my own free will.

". . . so you can stay here."

She realized the captain had been talking to her. "I'm sorry. I wasn't listening. What was it?"

He looked a bit annoyed. "As I said, we have no accommodations for a lady on board, so you can stay here."

"Thank you, sir. You're most generous, but I can stay anywhere. You needn't give . . ."

"No buts. You will stay here."

There was a rap on the door and when the captain acknowledged it, a young sailor entered carrying Cynthia's valise. He set it down and left.

There was a long silence during which Cynthia sat studying her folded hands before the captain stood up. "I must go on deck. We're sailing with the evening tide. Make yourself at home."

Cynthia looked up as he donned his cap. "Are there any other passengers on board?"

"We have only one passenger. A Georgian planter . . . and his manservant," he added as an afterthought.

He started out then turned back. "I'm going to lock the door from the outside. 'Tis for your own safety. A lovely, young woman on board is quite a novelty, you know."

He went out. Cynthia heard the key turn in the lock. I must have been wrong about him, she thought. He's been nothing but kind to me—even worried about my welfare. Then his words came back to her: "We have only one passenger."

Eleven

For a long time after the captain left, Cynthia sat where she was, too stunned to move. What have I done? she asked herself over and over. What have I done? Captain Tarrillton's words kept ringing in her ears—only one passenger! Why, I'm just cargo . . . *cargo*. When she fully realized the situation in which she had placed herself, she jumped up and ran to the door, but found it securely locked from the outside. She pounded on the door and screamed, then listened, but heard no sounds of footsteps coming to her aid. She turned to the window behind the captain's desk. I could break it and jump out, she told herself, then decided she would no doubt drown. She couldn't swim more than a few strokes.

She sat on the edge of the captain's oversized bunk, obviously built to accommodate his bulk. The sudden thought of even sitting on that fat, ugly little man's bed nauseated her. She stood up and started pacing. No plan for escape came to mind. She soon tired of pacing, so she sat in the chair. Realizing she was hungry, she took out the cold biscuits she had brought with her from the Courtneys and began to munch absent-mindedly on one. It felt pasty in her mouth. She looked around for something to drink. Seeing nothing, she began opening drawers and closets until she found a bottle containing a dark liquid. She uncorked the bottle and sniffed. It smelled very much like the captain had earlier. It must be rum, she decided. She had never seen or tasted any, but knew it was sometimes doled out on board ship.

She raised it to her lips and sipped slowly. The taste wasn't at all unpleasant, so she took a larger swallow. It burned all the way to her stomach and made her eyes water. She didn't choke, but it momentarily took her breath away. She set the bottle on the desk by the biscuits deciding to take only small sips hereafter. She ate all three biscuits and sipped sparingly of the rum, all the while trying to think of some way to get out of her present situation.

If I ever get out of this mess, she told herself, from now on I will think things through more carefully before I place myself in the hands of others. She scolded herself. You really should have more sense, Cynthia Fawley. Not every man you run into is going to be a Garrett Carver. Last night should have proven that to you. The thought of the previous night brought a lump to her throat. She sipped from the bottle to wash it away. It didn't help much so she started talking to herself.

"Get hold of yourself. What's done is done. You've got yourself into a fine pickle now and you'd best think of a way out."

She stood and turned to the window. Her head was reeling. She glanced at the bottle and found she had drunk more than she intended, but she didn't think it was enough to make her feel so queasy. It must be because I'm not used to it, she told herself as she groped for the bed. I'll just lay down for a bit, then I'll feel well enough to think what to do.

Cynthia awoke to deepening shadows in the little cabin. She could feel the ship moving beneath her. Oh, no, she thought, I haven't! She groped through the semidarkness looking for a lamp, which she found, but could find nothing with which to strike a flame. She made her way back to the bunk and huddled herself onto one end of it. Her head ached. She wished someone would come with something to eat and a cold drink of water.

She hadn't long to wait. There was a noise at the door and Captain Tarrillton entered carrying a lantern. Cynthia blinked at the light.

"Ah, I see yer awake. Well, we're underway." He bustled around the room lighting lamps. "Have been for some time. I was afraid you were going to sleep the night away." He took off his coat and hat and hung them by the door. "Be ye hungry?" He didn't wait for Cynthia to answer. "I've ordered the cook to send us something."

He sat down at his desk and looked at Cynthia. The bottle of rum was still sitting where she had left it. "I see ye've a taste for the bottle. Well, 'twon't matter. Ye'll still bring a pretty price in the colonies."

"I . . . I was thirsty. I could find no water. I would like something to drink and I am hungry."

"Good, good. Cook should be here soon."

Cynthia tried to avoid looking directly into his ugly face. She was afraid her fears would be too apparent, but in the silence, she could feel his eyes going over every inch of her body.

"Aye, a pretty price," he said.

Cynthia shuddered.

"Ye aren't taken with me, are ye?"

The question surprised Cynthia and she looked at him with her mouth agape. "I . . . well, I . . ."

"No need to think up a lie, lass. I saw the look on yer face soon as ya laid eyes on me." He gazed off into space. "It's always been that way with women, but maybe, just maybe this time 'twill be different."

Cynthia was too afraid to ask what he meant.

There was a knock on the door. "Come in," he growled as he pushed things to one side of the desk. A young boy entered, carrying a tray that was almost more than he could handle.

"Beg'n your pardon, sir. Cook tol' me to bring this to you."

"Good, lad. Sit it here."

The boy saw Cynthia then and almost dropped the tray. He regained his balance and proceeded in the direction of the desk. Setting the tray down, he reached to remove the cloth covering the food and stole another look in Cynthia's direction. She smiled at him but was afraid to say anything.

The boy fussed a bit longer until the captain dismissed him. "That will do, lad. About your duties now."

"Aye, aye, sir," the boy said as he backed out. Cynthia thought she saw just a hint of a smile for her as he closed the door.

She felt certain the boy would tell someone about her being in the captain's quarters—but what good would that do? No one knew she was his captive. No one except Mr. Mason knew but that she was a friend of the captain's and by now, even he probably thought she was Captain Tarrillton's paramour. Why, oh, why hadn't she told someone of her plan? At least then they might wonder why she hadn't been seen on deck during the day. Well, *if he keeps me locked up for long, they will wonder. Word might even reach Garrett that a young woman is on board. He might make an effor to pay his respects.* She paused in her thinking for a moment. *But this is ridiculous*, she told herself. *No one has done anything to me. I'm just being foolish. Mr.*

Courtney's attack last night has made me distrustful of everyone.

With that last thought, she turned to the captain and the food. She was ravenous and had expected some meager fare, but sitting on the desk before her was a veritable feast. There was roast beef with roast potatoes, Yorkshire pudding and horseradish sauce. One steaming dish held tiny carrots cooked in a sweet syrupy sauce. There was a plate heaped with steaming biscuits and a dish containing an assortment of fruits. There was water and milk to drink and a steamy pot of black coffee.

"Eh, I see yer surprised."

"Frankly, yes. I never expected such . . . such luxuries."

"Well, enjoy them now. We won't have 'em for long. Fresh things spoil rapidly. We only have them for a few days out o' port then it's to salted beef and pork and hardtack. Aye, ye'll get plenty tired of those before you see the colonies. Come, girl, eat." He motioned to the chair by the desk.

Cynthia got up from the bunk and, stumbling with the roll of the ship, made her way to the chair.

"Ye'll find your sea legs in a day or two," he promised as he set a plate in front of her. "Here, help yourself."

He began forking large amounts of food onto his own plate and Cynthia, forgetting him for the moment, began to do likewise. She felt as though she could eat everything on the tray.

They sat in silence for a few moments, each intent on his own plate.

"Have you a glass?" Cynthia asked. "I could use a drink of that water."

" 'Course ye could. I'd forgotten," he said as he opened a drawer of his desk and set a metal mug in front of her. "Will this do?"

Cynthia nodded gratefully, took the mug and filled and emptied it twice before her thirst was slaked. Then she filled it with milk. It tasted delicious. After draining the mug for the third time, she offered it back to the captain.

"I've another," he said.

Captain Tarrillton finished eating first and leaned back in his chair. Cynthia tried to pretend he wasn't there. She fussed with the food left on her plate, all the time thinking about how things had been with Garrett. She knew now that she loved him. She wondered how he felt about her.

Presently, Captain Tarrillton belched loudly and brought her out of her reverie.

"Ye'd better eat, lass. Ye'll be needin' yer strength before the voyage is over."

Cynthia glanced at him but could see only kindness and concern showing in his good eye. A shiver ran up her spine when she looked at him. What a cruel trick nature played upon you, she thought. No one should be so ugly.

"My countenance offends thee? Well, part was an accident of birth. The rest I've brought on meself."

Cynthia tried to pretend interest in her supper.

"The life of a ship's captain is a lonely one and one I'm suited to. Most people are put off by me looks. But enough of that, lass," he said as she laid her fork to rest. "Cook outdid himself. A truly fine meal, wouldn't you say?"

Cynthia nodded. "Yes, thank you."

He reached into his desk again and brought out a bottle of fine French wine which he set before her. He turned back to the drawer and lifted out two silver chalices. Cynthia was amazed that the disgusting little man had such impeccable taste.

"Would you care for some wine?"

"I . . . I . . ." She was about to say I don't think so, then changed her mind. She didn't want to do anything to antagonize him. "I think that would be lovely," she finally said.

"A very good wine, you know."

"Yes, I know. I . . . I'm honored you wish to share it with me."

" 'Tis no good to drink fine wine alone. It somehow loses some of its flavor." He leaned across the desk toward her. "Ale one can drink alone, or rum—but never wine, a good wine, that is. Also, 'tis best shared with a woman." He eyed her closely. "A young, lovely woman if at all possible."

"Thank you," she said. Then to change the subject: "I remember as a child we sometimes had wine with our meals. My mother would always let me have a little, but one rarely sees French wines in England nowadays. It's illegal, you know, since the war. For years all we've gotten is that horrible port. Not very palatable, I'm afraid."

He handed her one of the goblets. She lifted it to her nose and sniffed, then took a small sip and rolled it around on her tongue. It was exquisite.

"I see yer upbringing hasn't been remiss. You know how to savor good wine."

"It's delicious," was all she could think to say. He beamed and she thought she caught a glint in his eye.

The hour grew late and the wine was consumed in almost total silence. Cynthia purposely let the captain drink most of it. She still didn't trust him and the way he looked at her did nothing to convince her she should. She wanted a clear head should he decide to try something.

The wine finished, Captain Tarrillton wiped the goblets with the cloth that had previously covered the tray of food, then carefully laid them back in the drawer. As he did so, Cynthia stacked their dishes onto the tray. After all she had had to drink and the large meal she was feeling quite uneasy and looked about the small cabin for a place to relieve herself. Captain Tarrillton pointed to the foot of his bunk. Cynthia stood and weaved in that general direction. At the foot of the bunk she found a chamberpot.

"I . . . uh, I . . ." She didn't know what to say. She could hardly ask the man to leave his own cabin. She looked at him. He was obviously much amused at her discomfort.

Finally, he rose. "I'll be leavin' ye alone for a few minutes," he said as he picked up the tray. "This goes outside for the boy to pick up." He moved across the room. Pausing by the door, he put his hat on his head and slung his coat over his free arm. "I'll be takin' a turn on deck before I return."

Cynthia smiled her thanks as he went out, then stiffened when she heard the key turn in the lock a few seconds later. Then she relaxed and laughed at herself. I'll at least have a bit of warning when he returns, she thought.

She was sitting stiffly on the edge of the chair when the captain returned less than an hour later.

"I thought to find ye fast asleep," he said as he came in.

"I . . . I didn't know where you wanted me to sleep."

"Why, in my bunk, of course."

Cynthia felt the color rising in her cheeks. "Captain Tarrillton, I had hoped you realized that I have no intention . . ."

" 'Course not, girl," and he muttered something she couldn't hear. "But 'tis the only place for you to sleep unless, of course, you prefer to sleep 'tween the decks with the hands."

"But surely you have accommodations for passengers."

"You, lass, are no passenger. I thought I made that clear," he growled, then caught himself, "but even if you were, there are no accommodations. My first mate has given over his small cabin—the only other on this ship—to the Georgian. You, my dear, will have to sleep here."

"But, then, where will you? . . ." She left the question unfinished.

"I have a bedroll," he said. "I'll sleep on the floor tonight." He chuckled. "It seems that today I have acquired a reputation of sorts, thanks to you. My hands think that you and I . . ."

Cynthia gasped.

"Well, I haven't told them any different. I'll step outside a few minutes while you make ready for bed."

"That won't be necessary. I can sleep in my clothes."

"You'll sleep much more comfortable," he said as he opened the door. "Besides, I'll be on deck long before you wake in the morning."

He closed the door behind him. Cynthia stared at it for a moment. She was having trouble believing he was being so gallant after some of the things he had said or almost said to be more precise. Nevertheless, she did as she was told. She hurriedly removed her dress and her heavy petticoats and crawled into bed, pulling the covers up to her chin. The bedclothes reeked of the captain. She made a face but decided it was better than sleeping on the floor or, as he had said, between decks with the hands.

Captain Tarrillton came in and turned all the lamps off but the one on his deck. He removed a bedroll from a closet and put it on the floor then sat down at his desk.

"I won't be long," he said. "I just have to fill in the ship's log for today and go over my cargo lists."

At the word "cargo," Cynthia grimaced then turned her head to the wall. She could hear the captain's pen scratching in the silence and presently she heard him pouring liquid into a mug. She assumed it was the rum she had found earlier. After a long while, she dozed. She awoke, not knowing how long she had slept and found the lamp was still burning. She tried to stay awake, telling herself she would until she knew Captain Tarrillton was asleep. Her eyelids grew heavy. She forced them open not knowing if she had slept or not. The lamp was still burning.

Again and again she drifted in and out of sleep. Always the lamp was burning. Finally, she turned her head so she could see him. Too late she realized her mistake. He was sitting, staring at her lasciviously. Her eyes popped open in fright.

"I shee you been thinkin' 'bout me, too." His words came out slurred, his eyes were glassy, and Cynthia knew he was quite drunk. She had seen it often enough with her father.

"Of . . . of course I have," she lied as she pulled the covers tightly about herself. "You . . . you've been so kind to me." She tried to sound cheerful and sincere. "Just like a . . . a father."

She hoped that would give him second thoughts about what she knew he was surely thinking. He did seem to ponder what she had said for a moment.

"Aye, it's true. I'm rarely so kind." Then she saw his good eye light up. "Fathersh get to kiss their little girlsh goodnight, don't they?"

Before Cynthia had time to think, he was

lumbering towards her. In a split second, she had her knees drawn up to her chest and her back against the wall, the covers still somewhat around her.

"Whassa matter?" He tried to sound innocent, but the look on his face betrayed him. "Jus' wanna little kiss."

Cynthia's mind groped for something to say. Finally, "It's ah . . . it's late, Captain. You've had a lot to drink. Perhaps . . ."

"Why, you little she-bitch," he snarled, his speech suddenly losing its slur, his eyes clearing. "Yer probably running from the law or you wouldn't be in such a hurry to leave England. I take you on board, you fully knowing why and what to expect. You're mine—you understand—mine! Bought and paid for like the whore you are. I'll have that kiss and more besides." He lunged for her.

Cynthia planted her feet in the middle of his flabby belly and kicked with all her strength. He stumbled backward into the desk and just stood there, looking at her with hate for what seemed to Cynthia like an eternity. Then his eyes went glassy again and slowly, slowly, he crumpled to the floor, hitting his head as he went down.

In an instant Cynthia was out of the bunk and grabbing up her clothes. She stopped at the door. There was nowhere to go, no place to hide. She couldn't go to Garrett yet or he would probably insist they return her to England. No, they were still too close to land. Besides, even if she could go to Garrett, she had no knowledge of the ship or where he might be found. She turned back and looked at the bulk of Captain Tarrillton spread on the floor. She slumped against the door for a moment and tears slid from her closed eyes. She hastily wiped them away, laid her clothes on the bunk, then turned to the captain's bedroll, still unbound, laying in the middle of the floor.

She fought with the knots, then spread the thin blankets out on the rough planking. Turning to the man on the floor, she reluctantly examined his head where it had hit the desk. She was relieved to find it wasn't cut, but he would surely have a headache come morning. Then, inch by slow inch, she pulled and tugged until she had him onto the blankets and covered. She was breathing hard and perspiring from her efforts, so sat beside him on her knees for a moment to recover. Bright colors caught her eye from the closet he had left ajar and upon examination she found it to be a cushion embroidered with bright, gaudy, oriental designs. The greasy stains in the center of it told her he had probably used it on several occasions. She gently lifted his head so as not to disturb him and placed the cushion beneath it.

She then blew out the lamp on the desk and felt her way to the bunk. She pulled the blankets around herself and tried to sleep, knowing her only hope was that he, like her father had so many times, would remember nothing of what had happened when morning came.

Twelve

She knows she's too big to be sitting on Mama's lap rocking, but she does so love it. Mama seems to enjoy it, too. They both seem to know Mama isn't going to be with her much longer—but how does she know that?

Now they're in Brighthelmstone. Mama's not rocking her anymore. Papa says Mama needs her rest. Mama goes to a doctor every day. He sends her to the sea. Afterwards, Mama is sick—sometimes for a long time. She cries. She doesn't want Mama to be sick. She wants Mama to rock her again.

She's on Mama's bed. It's rocking. No, she and Papa are making it move. Papa's pulling her away from Mama, telling her that Mama is gone. Then Papa is gone. She has no one.

She finally sees Papa. They're together again. They're standing beside a large wooden box. She knows Mama is in the box and she's rocking from one foot to the other, marking time to a chant someone has started. It's a chant for the dead.

Cynthia opened her eyes with a start. She was still rocking and for a moment she didn't know where she was. When she remembered, she turned to look where she had left Captain Tarrillton. He was gone. There was no sign he had slept on the floor. She wondered briefly if perhaps she had dreamed the whole thing, but knew she hadn't.

She jumped up and ran to the door. It was locked as she had feared it would be. She leaned against the door for a moment and then decided she had better dress before someone came. She knew it must still be quite early, for though the sun was up, she felt a chill in the morning air. She looked about for a way in which she could wash up, and finding none, took the vial of perfume from her valise and splashed some on. As she pulled on her clothes she puzzled over the captain's behavior of the night before. He had, at one point, seemed so concerned for her, then he had come at her. She shuddered when she thought of what had happened, hoped it was only because he was drunk, and prayed that he didn't remember.

Using the toilette articles she had purchased, she brushed her hair till it was silky, then watching in one of the lamp bases, she pinned it up in a modish style and stuck the new bodkins in. She couldn't really tell how it looked, the image in the lamp base was so crazily misshaped, and she had no way to see the back of her head, but she hoped it was becoming. She refrained from using any of the lip rouge for either its intended use or on her cheeks. She had no desire to give Captain Tarrillton any thoughts, if it hadn't been the drink talking last night. She tucked her valise at the foot of the bunk, then busied herself for a few minutes longer straightening up. Having nothing else to do, she sat down in a chair to wait.

It wasn't long before the captain came in, trying to be quiet until he saw her. "Ah, I see you're up. I hadn't really expected to find you so, but I'm glad I do. I loathe laziness."

Cynthia smiled.

"Are ya hungry, lass? My, but don't you look pretty this morning? I trust you rested comfortably. Sleeping like a baby, you were, when I left you."

As his words came tumbling out one on top of another, Cynthia was trying to decide if he remembered the events of the night before. She finally decided either he didn't or he was ashamed and was nervously trying to make up for what had taken place. His face told her nothing. He seemed as concerned for her well-being as he had the previous evening. She realized he had finished talking only when he cleared his throat and said, "Would you, lass?"

She didn't know what his last question had been, so she smiled and said, "Yes, I am hungry. I would love some breakfast." He looked puzzled for a moment, but hurried to her side and offered his arm. "But aren't we going to eat here?" She saw the gleam in the captain's eye, but her last wish was to go wandering about the ship and take a chance on running into Garrett.

He must have thought her afraid of the men because his next words were, "I assure you, my dear, you shan't be bothered. The Georgian is not up and about yet—at least, I haven't seen his manservant—and the men are either on deck or in their hammocks. I shall personally escort you to the galley."

Cynthia stifled the hysterical laughter welling inside her. She knew she had nothing to fear from Garrett, except possibly his anger, and she was more afraid of the man beside her than she was of those under his command. She sensed something frightening in Captain Tarrillton, and even though the men she had seen the day before had made some pretty raw comments, they had been good-natured about it. She didn't feel she had anything to fear from the men, at least not yet. They had all just recently been in port. Perhaps in a few weeks, but then, how long did it take to get to the colonies? Surely not long at all.

Since he had said Garrett was still in his cabin and because she had no real desire to be closed up with the captain for another meal, she accepted his arm as she stood up and started toward the door. He stopped there and offered her her shawl which he had obviously hung there himself. Cynthia couldn't remember doing it.

They didn't see a soul as they left the cabin. The captain led Cynthia to the companionway and up onto deck. The men on deck looked up from their work as Cynthia and Captain Tarrillton came into view, but no one said a word. The captain patted her hand as she paused at the top of the companionway.

"No need to fear them, lass."

"I'm not afraid," she said. "It's only . . . well, I'm not used to so many men just looking at me."

He chuckled. "Better get used to it. It's going to be a long voyage, but not a one of them will bother you, I promise," he said as they strolled the deck toward the center of the ship.

"But how can you be so sure?"

"They wouldn't dare. They know I'd have 'em keel-hauled."

"Keel-hauled?"

"Now, don't go worrying your pretty head about that. It's a punishment, and a severe one, but every man on board knows I'd do it if any of them even tried to lay a finger on you."

"Then they still think? . . ."

"No, no. I set them straight this morning."

"You told them of our bargain?"

"Of course not. It matters not to me what they think of you, but I know it matters to you. I told them you were my niece. That way, you'll get more respect from them."

Cynthia warmed to him immediately. "Thank you, Captain," she said slowly as they came to a second companionway. She paused and scanned the horizon. "How far out to sea are we, Captain?"

"Oh, not far at all yet, lass. Not far at all."

As they descended into the galley, Cynthia wondered just how long she would have to wait before it was safe to let Garrett know she was on board.

They were seated in the corner at a long plank table before she remembered. "It won't work, Captain, telling them I'm your niece. I already told that nice Mr. Mason that I didn't know you."

"Aye, and neither would a niece of mine know me. I haven't seen my brother since we were little more than lads."

"Oh," she said as she turned to the food being set before them. As she ate, she wondered about the captain. He seemed to be two people locked into one body. She found it hard to overlook his hideous characteristics, yet he did seem to have a gentle, thoughtful side. On the other hand, he frightened her. His looks were enough to frighten anyone, but she had no doubt that he was trying to rape her the night before. It puzzled her. She wondered which was the real captain.

Her thoughts were interrupted by heavy footsteps on the stairway. She looked up just in time to see Jacob descending, then quickly bowed her head, thankful that she was in a corner and in the shadows. She hoped he hadn't seen her. She busied herself with her food until he left, carrying a tray with him.

"You're mighty quiet, lass," the captain said when he had finished his second cup of coffee.

"I told you I was starving." Then after a long

silence, she asked, "That man who came in? Who is he?"

"That's the Georgian's nigger. Probably bringing his master's breakfast to him. A disgraceful hour for a man to be having breakfast, but never did see a one of those rich planters worth his salt. They're all lazy, no-count women chasers. Too much time on their hands. They can buy all the niggers they need to do their work for them."

"But that's not . . ." She was about to say that's not fair, you don't even know Garrett Carver. The captain looked at her. "That's not true of all of them, is it?"

"All I've ever seen. A bunch of mealy-mouthed Mama's boys. Some of the younger studs have taken to going to England for their schooling. I've carried one over now and again, some of the ones not quite so rich, but they do like to be puttin' on airs."

"Then, this Georgian is a young schoolboy?" She almost choked over the words.

"Not him. He's older. Probably about ten years younger than me. I don't know about him. Never saw him till he hired me ship. Most of the cargo in the hold is his, too. He must be powerful wealthy, but he's not from around the coast or I would have heard about him. I know most of the coastal planters. He must be from several miles inland."

He lapsed into silence then and Cynthia finished her meal.

Garrett had been up since dawn and was starving, but Jacob had convinced him it would be more seemly if his servant were to bring him breakfast in his cabin. He had stormed at Jacob that it didn't matter anymore, they were on their way home on an American vessel, but Jacob had wanted to make sure, especially since he had seen more than one new hand on board ship. They had argued and Jacob had finally convinced him that a few more hours of play-acting wasn't going to hurt either of them.

Garrett let Jacob in when he heard a kick on the door. His friend set the tray down on the table, then turned to him. "She's on board."

"She's on board? Who's on board?"

"That Cynthia gal, that's who. I just saw her in the galley with the captain."

Garrett grabbed him by the shoulders. "Are you sure?"

"Pretty sure," Jacob said as he brushed Garrett's hands away. "Leastways, it looked like her. Can't be positive. They was sittin' in a corner in shadows."

"But what could she be doing here? I left her in Brighton. Even paid her lodging three months in advance."

"I tol' ya not to trust her."

"No, Jacob, she's no spy. I'm sure of that. What I'm not sure of is how she got here and why."

"We could ask around."

"Later. First, we'll eat. I'm starving. Later, I'll pay a visit to our good captain."

They were just finishing breakfast when there was a knock on the door. Garrett, who was closest, turned to open it. A young seaman stood in the passageway, twisting his cap in his hands.

"Cap'n . . . uh . . . beggin' yer pardon, sir. Cap'n wishes to pay his respects and asks if you'd care to join him on deck, sir?"

"Thank you," said Garrett. "I'd like that very much. As you can see, I'm not fully clothed yet. Tell Captain Tarrillton I'll be up presently."

"Aye, sir. I'll tell him."

Garrett closed the door and turned to Jacob. "Well, it seems I won't have to go about hunting up the captain after all. Where's my coat, Jacob?"

The black man shrugged his shoulders and glanced around. "Who knows? But I doubt it's lost. Just covered with somethin'."

Garrett started picking things up, looking under them. "Jesus," he muttered. "There's not enough room in here to cuss a cat without getting hairs in your mouth."

Jacob chuckled. "You noticed that, too, did you?"

"Yes, I noticed that, too."

"No need to get sarcastic, Garrett. Yer the one who's had that little gal hangin' on your coattails ever since we left London. Shoulda left her there, if you ask me."

"I didn't ask you," he said as he retrieved his coat from under a blanket.

"I know. If you had, I'da tol' you to leave her there."

"It doesn't matter now. She's here, at least you say she is, and I want to know why." He turned as he was going out the door. "For God's sake, Jacob, why don't you see if you can straighten this place up some while I'm gone?"

"Yassuh, Massa Carver. I do jus' lak you says."

Garrett stopped then looked at his friend sheepishly. "I'm sorry, Jacob. I didn't mean it that way. When I get back, we'll see if we can't stow some of this stuff more equally around the cabin so we have more room."

"I know you didn't mean it, Garrett. Just thought I'd slow you down a bit. Seems to me you're awful het up over her bein' here. Maybe you've gone sweet on her. Is that it?"

"Jacob," he said, smiling, "you know me better than that."

"I wonder," his friend said as the door closed. "I wonder."

141

Thirteen

Garrett momentarily shaded his eyes from the bright sunlight as he stepped on deck. A quick look around told him Cynthia was nowhere to be seen. He turned aft and sought the captain. He sighted the man, saw he was busy, so walked to the railing a bit unsure of his legs. He remembered that on the voyage over, one of the seamen had told him he would find his sea legs in a few days, but he hadn't. He wondered if he ever would. He leaned on the railing, thankful to have something to hold onto. This is the third time I've been on a ship, he thought, and I like it less each time. I wish there were any other way to get to and from England. There will undoubtedly be more voyages to make before the Crown recognizes the colonists rights, if it ever does. Then, too, there's the plantation. It's getting of a size that business will probably, on occasion, require my presence in London. I guess I should be thankful I'm not prone to seasickness, he mused.

The breeze blew his hair across his eyes. He brushed it aside and looked up at the billowing sails high above him. It was a perfectly clear day with puffy white clouds skittering across the sky. He knew they were making good time and hoped it would continue, although he realized there was always the possibility of the sails going slack for days on end. He had never experienced it, but had heard it talked about by others. He heard footsteps behind him and turned to face a young officer.

"Mr. Carver, sir, captain's apologies but he'll be detained a few minutes."

"Quite all right, Mister . . . uh? . . ."

"Mason, sir, Henry Mason."

"Thank you, Mr. Mason. You're one of the officers, aren't you?"

"Yessir, second mate, sir." Garrett noted a slight swelling of the young man's chest as he threw his shoulders back with pride.

"Good sailing weather we're having, isn't it, Mr. Mason?"

"The best, sir."

"Do you think it will hold?"

"I hope so, sir, although this time of year it's hard to say."

"Storms, Mr. Mason?"

"Oh, no, sir. Not much chance of encountering storms the likes of which we saw coming over. Even worse. We could be becalmed, sir."

"I've heard of that, Mr. Mason, but doesn't it usually occur much further south of our route?"

"Yessir, usually, although I've encountered it many times and many places."

"You've been at sea a long time, then?"

"Since I was a boy, sir."

"I understand we're favored with female companionship this trip, Mr. Mason. I'd venture to say you've not encountered that too often, eh?"

"Aye, sir. I mean no, sir. I mean, sir, I've not encountered it often, but you're right about the girl. I helped her aboard meself, yesterday. Captain Tarrillton's niece, she is."

"The captain's niece, you say?"

"Aye, sir. Must be his sister's offspring. She told

me her name. I didn't hear her too well, but I know it wasn't Tarrillton."

Garrett turned and saw the captain coming their way. No poor bastard, he thought, should be born to look like he does and he was for a moment consciously grateful for his own even features. He turned back to the young officer. "Well, Mr. Mason, it appears you're to be relieved of your duties here. Perhaps we'll be lucky and our weather will hold."

"Yessir, I hope so, sir—about the weather, that is." Sensing he had been dismissed, the young man turned and left just as Captain Tarrillton joined them.

"Ah, here ye be. Good morning, Mr. Carver."

"Captain."

"And did ye fare well on our first night out?"

"Quite, thank you."

"Your cabin, it's satisfactory?"

"Small, but we'll make do. We did on the way over."

"Of course you did. Harrumph, sorry I didn't get better acquainted then, but we should be favored with better weather this trip. In fact, if you like, it should be mild enough some nights to sleep on deck. I do at times and some of the men, too. Much more restful than below decks this time of year."

"Thank you, sir. I might try it." Garrett stood for some time scanning the horizon hoping the captain would mention the woman on board.

"You like to sail, Mr. Carver?"

"Frankly no, Captain. This is my third voyage, the first being many years ago when I went to America as a young boy, the second a few weeks ago. I've always admired the sea, the beauty of it and the power, but not from the deck of a ship, I've decided. I feel more at ease with my feet planted on solid ground where I can run my hands through rich, warm soil and call it home. I fear I wasn't cut out for a life at sea."

"Aye, I suppose 'tis a special man who is geared for adventure."

Garrett let the insult pass. He didn't care to argue the point with the man and he wondered if Jacob had indeed seen Cynthia.

"I trust, Captain, that my cargo is in good shape." He knew it was. He had checked it when he came on board the day before.

"Of course it is, Mr. Carver. You question my ability?"

"Indeed not, Captain. One reason I hired you was because I heard you not only knew your business but ran a tight ship."

"That I do, Mr. Carver, that I do. And the other reason?"

"I heard you could be trusted."

"Well, now, whoever told you that was only partly truthful," he chuckled at some private thought. "I know why you've come to England at this time and the secret is safe with me. It wouldn't do for me to blab about you around London and take money out of me own pocket, now would it?"

"Then there were no questions asked in London?"

"None."

"You've put on some new hands."

"Aye, I have, Mr. Carver, but how would ye be knowin' that?"

"Can they be trusted?"

"Trusted?" And he laughed so hard it shook his entire body. "Sir, I wouldn't trust a one of these bloody deck hands. Some'd sell their own mother if they thought they'd get so much as a farthing for her."

"Then they're ordinary seamen?"

"I'd say so, yes. They were brought on by a couple of me boys. I needed some extra hands, so took them on. But how observant of you to notice, Mr. Carver."

"Not me. It was Jacob, my . . . uh . . . my nigger. He's totally devoted to me, thinks of nothing but my safety. That reminds me. He tells me we have another passenger with us—a young lady?"

"Ah, so he did see her. I was wondering when you'd ask. A lovely young thing she is, too, my niece."

Garrett could detect no trace of a lie in the man's face. "Your niece?"

"Yes, the youngest daughter of me only brother."

"And she's going to America?"

"Aye. She was awaitin' for me in London. Seems she's betrothed to some young swag who was going to school over here."

"In London?"

"No, no, not London. The lad was schooled in Edinburgh. I'm Scottish, you know. Me brother has commissioned me to see the lass safely to the arms of her beloved."

"I'm sure you'll do so, Captain. I should like to meet the young lady and pay my respects, sir."

"Of course, Mr. Carver. I'm sure you would find her delightful, but unfortunately, she's indisposed. Poor lass has never sailed and is taken with a wee bit of seasickness. When she's feeling herself again, I'll let you know."

"Thank you, Captain. I'm sure she will relieve the tedium of the trip for all on board."

"Beg your pardon, sir?"

"No insult intended, I assure you, Captain. It will be most refreshing to have a lovely young face to look upon now and again."

"It is indeed, Mr. Carver." Garrett noticed a slight change in his voice, but could detect nothing in his face. "And, now, sir, if you'll excuse me, I'd best return to me duties. Good day to you, sir."

"Captain."

Garrett watched Captain Tarrillton stride aft, then turned to make his way back to his cabin. He paused outside the captain's door on his way back. Whoever the girl was, she was obviously close enough to the captain to be staying in his cabin. Garrett had been over the entire ship and knew there was no other place she could be staying. He started to knock, then changed his mind and walked on.

He entered the cabin he shared with Jacob and found his friend sitting cross-legged in the middle of the bunk shelling and eating peanuts, collecting the shells on a piece of paper.

"Well, did you see her?" Jacob asked.

"No. The captain says the girl you saw is his niece."

"Could be. I told you they was sittin' in the shadows, but I woulda swore it was her."

Garrett removed his coat. "Two things puzzle me. He says the girl is seasick, yet you say she was eating when you saw her. Seems to me if someone was that sick, they wouldn't be eating."

"Don't know. I've never been seasick."

"Also, the captain says she's his brother's daughter, but a young officer I talked with says her name isn't Tarrillton."

"Nothin' so strange in that."

"I suppose not. But you seemed so sure it was Cynthia."

"You'll have to prove to me it wasn't."

"But why . . . how did she get here?" He sat

147

down on the bunk and helped himself to the peanuts. They sat in silence, shelling and eating peanuts for a few minutes.

"You gave her money, didn't you?" Jacob asked.

"Only enough for a few days. Not enough to pay her passage."

"Maybe she had money."

"No, but the rent money—she could have gotten the rent money back."

"That'd explain how. What I wanna know is why."

"She's running from her husband. She's terrified of him." He hadn't intended telling Jacob, but it was out now. "That day at the cattle market, he was putting her up for auction."

"That explains it, then," Jacob said as he threw his long legs over the side of the bunk, stood and stretched.

"Not to me, it doesn't. If it is Cynthia and she's a paid passenger, why is she staying in the captain's quarters?"

"Maybe she chose to stay there."

Garrett scowled at his friend, then turned his attention back to the peanuts.

"Well, she took up with you easy enough, didn't she?" Jacob chided.

Garrett made to get off the bunk then settled back. "Thanks for the compliment, friend. No, it must be his niece, just as he says. I suppose we'll find out. No one can be seasick for three months, can they?"

Jacob shrugged and sat on the edge of the table. "What'd he want with ya, anyway?"

"Damned if I know." He abandoned the peanuts and leaned back against the wall. "All we talked about was the girl and the new hands you saw. He says they're just ordinary deck hands. I expect he was just trying to be friendly like. Even apologized for not getting better acquainted on the trip over."

"Now why do you suppose he'd want to go and get friendly all of a sudden?"

Garrett shrugged his shoulders, deep in thought now. "Unless . . . unless, the girl is Cynthia and he wants everybody on board to think she's his niece."

"But why?"

"I don't know, Jacob. There's something missing. There has to be. I see no reason for Captain Tarrillton making a point of telling me the girl is his niece."

"Me neither, but let's think on it. There must be a reason."

"Think on it, hell, I'm gonna go find out." He stood up. "The girl's in his cabin now. Has to be. I didn't see her on deck."

"Now, hold on, Garrett. If it is Cynthia, she knows we're on board. If she wants to see you, she'll find you. The ship's not all that big."

"How does she know we're on board?"

"You told her we were sailing from Worthing, didn't you?"

"Yes, but how did you . . . ?"

"She told me the day we went to the old fort. And this is the only ship that was anchored off Worthing. I told her that much. If she wants to, she'll find you—if it's her."

Garrett sat back down, brooded for a few minutes then looked up at his friend and smiled. "Thanks, Jacob."

Jacob spread his hands and with a blank look on his face said, "I'm only looking out for my own black carcass. If the captain were to put you in irons for raising a ruckus, what would become of me?"

Garrett looked at the floor. He knew Jacob was lying but loved him the more for it.

"Now, if it's all right with you, I think I'll go on deck for a while myself," Jacob said as he walked toward the door. "Maybe the captain's 'niece' is up and about now."

"Or maybe he has her locked in."

"Now there you go again. I swear to God, Garrett, I've never seen you get so het up over a filly before. You ain't even thinkin' straight today. If it is Miss Cynthia, she ain't locked up or I wouldn't've seen her in the galley this mornin'."

Jacob left, shaking his head as he went out. Garrett watched him close the door, then stretched out on the bunk, his hands behind his head. He wished he knew what was going on. Jacob was right. He wasn't thinking straight today. At times, his head felt as though it were filled with cotton.

Fourteen

Cynthia stretched lazily, ran her hands behind her neck, lifted her damp hair and spread it on the pillow. It was warm in the cabin. She had stripped to her chemise. She ran her hands slowly down her body and the movement brought the unbidden image of Garrett before her. Her thoughts drifted. She remembered the pleasures he had introduced her to when they were in Brighton. She longed for him now, for the feel of him, the smell of him. She longed to see those laughing blue eyes she had come to love. Reluctantly, she pushed the thoughts from her mind. She couldn't think about Garrett yet, but soon—soon now she was sure it would be safe to let him know she was on board.

She had been at sea for over a week. Her life had taken on a pattern. There had been no further advances from Captain Tarrillton and she had decided it was, after all, the drink he had consumed their first night out. He was playing the role of doting uncle to the hilt. He still locked her in when he wasn't present, still insisting it was for her own safety, but she had no desire to be wandering about the ship anyway. She didn't want to chance running into Garrett. She hadn't seen him as yet, but she had seen Jacob on more than one occasion, each time being extremely cautious that he didn't see her. She had worried that Jacob had seen her that first morning in the galley, but when Captain Tarrillton made no mention of it, she assumed everyone on board thought her his niece.

She found the mornings and afternoons were her own. The captain always showed up to escort her to and from meals and always when the galley was empty or nearly so. Their evening meal was sometimes taken in the cabin. She did not know or care what the captain did or where he was in the meantime. She was thankful for the privacy, but she was bored beyond words. Aside from two books Captain Tarrillton had given her to read, she had nothing to do, but consoled herself with the thought that she would now be forever free from Walter. She knew he would never believe her capable of putting an ocean between them. She smiled when she thought of Walter searching all of England for her. She knew he would. He wouldn't easily give up a valuable possession.

The vision of Walter faded and she was with Garrett. She didn't fight it this time, but let the dream envelop her. Even as one part of her was consciously aware that she was drifting into sleep and should cover herself in case the captain came in unexpectedly, another part of her told her the afternoons were hers and welcomed sleep as a way of passing the time.

Garrett was caressing her. She was wild with desire. She docilely let him remove her clothing, then he just stood and looked at her. She called upon all her instincts to entice him to join her. He laughed and turned away. She called out to him, but he was gone. She called again then sank back and cried.

Her sobbing woke her, but she refused to open her eyes until some sixth sense told her she wasn't alone. Her eyes flew open. Captain Tarrillton was standing beside the bunk watching her. She hazily wondered if this weren't more of the dream. Cynthia glanced down and tried to cover herself with her hands, pulling the chemise closer.

"Don't," he roared, then smiled. "You're too beautiful to be hidden."

Her mind still fuzzy from sleep, Cynthia obeyed meekly, looking at him quizzically.

He began jerking at his clothes.

Cynthia closed her eyes. It's a dream, she thought. A nightmare.

"Don't close your eyes," he ordered. "Look at me. Am I so disgusting you can't look upon me?"

Yes, her mind screamed, but she obediently opened her eyes and looked at him. The sight of him nauseated her and, fully awake at last, she reached out for something with which to cover herself. There was nothing. She was lying on the blankets. Her clothing was not where she had left it. Terrified, she tried to sit up. Still half dressed, the captain grabbed her shoulders and pinned her to the bed.

"Oh, no, you don't. I'll not give you that advantage again," he said, all the while smiling.

"You . . . you do remember. You weren't drunk."

"Only drunk enough to give you the advantage. It won't happen again."

"But . . . but you've been so kind to me."

"Aye, and now 'tis time to give me a wee bit o' kindness in return."

When he shifted his weight, Cynthia tried to squirm out of his grasp. He laughed sadistically. "Ah, a fighter, are you? Well, we'll have to take some of the fight out of you." An evil glint came into his good eye.

"Please don't do this," she begged. "Please don't."

His face turned red, the scar a deep purple. "Don't beg," he hissed as his fingers dug into her arms. "They're always beggin'," he said as his gaze shifted to somewhere over her head, "beggin' me not to touch 'em like I was diseased. Even some I paid for changed their minds when they saw me. Like my money weren't no good. But I showed 'em, I did. Showed 'em what it's like to have a real man." His gaze shifted back to her. "And now, lass, I'm goin' to show you."

Cynthia closed her eyes. She sensed any struggle on her part would only infuriate him further and she knew she was no match for his bulk.

"Open your eyes, bitch," he growled. "You'll not go pretending I'm some dandy. You'll know you've been taken by Jack Tarrillton, by God."

Cynthia remained still. He hit her. She opened her eyes and he grabbed her hair in one hand, forcing her head back as he stretched full-length beside her. He threw one leg over her, pinning her down, then he tried to kiss her. Cynthia shuddered and turned her head away from the foul stench of him. He jerked her head around to face him and kissed her full on the mouth, his tongue probing, his lips moist and bruising. Her left arm was pinned between them. Cynthia brought the right one up to hit him. He grabbed it and neatly folded it back and under her so that she was held fast by her own weight.

Finally he reared back and looked at her. "Shoulda taken you while you was sleepin'."

Cynthia looked at him in horror.

He chuckled. "A little somethin' in your tea and you sleep like a baby," he said as he ran his hands up and down her body. "I've watched you every afternoon and I've waited—waited for you to learn to like me, but when I saw you today in that skimpy little shift, I could wait no longer."

Cynthia felt sick. So that was why she had no trouble sleeping these long afternoons away and she had thought it the warmth of the cabin and the tedium.

"I know about the Georgian, too," he continued. "You called his name in sleep more than once." His hands continued to roam.

"You, you bastard," she hissed. "Leave Garrett out of this."

"Oh, I intend to, lass. I fully intend to. He has no idea you're on board, so I may surprise him later, but not before I'm finished with you." His voice turned surly. "You're mine, you understand? Bought and paid for with your passage and I intend to make good on my investment, now *and* when we reach the colonies. But," he said, his voice changing again, "if you try to love me just a little, lass, mayhap we can shorten your servitude."

"Never!"

"Never?"

"You filthy, stinking bastard! What you want isn't love."

He stood up, then turned and slapped her with all his strength. The power of it threw her back against the wall. She sat holding her cheek, too stunned to move.

"You're mine," he said again. "And ya'd best be rememberin' it!"

Suddenly there was the sound of running feet in the passageway and loud knocking on the door.

"Captain, Captain, come quick," a voice yelled. "There's a fire in the galley!"

Cynthia flung her face into the pillow and sobbed in relief.

She heard the captain moving about the cabin

quickly putting on what clothes he had taken off but ignored him until she heard him unlock the door. She raised herself on one arm. "I'll never, never eat or drink another thing you give me."

He paused only a moment. "Then you'll die," he said unconcernedly.

"I'd rather."

He left then and Cynthia sobbed into the pillow until no more tears came. She relived the entire afternoon over and over but found no way she could have changed the events. She grew cold and crawled beneath the covers, tried to force herself to relax and wished her head would stop pounding. At long last, just as the cabin was growing dim with nightfall, she slept.

When they heard the cry of "fire," Garrett and Jacob joined the crew running toward the galley. Garrett paused briefly outside the captain's cabin. Jacob turned and grabbed his arm.

"No time for that now. You know what's in the hold beneath the galley! It could blow us all sky high."

Garrett nodded, then he and Jacob took the stairs two at a time.

Smoke was filtering up from the galley as they raced the length of the ship. By the time they got there the fire was under control and almost out. Everyone breathed a sigh of relief, and Garrett and Captain Tarrillton exchanged a knowing glance.

Back on deck, the captain smiled benevolently. "No harm done. 'Twas a minor thing."

Garrett rubbed his eyes still stinging from what little smoke he had encountered. "Are you sure? Shouldn't we check the hold below the galley?"

"We can if you like. I'll accompany ye myself—but I'm sure all is well."

Half an hour later when Garrett had determined for himself that all was secure below decks, he and the captain stood at the railing enjoying the fresh air after the stuffiness of the hold.

Captain Tarrillton turned to leave. Garrett laid a hand on his arm. He immediately noticed a change in the man's attitude at being touched.

"Beggin' your pardon, Captain"—he removed his hand—"but I was wondering about your niece. Is she feeling better yet?"

"Some," he said. "Some better, Carver. Another few days and I'm sure she'll be wantin' to be out and around."

"I'm glad to hear that, Captain, because if she weren't your niece and you're holding some young woman against her will, I'd be obliged to report it to the owners of the ship."

Garrett could sense the man beside him bristle.

"Now why would I be doin' a thing like that?" Captain Tarrillton asked, avoiding Garrett's eyes.

"I don't know, sir, you tell me."

The captain turned on him, his face twisted with rage. "You doubt my word?" he roared. "You'll be meetin' the girl soon, Carver. When you do, draw your own conclusions." He paused. "Until then, if I were yerself, I'd not be thinkin' o' bandying tales about Jack Tarrillton. Because it appears to me, Mr. Carver, there are secrets you want kept. Aye, and they're safe with me, but I'll tolerate no more threats from the likes o' you."

He stalked off and Garrett was left standing in the twilight knowing no more than he knew before. And, he thought as he leaned against the railing, I might just have jeopardized my whole mission. As he turned to make his way to his cabin, he decided the captain's bark was probably worse than his bite. The man could ill-afford to be in bad with the ship's owners and Garrett felt they both knew it. Garrett also knew the owners' backgrounds had been closely scrutinized before the hiring of the ship had been done.

Fifteen

It was mid-afternoon. Cynthia sat looking at the pitcher of water from across the room. She had had nothing to eat or drink in three days except a small sip, now and then, of the captain's rum. She had thought that safe enough. After her refusal all the first day, he had even stopped coming to escort her to the galley, but had brought water. Each day she had used the water to bathe as best she could, but she still felt dirty from his touching her. She had even doused herself and her clothing with all the perfume in the small vial but couldn't rid herself of his foul stench.

She knew she was growing weak and knew she needed the water, but was terrified to drink anything he gave her, even though he assured her it was harmless. She had seen very little of him since that day, but when he did come to the cabin he acted as though nothing had happened and each time he had brought the water he'd told her how concerned he was for her welfare.

She turned her back on the water, telling herself she would rather die than be at his mercy ever again. If I die, she thought, he'll not make good on his investment and she smiled thinking of it. Then a frown creased her brow as she thought of all her life she could remember up to the present. If I die, I'll have lived for naught and he might well get away with it again and again with some other stupid fool.

"No, I must live," she said aloud even as she turned back to the water. "I must live and when I get the chance, I'll go to Garrett and . . ." She stopped. And what? she asked herself. Tell him I'm an idiot? Better that, she thought, as her hand rested upon the handle of the pitcher, than a slow death.

She raised the pitcher and sniffed but could detect no strange odor. She put the rim to her mouth, took a small sip and rolled it around her tongue. It had no noticeable flavor. She then took several swallows, returned the pitcher to the desk and moved to the bunk. She sat down and waited.

When several minutes had passed, she felt no different, so retrieved the pitcher and drank deeply. Finally satisfied and feeling overly full, she returned to the bunk and lay down. She gazed at the beams overhead waiting for her body to tell her she had been tricked by the captain. After all, she thought, I didn't taste any difference in the tea I drank and he did say he had put something in it. She waited. Nothing happened. She chided herself for thinking he'd try again so soon now that she was fully aware of his deviousness.

It was hot and stuffy in the cabin. She was feeling uncomfortable as though she had just eaten a large meal, but she refused to entertain the idea of even loosening her clothing. Fighting sleep, she counted the beams over and over. In the grain of one she found a face. It reminded her of a girl she had once known. She searched for more images, but found none. Still feeling very much herself, and by now sure the water hadn't been drugged, she got up, crossed the cabin and got one of the books the captain had given her to read. She made a face as she picked it up. She had already read it, had found it boring, but decided anything was better than just sitting. She sat down at the captain's desk and opened the book. After reading the same passage three times, she flung the book aside.

"I have to get out of here," she said aloud. But how? she thought, and at what price? She walked to the door. Maybe he had forgotten to lock it this time. She reached out, but knew it wasn't true even before she tried it. "Oh, God," she cried as tears filled her eyes.

She stumbled back to the bunk and fell on it in a heap, sobbing into the pillow. She condemned herself over and over for having been so stupidly gullible. She thought back to how naive she had been. Had two years with Walter taught her nothing? The thought of it made her sit up and dry her tears. Of course she had learned from Walter, but how to use her knowledge here?

She thought about Captain Tarrillton and the little she knew of him. His one inherent weakness seemed to be his need for love and approval from her. Well, she thought, it will be no easy task, but perhaps I can act as though I care for him long enough to win his trust. She knew she must have the freedom of the ship in order to reach Garrett and she felt he was her only haven. She became nauseous when she thought of what his decision might entail, but told herself it was the only way. Captain Tarrillton could do no worse to her than Walter had done and she had lived through that. She knew if she didn't do something, she was at his mercy and by drugging her he could very possibly have his way in the end.

"Then the decision is made," she said aloud, sounding more determined than she felt, but feeling better for having said it.

She lay down again and calmly tried to think of

how she might use her womanly wiles to have her way. She soon grew drowsy from the gentle rocking of the ship. She instinctively tensed herself to fight sleep, then relaxed and let it come.

Awakened by the smell of food, she was sure she was dreaming, but opened her eyes and looked around. She was alone and on the desk was a covered tray. She jumped up and removed the cover. Before her sat a bowl of thick soup, some hard rolls and a bottle of unopened wine. It smelled heavenly and made her mouth water. Without even sitting down, she took a spoonful of the soup and sniffed it, then laughed at herself for being so childish. She put the spoon to her lips and found it to be only lukewarm. She gulped it hungrily and dipped the spoon for another bite before sitting down. She ate greedily then, roll in one hand and spoon in the other, dripping occasionally on her dress and not caring. She ate until she could hold no more. The bowl was still half-full. She pushed it aside and reached for the wine.

She struggled for some time to remove the cork, and was at last rewarded. There was no glass on the tray so she tipped the bottle and drank from it. The wine was not as good as that of the captain's private stock, but she found it to her liking. She took several more drinks before replacing the cork. She was just setting the bottle back on the tray when she heard the key in the lock. Remembering her decision of earlier in the day, she forced herself to smile when Captain Tarrillton came in.

"Ah, lass, 'tis good to see you've come to your senses. Going without food and water will do harm to no one save yourself."

"Yes, thank you, Captain."

"Is there anything else you'd be liking, girl?"

"A bath," she blurted without thinking.

Captain Tarrillton roared with laughter. "A bath, is it? Surely, lass, you realize there's no way for you to have a bath."

"But surely you bathe."

"Aye, on deck. We pour sea water over one another."

Cynthia knew her face was crimson.

"I'll think on it, lass. Mayhap we can come up with something. Now, if you'll excuse me . . ."

Cynthia stood up to be out of his way. He opened a desk drawer and removed an instrument she had never seen before.

"I came in for this. I want to take a reading before the sun sets."

"What is it?" asked Cynthia trying to show an interest.

"This, lass, is a gift from heaven for sailors. It's fairly new. An invention by one of our Americans, a Mr. Godfrey. It's called a sextant."

"What's it for?"

"By taking readings on the sun and stars and using charts, I can tell exactly where we are. Would you like to come up on deck with me and see how it works?"

"Some other time. I'm really not very presentable." He seemed to be in such a benevolent mood, she was hoping he would leave the door open.

"But there's no one about much this time of day, lass. Most of the lads are in the galley and I assure you, those on deck won't notice whether you're presentable or not. They've not seen a woman for a fortnight and they won't be noticin' how you're dressed."

"Thank you for the compliment, Captain, but I really would like to bathe and wash my clothes first, if you don't mind."

"Have it your way, lass." He strode across the room, stopped at the door and turned. "I'll be speakin' to the cook. Mayhap he has a tub he can spare for you."

He went out. Cynthia waited breathlessly, then she heard the key in the lock. She stamped her foot in disappointment, but knew she could do nothing.

An hour later she was on her knees beside a large tub of hot water scrubbing everything she could think of. Wadded on a towel beside her, with rivulets of water spreading out from them, were the sheets and pillow slip from the bunk. She had just put the dress Garrett had given her into the tub. She slowly got up and looked down at the dress she had on. It was spattered with food stains as well as the wash water and she wanted to wash it also, but had only the apricot-colored gown she had bought in Brighton into which she could change.

Deciding she didn't want to wear the gown, she went rummaging in the captain's closet hoping she could find something with which to cover herself while she washed the dress she had on. She didn't know what she was looking for, perhaps some sort of dressing gown, but when she found none, she drew out a pair of breeches and shirt, both of which were in a corner as though they had been discarded. They were old, but she noted they were of good quality. She held them up for inspection and found no holes, although one of the shirt sleeves had a neat mend up high toward the shoulder and a stain Cynthia thought might have been a bloodstain, although the shirt evidenced numerous scrubbings.

She shrugged, tossed the clothes to the bunk and quickly stripped, dropping her own clothes near the tub. She pulled the shirt on. Though it was much too big through the shoulders, she found the sleeves were only a bit too long. The pants fit her much the same, with the legs being only slightly long. Sized as they were, she knew they had to be the captain's, though from a day when he had been less portly. She tucked the shirt in then looked around for something with which to tie the pants snugly about her. Seeing nothing close at hand, she returned to the closet. Reaching to the farthest, darkest corner she felt something like a cloth band and pulled it out. As she pulled, she realized the band was tied around something. When it came into view she saw the band was a sash. It was tied to a sword scabbard which held no sword. It looked to be almost new. She briefly wondered what could have happened to the sword before untying the sash and placing the scabbard back in the closet. The sash was quite long so she wrapped it around her waist twice before tying it. She turned back to her laundry just as the captain came in.

"Eh, lass, I see ye've made good use of the tub and water, though I thought ye meant to bathe."

Cynthia felt her anger rising. She knew he had come in purposely to catch her in the tub. She choked back angry words and said instead, "I did. I mean, I do, only I haven't any clean clothes."

She noticed he was eyeing her critically.

"I . . . uh . . . I hope you don't mind," she said, indicating the clothing she had on.

He came across the room, stopped directly in front of her, looked her up and down, then walked around her in a circle.

Cynthia waited expectantly, her bare toes working at the floor.

"Where did you get those?" He spoke so quietly for a moment Cynthia wasn't sure he'd spoken at all.

She glanced at him. His face looked younger, his eyes told her his thoughts were far away.

"I . . . I found them in your closet, Captain. If it's not all right, I can change back into my own."

Instantly his mood shifted. "All right? 'Course it's all right, lass. More women should take to wearin' breeches. By God, if they shouldn't."

Crimson with embarrassment, but somehow pleased, Cynthia knelt beside the tub again. "I'm almost finished, Captain," she said as she rolled up her sleeves. "Is there any place I can hang these so they'll dry?"

"We can string a line on deck." He sat down on the bunk. "They ought to dry in no time at all."

Cynthia forced herself to smile at him, then bent over the tub. In a few minutes she was finished. The brown dress Garrett had given her had fairly soaked clean while she had changed and the second dress she gave only cursory attention. The captain watched her all the while. She didn't like washing her under things in front of him, but there was no way around it. After all, she thought, they're going to be hanging on deck for every jackanape to see. She was thankful it was almost dark.

"I'm ready now, Captain," she said as she caught the corners of the towel into a bundle and stood up.

He opened the door for her, bowing low as he did so, and they left the cabin.

Sixteen

Garrett was standing on the starboard side and a bit aft of the gangway when they came on deck. Even dressed as she was, the girl moved with a certain familiarity and he was sure it was Cynthia, though he couldn't see her face. His first impulse was to step forward and confront her, but he held himself in check—even stepping back a few paces.

The cool air washed over Cynthia as she stepped onto deck. She inhaled deeply and immediately felt refreshed. The captain led her toward the bow of the ship, motioning to two seamen as they walked. He gave them orders to string a line from the rail to the foremast and they ran ahead.

It took her no time at all to secure all the washed articles to the line and they whipped away from her as though they longed to be free. She knew they would dry quickly. The captain never left her, so when she had tied the last item in place, she sat down beside him.

"Could we sit here for awhile?" she asked, afraid to suggest that he leave her to herself.

"I have me duties, lass, but you may sit here if you like. I'll be able to see you when you're ready to go below. I'll escort you."

"Oh, that won't be necessary, Captain," she said, trying to conjure up the smile she had always given Walter when she wanted him to believe her. She slanted her head and teased him with her eyes. "I still need my bath, you know."

In the fading light she saw a kindling of hope in his good eye and his face was all smiles. He leaned close and spoke as though they were in a crowded room, "Do ya mean, lass?"

"I mean nothing," she said. *Fat pig,* she thought, flashing him another smile. "It's just that I've been thinking. We've a long voyage ahead of us. 'Twould be a shame to waste all that time being enemies."

"My thoughts, exactly, lass," he said as he grabbed her hand and drooled over it. " 'Tis a wise young woman ye be. I'll have clean water brought immediately."

"Oh, no, Captain."

"Jonathan," he corrected her, wagging a finger in front of her face.

"Please, Jonathan, I'd like to sit here for a while and enjoy the breeze in my face. Besides," she lowered her voice to a confidential level, "there's really no hurry, is there?"

"Of course not, my dear," he said, patting her hand. "You sit here as long as you like. Your bath will be ready when you are."

"Thank you, Jonathan," she cooed as she watched him heave his huge bulk to a standing position. She smiled up at him. He gave her a leering glance, a small salute, and strutted off.

Cynthia covered her mouth with her hand to keep from giggling out loud. He looked utterly ridiculous. She knew what she was letting herself in for with the captain, but still felt it was the only way she had of ever getting to Garrett and putting some sanity back into her life. She pushed thoughts of the captain and what lay ahead to the back of her mind and sat, with her arms wrapped around her legs, watching the rise and fall of the horizon.

Garrett saw the captain leave her and head his way. He hoped he wouldn't be seen. He wanted an opportunity to speak with Cynthia alone. He crouched down a bit as the captain went by.

He watched Cynthia a few minutes longer, waiting for the captain to get busy enough not to notice him, then he slowly moved as close to her as he could before having to show himself in full view of the quarterdeck. The last few feet he strode across purposefully.

She was lost in thought when she heard footsteps behind her and turned, too late to pretend she hadn't seen him. She hadn't wanted him to find her like this. She jumped up and started to rush into his arms but something in his face held her where she stood.

"Madam Faucieau, isn't it?"

"Oh, Garrett, I . . . let me . . ."

"Or is it something else, Tarrillton for instance? He says you're his niece."

"I'm not."

"That much I believe. I just saw the two of you together. It's not hard to guess what you are to him." She saw cold hatred in his eyes.

"And just what is that supposed to mean?"

He went on as though he hadn't heard her. "But why me? What did you want from me?"

Cynthia squared her shoulders. "If you recall, Mr. Carver, I had no choice in the matter. You carried me off."

"Ah, but I offered to see to your safe return to London. You practically begged me to take you with me. And all those lies about a husband in London and your poor dead parents. What were you really running from in London, Cynthia, or whatever your name is?"

This isn't going at all right, she thought. She lowered her head. "I . . . I told you the truth, Garrett. That morning in Brighton I told you the whole truth."

"You surely don't expect me to believe that, love. Not after I've seen you and the captain together and you are staying in his cabin. How long have you known him, Cynthia? Was I just a means to get to him? Does he pay well to have you as a traveling companion?"

Garrett saw the hurt look on her face turn to one of anger. Needing to collect his thoughts, he turned and walked to the railing. You dolt, he scolded himself, you were going to give her a chance to explain. In an instant his anger had subsided. He felt her at his side.

"Cynthia, I . . ."

"Well, Mr. Carver, I see you've met my niece."

They both turned to see Captain Tarrillton scowling at them. Cynthia looked at Garrett to see the muscles working in his jaw.

"Yes, Captain, so I have. She's quite comely, although the fading light doesn't do her justice. You see, we've met before."

"Yes, she told me." The captain focused his attention on Cynthia. "Your bath is ready, my dear, just the way you like it."

She felt Garrett bristle. She looked at him but could detect nothing in his face. He wasn't even looking at her.

"You'd better hurry before the water turns tepid," the captain continued. "And put on that pretty gown you have. I'm sure Mr. Carver will find it more appealing than what you're now wearing."

Cynthia opened her mouth to say something, then closed it. So he had gone through her things, had he.

The next thing she heard the captain say amazed her.

"You will join us later for a drink, won't you, Mr. Carver? It's so seldom we're able to entertain and now that my, uh, niece is feeling better, I'm sure she would enjoy the diversion."

Garrett's answer suprised her even more.

"I'd be delighted, Captain."

The captain turned to Cynthia. "Well, along with you, lass. You don't want to keep us waiting all night, now do you?"

Not knowing what else to do, Cynthia left them. At the gangway she turned and saw they were still talking, then Garrett threw back his head and his familiar laughter drifted to her. She could only guess what they were laughing about. She turned and stamped down the stairs, pushing a sailor out of her way before he could move, and made her way to the captain's cabin.

Garrett watched her leave, laughed absently at something the captain was telling him, then excused himself saying he wished to change. He walked aft slowly, hoping the captain wouldn't think he was following Cynthia. He still wanted to talk to her and give her a chance to explain, but he wanted time to think first.

"Mr. Carver?" He heard the captain shout and turned. "Shall we say in an hour?"

"In an hour, Captain."

Hot tears stung her eyes as she slammed the door behind her. She brushed them aside harshly and saw the tub, now filled with clean water, was sitting where she had left it. Her gown, the gown she had bought in Brighton was lying on the bunk. She had wanted to save it to wear for Garrett.

"Well, I will wear it for him," she said as she jerked at the sash. "For him and the captain. I wonder which will appreciate it more?"

Having untied the sash, she quickly stripped and stepped into the tub of hot water. Remembering the soap she had purchased in Brighton, she started to get out again when she saw the small bar lying with a towel on the floor beside the tub. She sat down slowly, reached for the soap and began to scrub gently. She would have liked to wash her hair, but didn't know what effect sea water would have on it. Since the tub was rather small, she decided to wait and see if she couldn't use fresh water on her hair. A thorough brushing would have to suffice for the time being. In a very few minutes she was glad of the decision. The soap was leaving a scum floating on top of the water.

She hurriedly finished washing and rinsed herself off as she stood up. She reached for the towel and dried as much of her body as she could while still standing in the water, then, drying one foot at a time, she stepped out of the tub. At least, she thought, Garrett will keep the captain busy until I'm dressed. She had wrapped the towel about herself and just loosened her hair to brush it when there was a knock at the door. She knew it wasn't the captain. He never bothered to knock.

"Maybe it's Garrett," she said aloud and rushed for the door.

But when she opened it, she was disappointed to find it was the young boy who had brought dinner that first night. He was carrying a bucket in either hand.

At the sight of her, his mouth fell open and he blushed. "Uh . . . uh . . . b-b-beg'n your pardon, ma'am," he stammered as he turned his head. "But Captain Tarrillton said I should remove the water and tub. I . . . I didn't know . . . I mean . . ."

Cynthia closed the door part way and stood behind it. "It's all right, boy. If you'll just wait a minute, I'll slip into something."

"Yes, ma'am."

Cynthia closed the door and looked around for something with which to cover herself. The gown was there, but she didn't want to put it on yet. She grabbed a blanket that was folded on the foot of the bunk and threw it about her shoulders, then she let the boy in.

"Is Captain Tarrillton still talking with Mr. Carver?"

"No ma'am. Mr. Carver's no longer on deck." He bent to fill a bucket from the tub.

Cynthia stood in silence thinking as he filled the second bucket. He paused at the door. "I'll be back in a few minutes, ma'am, soon as I dump this overboard."

Cynthia nodded as she closed the door behind him. As soon as he was gone, she threw aside the blanket and pulled on the gown, paying no heed to how it or she looked. She had to find Garrett. She knew she could make him understand.

As she fought the buttons she was thinking of how Garrett had looked at her and her hopes of making him even listen to her began to fade. What if he doesn't believe me, she thought, what then? She wouldn't think about it now. She hadn't the time.

"I have to make him believe me," she said aloud as she finally closed enough buttons to be decent. "I have to, that's all."

She was stepping into the slippers that matched the gown when there was another knock on the door. She admitted the boy and stood to one side as he entered.

"You look lovely, ma'am," he said, his fair skin

flushed. "I hope I didn't rush you."

"Not at all," she said laughingly, feeling happy for the first time in days.

"Well, lass, I see a bath has improved your humor."

She whirled about to find the captain standing in the doorway. She wondered how he had come up so quietly or perhaps in her preoccupation she just hadn't noticed.

The excitement drained from her body which felt as though it had just been beaten. She turned away from him. "Yes," she said sullenly. "It does seem to have helped."

She walked over, picked up her brush and began to run it absently through her hair. I'll have another chance, she thought. Maybe even tonight if I play my cards right. Her spirits lifted again.

As soon as the boy left, she turned back to the captain. "Well, Jonathan, shall I put my hair up or leave it down?"

He was obviously pleased that she had asked his opinion. "It becomes you either way, lass."

"And the things hanging on deck. They should be brought in."

"I took care of it. They'll be here shortly."

He walked over to his desk and sat down, made some notations in the ship's log then closed it. He looked up at Cynthia who was still brushing her hair.

She was wondering if it would make any difference to Garrett how she wore it. She felt the captain's eyes on her and turned.

"Is there something you wanted, Jonathan?"

"A great many things, lass," he leaned back in the chair. "But most important right now is I want you to know it's going to be tonight."

Cynthia felt her heart skip a beat.

"Sit down," he ordered.

She sat in the chair opposite him.

"I don't know what there is between you and Carver, but I can guess, especially since you call his name in your sleep. What I can't understand is why he left someone like you behind."

Cynthia opened her mouth to say something. He waved her to silence.

"It doesn't matter to me. What does matter is that, as of now, you're mine. I think you've finally realized that or you wouldn't be trying to make up to me."

Her mouth opened in protest. He silenced her again.

"You don't expect me to believe you've had a change in heart as you pretended to up on deck, now do you?"

Cynthia looked at the floor.

"I'd like to believe it, lass. Given time, mayhap I could convince myself you care a little, but not with Carver on board. After seeing you with him I'll always believe you're only playing up to me to get to him, though why you'd want to I don't know."

She wondered what he was leading up to.

"I am the law on this ship," he shouted as he pounded a fist on the desk. "And if you value his safety, perhaps even his life, you will do as I say."

"But how could you hurt Garrett Carver?" She tried to sound interested, but not overly so. "If any harm should come to him, you surely would have to answer to someone. He seems to be a wealthy, prominent citizen in the colonies."

"Bah! His money means nothing to me, though he does seem to have no lack of it. There are others who would pay plenty to know of his activities of late and to get their hands on the cargo he's bringing back from England."

"His activities? His cargo? I'm sorry, Cap . . . er, Jonathan, but I don't know what you're talking about."

"He's a spy, lass, a bloody spy, but you needn't worry your pretty head about that so long as you do as I say."

Garrett a spy? Too stunned to think straight, she heard herself asking, "What is it you want me to do?"

Just then, the boy returned with two seamen to remove the tub. With them were the clothes Cynthia had hung to dry a short time before. She motioned for them to lay them on the bunk, then she and the captain sat in silence while they struggled through the door with the tub.

As soon as they left, the captain stood up and started pacing. "To begin with, he knows you're not my niece, so there's no use trying to pretend. I don't care what he comes in here thinking, but by the time he leaves, I want him to believe you're my woman. Do you understand what I mean?"

"But Captain, Jonathan, I . . ."

He leaned forward, placed his hands on either side of her chair and looked directly into her eyes. "Do you understand?" he asked quietly as he raised a hand to her cheek. "Remember, his safety depends on you."

"But what makes you think I should care what happens to him? As you said, he left me behind."

"You care all right. Of that, I'm sure. You'll do what I ask?"

She nodded.

"Good," he said, obviously pleased with himself for having so correctly guessed their relationship. He began to stroke his chin. "I may give him the opportunity to buy you later, but not before we reach the colonies. Till then, you're mine."

Having settled things in his own mind, the captain turned to his closet and stripped to the waist. Cynthia watched him, horrified for an instant, until she realized he was only changing his shirt. She noticed a white scar on his upper right arm, then turned away. Finding the hairbrush still in her hand, she began to run it through her hair.

She couldn't believe Garrett was a spy. He was British. He loved the colonies. Surely a subject of the Crown would have no reason to spy in England. Then she remembered something she had heard about taxes in the colonies. Had Garrett told her? No, it had to have been Walter or perhaps something she had just overheard. Damn, she thought. I wish I had paid more attention to Walter and his friends. They were forever talking politics and about the possibility of war in either one place or another. Had they ever talked about the possibility of war in the colonies? Of course not, she decided. It was just too preposterous.

Upon returning to his cabin, Garrett changed quickly then sat down at the small table to wait and think. He wished Jacob were here to talk things over with. Jacob always seemed to help him think more calmly, especially lately where Cynthia was concerned. He would have sought Jacob, but had no idea where he was. He thought he might have made friends with one of the deck hands.

When it was time for him to go, he had still reached no conclusions about Cynthia. He found it hard to believe she was Captain Tarrillton's whore, but everything seemed to point to that. As he stood, he decided to leave judments in God's hands. He wanted Cynthia and if given the opportunity, he'd give her a chance to explain.

He knew he would have to tread easily. He didn't dare cross the captain just yet. The man knew too much about his activities and Garrett didn't think him entirely trustworthy.

He stood outside the captain's door for a moment hoping to overhear some snatch of conversation which might tell him what to expect. When he heard nothing, he knocked.

Cynthia was so deep in thought when the knock sounded, it startled her. She jumped, returned to the present, then stood to greet their visitor. Captain Tarrillton, hurrying to button his coat, walked slowly to the door and opened it. As he did so, he gave Cynthia a warning glance.

In the few days she had spent with Garrett, she had never seen him look so splendid. He had obviously dressed with care. One glance from him and she knew he approved of her gown. She wanted to twirl around and show him how becoming it was, but knew she didn't dare, so she courteously acknowledged his arrival.

"Mr. Carver," the captain was saying, "please come in."

"It's Garrett, Captain. Please call me Garrett." He never took his eyes off Cynthia. Lord, she's lovely, he thought. He crossed to her and took her hand in his. "I'm glad you're feeling better. The captain told me you suffered from seaksickness."

She cast a swift sideways glance toward the captain and saw he was not pleased with their touching. She pulled her hand away, then looked back to Garrett. "I'm much better now, thank you." Then, remembering the captain's warning, she sidestepped Garrett and moved to his side. "Jonathan, I'm terribly embarrassed. I couldn't reach some of the buttons and I'd forgotten until just now. Could you please do me up?"

The captain beamed his approval as she turned to let him button the gown. Definitely a good beginning, his look told her. She dared not look at Garrett.

"Women," he said as his clumsy hands fought the buttons. "They couldn't get along without us, could they, Mr. . . . er . . . Garrett?"

Garrett was fighting for control. "I wouldn't know, Captain," he said through clenched teeth. "Some seem to do quite well for themselves." He forced a smile.

Cynthia looked at him just in time to see the hurt and anger on his face give way to resignation. She reached out to him. "Don't, Garrett . . ." The look of cold hatred in his eyes stopped her and held her in a trance. It slowly changed to a cool aloofness. A few awkward moments passed.

Cynthia had forgotten all about the captain until Garrett looked over her shoulder and spoke to him. "We were going to have a drink, Captain?"

She turned. Jonathan was obviously enjoying the situation in which he had put them. She had never before in all her life wanted so badly to kill someone.

"Yes, Garrett. I have some very fine Scotch whiskey. Would that be to your liking?"

Garrett moved around Cynthia. "I'd like that fine." He looked around the room. "A comfortable cabin you have here, Captain," he said as the drinks were being poured. His eyes stopped momentarily as he looked at the oversized bunk. Cynthia felt herself go crimson. She was watching Garrett and hoped he wouldn't look her way.

When he didn't, she turned her back to the both of them and tried to gather her thoughts. My only hope, she told herself, is to try to get the captain drunk so I can talk to Garrett. She stood that way for some time until she heard the captain.

"I say, Cynthia, dear."

She turned. "I'm sorry, Jonathan. Did you say something?" She avoided Garrett's eyes and tried to smile.

"Would you like some wine, my dear?"

"Yes, anything, Jonathan. Anything would be fine."

While the captain was busy pouring her wine, she stole a look at Garrett. He was regarding her over his glass. Please, she tried to beg with her eyes, please don't believe any of this. He cocked one eyebrow, tilted his glass in a salute then drained it. Damn you, she thought, you're always ready to believe the worst.

She took the goblet offered her by the captain then withdrew and sat on the edge of the bunk. She didn't feel like making small talk. She watched as the captain refilled Garrett's glass, then his own. They were engaged in a discussion about shipping routes and cargoes. She didn't wish to follow the conversation. They were seated one on either side of the desk. Now they were peering at a map. Garrett stole occasional glances in her direction and once or twice she tried to will him to know what she was thinking. It can't work, she decided, because he's shut me out.

The conversation ended abruptly when the captain suggested a game of Hazard. Cynthia declined when he asked her to join them. The look he gave her suggested she shouldn't cross him, but she stood her ground. She knew she couldn't concentrate on a game and play the role he wanted.

She stood and walked toward him. "I'll play

hostess, Jonathan and freshen your drinks. I'm not very good at the game, anyway."

He was momentarily appeased. As she purposely reached across him a few minutes later to fill his glass, she let one supple breast brush against him. He smiled his approval. She forced a smile in return.

The evening wore on in almost absolute silence except for the rattle of the die. The men bet small amounts at first, then larger sums. She was amazed at the apparent wealth of both, and the contrast between the two entranced her. The captain was greedy, jubilant when he won, ill-tempered when he lost. Garrett seemed to be playing entirely for fun. He played with cool calculation and didn't seem to notice he was losing more than he was winning. She kept her post beside or behind the captain at all times and kept their glasses filled. From time to time, she would rest a hand on his shoulder and he would pat it approvingly. How many times, she thought, did I play this same role for Walter? She kept watching Garrett, but he only occasionally looked her way. When he did, she could read nothing in his face.

The captain was growing bored with the game. She could feel it and knew he was deep in his cups when he said, "I've got it. For a little excitement, how 'bout if I wager you for the wench. Eh? What do ye think of that?"

Cynthia was sure her heart came to a full stop. Garrett seemed to consider the proposal for a moment. "I like the idea, Captain, but I haven't anything of equal value to put up for her."

The captain rubbed his chin, obviously having some difficulty thinking this out. "Your nigger! By God, you can wager your nigger against her."

"Sorry, Captain. I need him more than I need her."

Anger flared in Cynthia before she realized Garrett could give no other answer. Jacob was a free man.

"But tell me, Captain," she heard Garrett saying, "how can you wager her without asking her permission?"

The captain threw his head back and roared, "Ask her permission? Why should I? She's bought and paid for, man, like one of your niggers. Even came to me of her own free will."

Cynthia found her voice. "That's not . . ."

"Not what?" he growled as he stood. "Not what?"

Garrett stood, too. "I think I'd better be going."

"Sit down, Carver," ordered the captain.

Garrett stood where he was. "As I said, Captain, I have nothing to wager for the lady." His hand went to his head. "And I fear I've lost track of my drinks."

"I said sit down!"

Garrett turned and started toward the door, his steps a bit unsure. The captain heaved his huge bulk around the desk and caught his arm. Garrett whirled and in an instant, the captain was spread-eagle on the floor.

Cynthia just stood and stared for what seemed an eternity, then she ran and wrapped her arms about him. "Oh, Garrett," she sobbed against his chest. "It's not like he said. It's not. He made me do it. He said if I didn't that you . . . you . . ." She pulled back and looked at is face. "Oh, Garrett, he'll kill you for this."

She realized he wasn't holding her. She looked at him intently and knew he hadn't heard her. His eyes were glazed with drunkenness and there was a look of disgust on his face. He forced her arms from around him and pushed her away.

182

"Go back to your captain, whore. He needs your attention."

Cynthia crumpled to the floor, sobbing as he weaved through the doorway and disappeared. "He didn't mean it . . . he didn't mean it."

She heard a noise behind her and turned to find the captain pulling himself up by holding onto the edge of the bunk. He was in a rage with murder written all over is face. She knew he was going after Garrett. She looked about for some way to stop him. Her eyes rested on the wine bottle, still over half full. She jumped up, grabbed the bottle, raised it high and brought it down on the captain's head. He slumped forward onto the bunk.

By some miracle, the heavy glass bottle did not break, so she set it carefully back on the desk, then turned and with much effort, heaved the captain's inert body onto the bunk. She returned to the desk, sat in the captain's chair, laid her head on her folded arms and cried.

Seventeen

Cynthia's head was pounding as she sat nursing her bruises from the Captain's latest assault. It had been three weeks since the night Garrett had come to the captain's cabin. She hadn't seen him since. She had seen no one but Jonathan Tarrillton. He had remembered everything the next morning and he hadn't forgiven her. He had beaten her, but during all this time he had never again drugged her or tried to rape her, though he did seem to get pleasure from ripping her clothing whenever he assaulted her. She couldn't fathom the change in him but was thankful he left her with no more than bruises. She didn't know what fate had befallen Garrett, but assumed he was either dead or in irons.

Three weeks, she thought, it seems like a lifetime. She glanced around the cabin. It was a shambles. The captain had let no one in and seldom went out. Food scraps lay about the desk, stinking and moldy. The few clothes she had brought lay in shreds about the room. She was reduced to wearing his pants and shirt she had found. He had never ripped them off her as he had her own clothing, but neither had he denied her wearing them. It was as if they held some special meaning for him. Cynthia had noticed the carefully-stitched rip in the sleeve coincided with the scar on his arm. She surmised he had been wounded, but wondered why he had kept the clothes all these years.

She touched a particularly tender spot on her cheekbone and her wonderings of the captain's past gave way to hatred of the man. She detested the sight and smell of him. She laughed hysterically when she thought about that. She knew she now smelled as foul as he ever had. She was glad she didn't have a mirror. There was nothing to remind her of how horrible she knew she must look. Her hair was tangled and matted, her brush having long been misplaced. She had lost weight and knew it was getting worse each time she wrapped the sash about her waist to hold up the pants she wore. Her legs and arms were covered with grime and filth. Most of the time she didn't care. It was only at times like now when she fully examined herself she even noticed.

There had been knocks on the door in the middle of the night the last few days and conversations had been in hushed whispers. She heard the word fever over and over so at first opportunity had looked at the ship's log. His scrawled hand told her nothing more than "fever on board," but she guessed that was why he seldom left the cabin. Today and yesterday he had been called away more often. She guessed the fever was getting worse, but his more frequent absences had give her little reprieve. She thought of Walter and almost wished she were back with him. She had at least learned a few tricks to use with Walter. The captain, she had decided, was a hopeless sadist. He found sheer joy when he had last beat her and when she tried to kick him in the groin he had left her with the threat of something "worse to come" ringing in her ears.

She lay back on the bunk wearily, deciding that if left alone the bruises would eventually heal themselves. She pulled a coverlet over her, closed her eyes and willed her head to stop pounding. In an instant, her eyes were open. "Maybe he'll die of the fever," she said. "I wish for him a terrible death." She giggled, then forced her body to relax, wanting nothing more than a cool cloth for her head and peaceful sleep.

She had finally reached a state of relaxation and her head was feeling a little better when she heard the key in the lock. She cringed, but refused to open her eyes. She did so only when she heard more than just the captain's footsteps. He was standing over her, legs spread, hands on his hips, a malicious grin on his face. Behind him stood five of the hairiest, dirtiest men she had ever seen. She pulled the coverlet closer. He reached down and yanked it away. There was a guttural sound from those with him.

"See, boys, not much to look at, but I have no doubt she would satisfy a man's hunger."

Cynthia looked at him in horror.

"She's all yours, boys. No need to be gentle, but leave her alive. I have an investment in her. And remember, this was none of my doin'." He turned and walked to the door.

"Jonathan!" she screamed.

He turned, one hand on the latch. He had never before looked so evil.

"Jonathan," she begged. "Jonathan, please not this. Please. I'll do anything."

A crazed look came into his eyes.

"What you can't do yourself you get others to do for you, Captain? Is that it?"

A murderous look crossed is face before he threw his head back and laughed, then went out, closing the door behind him. Cynthia sat there dazed, his laughter echoing through her mind. One of the men moved toward her. She grabbed the coverlet to her and looked from one face to another.

"Please," she begged as she pulled her legs up protectively and backed up against the wall. "Please, no."

The one who had moved toward her and seemed to be the leader laughed. The others joined in, then as if by signal, they lunged for her. She struggled, but they easily lifted her and flung her to the floor. Four of them spread-eagled her while the leader stood between her legs and tore at his pants. When he came into full view, she pleaded again. They weren't listening.

He stood there for a moment, taunting her with the inevitable, then he slowly sank to his knees.

"Let's get her clothes off," said one.

"In a minute," he said slowly. "There ain't no hurry."

There wasn't another sound until he reached up and cupped both her breasts in his hands, then there was a groan from one of his mates. He grinned. She saw broken teeth and spaces where teeth should have been. He bent to kiss her. She turned her head from his foul breath. He grabbed her hair and forced her to kiss him. The four holding her cheered. Cynthia screamed. It was muffled by his mouth. She tried to pull away but found she was held securely. She bit his lip.

He reared up, wiping the blood from his mouth. Cynthia thought she heard someone coming but couldn't be sure. As she took a deep breath and opened her mouth to scream again a hairy fist smashed into her face.

The five sat in silence looking at one another until the footsteps died away.

"Come on, lads, let's get outa here," said one.

"But what about the girl?" complained the leader

as he sat back on his heels.

"You done smashed her a good 'un, mate. Could be your broke her nose or jaw. Bloodied 'er up some, anyhow. She ain't no good to us now."

The others nodded agreement.

"Friggin'd bring more pleasure to my way o' thinkin'," another said as they let go of Cynthia. The four of them stood to leave.

"She'll come 'round, mates, you'll see. I didn't have no choice, did I? I couldn't let 'er 'oller when someone might hear."

One of his friends tried to pull him up. "Come on, mate, it's over. Let's get outa here."

He shrugged his friend off. "Do whatcha will." He unsheathed a knife. "I'm gonna wait till the bitch comes 'round." He put the tip of the knife under Cynthia's chin. "I'll have 'er all to myself then. I won't be needin' you boys."

The four hesitated a moment, then one motioned toward the door with his head and, after checking the passageway, they hurried out.

While waiting, he began to expertly twist the knife at the shirt and pants buttons. They popped off easily. Working from the bottom up on the shirt and the top down on the pants, he was almost finished a few minutes later when Captain Tarrillton came stumbling in.

"You still here, Beall?"

"Yessir. We had to . . ."

"Left her alive, didn't ya?"

"Yessir, we . . ."

"Then get out, Beall." He paused as he looked at Cynthia. "Nice touch, Beall, puttin' her clothes back on."

"But, sir?"

The captain turned on him. "I said get out, Beall."

The sailor left then, but not before giving Cynthia a resentful kick.

Captain Tarrillton lumbered to his desk and sat down. A moment later his head collapsed onto folded arms.

Startled to wakefulness, Garrett sat up and listened. Nothing. He had thought he heard Cynthia screaming. He rubbed his hands over his face. It must have been a dream, he told himself. He swung his legs over the edge of the bunk, started to get up, then decided it took too much effort, sank back. He glanced around for Jacob. He was gone. At least, he thought as he lay back, we've been spared the fever so far.

The sickness had struck swiftly, without warning. Six men had fallen ill within hours of each other. By the time Garrett heard of the strange fever, the cook had bled three of the men. Infuriated, Garrett had ordered what he considered a heathenish practice stopped. He and Jacob had worked together to wrap the sick men in wet blankets to lower their fever, something they had learned from one of their blacks. Still, two of those who had been bled, died. When no one, including Captain Tarrillton, interfered with his taking command of the situation, Garrett realized what little he and Jacob had learned in the slave quarters about treating the sick was more than anyone else on board the *Providence* knew.

He almost regretted having taken charge two weeks ago—or was it longer? He didn't know. Day had run into day, week into week. Tending the sick had become a burden. He was tired. There was more sick now, possibly as many as a fourth of the crew, and more deaths. Those who had been stricken first didn't seem to be getting any better and Garrett was at a loss for how to help them. He and Jacob had tried everything they had ever heard about. Still, the fever persisted. Some had developed a rash on their chest and abdomen, others a racking cough, still others complained of stomach pains. It seemed to affect everyone differently. One man Garrett was particularly concerned about had lost all his hair and was, when Garrett last saw him, at death's door.

His thoughts drifted aimlessly back to Cynthia. He hoped she wasn't sick. God, he wished he could forget her. He never should have gone to the captain's quarters that night. It had been a mistake, but he kept hoping he was wrong about Cynthia. Something she had said just before he left about the captain forcing her—he couldn't remember what it was. It didn't matter, he told himself at the time, because her actions had belied whatever it was she had said. But now, he wondered. He thought of his own actions and wished he had overcome his pride and tried to see her the following day. Instead, he had buried himself in his work, writing and rewriting the numerous reports he would have to present when he got home. The time had been well spent. He was almost finished when the fever struck.

He turned onto his side, lay there a few minutes longer, then decided he'd best clean up, shave and go relieve Jacob. They had little enough help from anyone in the crew. Everyone was afraid to be near the sick. Only young Mr. Mason had agreed to relieve them occasionally. He stretched and stood barefoot before the small mirror Jacob had hung on the wall. The eyes looking back at him were red and puffy from hours of sleep. He had at least three days growth of beard. He stuck his tongue out. It looked pink and healthy. At a noise behind him, he turned and found Jacob watching him from the door.

"How long?"

Jacob grinned as he closed the door. "It's good to have you back, old friend."

"How long, Jacob?"

"Two and a half days. I thought you was gonna sleep all the way home."

"Jesus," he swore. "Are many more sick?"

Jacob walked over and sat on the bunk before answering. "Three. It seems to be slowin' down some since no one'll go near 'em and everone is fearful of havin' anything to do with anyone else, lest he should be next. Four died yesterday. One more just now. I sent that Mason fella to tell the captain."

"The one who lost his hair, the one known as Curley, is he? . . ."

"Some better, I think. He opened his eyes this morning and took some water. He's resting easier."

Garrett turned back to the mirror and ran a hand over his beard. "I'll get cleaned up and go tend to them. You'd better get some rest."

When there was no response from Jacob, he turned and found his friend lying sideways, feet still on the floor. He made Jacob more comfortable before pouring water with which to shave.

Cynthia was on the edge of consciousness. She knew someone was bathing her face, but she couldn't see him yet. She felt pain and from somewhere a voice was telling her everything was all right now. She reached out. A hand took hers gently. She pulled it to her. A cool cloth was put on her head. After a few moments she forced her eyes open. The young officer she had taunted her first day on board was bending over her. She opened her mouth to speak but he silenced her with a hand touched to her lips.

"Don't try to talk now. You're gonna be all right,

I . . . I'm sure. You just lie still. I'm going to get help."

He had moved to the door before Cynthia could speak. "Captain . . . Captain Tarrillton . . . where . . ."

"The captain's down and out, miss. Likely the fever, I'm thinkin'. Now don't worry. I'll be right back." Then he was out the door.

Cynthia closed her eyes and waited. She wished she had some of the captain's drugs to ease the pain.

Garrett had just lathered his face when someone started pounding on the door, shouting his name. He glanced at Jacob as he stepped to the door but the noise hadn't bothered him.

He jerked the door open, ready to silence whoever it was, and found Henry Mason standing there looking very white. He stepped into the passageway and pulled the door closed behind him.

"Mr. Carver, you have to come right away. It's . . . it's . . . it's an emergency, sir. Blood and . . . and . . . a real mess . . . I don't know what to do."

"Now, calm down, Henry. Calm down. Did someone have a fight?"

"No, sir. It's the girl. She's . . ."

Garrett grabbed him by the shoulders. "Where is she?"

"Captain's cabin, sir."

Garrett took off at a near run, Henry Mason following close on his heels.

"I just found her there, sir, when I went to report to the captain about the death. She was so still and so white, I thought at first she was dead. There's so much blood. I covered her up and when I realized she was alive, I began washing her face. She came around a little and I told her I was going for help."

Garrett only heard snatches of what Mason was

saying. I'll kill him, he was thinking. Cynthia tried to tell me. I wouldn't listen.

As he entered the captain's cabin, he stopped only momentarily to view the scene. Cynthia was lying on the floor, a blanket covering her still figure. Captain Tarrillton was at his desk, his head resting on folded arms. Garrett moved to Cynthia's side. He was shocked by the change in her. There was a small pool of blood to one side of her head. Her eyes were sunk back with dark circles under them. A bruise was plainly visible high on her left cheek, dried blood was at the corner of her mouth, and her face showed evidence of not having had enough to eat.

"Holy Jesus," he swore softly. He turned to the captain's desk. Mason had moved to the captain's side and was trying to rouse him. He looked up at Garrett.

"It's the fever, sir. He don't even know we're here."

Garrett lifted the blanket from Cynthia, looking for more wounds. Mason had implied there was lots of blood. What he saw sickened him. He let the blanket drop. He sat back on his heels, fighting the nausea. Tears came to his eyes.

Cynthia moaned and he once again focused his attention on her. Her eyes were open. She was trying to say something. He leaned closer to be sure he heard her.

"Oh, Garrett," she whispered. Her eyes fluttered then took on a crazed look. "He let them, Garrett. He *let* them!" She said through clenched teeth, then closed her eyes again. Tears slid beneath golden lashes.

Garrett cried unashamedly as he wrapped the blanket around her and gently picked her up in his arms. She moaned at being moved but looked at

Garrett and tried to smile.

"You look just like Saint Nicholas," she whispered and snuggled her head against his shoulder before he felt her go limp.

He turned to the young officer. "I'm going to need your help, Mason."

"Yessir—but what about the captain?"

"Let the bastard rot." Garrett strode out the door. Henry Mason followed.

Eighteen

Henry Mason grew so concerned over possible consequences if he didn't report the captain's illness, Garrett finally let him go, but not before Cynthia was made as comfortable as possible and not before fresh water, towels and blankets were brought to the cabin. He had put Cynthia on a mat on the floor. He knew it to be no less comfortable than the bunk and he hadn't the heart to waken Jacob.

As soon as Mason left, Garrett carefully removed the blanket from around Cynthia. He was appalled at her emaciated condition and fresh bruises were showing a pinkish-purple all over her body.

"Lord," he said aloud, "what she must have been through these last three weeks." He clenched his fists and ground his teeth. I'll kill them, he thought, all of them, if the fever doesn't do it first. He didn't know who the "them" were that Cynthia had alluded to, but he secretly hoped the fever would spare the captain for him.

The bleeding had stopped, for which he was thankful. His knowledge of anatomy was limited, and the internal injuries which he feared she might have was beyond him completely, so he slowly, methodically began to examine her for any visible open wounds that might become infected. Looking closely at the bruises on her wrists and ankles, he found the skin was not broken but felt certain the marks were left by strong hands rather than bonds. He shook his head to try to clear it of the vision that came to him. He had a strong desire to lift her and cradle her close. Instead, he wiped the tears from his eyes and gently began to wash her from head to foot. He cleansed the wounds on her face thoroughly using some of his shaving soap. She moaned while he was trying to remove the filth from her legs. He saw why in a few moments. Her legs were badly bruised and chafed.

At last, feeling she was clean, he rubbed ointment on the marks on her face and put powder on the chafed parts of her body, then having nothing else in which to dress her, dug down in his trunk for one of his oldest, softest shirts.

He gathered all the soiled towels, placed clean sheeting beneath her, then stood looking at her for a moment before covering her with a clean blanket. She looked so small and vulnerable lying there in his shirt which came almost to her knees. He knelt and covered her with the blanket. She opened her eyes.

"Garrett?"

"It's all right, little one. I won't let them hurt you again."

"Garrett. . . ." She tried to smile. "You haven't shaved yet."

He touched his hand to the almost-dry lather. "I guess I forgot. But how do you feel? Are you in pain?"

"I don't think so." She looked around. "Where am I?"

"You're in my cabin. It's small, but we'll make do. Are you hungry?"

"Famished. I don't remember when I last ate." Tears came to her eyes. "Oh, Garrett, it was awful."

"Do you want to talk about it?"

She wiped the tears from her eyes. "No. I don't even want to think about it. I want . . . I want something to eat."

He stood. "I'll find something. Can you wait till I finish this?" He pointed to his face.

"I can't wait."

Garrett moved to the small mirror and picked up his razor. "This won't take long," he promised.

A few minutes later, as he wiped the last of the lather from his neck and around his ears, he stole a look at Cynthia. Her eyes were closed. She was crying silently. Undecided whether he should say something or pretend he hadn't noticed, he finally spoke quietly. "Are you in pain? I can get some laudanum."

Cynthia opened her eyes. "No, no pain. Not the kind laudanum would help." She smiled wanly and reached out to him. He moved to her side and knelt.

He looked into her green eyes for a long time and tried to understand the pain he saw there. Her gaze held his until he could no longer bear seeing her torture. He shifted his eyes away from her face.

"I . . . uh . . . I wish there were some way I could help you."

"Hold me, Garrett. Please just hold me." She spoke so softly that for a moment he wasn't sure he'd heard her correctly.

He looked at her. "I'm afraid I'll hurt you if I move you."

"Love never hurts, Garrett," she said matter-of-factly. "But . . . but . . . after everything . . . maybe you . . ."

Garrett quickly bent to kiss the tears from her cheeks. "Lord, Cynthia, don't even think it. So much of it's my fault."

"No, Garrett," she whispered against his cheek.

"Not your fault. Not this. He did it."

Garrett raised his head and could see her anguished thoughts were somewhere else. In a moment she was back with him.

"I'll lay beside you," he said. "Then I won't have to move you."

She raised the blanket and he moved in beside her. He slowly slid his arm beneath her and held her close, her head just below his chin. They lay that way in silence for some time, then Cynthia began to sob uncontrollably. Garrett caressed her and soothed her much as he had many weeks ago in Brighton. Eventually, her sobbing ceased and finally he knew she slept. He kissed her lightly on the forehead then slipped away from her.

Later, he thought as he looked down at her, later the physical pain will be real again.

Many times during the next three days Cynthia wished she were dead. Even the slightest movement cause her agony. Over and over she refused the laudanum Garrett brought her, even though he assured her it would ease the pain. By the fourth day she was feeling much better and found she could get up from the bunk, to which Garrett had moved her, with a minimum of discomfort by using a sideways rolling motion instead of trying to sit up first. By the end of the week she was moving around with relative ease. The overall soreness was gone and some of the bruises were healing.

Jacob had practically moved out. She didn't know where he was sleeping, but he stopped by every day to see how she was doing. She always welcomed his cheerful face and nonsensical chatter.

Garrett was always there when she needed him. He was sleeping on the mat on the floor. He hadn't touched her since he had lain beside her except to tend her wounds or to move her to a more comfortable position. He had never questioned her about what had happened and she sensed he was waiting until she was ready to tell him.

It's time, she thought, as she pulled Garrett's brush through her hair. I can feel the rift between us growing wider each day. She was sitting at the table still dressed in one of Garrett's shirts. He had kissed her on the forehead a few moments before and gone to tend those down with the fever. She recalled their conversation of the night before.

"But, Garrett," she had protested when he was leaving to minister to the sick. "Aren't you afraid you'll get the fever?"

"It's a possibility," he'd said, "but I think I would have gotten it before now, don't you?"

She had thought about it for a moment, then asked, "If you get sick, what will happen to me?"

Garrett had thrown back his head and laughed. The first time she'd heard him laugh in weeks. "Now I know you're getting better. You're starting to think about yourself again. Not a thought of what might happen to me."

Warmed by the thought of Garrett's laughter, she smiled. You really are getting spoiled, Cynthia Fawley, she told herself. Still, one thing puzzled her—Garrett's treatment of her the last few days. He acted more like a loving brother than the lover he had been. She wasn't sure what she expected from him, but knew it was more than kisses on the forehead.

She sat for a long time thinking back over the events of the last few weeks, sorting in her mind the things she would tell Garrett. She finally decided to tell him everything. She owed it to herself, she decided, to have him think better of her than he now did. She hesitated for a moment to examine what he did think of her.

All of a sudden she giggled with delight. She jumped up and danced around the small cabin. Her heart beat wildly. "He loves me," she spoke softly as she made one final turn and sat down.

In a moment the mood had passed. She sat subdued. What difference does it make? I'm married. Besides, my body has been ravaged by others. He couldn't possibly want me after those five . . . her thoughts drifted.

She was sitting, staring at the brush in her hands when Garrett came in with their midday meal. He set the tray in front of her.

"What's the matter? You all right?"

"I'm fine." She looked up and tried to smile. Seeing him standing over her looking so concerned brought tears to her eyes. She turned her head away. Garrett pulled her up from where she sat and held her close. Being held like this is a little like heaven, she thought. Garrett ran his hands over her back. I love him, but he deserves better.

"What is it?" he asked.

Cynthia shook her head. "It's nothing," she said choking back the tears that threatened. "Nothing."

Garrett held her at arms length. Cynthia kept her head down.

"Cynthia, look at me."

She raised her head. Green eyes met blue.

"We have to talk."

She nodded.

"Good," he said. "Sit down."

She sat.

He paced the room twice tying to gather his thoughts. He didn't know where to begin. He wanted to tell her they would go back to London on the first ship they could book passage and he'd pay her husband whatever he wanted for her freedom. But where to begin? Her reticence this week had been provoking. He had tried to understand how she must feel after all she'd been through, but knew he never could. He had wanted to comfort her but she had withdrawn herself, or so he felt.

Cynthia took a deep breath. I want him. I love him and I want him but I can't hurt him. We could never marry and have a family, living as other people do. He should have that. I can't give it to him. He was right. I should have stayed in England. A fine thing to think of, she told herself, when you're in the middle of the ocean.

She sighed. "What do you want to talk about?"

Garrett stopped pacing and sat in the other chair. "Christ, I don't know." He took her hand in his. She had never seen him look so beaten. "I just really don't know, Cynthia. It's like there's a wall between us."

"I know."

"What happened to the easy relationship we had in Brighton? Can't it be that way again?"

She pulled her hand away. "No. Too much has happened." Her voice was rising in crescendo. "Nothing can ever be the same again. Nothing! Nothing! Nothing!" She was shaking when she finished and her eyes had a wild look in them.

Garrett stood and tried to pull her to him, as much for his own comfort as hers. She pushed him away.

"Don't touch me!" she screamed. "Don't touch me. I'm dirty. I'm . . . I'm vile. I'm . . . I'm . . . tainted!" She laughed loudly.

Garrett watched her and waited, feeling the storm had just begun.

"I have been mauled. I have been beaten." She

was counting on her fingers the things that had happened to her. "I have been drugged. I have been raped—after they knocked me senseless but it doesn't matter, it still happened and it's not something one keeps count of, is it?" She laughed, but tears were streaming down her cheeks. "Did you hear that?" Her eyes took on a faraway look. "The worst was in Brighton—and I didn't even get the money back." She laughed hysterically. "So much in so short a time. So much . . . so little time."

She was silent then. Garrett reached out for her.

"Don't touch me!" she hissed as she moved away from him. "Didn't you hear what I said? Don't you see that I have to protect you. Can't drag you down, too." She looked around wildly. Garrett saw her eyes rest on the knife on the tray. He moved slowly toward the table. When she lunged for the knife, he grabbed her. She fought him, screaming.

"Let me go! Let me go! I have to. It's the only way."

Garrett slapped her. She looked his way. Her eyes were glassy and unseeing. He slapped her again. She began to cry. He smoothed her hair and caressed her back while she sobbed into his chest. The tears on his cheeks flowed unheeded. He kissed the top of her head.

"I'm sorry. So sorry. It's . . . so much of it's my fault."

Cynthia shook her head against his chest. "No, my fault." Her voice was muffled. "You tried to warn me. It was my decision to go as a bond servant. My own doing. You tried to warn me."

Garrett stepped away from her so he could see her face. "Bond servant?" He raised her chin and made her look at him. "Cynthia, did you say bond servant?"

She nodded.

"Then you've been Tarrillton's . . ."

"Prisoner," she finished for him.

He pulled her to him. "My God, how you must hate me."

"Hate you? Why would I hate you?" She spoke as though dazed.

"Never mind," he said. "It doesn't matter now. Not now or ever." He picked her up and swung her around. When he set her down he embraced her. "I love you, Cynthia, and nothing else matters. Nothing at all."

"But how can you after . . . after everything?"

"I can and I do. What's happened is behind us. It seems I've loved you since the first day I saw you. I only realized it when I was going to leave you behind. I came back that day in Brighton, but you were gone. I should have waited but I thought . . . well, it's of no consequence. We'll start over now that you're here."

She pushed against his chest so she could look into his face. It was the shining face of a youth who has just been granted his most ardent wish. "You really want me? After all the oth . . . after all that's happened?"

He pulled her to him. "Cynthia, my beautiful Cynthia, I've never wanted anything more in my life. Besides, I don't think there were any others. I don't think you were raped. I saw no evidence of it when I helped you that afternoon."

"And you let me go on believing I had been? All this time?"

He pulled back and looked at her. "My love, I didn't know what you believed. We . . . we've hardly talked about . . . about anything that's happened."

She pursed her lips in thought. "I guess that's my fault."

"Or both our faults. I felt you would tell me when you were ready, but I had no idea you believed you'd been raped. Otherwise, I would have put your mind at ease that very afternoon."

"But, Garrett, there's still Walter."

"I know. I know. We'll work it out. I'll pay him whatever it is he wants for your freedom. We'll return to London as soon as I've concluded my business affairs at home."

He stood holding her for a long time and at last Cynthia began to accept the idea. "Garrett, I love you."

"I know."

Nineteen

In the days that followed, Cynthia and Garrett reveled in one another. They spent hours exploring and enjoying each other's bodies and minds. Cynthia had never felt such freedom or ease at being with a man. She learned a man could be her friend.

When she felt the time was right, she related to Garrett all the horrors to which she had been subjected. With the telling, she found some of the inner wounds less hurtful and when Garrett embraced her tenderly, she knew it was all right, that it didn't matter to him—not the way she had feared.

She luxuriated in his love for her.

One day he presented her with clothing about her size which he had gotten from what he described as "a jaunty little sailor." After that, Cynthia began helping him and Jacob tend the sick. On the third afternoon she helped, Garrett was comforting a dying man. Cynthia moved to his side to see if she could be of aid. When she saw the dying sailor she turned ghostly white.

"I'm glad he's dying," she said, turned and left the area.

Garrett found her a few minutes later standing at the railing on deck, the wind blowing her golden hair. He paused a moment to drink in her beauty before he walked up to her. Afraid to touch her, he leaned on the railing beside her. Her knuckles were white where she gripped the railing. He watched her out of the corner of his eye. She was staring at the horizon but her eyes were unfocused.

"He's dead."

"Good."

"He was one of them."

"Yes. I hope they all die."

Garrett waited for some sign that she needed his comfort.

"How long was he sick?"

"A long time. Since the night that . . . since that night."

She relaxed her hold on the railing and turned to Garrett. "I'm going to get sick, too, aren't I?"

"I don't know." He searched her face for some sign of fear. He found calm resignation. He took her in his arms. She was rigid. "Lord, Cynthia, I hope neither of us nor anyone else gets sick."

She pushed away from him to see his eyes. "Tell me the truth, Garrett."

He turned back to the railing, she beside him. He chose his words with care. "It's a strange sickness, Cynthia. I've never seen it before, though I've seen similar symptoms. I don't know anything about it: what it is, why some get it and some don't, why it affects people differently, deadly to some and not others. I wish I knew, but I don't."

Cynthia sensed he was being truthful. She let her shoulders relax and permitted Garrett to hold her. They stood in silence for a long time. Tears rolled down her cheeks.

"Garrett, . . . I . . . I don't want to die. Not when I've just found you."

He held her tighter. "You won't. I won't let you."

"But how . . ."

"Hush now. Don't think about it. It's been a long

time. Chances are you won't even get sick." Oh, God, he prayed silently, let me be right.

Cynthia didn't help with the sick the next day and Garrett found himself wondering if "this were one of them" each time he stopped at a hammock. Jacob finally sent him away late in the day telling him to go rest. Garrett knew he didn't need rest. He needed answers. He appreciated Jacob's concern, but he didn't return to his cabin. He went topside. He needed fresh air. He needed to be alone. He needed to think.

Garrett stepped on deck to a perfectly beautiful day. Despite the many who were sick, the ship was under full sail. They were making excellent progress. He tried pacing much as he had seen the captain do, but found he was hindered by the roll of the ship. Tarrillton, he thought as he steadied himself with one hand on the rail. I wonder if he's dead. What of the others who had assaulted Cynthia? Were they all sick? Who were they? That gnawed at him. He pushed it from his mind. What was the sickness? Was there any better way of treating it than what they were already doing? Why did some get it and not others? Would Cynthia become its next victim or had it been long enough? How long was long enough?

Finding no answers, he turned to go below. He encountered Henry Mason at the companionway.

"Oh, Mr. Carver, sir, I've been looking for you."

"Mason, I do wish you would call me Garrett."

"I'll try, sir, and . . . and you call me Henry."

"All right, Henry. You said you were looking for me?"

"Yessir. It . . . ah . . . it would seem, sir, . . . uh, Garrett, that we are now in command."

"We, Henry?"

"Yessir . . . er, Garrett. I just helped the first mate below. He's in a terrible way."

"Good Lord," said Garrett as he ran his hand through his hair. "What next? The captain, Henry, how's he?"

"He still don't know much, though he does rally at times."

"How about the crew, those who aren't sick? Can you handle them?"

"They're all good sailors. We've never had any real trouble on board. I think I . . . Yes, I can handle them."

"Well, the ship's yours, Captain Mason. I know nothing about sailing. I'll keep doing what I've been doing. If you have any trouble with the men, Jacob and I will do what we can to help."

"Thank you, sir."

Garrett arched an eyebrow at him.

"I mean; thank you, Garrett."

Garrett watched as Mason strode aft to take command. He had a new, self-important lift to his step. Garrett smiled, then turned to go below.

When he opened the door, he saw that Cynthia was sleeping so he let himself in as quietly as possible. Still, she roused. She raised up on one elbow, ran a hand over her eyes and shook her hair loose.

"I guess I dozed off."

"Are you feeling all right?"

"Fine." When she noticed him eyeing her critically, she added, "Really. It's just there's nothing to do. The motion of the ship . . . the closeness of the cabin . . . I grew drowsy."

Garrett reached out and felt her forehead. He detected no fever.

"Really, Garrett, I'm fine. Just sleepy."

Satisfied that she wasn't ill, he sat on the bunk beside her.

"Are you hungry? I can get us some supper."

"No. Maybe later."

Garrett gave her a quick, furtive glance.

"Now stop looking at me that way, Garrett. I'm fine. I really am."

"Okay, okay." He laughed. "I guess I am overreacting."

She reached a hand up to his forehead. "How are you?"

"I'm all right. Just tired."

"In that case, you rest and I'll go get the supper." She slid smoothly off the bunk, put her hands against his chest and pushed until he reluctantly gave in and lay down.

"I'm not that tired," he teased.

Cynthia giggled, then snuggled up beside him. Within seconds their clothes were scattered about the small cabin.

Garrett pulled her to him gently. Cynthia wrapped her arms about his chest and lifted her face to his with lips parted. His mouth claimed hers hungrily, their tongues doing a dance as their hands began their own explorations. He softly caressed her back and buttocks then moved his hand to cup a smooth, silky breast. Cynthia moaned and began to move against him. The fire within him raged and he struggled for control as he pulled her against his lean frame.

Cynthia felt him hard against her belly and a fiery sensation flooded her body. She rolled onto her back as Garrett's warm, moist kisses traveled over her neck and shoulders. His hand moved from her breast and inched down her body on waves of caresses. The fire within her spread.

As he moved over her, she spread her thighs willingly and her body arched up to meet him. His mouth was again hot upon hers, tongue probing, claiming as he thrust deep within her. He lay very still for a moment, then slowly he began to move, loving her, caressing her with every part of his body.

Slowly their passions mounted. Cynthia clung to Garrett fiercely so as not to lose touch with reality. One last crest of uncontrollable pleasure and they were drawn into an all-consuming ecstasy.

They lay breathless for what seemed an eternity and their hearts beat as one. Finally, Garrett raised up and looked down at her smiling.

"God, I love you. You're so beautiful," he said hoarsely.

"Cynthia ran her hands through his dark hair, then pulled his head down till their lips met, warm and loving. She began to move against him slowly, teasingly until he sighed and drew away.

"You are a little minx, you know that?"

"I've had an excellent teacher since meeting you. Besides, you love it."

Garrett smiled and leaned back against the wall.

Cynthia caressed his chest and openly admired his lean, muscular build. "Wouldn't it be fun to live like this always, have absolutely nothing better to do than love one another?"

He pulled her to him. "We will one day, my love, we will."

Over supper Garrett told her that Henry Mason was now in command.

"Who is Henry Mason?" she asked around a piece of bread.

"The young officer who helped you."

Cynthia remembered as she swallowed the half-chewed bread. "Oh, my God, Garrett. Are we ever going to make it to the colonies? First the captain sick and now this . . . this boy running the ship. Can he do it?"

Garrett laughed, as much to hide his own concern as to reassure her. "I certainly hope so. I know I couldn't sail a ship." He picked up a piece of dried meat. He felt her staring at him, so added, "He seems capable enough, just inexperienced. I'm sure he'll do fine."

They finished the meal in silence.

Sometime in the middle of the night Garrett was awakened awash in his own perspiration. He kicked the blanket back before he realized the source of heat was Cynthia's body. She was burning up with fever.

"Oh, God, no," he mumbled as he felt his way from the bunk and hunted for a lamp. He pulled his pants on, fastened them, then carried the light closer to the bunk. Her face was flushed. She was shivering. He sat the lamp down and tucked the blanket close around her. She continued to shake. He got the blanket from the mat on the floor and covered her with that, then he placed cool, wet cloths on her head and bathed her face.

He went for more water. When he returned he found Cynthia half in, half out of the blankets. He tucked one around her then saturated the other. He wrapped her in the wet one and continued to bathe her face. She opened her eyes once and her look told him, "See, I knew it would be this way." He grabbed her fiercely by the shoulders.

"You can't die, Cynthia. You can't. I won't let you. Do you hear me?"

He thought he saw a slight nod of her head, so he sat back and continued to bathe her face.

The remainder of the night he spent wrapping and unwrapping her with wet blankets. *I only hope she's* had enough time and put on enough weight to fight her way through this, he thought.

At dawn she was resting easy and Garrett thought she felt cooler, so he removed the wet blanket, wrapped her in a dry one and sat down at the table. Midmorning Jacob found him there, his head resting on folded arms.

Jacob looked at Cynthia then shook Garrett. "Garrett, wake up. Wake up, Garrett. How long she been sick?"

Garrett raised his head and tried to blink the room into focus. He shook his head to clear it.

"Oh, Jacob," he said. "How . . . what . . . what time is it?" He looked at Cynthia then rushed to her side. Her face was flushed with fever. Her skin felt dry to the touch. "Wet blankets, Jacob. We need wet blankets. I shouldna slept so long. Shoulda took care of her. Blankets, Jacob!" he screamed, "Wet blankets!"

Jacob reached for the wet blanket that had been dropped on the floor. He helped Garrett wrap it around the girl. She shivered slightly.

"That's all we can do, Garrett," he said softly. "That and wait."

"I know, Jacob. I know. But why her? She's been through so much. Why her?"

Jacob took a firm hold on Garrett's shoulders. "Come on, friend. You need rest."

Garrett shook his head. "She needs me."

"Won't do her no good if you get sick, too. Come on. Rest."

Garrett still resisted.

"I'll stay with her." Garrett looked at the large black man hovering over him. "I'll stay, Garrett. I'll do everything for her I can. You know that."

"I know. I know." Garrett let himself be helped

up and moved to the mat in the corner. "Thank you, Jacob. I am tired." Garrett lay down, then sat up again. "But what about the others, Jacob?"

"They'll be all right," his friend assured him. "I got that cook fella helpin' me with 'em, and I told him if he did any more bleedin', I'd cut off his ears and bleed him." Jacob grinned. "I think he believed me."

Garrett lay down. "Is it ever gonna stop, Jacob?"

"Has to eventually. Seems to be peterin' out some now. Only had one sick all week till this, and some of those first sick are about well. I'd say the worst is over."

"I hope you're right, Jacob," Garrett mumbled and closed his eyes. He heard Jacob moving around, but willed himself to sleep. He knew Cynthia was in capable hands.

Two days later Jacob had two patients. He now knew the initial signs of the fever. He had watched Garrett repeatedly begin to do something and then tire easily. Garrett had continually fallen asleep whenever he was sitting idle and would wake up not knowing how long he had slept. He had trouble remembering and doing even the simplest things. Jacob hovered over his friend like a mother hen, trying to help him but at the same time allowing him the dignity to do what he could on his own. When the fever commenced on the second day, he worked tirelessly to keep Garrett as cool as possible. Between taking care of both Garrett and Cynthia the next few days, he got little rest. At the end of the week, Cynthia developed a rash across her chest and abdomen. He knew then that she would be all right. He had seen it among the sailors he and Garrett had treated. Those who developed no rash were the sickest. Some of those had died.

By the tenth day after Garrett's fever had commenced, he showed no signs of progress. Jacob was worried. He was pacing the cabin trying to think of something more to do when he saw a movement from the bunk. He hastened to attend to Cynthia. Her eyes were open.

"Garrett . . . I . . ." Then realizing it was Jacob with her, she asked, "Where is he?"

"He's down sick, Miss Cynthia. You been sick too."

"I . . . I know." She closed her eyes then opened them again. "How is he, Jacob?"

"I'm right worried, Miss Cynthia. He ain't developed a rash like you done."

"A rash?"

"Yes, miss. Those what get the rash don't get so sick as those what don't."

"Oh." Cynthia could feel herself fading away, but she struggled to stay awake. "A rash, did you say Jacob?"

"Yes, miss. You know somethin' 'bout rashes, miss?"

"Let me think . . . all right?"

"Yes, miss."

She closed her eyes again. Jacob reached out and shook her awake. "You know somethin' 'bout a rash?"

"In a minute, Jacob."

He waited. She was sleeping again.

"Miss Cynthia," he shook her. "Miss Cynthia, what about the rash?"

She peered at him from behind glassy eyes. "Rash?"

"Yes, Garrett's got no rash. I fear for his life."

"It's simple, Jacob. Hot towels."

"Hot towels?"

214

"Of course. Mama said so. Brings out the rash." She closed her eyes.

Jacob shrugged his shoulders. She was sleeping again. It didn't make sense, but what had he to lose by trying it?

It didn't take long to get hot water and wrap the inert Garrett in hot towels. Jacob watched and waited. At first sign of the towels cooling, he replaced them. By nightfall, Jacob was exhausted, but Garrett's chest and abdomen were a bright red, and he felt cooler. Jacob got down on bended knees and gave thanks. Tears streamed down his black face. He covered Garrett with a warm blanket, then lay beside him and slept.

Twenty

Cynthia forced herself to swallow the broth Jacob was spooning her. She knew she needed the nourishment but she wasn't hungry. It had been over a week since her fever broke. She still didn't have the energy to feed herself a full dish of broth. She was, as far as she could tell, normal in all respects, but the fever had sapped her strength and left her with no appetite. She pushed Jacob's hand away.

"Miss Cynthia, we been over this time an' ag'in. You need to eat to gain your strength back."

"I know, Jacob. I'm just not hungry."

"Will ya please jus' try a little more? Don't want Garrett thinkin' I didn't take good care o' ya, now do ya?"

She looked at the mat where Garrett lay. "How is he doing, Jacob?"

"He's comin' right along since his fever's down. It'll take time, though, longer than what it tuck you. It's a good thing you tol' me 'bout usin' hot towels. He woulda been dead by now."

"Hot towels?"

"You don't remember?"

Cynthia shook her head.

"When Garrett was bad sick, you woke up long enough to tell me to put hot towels on him to bring out the rash. Said your mama tol' you that. I thought you was crazy, but I did it anyway an' it worked."

"I'm glad it worked, Jacob, but I don't recall my mother ever telling me anything like that."

"Well, the Lord works in strange ways, Miss Cynthia. Most likely it was him what helped us. Now eat this here soup."

Cynthia opened her mouth obediently and continued to down the warm broth. When Jacob was satisfied she had eaten enough, he set the dish on the tray.

"I'll be right back, Miss Cynthia, soon's I take this to the galley."

"Jacob, what happened to the almost perfect English you were speaking in Brighton? You've dropped it lately."

"It's a lot of work to speak that way all the time, Miss Cynthia, but I can if that's what you wish."

"No, it's all right. I was just wondering."

"Well, I don't feel as how I have to be so proper around you anymore, not after all we been through, that is."

"I'm glad you feel that way, Jacob. Will you please help me up before you go? I want to try moving around some more today. It seems to help."

"I ain't sure you oughta be movin' 'round so much yet, Miss Cynthia, 'specially when I ain't here. You been mighty sick."

"It'll be all right, Jacob. Just help me up. If you don't, I'll get up by myself while you're gone.

"Lordy, Miss Cynthia, you are one stubborn girl. Come on. I'll help you."

Cynthia threw back the covers. She was dressed in Garrett's shirt which only came to her knees, but she had long ago lost any modesty with Jacob when she realized he had cared for her. She knew what that had entailed. Jacob picked her up easily and set her in one of the chairs, then he picked up the tray and left, reassuring her he'd be right back and warning her not to try anything foolish.

In the days that followed, Cynthia began to feel her strength returning. The exercise of moving around the cabin was helping more each day. She could move around quite easily once she was up, but she continued to need Jacob's help getting in and out of the bunk. On occasion she and Garrett were awake at the same time. Then they would talk. She looked forward to their short conversations. There were times Garrett's mind wandered. She hoped the fever hadn't addled his brain.

Finally came the day when she was able to get herself out of bed. She woke up feeling extremely well, but waited until Jacob left to get their breakfast before she tried getting out of bed. After some effort she succeeded and was sitting at the table waiting for him when he returned.

"Well, well," he exclaimed. "Isn't that a sight to behold, a pretty lady waiting at my breakfast table."

"I know I'm not completely well yet, Jacob, but it's time I started helping. The first thing to do, I think, is to clean this cabin. We'll work at it slowly, though. I still tire easily."

"You're right. It does need some cleaning. I'll do all I can, though I am tired this morning. Didn't sleep well last night. Garrett was restless. His fever was up some."

"Oh?" Cynthia turned to Garrett. "I didn't even hear him. Is he . . ."

"I think he's all right. He finally fell into a deep sleep just before dawn. He'll probably sleep most o' the day."

Cynthia tackled the tasks she felt capable of handling but rested frequently throughout the morning. She kept a close eye on Jacob. She napped in the afternoon and when she awoke she found him sleeping at the table. She called to him but he didn't move. She got out of bed, walked to his side and shook him. He raised his head. She could tell he was ill.

"Jacob, you're not . . ."

"I'm afraid I am, Miss Cynthia. I tried hard not to be but I have all the symptoms. I saw it in Garrett. I'm so tired . . . I keep falling asleep."

"Come on. I'm going to get you into bed."

"Jes' spread me a blanket on the floor, Miss Cynthia."

"Nonsense, Jacob. You're going in the bed. I'm almost well. I'll sleep on the floor. And don't you worry. I'll take care of Garrett."

By the time she got Jacob into bed she was shaking from her efforts. I'm really not very strong yet, she told herself. She sat down at the end of the bunk and debated a long time whether or not she had the strength to remove Jacob's clothing and whether or not she ever should. She finally decided she had to. When his fever started she knew it would take every ounce of her strength to keep him wrapped in wet blankets as she had seen him and Garrett do with the sick sailors. With his help she removed his clothes, save for his underwear, and covered him with a warm blanket. He murmured his thanks then was sleeping again.

Cynthia sat at the table wondering what Jacob had done with her clothing and decided she would look for it as soon as she was rested. She knew she had to go get their meals. She couldn't do so wearing nothing more than Garrett's shirt.

"Cynthia?"

She turned to find Garrett watching her. She rushed to his side. "How are you feeling? You've been sleeping all day."

"I feel some better. Where's Jacob?"

"He's . . . uh . . . he's resting." No need to worry him yet, she thought.

"I'm sure he's exhausted after taking care of both of us. And you, you're all right now?"

"Almost. I was just going to look for the clothes you got me. Do you know where they are? I'd like to get some fresh air."

"I don't know where they are. Besides, you shouldn't be out and around yet. The fever . . . you might get sick again."

"Oh, posh. I'm fine."

He smiled feebly. "I just don't have any strength. Don't feel like I can even raise an arm. I want to sleep all the time."

"It's going to take awhile, but with the proper care you'll be fine."

"We owe Jacob a great deal."

"I know."

Garrett slept again. Cynthia started rummaging through bags and finally the trunk before she found the clothing Garrett had given her. She put it on then sat down to rest before making the trek to the galley.

Not wishing to wake either Garrett or Jacob, she left the cabin silently. She traversed the passageway quickly, shuddering when she passed Captain Tarrillton's cabin. I hope he's dead, she thought. She stepped on deck and breathed deeply. The fresh air seemed to revitalize her. She walked to the railing. From the corner of her eye she saw a figure approach her. She wanted to run but turned and faced it head on. To her relief, it was the young officer Garrett had told her was now in charge.

She smiled. "Mr. Mason, isn't it?" she asked when he was close enough to hear.

"Yes," he tipped his hat. "I'm glad to see you out and about. You're feeling well?"

"Quite well, thank you."

"Everyone else seems to be getting well, too, and just in time. We should be home in another five days."

"Five days? We're that close?"

"Yes, ma'am. It's been a long, hard voyage. It's going to be a joyful homecoming—except, of course, for those families who lost men."

"How many died?"

"Eight altogether. But some of them, I think, didn't have families, leastways not in America."

"I see you're still in command. That must mean the captain was . . ."

"Oh, no, ma'am. The captain pulled through. He should be relieving me tomorrow or the next day."

Cynthia gripped the railing. She felt herself go numb.

"Are you all right, miss?"

"I . . . uh . . . I'm fine. I'm just . . . just . . . I'm on my way to the galley to get some food. If you'll excuse me, Mr. Mason."

Cynthia turned and practically ran toward the companionway leading to the galley. *Of course he can't know what the captain did to me,* she thought. *He only knows about the others. Only Garrett knows the whole story. I'll just have to stay out of his way. I'll get enough food to last till we reach the colonies. Dried, everything dried. Garrett will just have to eat it, even though he needs broths now. I should have told Mason not to mention to the captain that he saw me.* She turned. He was gone. She scrambled down the narrow stairway and into the galley. She cajoled the cook into giving her the food she felt would be needed then hurried back to the cabin, passing the captain's quarters as quietly as possible.

She found Garrett and Jacob still sleeping, so she closed the door silently then leaned against it. It has no lock, she thought. How can I keep him out? She set the food down then shoved and pulled the table until she had it in front of the door. She looked around for something more and spied the trunk. She struggled with it until she had it in place under the table.

The noise hadn't wakened either man. She sat down. She was trembling more from fright, she decided, than from exertion. She sat for a few minutes before it occurred to her. Water. I'll need a supply of water—lots of water if I'm not mistaken about Jacob.

She felt exhausted, but forced herself into motion. She moved the table and trunk enough to open the door. Taking what containers there were, she left to find water, realizing she didn't know where it was. I'll ask Mr. Mason, she decided.

She was halfway up the companionway when a shadow loomed over her.

Cynthia tried to sort it out later, but all she could remember was falling when she looked up and saw Captain Tarrillton. She came to in his cabin. Her hands and feet were bound.

"You'll not get away from me again," he'd said.

Cynthia had tried to free herself during his absences but to no avail. He came in twice a day to feed her. He never approached her for any other reason. She knew he slept in the cabin but she seldom saw him unless she happened to wake in the middle of the night. Except for the necessary, they were silent.

She couldn't help but worry about Garrett and Jacob, abut she was afraid to ask Captain Tarrillton of their condition. She knew he hated Garrett enough to kill him. She didn't want to remind him of their relationship. Finally on the day they dropped anchor she knew she had to ask. When the captain came into the cabin late in the day, she took a deep breath.

"Has Mr. Carver gone ashore yet?"

He turned, obviously surprised that she had spoken. "The Georgian?"

She nodded.

"He's dead."

"Dead! But he was almost recovered."

"Took a turn for the worse. Died two days ago."

"And you didn't tell me?"

"Saw no reason to. His nigger's hanging on, though he's mighty sick. Someone came and took him earlier. Poor bastard probably won't live to see home."

Cynthia turned her head and let the tears flow. Her chest felt as though it would burst. She knew vaguely when the captain untied her and left. She cried until there were no more tears. She felt drained.

Suddenly she knew she had to find out for herself. She stood up cautiously. Her legs were weak. She had hardly stood on them for the last five days. She walked to the door slowly, and much to her surprise, found it unlocked. It must be true, she thought, or he wouldn't give me the freedom of the ship. Still, she had to see Garrett's cabin. She made slow progress along the passageway, one hand on the wall for support. She encountered no one. At the door to the cabin, she paused, fearful of what she would find. She leaned her head against the door and prayed it wasn't so, then slowly opened it.

The cabin was empty, all signs of Garrett and Jacob having ever occupied it were gone. A strange trunk sat at the end of the bunk which was neatly made up. Cynthia turned and fled.

Two days later Captain Tarrillton and a grief-stricken Cynthia were rowed ashore. Cynthia had been in a daze for the last forty-eight hours. She didn't know where they were going. It didn't matter now that Garrett was gone. She tried to force her mind to function. As much as she wanted to, she knew she wasn't going to die. She was having some trouble, but found that with effort she could concentrate on the things at hand.

To her amazement, they were anchored in the middle of a river. She had expected the ship to be anchored off-shore as it had been at Worthing. They stepped ashore onto a wooden wharf. There was a high bluff directly in front of them. As they made their way around cargo dispersed about the wharf she watched, with some interest, cranes lifting the heavy cranes to the top of the bluff, where four stately pines stood.

The captain nudged her, then led the way to a wooden staircase built into the side of the bluff. Cynthia was shaking-tired by the time she reached the top but Captain Tarrillton would give her no rest. He led her a short distance to a building where he met with a man. Cynthia sat on a tree stump while they talked.

Before her was a town bustling with activity. It was larger than she had expected for she knew from what Garrett had told her it was Savannah. The thought of Garrett brought tears to her eyes. She brushed them aside. There's no one but me now, she told herself. I have to take very good care of me. She forced her attention to the town spread before her. Even from where she sat she could see it was a prosperous town, sporting many fine homes.

Captain Tarrillton walked by. She rose to follow. He turned to her.

"Yer his now, lass." He nodded toward the man he'd been talking to, then turned to go. He paused. "Good luck to ya, lass."

Cynthia stifled the hysterical laughter that threatened, then turned to regard her new . . . what? she thought in a panic. He was a short, slightly-built man, not much bigger than herself.

"Mistress Fawley?" He seemed civil enough. "I'm Elijah Jameison, yer new master. It would seem the first order o' the day is to find ye some decent clothing."

Cynthia looked down at herself. She hadn't noticed or thought about how she must look. Her bare feet were filthy. The clothing she wore wasn't much better. "And a bath, sir?" she questioned meekly.

He laughed. "Aye, girl, and a bath. Come along."

Twenty-One

Ensconced in his favorite chair before the fireplace in what had originally been designated as the library at Garidas, but had in the truth become his office, Garrett sipped brandy, savoring its fluid warmth. Almost a fortnight had passed since he and Jacob had been carried ashore. Aaron and Micah had been waiting in Savannah for over a week for the arrival of the *Providence* and Garrett welcomed their presence the morning the ship dropped anchor. Jacob's fever broke the last night on board so Garrett insisted they head home immediately where both could recuperate more comfortably. Though the trip would normally have taken two days, they had taken four in deference to Jacob's illness and his own weak condition. Jacob was still abed, but was rapidly becoming himself again, and Garrett could feel his own strength returning with each passing day.

He pushed himself out of the chair and walked to the window. She would have loved it here, he thought, as he looked out across the wide lawn and beyond the brick fence to the flagstone drive curving in front of the house. He still couldn't believe she was dead. He kept thinking he had talked to her, that she was well, but he knew several days had passed when he had been unable to separate reality from feverish dreams. If anyone but Henry Mason had told him, he wouldn't have believed it, would have demanded proof.

He recalled Mason's words. "I saw her just shortly before it happened, Garrett. She was on deck. I thought she looked fine at first, then all of a sudden she turned pale and hurried off. Not long after, I heard she had fallen, broken her neck. I blame myself to some extent. I should have seen to her safety, but other duties were pressing at the time."

"Did you see her, Mason? I mean after . . ."

"No, only the shroud, but there was no mistakin' her size."

Garrett shook his head to clear it of the vision of Cynthia's small shrouded body slipping into the Atlantic. He hadn't told Jacob yet. He would have to soon. Jacob was probably already wondering why he hadn't seen her.

He focused his attention out the window. It had turned unseasonably cold for October and before him was a kaleidoscope of color. The leaves were beginning to show shades of gold, copper and many hues of red and brown. The brilliant red foliage of the sweet-gum trees made them easily discernible. Far to the northwest he could see the mountains. The colors blended there and a bluish-gray haze hung on the peaks. His gaze returned closer to home. Along the drive were pine and oak seedlings that hadn't been there when he and Jacob had left over half a year ago. Other brushy plants he could give no name to were creeping in around the edges of the lawn. We've been gone too long, he thought. The forest is longing to reclaim Garidas.

He returned to his chair and the warmth of the fire. He thought about the land and the home he had come to love. He recalled how thrilled he and Jacob had been when they completed the house two years earlier and the strange name given it by a black from Hispanola. The girl, just recently purchased, spoke no English, but some strange dialect, a mixture of French, Spanish and Indian. She had called the half-finished house Garidas. Garrett had assumed it was either Spanish or Indian or a combination of the two, but he liked the sound of it. The name had stuck. He remembered how amused he had been when he found out later Garidas was distorted French for garrets.

He gazed fondly at the new volumes he and Jacob had brought back from England. They had been carefully placed on the shelves. He noted, with some satisfaction, that most of the shelves were gradually being filled with the fine volumes he and Jacob most enjoyed. They had already acquired Homer, Dante, several volumes of Shakespeare, his contemporary Bacon and numerous others. He felt as though he should be reading some of their newest possessions, but as yet he had no inclination to do so. He stood up abruptly and left the library-office.

It was cold in the main hall. He shivered slightly. Gathering his shawl closer, he paused to observe the room he had worked so hard to plan. It was two stories high and ran the full width of the house, front to back. Four identical fireplaces, now cold, were used to heat the large room when occasion dictated. He smiled when he remembered the discussions he and Jacob had had over the plans for the house, particularly the placement and number of fireplaces.

"It just ain't practical, Garrett," Jacob had argued. "The whole thing's crazy. Never saw a house built like that."

"Maybe it looks crazy on paper, but it'll work, Jacob. Trust me. We'll have four large chimneys. They'll be shared by back-to-back fireplaces downstairs and by those in each of the bedrooms upstairs. I tell you, it'll work. There's no reason to build more chimneys than we need. We need four. Any less than that won't heat this room in winter."

"And those stairs," Jacob changed the subject. "What's gonna hold 'em up?"

"Don't worry, Jacob, they'll be sturdy," Garrett said as he pored over the final plans. "Mr. Trent didn't think it'd work, either, till I showed him the ideas Jeremiah and I came up with."

"Jeremiah? The ol' blacksmith? He don't know nothin' 'bout buildin' houses."

"That's true, Jacob, but he does know about working with metals."

Unconvinced, Jacob had stalked off mumbling to himself, but when the house had been completed, he was as proud of its unique design as Garrett. The twin, free-flying stairways, elegant works of wood and iron, placed on either side of the front door were especially impressive as they rose in long, sweeping curves to the second floor balcony which encompassed the room. Off this balcony were the bedrooms. Because of the physical separation by the large room, the areas of the house had come to be called the main hall, the east wing and the west wing, the stairs also being designated east and west. It was the west stairway for which Garrett now headed.

Jacob had insisted his room be on the west side of the house. He wanted the afternoon sun as well as the heat rising from the first floor kitchen for warmth in winter. He'd told Garrett, in jest, that age should have preference, that his old, creaking bones needed the extra warmth. Garrett smiled when he thought about it as he climbed the stairs. Though older than his own thirty-three years, he realized he didn't know how old Jacob was. He had never thought of him as an old man.

He rapped lightly on Jacob's door. There was no answering call so he opened it quietly. There appeared to be no one in the room.

"Jacob?"

"Over here."

Garrett went into the room. Jacob was in the far corner rummaging in his closet. Clothes were lying on the bed.

"What are you doing out of bed?"

Still in his nightshirt, Jacob turned. He was holding one boot. "Can't seem to find my other boot."

"What are you doing out of bed, Jacob?"

"Confound it, Garrett, I'm tired of layin' abed."

"It's only been three weeks, Jacob. You're not strong enough to be up and around yet."

"Well, I am up, as you can see. 'Sides, I wasn't very sick. Not like you and Miss Cynthia." He looked thoughtful for a moment. "Haven't seen her since I got sick. Leastways not that I remember. She musta been in while I was sleepin', huh?"

Garrett moved across the room and took Jacob's arm. He was trembling. "I tell you, Jacob, you're not well enough to be up yet."

"I am kinda wobbly at that. Maybe I'll jes' rest a little while. But later, you tell Miss Cynthia to come see me."

"Come on, let me help you back to bed."

Nothing was said as he got Jacob into the bed and covered. As he put the clothes away, he stood in the doorway of the closet for a moment. How to tell him, he thought. Once Jacob had learned the whole story he had come to like Cynthia a great deal. Garrett knew he had been happy for them. He closed the closet door. Jacob appeared to be sleeping. He decided he would wait until later to tell him. He was almost to the door when he heard Jacob.

"What happened, Garrett? Where is she?"

Garrett turned. Jacob was raised on one elbow. "She's dead, Jacob."

Confusion clouded the black man's face. "She couldn't be, Garrett. She was up and around before I ever got sick."

"She didn't die of the fever, Jacob." Garrett moved a chair close to his friend's side. "She fell and broke her neck." Jacob lay back on the pillow and Garrett repeated what Henry Mason had told him.

"Bet that bastard of a captain's behind it," Jacob spat when Garrett had finished.

"I doubt it. She was an investment for him. Come to think of it, I didn't see Captain Tarrillton the day we went ashore. I don't even know if he survived the fever."

"He survived all right. His kind always do."

"Perhaps you're right, Jacob. I'll find out when I go to Savannah next week to report to Alex McDaniel."

"Think you should be travelin' yet?"

"I have to. Alex needs the information I have. Besides, our cargo has to be seen to."

Garrett stood up. "You rest now. I'm going for a ride. I'm anxious to see everything again."

"You up to that?"

"I think so. I've been taking short rides daily the last week, always close to the house." He paused at the door. "I plan to be gone all afternoon, but if you like, I'll have supper with you. We can talk then."

Jacob nodded. Garrett closed the door and walked around the balcony to his own room.

It was still warm from the morning fire. Coals were smoldering on the grate. He knew when he returned late in the afternoon he would be greeted by a cheerful fire and a warm bath. He crossed the room, opened the big double closet and removed the clothes he wanted. Tossing them over one arm, he bent to retrieve his riding boots. Both he and Jacob spurned the idea of having personal servants, but the household help banded together to tend to their needs. Garrett knew Munsy was behind it. Having been their first slave purchase, she had been with them almost from the beginning. Bought as a cook, she now had full charge of the house. When Garrett offered her freedom, she had taken the papers, but, with feet firmly planted and hands on her wide hips, she informed him she was "stayin' on." He never questioned her reasons. Whatever they were, he was grateful. The house ran smoothly under her firm hand.

For a time he had entertained the idea that she and Jacob might one day marry. He had abandoned such thoughts years ago. They had become friends, but neither had ever shown any romantic interest toward the other. Since they got home, she had fussed over them like a mother hen.

Garrett closed the door to his room, descended the east stairway to the main hall, crossed and entered the kitchen. Munsy was sitting at the table where the three of them often took their meals, drinking coffee. When he came in she pushed her short, plump figure into motion, moved to the fireplace and pushed the crane holding the coffee pot over the flames.

"Munsy . . ."

"Goin' ridin', Mr. Garrett?"

"Uh-huh."

"Want some coffee 'fore ya go? Jes' made fresh." She was already reaching for a cup.

"No thanks. Just had some brandy."

She pulled the pot from over the heat. "We-ell, I s'pose that'll warm yer innards, too."

Garrett laughed. "You know it does, Munsy."

"Sure good to hear you laugh, Mr. Garrett. Ya ain't been doin' much o' that since ya got home."

"I know, Munsy, but I'm better now. Almost normal."

"I should say so . . . the way ya put away yer dinner."

Garrett raised one eyebrow at her in mock disapproval. She laughed good-naturedly. He walked toward the back door, pulling on soft doeskin gloves.

"Where's Daniel?"

"Mos' likely in the stable. He knows you been goin' ridin' ever' day after dinner. You go along now. I'll have hot coffee for ya when ya get back."

"I won't be back till supper, Munsy," he said as he shrugged into his cloak. "I want to see everything that's been going on while we were gone."

She eyed him sternly. "Mr. Garrett, you ain't well enough to be out in this cold so long."

"I'm fine. And don't go raising your eyebrows at me. Keep an eye on Jacob. I found him trying to get out of bed awhile ago."

"That ol' man ain't got good sense—no more'n you do if you go out today. Why don't you wait a few days? It's bound to warm some again."

"I'm going, Munsy. Have a supper tray ready for me with Jacob's. I promised to eat with him tonight."

"Whatever you say, but you wrap up good, ya hear. Feels like hog-killin' weather out there, sure."

Garrett laughed and stepped out the door into the cold, crisp air. He inhaled deeply and walked the short distance to the stable, knowing he would find

Daniel waiting for him.

Daniel had been with him for twelve years, only two years less than Munsy. He came as a belligerent youth, but once Garrett explained the system, he had become a more than willing worker. As the years matured him, Daniels began to show a great deal of common sense as well as a remarkable ability to handle people. Garrett had given him his "free" papers over three years ago and at the same time offered him the position as general overseer of Garidas, a job he had handled well as a servant for two years. Daniel accepted the job gratefully. Garrett had never been sorry for his choice. Daniel had become a loyal friend.

Garrett entered the stable and waited a moment for his eyes to adjust to the dim light. Temple, his tall chestnut mare, saddled and bridled, stood pawing the hard dirt. Noises came from her empty stall.

"Daniel?"

His nearly bald, black head popped up, shining in the dim light. "Yessir?"

"Daniel, what are you doing?"

"Thought she might like some fresh hay in her stall, that's all."

"And what have you planned for the stable boys to do?"

Daniel smiled, shrugged his shoulders and came around the corner of the stall. Garrett walked over and let Temple nuzzle him. He had intended riding out alone, but now changed his mind.

"Daniel, saddle Wenny. I want you to ride with me."

"Yessir." Daniel, tall and gaunt, moved swiftly to a back stall and brought out the small gray.

"You're limping."

"Oh, it's nothin', Mr. Garrett," he said as he placed the bit in Wenny's mouth and proceeded to bridle him. "Ax head come off last night when I was choppin' wood for Sally. Dropped on my foot. It's jes' bruised. Be okay in a day or two."

Garrett knew Daniel had been courting Sally, the girl from Hispanola, for over a year. "Well, you take care of it, you hear?"

"Will do, Mr. Garrett."

"You and Sally set a date yet?"

"Not yet. We was waitin' till you got home." He paused, holding the saddle. "I . . . uh . . . I'd like to talk to you sometime, Mr. Carver, 'bout Sally's papers."

Taking note of the "Mr. Carver," Garrett straightened. He knew he should have expected this. "How much time does she owe me, Daniel?"

"Somethin' over four years. You tol' her and some others 'fore ya left they was startin' their five years."

"I'll check the book, Daniel. We can talk, but I won't promise anything."

"No, sir. I mean . . . I know ya can't jes' give it to her, or others'd 'spect the same thing, but I've saved some money. I thought maybe . . ."

"I'm sure we can work something out we will both agree to. All right?"

Daniel beamed. "All right, Mr. Garrett. Ya know, it really wouldn't matter much, 'cept Sally wants youngins right away and . . . well . . ."

"I understand, Daniel. I wouldn't want my children born in slavery, either."

There were a few silent moments. Garrett untied Temple and led her to the door. He turned back and found Daniel watching him.

"Thank you, Mr. Garrett," he said huskily.

"Wish there was more men like you, sir."

"There are, Daniel," he said quietly. "There are." He walked out into the bright sunlight. Daniel followed.

Garrett was mounted before he noticed Daniel's meager clothing. "We'll be gone all afternoon, Daniel. Go dress warmer. I'll meet you at the river road. And Daniel," he leaned over and laid a hand on the black man's shoulder. "We'll talk tomorrow."

Shading his eyes from the sun, Daniel looked up from tying Wenny to a railing and smiled. "Tomorrow, Mr. Garrett."

Twenty-Two

Dawn was breaking. Warm and comfortable, wrapped in luxurious furs, an iron warming pan at her feet, Cynthia was convinced indentured servitude was not as frightening as Garrett said it would be. She smiled when she realized that in the two weeks she had been in Savannah she had served no one but herself. She had grown stronger. She felt completely healthy. Elijah Jameison had been nothing but kind since her arrival. He saw that she had proper clothing, decent meals and a place to stay. He made no demands on her, though Cynthia suspected he was a womanizer. Their rooms adjoining, she knew there were several nights he never returned to the inn.

They were now making ready to leave Savannah. After seeing to her every comfort in the coach, he was tending to last minute details of loading just-delivered supplies he had purchased. She could hear him giving orders in a firm voice.

Under the furs she hugged herself then ran her hands down over her stomach. She knew the child was Garrett's and considered herself extremely fortunate to have a part of him left her. The thought of Garrett still brought pain. Nights are the worst, she thought, when I long for his closeness. We had so very little time. She blinked away the threatening tears and tried to think of the child, his child, their child.

When she first realized she was pregnant, she had been exhilarated. Exhilaration had quickly given way to concern and fear. She knew the child had been conceived before her illness and concern for its well-being became her constant companion. Fear that her condition would soon be discovered engulfed her. What would happen to her once she was found to be pregnant? The last two weeks her fear had been somewhat allayed. Elijah Jameison seemed such a kind, understanding man. I hope it's a healthy child, she thought, and grows to be like its father, gentle and compassionate.

She gathered the furs closer as if to find comfort in them and felt their softness against her cheek. Brought back to the present, she marveled at the richness of this new land, where valuable furs were used as lap robes. She wondered again what lay ahead for her at Mountview, Elijah Jameison's oft-spoke-of plantation. There had also been references to a Mrs. Jameison and Cynthia hoped she would be as kindly disposed as her husband.

He opened the door and stepped in, seating himself opposite her.

"Be ye cold, girl? Ye have the furs held so close."

"I'm quite comfortable, thank you, sir. I was just marveling at their luxuriousness." She rubbed one against her cheek. "They're so soft."

"Aye, and remarkably abundant hereabouts."

The coach made a rocking motion as the driver climbed to his seat, then with a sharp whistle and the crack of a whip, they moved forward. Going slowly at first, they gained momentum once they rounded a corner, skirted the South Common and headed north along Bull Street. They passed the public draw-well and crossed two squares before coming to the river. Here they turned west.

They quickly left the town behind and travelled beside open fields. Cynthia looked closely, but could see no houses.

"Where are the houses? Who farms the land?"

"Many farm it. They'd be livin' inside the palisades."

Beyond the fields, they plunged into dense forest. Cynthia was awed by the wildness of the tangled underbrush which was contrasted by the smoothness of the road.

" 'Tis the stagecoach road," he commented. "We'll follow it most o' the way."

Though it wound first one way and then the other following the course of the river, it was a good road, allowing ample room for easy passage. Logs were laid to cover soft bottoms and from an occasional high, open spot the untamed, unclaimed wilderness which surrounded them could be glimpsed.

It was nearing midday. They had seen several log cabins nestled along the riverbank the last few miles and one substantial-looking house far off the road to their left.

"We'll be comin' to Moss Creek crossin' soon, Mistress Fawley, where's a small roadhouse. We'll be eatin' there and restin' for a spell."

Cynthia was thankful when he handed her out of the coach. She paced back and forth in front of the small log building. A weathered sign told her this was "The Wren's Rest."

Elijah Jameison came around the supply wagon, checking the ropes which crisscrossed the canvas covering. Seeing Cynthia, he rubbed his hands together briskly and walked up to her.

"Ye should ha'e gone on ahead, girl. 'Tis cold out here and ye just gettin' well."

A little surprised that he knew of her illness,

Cynthia glanced at him out of the corner of her eye.

"The captain told me," he said as he took her elbow. "Now, let's be gettin' ye inside afore ye take a chill."

"I only wished to stretch my legs, sir," she said as he escorted her through the door. "Besides, I'm fine now. You needn't pamper me."

Seated at a long wooden table with steaming mugs of cider in front of them, Cynthia tried to continue the conversation started earlier. "I really am fine, Mr. Jameison. I intend to be a good servant to you."

"I'm sure ye will be, girl. I'm sure ye will be," he said, then drained his mug and banged it on the table demanding a refill.

They were served a thick, savory venison stew, fresh rolls, hot from the oven and mugfuls of scalding black coffee. Cynthia watched as he removed a small flask from an inside pocket and poured a generous amount of its contents into his coffee.

He smiled and offered her some. " 'Twill ward off the chill," he promised.

She shook her head and raised a spoonful of the stew to her mouth. It was delicious. She ate ravenously, but sipped the coffee sparingly. It was all she could do to keep from making a face at its harsh bitterness.

Elijah Jameison came to her rescue. "It seems ye ha'e no taste for our coffee, girl. Would ye be likin' some tea? If they ha'e none in the house, I'd see to fetchin' ye some from the supply wagon."

Cynthia smiled her gratitude and nodded. He motioned to the young girl who had served them. She moved swiftly to their table and curtsied.

"Yes sir?"

"Mistress Fawley would be likin' some tea. Ha'e

ye any, girl?"

"Right away, sir."

"And girl?"

She paused. "Yessir?"

"I'd be havin' some more coffee."

"Yessir."

The girl disappeared and returned immediately with a steaming pot of tea and more coffee.

Cynthia relished the aroma of the tea as the girl poured. She stirred sugar and milk into it, poured some into the saucer, raised it to her mouth and sipped, delighting in the taste. Replacing the saucer on the table she looked at her master.

"Thank you, Mr. Jameison. It's truly a heaven-sent brew."

"I shall have to remember."

"You have tea in the supply wagon, but you drink coffee?"

"Aye. The tea's for Mrs. Jameison. We been married for six years and she has yet to develop a taste for coffee."

This was the first time he'd ever made a direct remark to Cynthia about his wife. She decided to pursue the conversation.

"Your wife? Does she like the country?"

"Aye, very much so, though she does find it a wee bit lonesome. We have but few neighbors with whom we visit and there are great distances between us."

"But surely your children keep her occupied."

He set the coffee mug on the table and sighed. "Ah, if it were only so."

Cynthia could see signs of inebriation.

"We have no wee bairn as yet."

"I . . . uh . . . I'm sorry. I didn't mean to pry."

" 'Tis all right, girl." He brightened. "Our childless status may be changin' quite soon. Mrs. Jameison chose not to make the trip to Savannah with me, a choice no doubt hard for her to make with her bein' so lonely, because . . . uh . . . she told me she may be with child. She dinna want to take a chance. Travelin', ye know, is hard on a woman with child."

"Yes, so I've heard," Cynthia said, thinking again of her own child and wondering if she could tell Elijah Jameison. She decided not, at least, not yet. Perhaps Mrs. Jameison would be the one to tell. She would wait and see.

Their journey was resumed after a brief rest. A little unsteady, Elijah Jameison handed Cynthia into the coach. Sure that the day had turned colder she quickly gathered the furs about her. She felt for the heat of the warming pan with her feet and was glad to discover the coals had been replenished during their stop. It was toasty warm. She snuggled down into the furs as the coach moved forward.

His tongue loosened by the liquor he had consumed, Mr. Jameison regaled Cynthia with tales of the country through which they traveled. She was amazed and a little frightened to hear there were Indians in the area. She had seen no evidence of savages. Her fear must have shown. He tried to reassure her.

"Ye needn't worry about the savages, girl. There's ne'er been a major Indian uprisin' in Georgia, tho' it has been a wee bit touchy at times. Cherokees went on the warpath six, seven years ago. Stirred up by the French, they were. Fightin' to the north and east o' us but ne'er in Georgia. The French also tried to incite the Creeks. Some traders were ambushed up north o' Augusta, but Governor Ellis was able to convince the Indians that we're their friends. Besides, they need our trade. Aye, and it coulda got bad in sixty-two when the Spanish joined the French in raids on the river, but Governor Ellis, bein' as he was on good terms with the Indians, again convinced them to stay out o' it. And ye needn't worry about living at Mountview. We're but a short distance from Fort Augusta."

He took another drink from the flask.

"It . . . uh . . . it all sounds so violent," Cynthia said.

"Aye, I suppose 'twould to you, but to my way o' thinkin', it's safer than bein' on the streets o' London."

He tipped the flask again and drained its contents. Within minutes he was peacefully snoring.

Cynthia, somewhat reassured by his words, found herself dozing and waking time after time, never knowing how long she had slept. The afternoon waned. Just as the sun was setting the driver called out, "Bent Tree Road comin' up, sir."

Eliljah Jameison slept on. Cynthia reached out and shook him. "Mr. Jameison, Mr. Jameison, sir!"

He roused. "Um . . . uh . . . yes? What is it, girl?"

"The driver, sir, he just called Bent Tree Road."

He rubbed his hands across his face. "Ah, good. 'Tis our stop for the night, girl." He leaned over and looked out the window. "Bent Tree tonight, Birdsville on the morrow and the next day home." He settled back into his seat and smiled at her. "Be ye tired, girl?"

She returned his smile. "A little. Mostly, I'm anxious to stretch my legs."

"Shortly, girl, shortly."

The coach halted before a long, low building hugging the hillside. Handed from the coach by an overly cheerful Jameison, Cynthia hurried up the stairs and across the rough plank porch taking only cursory notice of the hand-hewn sign proclaiming her arrival at Bent Tree Inn. Remembering Mr. Jameison's admonition about her standing out in the cold at their midday stop, she pushed on the door and entered. She was standing by the fire in a large common room when he joined her.

"A right cheery place, wouldn't ye say, girl?"

She turned and found him eyeing her critically. She turned back and held her hands out to the fire. "Yes, it does appear so."

"A wee bit rustic, perhaps, but the owners are most accommodating. Supper will be here shortly. I've secured a room, girl. Would ye care to freshen up a mite?"

"Yes, I think I'd like that, sir. Thank you."

He led Cynthia around a corner and down a hallway, showed her which room then turned and left. She returned to find him in heated conversation with a traveler who was obviously his social equal. He motioned her away. She moved to the end of the table and sat opposite one of his drivers. Generous plates were set before them. The man across from her ate as though in a trance. Cynthia strained but could hear only snatches of conversation from the other end of the table.

". . . I tell you, Wright'll know how to deal with 'em. . . . Sons of Licentiousness? . . . Does he really? . . . Back, you say . . . stupid . . . crazy ideas . . . blacks . . . step above apes. . ."

She finally gave up and turned her attention to the man opposite her. He was clean shaven with a healthy, robust look. "I . . . uh . . . I'm Cynthia Fawley."

The man jumped as though a shot had been fired. His gray eyes studied her for a moment before he spoke. "Know that." He returned his gaze to his plate.

After a few minutes, Cynthia tried again. "What's your name?"

"Roland," the man answered without looking up.

"Roland? Roland what?"

"Jes' Roland."

"But everyone has a last name."

The man looked up. His eyes were penetrating. They appeared to have changed color. "Not at Mountview they don't. They have the name Mr. Jameison gives 'em. Mine's Roland. Nathan Tolliver wasn't fancy-soundin' enough for him. I'm Roland." He resumed his meal.

"You . . . uh . . . you weren't driving the coach."

"No ma'am. 'At was Shires."

"Shires?"

He nodded.

"Strange name."

He shrugged.

"Where is Shires, Mr. Tolliver? Why isn't—"

He reached out and grabbed her wrist, at the same time casting a glance to the other end of the table. "Don't ever call me nothin' but Roland. Leastaways not where Mr. Jameison can hear. As for Shires, he's black. He ain't allowed in here."

"But why can't I call you—"

"Jes' don't, that's all." He let go of her and stood up.

"Very well, but—"

He gave a nod. "Evenin' Mistress Fawley." He turned and walked away, placing his hat on sandy-colored hair as he went out the door.

Cynthia shrugged off his ominous-sounding words, stood and moved to Elijah Jameison's side. "Excuse me, Mr. Jameison."

He glanced up, his look telling her she had just overstepped her bounds. "Aye, girl? What is it?"

She tried to rectify what she decided must be a breach of etiquette. "It's been a long day, sir. If there's nothing I can do for you . . ."

He waved her off. "Aye, it has been a long day. To bed with you, girl."

As Cynthia opened her door, she heard loud guffaws from the common room.

Twenty-Three

Garrett leaned forward in the saddle, letting Temple have her head, as they raced down the winding drive toward the river road. The cold air stung his face as he rounded one familiar curve after another. The house set over a mile distant and was not visible from the river. He liked it that way. The long, winding drive had been painstakingly carved from the wilderness to avoid cutting down more trees than necessary. Through sheer determination and hard work the drive and that part of the river road running through Garidas were kept clear. There were few travelers to this part of the colony and even fewer visitors to Garidas. Garrett didn't miss society. He rather enjoyed the solitude his way of life had brought, still he had wondered how such isolation would have affected Cynthia.

When he reached the river road, he reined in, dismounted and led Temple to the small cabin he and Jacob had shared their first few years on the land. He knew Daniel would be along shortly, yet he wanted to spend a few minutes alone where he always felt he had his beginnings in this new land. He never wanted to forget how it was those first years. It helped him keep his perspective.

He tied Temple to the crude railing out of the wind and entered the cabin. Strange, he thought, that I haven't ridden this way since I got home. How many years has it been? he wondered as he removed his gloves, crossed to the fireplace and struck a flint to the expertly-laid kindling. He knew Munsy had been onto him about the cabin for years. He never failed to enter but that it was ready for him. He didn't know who she had tending it, but he decided long ago she had taken on the care of the cabin as an extension of her household duties when she discovered he used it on occasion. Neither of them ever spoke of the service rendered here, but he was certain each knew how the other felt.

Within seconds the kindling was blazing and crackling. He took a small log from the seemingly endless supply by the hearth and settled it in the flames, then stood and looked around. He was aware that on rare occasions lone or lost travelers had spent the night here, yet the small room was unchanged, ready for occupancy. The built-in bunks opposite one another at the far end of the room were neatly secured, their feather beds rolled in a blanket at the foot of each. The feather beds were fairly recent traditions, having replaced straw ticks. The rope webbing in the bunks had been kept taut over the years and replaced when worn. He walked to the pile of furs kept on a small table between the bunks, returned to the fire with one, spread it in front of the hearth and sank down.

How often he had sat in this exact spot after working from before first light to last when he was little more than a boy. The years rolled away for him. He could almost hear Jacob moving in the room behind him. Staring into the fire, so many memories flooded his mind he had trouble sorting them. He closed his eyes and remembered Jacob's excitement when he had come home from Savannah with one of the first copies of the *Georgia Gazette*.

He recalled handing the paper to Jacob who passed it back with tears in his eyes. He asked Garrett to read it to him. He didn't know how to read. Garrett could see them poring over the paper night after night in front of the fire as he taught Jacob the words. He relived it all, the good times, the bad, the happy sharings of knowledge.

He opened his eyes. The small log was little more than glowing embers. In the stillness he could hear hoofbeats coming from the direction of the big house. He stood, replaced the fur and walked to the door. With a hand on the latch, he looked over the room again and suddenly thought of Cynthia.

"We could have been happy even here," he said aloud, then opened the door and stepped into the bright sunlight. But she's gone, he thought as he pulled on his gloves. I can't dwell on that. I mustn't. She touched my life, was a part of it for a short time, but like this cabin and the time spent here, it's over. I can only draw on the memories and gain strength from them.

He mounted Temple. She fairly danced under him. "Easy, girl," he said as he patted her neck and held her to a walk. "We have to wait for Daniel."

He was waiting at the junction of the drive and river road when Daniel rounded the last curve. Upon seeing Garrett, Daniel urged Wenny into a lope. Garrett held Temple until Daniel was beside him then they raced westward toward the frontier and the outer boundaries of Garidas.

Where the road curved down to the river and crossed it, Garrett and Daniel continued westward, following little more than a trail into the dense forest. Within fifty yards they had cleared the forest and were in open field. Garrett reined Temple to a stop.

"Daniel, that track needs to be cleared."

"Yessir, Mr. Garrett."

"How did you get the wagons down to the road?"

"We tuck 'em 'round t'other way, Mr. Garrett."

"Wasteful, Daniel. Wasteful."

"I know, sir, but we had so many down with summer complaint 'bout the time harvest started here we couldn't spare the hands to clear the roadway. I decided it was more important to get the cotton out o' the field even if we did have to go the long way 'round. We'll clear it come spring plantin'."

Garrett scanned the field and the workers who were turning the soil. He had been wrong to chastise Daniel. He knew the man had been short-handed the last few weeks. His and Jacob's coming home sick hadn't helped.

"You're right, Daniel. Sorry."

He loosened the reins and rode across the field, stopping to speak to some of the hands. They'd be finished with this field in another day then move on to other jobs. Garrett could see Daniel had things under control. They rode on.

"Think you can spare Ben tomorrow, Daniel?"

"S'pose so, Mr. Garrett. You got somethin' special you want him to do?"

"I plan to ride over to Birdsville tomorrow. Thought I'd take Ben with me. It'll pacify Munsy if I don't go alone."

Daniel smiled. Everyone knew how Munsy mothered Mr. Garrett . . . Jacob, too. "Right, Mr. Garrett. I'll tell him tonight. You be leavin' early?"

"Just tell Ben to be at the house about breakfast time."

"Yessir. You be gone all day?"

"Probably two days. Don't think I'm up to ridin'

both ways in one day yet." Garrett glimpsed Daniel's crestfallen look. "Have breakfast with me in the morning, Daniel. We'll talk about Sally's papers then."

Daniel smiled his appreciation as they paused and looked back at the field they'd cleared for cotton only three seasons before.

"It was a good crop, wasn't it, Daniel?"

"Seemed to be, sir. Got a good price, too, though . . ."

"I know. You and Jacob thought I was crazy for plantin' cotton."

"Yessir. At the time . . ."

"But it's a dependable crop, Daniel. The price doesn't fluctuate like that of tobacco. Someday, everyone around here will be growin' cotton."

"If you say so, Mr. Garrett. What I was gonna say, sir, is even though we got a good price, we ain't growin' enough to make much profit."

"I know, Daniel. I wanted to try it first, see if you and Jacob were right. Next year we'll clear more land. Our new agent in London says he can sell all we can ship him."

"Yessir. Maybe in two, three years."

"That's what I thought, Daniel."

They turned their horses to leave.

"By the way, Mr. Garrett, a Mr. Carruthers stopped by a few weeks ago. Said he'd buy any spare cottonseed we had."

"We won't have any to sell if we increase our acreage, Daniel. But you see what I mean? Cotton is the up and coming crop."

"Yessir."

"Carruthers? Do I know him?"

"Said he made your acquaintance in London, Mr. Garrett. He's from someplace south o' here. Was on his way to Fort Augusta he said on business."

Carruthers. Garrett mulled the name over in his mind as they rode. Then he recalled the pompous little man he had met at a dinner in London, a few days before the cattle market meeting. He had been a brash boor, forcing himself on everyone at the gathering. Garrett certainly wanted no business dealings with him.

"What did you think of Carruthers, Daniel?"

"Didn't much like him, sir. He kept insisting on talking to the white folks. I don't think he ever did believe I was the overseer."

"Well, should Mr. Carruthers ever return when I'm not here, tell him that at no time in the foreseeable future will we have anything here at Garidas to sell him."

"Yessir. You think he's a troublemaker, Mr. Garrett?"

"I don't know, but I think he could be."

Their next stop was the west tobacco barn. Garrett and Daniel rode into the barn and dismounted. Men were everywhere, lifting the long poles from their racks and tying the cured tobacco into bundles.

"This is the last of it, Mr. Garrett. All the other barns been cleared."

Garrett walked over and inspected several of the bundles. "Looks like prime tobacco, Daniel."

"Mostly all good this year, sir. Mostly all good. Not much sortin' to this crop, no sir."

Garrett looked up. Daniel was beaming. "You've done a fine job, Daniel."

"Thank you, sir."

They walked and watched for a few minutes, both stopping occasionally to inspect the dried plants, each nodding his approval from time to time.

As they mounted to leave, Garrett turned to

Daniel. "Noah started on the hogsheads yet?"

"No sir. Gonna start tomorrow. Jes' finished cuttin' the saplin's last week. Noah and Zeke been strippin' and splittin' what they need to start with and gettin' the slats ready. Be half done 'fore Christmas. Ever'thin' else 'bout finished up. Munsy got the spinners goin' t'other day."

"Yes, I know."

The afternoon passed quickly as they rode from field to field talking to the hands and inspecting the harvested crops. It was dusk when they came to the lane which ran between the people's cabins in back of the big house. Their last stop was the carpenter's shop where they viewed Noah's last minute preparations for the next day.

Garrett was pleased with the way Daniel had handled the work at Garidas during his absence, but he was exhausted as he lowered himself into the tub Munsy had waiting for him. Maybe I'm not ready for a trip to Birdsville, he thought. He leaned back and let the warm water soothe him. No, he argued with himself, I'll be all right after a good night's sleep. It's been so long I need to hear the news. Maybe Thaddeus will have a recent issue of the *Gazette*. Leastways, he can give me the news.

Bathed, dressed and feeling refreshed, Garrett traversed the balcony to Jacob's room. He found his friend sitting up in bed looking much rested. Nancy, one of the kitchen helpers, was fussing over a large tray, laden with several covered dishes.

"Nancy, you didn't carry that heavy tray up, did you?"

The small girl turned. "Oh, no, sir. Sam brung it up for me. I'se jus' gonna set some o' these dishes over by the fire till you're ready for 'em."

Garrett nodded and pulled a chair up beside

Jacob. "Well, old friend, you're looking much better."

"Ought to. Slept the whole afternoon."

"It seems to have done you some good."

"Consarn, Garrett! Wish I could get over feelin' so helpless."

"In time, Jacob. It takes time."

Nancy finished and turned to them. "Would you like me to stay and serve, sir?"

"That's all right, Nancy. I'll take care of it." The girl turned to leave. "And Nancy?"

She turned back. "Yessir?"

"Tell Munsy I'm going to Birdsville tomorrow. If there's anything she wants, she can tell me at breakfast."

"Yessir." The girl left in a rustle of skirts.

"There you go, Garrett," Jacob accused as the door closed, "spoilin' our supper."

"Spoilin' our . . . what'd I do?"

"You know 's well as I do that ol' biddy hears you're plannin' a trip to Birdsville, she'll be right up here."

"That's not kind, Jacob," Garrett said with a smile.

"S'pose not, but it's true. Look at how she's babied us since we got home. Gettin' to be a real pest. Mark my word. 'Fore we're through 'ith that first dish she'll come roarin' in here 'thout even knockin'."

Garrett laughed as he set the tray across Jacob's lap and pulled a small table up to his own chair. "Why are you so hard on Munsy, Jacob? You love her as much as I do . . . and we both know it."

"Harrumph," was all Jacob said as he unfolded the large napkin and reached to tie it around his neck. He avoided Garrett's eyes as he fumbled the knot twice.

"Come on, Jacob, eat up. It's delicious."

"Consarned it, Garrett, I can't tie this damn thing."

"Just tuck it in your nightshirt. Your soup's gettin' cold."

Disgruntled, Jacob obeyed. Garrett watched him out of the corner of one eye. Soup dribbled down his chin. He threw his spoon down and pushed the soup away, sloshing it onto the tray.

"God damn it, Garrett, bein' sick is inhuman."

Garrett leaned back in his chair. "Jesus, Jacob! I'll be glad when you get out of that bed.

"Well, that makes two of us."

"Maybe by the time I get back from Savannah."

" 'Fore ya leave. Ya can lay odds on it."

Silence followed. Jacob laid his head back and closed his eyes.

"You're not eating?"

He raised up and looked at Garrett as though he thought him daft. " 'Course I am. I'm hungry. Jes' waitin' for you to get to somethin' more substantial that won't run down my front."

Garrett smiled, walked to the fireplace and returned with one of the covered dishes, a towel protecting his hands. He set it before Jacob who immediately removed the cover and attacked the large slab of ham, yams, green corn and small whole beets. Garrett was glad to see Jacob show such interest in food again. He had hardly sat down to resume his own meal, however, when the door flew open with a bang.

Munsy stormed into the room and planted herself before Garrett, hands on her hips.

"Tol' ya," Jacob said quietly.

Munsy glared at him then turned her attention

back to Garrett.

"What you mean you goin' to Birdsville tomorrow?"

Garrett laughed lightly. "Munsy, as much as I'd like to let you pamper me all winter, I can't. There's work to be done . . . and . . . uh . . . I thought you might need some supplies."

"Supplies! Work! Devil's work, dat what!" She walked to the far side of the bed, picked up the coverlet at the foot of the bed and began to fold it. "Liberty Boys bring ya a passle o' trouble, Mr. Garrett."

Garrett's mouth fell open.

"Ya think we don't know? Blacks know ever'thin'. Aaron and Micah heared all 'bout them Liberty Boys when they was waitin' fo' ya in Savannah."

"Then you know there are no Liberty Boys here on the frontier."

"Not yet they ain't." She dropped the coverlet, put her hands on her hips and stared at him. "But you right smack in the middle of it, ain't ya, Mr. Garrett?"

Garrett looked at Jacob, who quickly cast his eyes toward the ceiling, then he looked back at Munsy.

"Yes, I am, Munsy, as you say, smack in the middle . . . Jacob, too. I don't know how it will end, but we're on the right side. It's a natural extension to what we're doing here at Garidas."

"How dat, Mr. Garrett?" Her black brow was furrowed.

"Well, Munsy, the Liberty Boys want the colonies to be able to choose their own leaders, make their own laws, be represented in parliament. In short, they are advocating freedom from a tyrannical, and some say insane, king."

" 'S'at what you want, Mr. Garrett?"

"That and more. I advocate freedom for everyone, black and white."

She looked from Garrett to Jacob and back. "Advocate?"

"That means I agree with and support the idea of freedom."

"I know dat, Mr. Garrett . . . and these Liberty Boys, they believe like you do—in freedom for ever'one? They not jus' riffraff?"

Garrett chuckled. "Well, not all believe as I do, but some. Maybe enough. And most of them are reputable, respected landowners."

Munsy walked to the door. "That case, Mr. Garrett, I be needin' some needles and thread, since you be goin' to Birdsville tomorrow on important business like freedom." She opened the door and left. Garrett could hear her whistling as she descended the stairs.

Behind him, he could hear Jacob letting his breath out slowly. He turned and surveyed his friend.

"What are you so relieved about?"

"I was afraid you was gonna sick her on me—now that she can see for herself that you're well and back in harness."

The two men laughed easily as they returned to their supper. Over the remainder of the meal Garrett told Jacob of the profitable year Garidas had seen under Daniel's hand. They made plans to purchase more blacks at first opportunity and they agreed as a bonus for Daniel's fine work, they would give Sally her papers.

Garrett crawled into bed thinking how he would mark Daniel's bonus on the books so it would appear as a simple cash transaction. He fell into a fitful sleep surrounded by golden hair, caressed by laughing green eyes. Sometime late in the night he awoke himself with his own laughter. He knew immediately where he was, yet he could see Cynthia in front of him huddled in a coverlet afraid he was about to rape her. He laughed again. That was in England, his sleep-muddled brain told him ... England. He turned his face into the pillow.

Twenty-Four

Cynthia was awakened by a noise behind her. She was surprised to find light in the room. She turned and discovered Elijah Jameison standing on the far side of the bed, his back to her. It took her a moment to realize he was undressing. She instinctively pulled the covers to her chin. Why hadn't she locked the door?

"Mr. Jameison?"

He turned. "Ah, sorry, lass. I dinna mean to waken ye just yet."

"Just yet . . . but . . . is it morning?"

"Mornin'? Oh, no lass. Ye've only been sleepin' but a wee bit o' time."

"Then . . . then why are you here?" She held the quilts closer.

He sat on the bed, pulled off his boots, then turned to her. "I could lie to ye, girl, and tell ye 'twas the only room, but I won't. Ye need to be understandin' the way o' things."

"Understanding?" She shook her head to clear it of sleep. "Understanding?" Her voice rose with each word. "I understand all too well, you . . . you . . ."

He slapped her. "Hush, girl. Ye want to be wakin' ever'one?"

Tears came to her eyes.

"I paid the captain hard cash for yer passage, lass and ye'll be doin' my biddin' for some time to come.

It'll be easier on ye if we have, shall we say, a harmonious relationship?"

Cynthia nodded, then cast her eyes downward as Jameison stood, unbuttoned his pants and let them fall to the floor.

"But why now? I . . . I've been with you for . . . for a fortnight." Her mind raced, seeking an escape.

"Aye," he said as he climbed into bed, "that you have, but I'm well-known in Savannah."

"And word might get back to your wife?"

He raised up and glared at her. "We'll not be speakin' o' Mrs. Jameison again, lass." He paused and looked away. "But yes, she might somehow hear, then I'd be obliged to sell ye. That I would be loath to do."

"But you had women in Savannah!"

He cocked an eyebrow and peered at her out of the corner of one eye. "Aye, and what mon doesn't when he's away from his wife? They're nice girls, too, all o' 'em, but I wouldna be takin' 'em home wi' me." He paused a moment, then spoke quietly. "I'll be havin' ye now girl, with or without your consent."

Cynthia nodded again. The solution, her brain screamed. Why didn't I think of it before? I could have enticed the man. He was panting after every skirt in Savannah. It'll work, she told herself, as he pulled her to him. It has to. I don't have to tell anyone I'm pregnant for a while. By then, perhaps I can convince Jameison the child I carry is his. A small sacrifice to pay if it will insure the child a decent beginning.

"Ah, lass," he whispered against her neck. "I hoped ye'd be receptive to the idea. Ye won't be sorry, I promise." His hands roamed freely under her chemise.

Cynthia closed her eyes and thought of Garrett, trying to convince herself he was the man next to her. When Jameison's face kept appearing behind closed eyelids, she abandoned the effort and suffered his attentions, thinking of anything but what was happening to her.

Within minutes she knew he was aroused. He raised over her and easily slipped off her chemise.

"My God," he breathed, "yer more beautiful than I envisioned. A veritable feast for any mon."

She closed her eyes tighter as she felt him between her legs.

"Come, girl, open yer eyes. I'm not repulsive and I know I'm not the first mon ye've had. Captain Tarrillton told me ye were recently widowed. Open yer eyes, girl! Look at me!"

I must make the effort, Cynthia was thinking. I've some years service with this man and . . . and the child. Think of the child. He must find me agreeable. She opened her eyes and smiled, reached her arms up and pulled him to her.

"I'm sorry, sir," she spoke quietly against his ear. "I was remembering my husband. You're very much like him."

"Call me Eli," he whispered back. "And ye? Ye shall be my beautiful Helen."

Cynthia smiled secretly. It's better this way. When I tell him he's to be a father he'll suspect nothing on my part.

Later, irritated by his snoring, she stole from the bed. Finding the room cold, she completed a hasty toilette then, much as she hated the idea, returned to lay beside Elijah Jameison. She lay awake for what seemed like hours before sleep finally overtook her. She dreamed of security in strong, loving arms.

Cynthia awoke to loud, insistent knocking on her

door. The room was flooded with sunshine, the bed empty save for herself.

"Yes?" she called. "Yes? Just a moment."

"Come along, Helen. Ye've only time for a quick meal before we leave."

So he's found a name for me, too, has he? she thought. Well, I'll not let him. "There's no Helen in here. You must have the wrong room."

The door opened. He stepped in, closed it behind him then leaned against it. "My people go by the name I give them. For ye, I have chosen the name Helen. I told you that last night. I have no Helen on my plantation."

"But that's ridiculous. I have a perfectly fine name. Cynthia, Cynthia Fawley."

"I happen to like the name Helen. Now, get yerself dressed and fed before ye cause us delay." He turned to leave, then paused. "Henceforth, Mistress Fawley, ye shall be Helen. I'll call ye none other. I expect silence from ye unless yer spoken to. I demand obedience. Should ye find occasion to cross me, the punishment is harsh. Do ye understand, girl?"

Cynthia nodded. She could feel a knot of fear growing within her. He left. As she rushed to dress, she wondered at the power the man seemed to wield. And he enjoys it, she thought. He gets uncommon pleasure from having power. He could be dangerous. I'll not let him beat me down. I'll fight him in every way I can save one. As deplorable as it is, I must convince him the child I carry is his.

In the coach Elijah Jameison was as talkative as he had been the day before. It rankled her when he called her Helen, but she decided that was one concession she had to make. There was no way to fight him in that. There would surely be other ways.

Cynthia was dozing, but woke suddenly when the coach came to a halt. The sun told her it was past midday. They were stopped before a small, clapboard-gabled structure.

"We're here, girl. Birdsville."

Cynthia gazed out the window at the few scattered buildings. "Is . . . is this all?"

"Aye. Well, almost." He stepped out of the coach. "Come, girl, see for yourself."

Cynthia let him help her out. As she turned, her eyes widened in amazement. Not far from where they stood was the grandest home she had seen since her arrival in Georgia.

"Impressive, isn't it, girl?"

She nodded. "Your . . . your friends, they live there?"

"The Gilmores? Nay, girl. That's the home of Francis Jones. He's probably the richest, most powerful man in this part of the colony. We're on his land now and have been the last few miles. The Gilmores' land borders his just north of here. Come. We'll eat before going on."

Cynthia followed him to the wagon where he retrieved a bundle of papers. He told her the small building they entered served as a post office as well as an inn for stage travelers. He laid the papers on a counter just inside the door, then led Cynthia into a small common room. The room was empty except for a thin, young man tending the fire.

"Theren, Theren Ewen."

The young man turned. "Ah, Mr. Jameison. Good to see you again, sir. How was your trip?"

"Fine, fine. Where's Bird?"

"In the stable, sir. His mare's about to foal."

"I see." They sat down by the window closest to the fire. "Well, mon, bring us something to eat and

263

tell Mr. Bird I've left him ten copies of the *Gazette,* compliments of Mr. Johnston."

"I believe, sir, the *Gazette* came in on last night's stage."

Jameison scowled.

"But . . . but in these troubled times, everyone wants the news. I'm sure he'll welcome them. Did ye leave any off at Overby's place?"

"Overby? Thaddeus Overby? I'd not give the mon the time o' day. Nay, I was asked to deliver them to Mr. Bird. Whom he favors with them is his business."

"Aye, sir. I'll . . . uh . . . I'll have you some dinner shortly."

"And ale, lad. Bring me some ale now."

"Aye, sir."

Garrett was tired when the Jones' house finally came into view. He and Ben had traveled the last few miles in silence, the sun at their backs. It had seemed a longer journey than usual. He knew he needed rest.

"We're almost there, Ben."

"Yessir. You all right, sir?"

"I'm tired, Ben. I'll be fine soon as I get some rest."

"Yessir. Maybe, sir, we shouldn't leave early tomorrow lak you said."

"We'll see, Ben. If we don't, Munsy'll be fit to be tied."

"Oh, no, sir. She tol' me to tak' good care o' you even if that meant layin' over an extry day. She won't worry none 'lessin' we're gone longer than that."

Garrett smiled. Thank the Lord for Munsy, he thought. "What would we do without her, Ben?"

"Sir?"

"Munsy. What would we do without her to keep

264

us all in line?"

"I don't know, sir. She's been lak a mother to me 'bout as long's I can recollect."

"Me, too, Ben. Me, too."

They lapsed into silence again until they were almost to the post office.

"Want I should stop here, Mr. Garrett and see if there's anything for Garidas?"

"Huh? Oh, no, Ben. Doubt if there is. We can check later."

"We stayin' at Mr. Overby's?"

"Uh-huh. He'll have all the news and he's easier to talk to than Bird. Not as busy."

Cynthia looked up from her plate. The movement of the riders caught her eye. The taller of the men turned to speak to his companion. Cynthia dropped her fork. She half-rose from her chair and craned her neck for a better view. They disappeared around the corner of the building.

"Is something wrong, girl?"

She sank back into her chair and focused her attention on Elijah Jameison. "What? Wrong? Uh, no, it's just . . . it's just . . ."

"Ye look like ye've seen a ghost, girl."

"Oh, no, sir, it's . . . those riders. . . ."

"Riders?" He turned to look.

"They're gone now, sir, but one reminded me of . . . of a man I helped nurse on board ship. Of course, it couldn't have been him. He died of the fever, but the resemblance startled me."

"I should say it did. Yer tremblin'. Let me get some rum for you."

"I'm sure I'll be all right, sir, but yes, some rum might help. Just the memories . . . and . . . and remembering about the fever. It was a nightmare."

Garrett was relieved when they reined in at the

small, unpretentious roadhouse run by Thaddeus Overby. He gave Temple into Ben's care and pushed open the rough plank door. Faint odors of smoke, unwashed bodies, spilled drinks and cooking meat greeted him. The round, boisterous proprietor glanced up from his work, then pushed his way toward Garrett, wiping his hands on his apron.

"Garrett. Garrett Carver!" His red, perspiring face lit up in welcome.

"Thad." The man was in front of him now and grasped his hand in a bear-like paw.

"Lordy, Garrett, it's been nigh onto . . ." He paused a moment to figure. "Nigh onto a year."

"That it has Thaddeus."

"I heard you'd gone back to England."

"Yes. For a visit. I'm glad to be home."

"Didn't like it, huh?"

"It was interesting, but no, I didn't like it."

"Saw your sister?"

"Yes. She's well. I . . . uh . . . can we talk later, Thaddeus? Right now, I need a place to clean up, a strong drink and some rest."

Thaddeus cocked his head to one side in scrutiny. " 'Course, Garrett. 'Course. You know the back room is always ready. Go along. I'll bring you some hot cider."

"Brandy, Thaddeus. I'd like some warm brandy."

"Sure, Garrett, sure. I'll be right in." He turned to go, concern clearly showing on his face.

Garrett turned to the door on his left, then paused. "Thad, Ben's with me. He's stabling our horses. See that he's taken care of, will you?"

Thaddeus nodded, then waved him off.

Garrett had hardly removed his cloak when there was a knock on the door. He opened it to find a pretty, dark-haired young woman standing before him.

"Afternoon, Mr. Carver. Papa tol' me to bring you this here hot water."

"But you're not . . ."

"Oh, yes, I am," the girl said as she moved into the room, pushed the door closed behind her and poured steaming water into the washbasin.

"Mourning?"

The girl faced him, beaming with pleasure. "You remembered!"

"Well, yes, but my how you've grown."

Mourning lowered her eyes.

"You were away for a while, weren't you? Savannah?"

"That's right, with Mama's sister, but I been home almost a year now. I hear you've been to England."

Garrett nodded. He wished Thaddeus hadn't sent her. His head was beginning to ache.

"I'd love to go to England. Not right away, of course, but someday. Maybe . . . maybe on my honeymoon."

"Oh? You have plans, girl?"

They both turned to find Thaddeus at the door. He set a tray on the table.

" 'Course not, Papa. I only said someday . . . but I will be sixteen come spring."

"I know, girl. I know. Now off with you. Your mama needs help in the kitchen."

"Yes, Papa. Good day, Mr. Carver. I will see you again, won't I?"

"Yes, of course, Mourning, and thank you for the water."

The girl curtsied, then slowly closed the door as she left. Thaddeus burst into laughter.

"I do believe, Garrett, she was toying with you."

"Oh? I hadn't noticed. She is an attractive young

woman, Thad."

"Aye. That she is. But what's wrong, Garrett? You look awful."

As he removed his shirt and washed, Garrett told Thaddeus of the voyage and of Cynthia.

"Terrible business, a sickness on shipboard. No way to steer clear of it. I'm . . . I'm sorry about the girl, Garrett."

"Thank you, Thaddeus. I still find it hard to believe she's gone."

They were sitting on the edge of the bed, Garrett sipping the warm brandy.

"You sure you don't want something to eat?"

"Later, Thad. Right now I need rest. The ride in tired me more than I thought it would."

"Sure. Sure." He pushed his bulk to a standing position and picked up the tray. He paused at the door. "Elijah Jameison's coach passed by less than an hour ago."

"Yes, I saw it at the inn."

"He's been to Savannah. Perhaps he knows something of this Captain Tarrillton. Would you like me to inquire?"

"As many ships as there were in the harbor, it's a long shot, but yes, if you would. I don't particularly care to talk to the man myself."

"I know. I'll tend to it. Now you rest. I'll wake you for supper. We'll have a good talk then and I'll catch you up on the news."

"Thanks, Thad." He stretched out on the bed. "And I would like to see any back issues of the *Gazette* you have."

"I have some dandies, Garrett, some dandies — like the one about Patrick Henry's speech last . . . but later, right?"

Garrett smiled and nodded.

Thaddeus closed the door quietly as he went out.
Garrett could feel the effect of the brandy. He pulled a blanket to his chin and closed his eyes.

Twenty-five

Some miles out of Birdsville the coach came to a stop before a modest home. The Gilmores were out of the house to greet them before they could alight, the supply wagon having been sent earlier that morning from Bent Tree with instructions to Roland to inform the Gilmores of their pending arrival. Children, black and white, were everywhere, jumping up and down, running among the adults and horses. Cynthia had never before seen so many black faces in one place. Elijah Jameison took her by the elbow. They met the Gilmores halfway between the coach and the house.

Thomas Gilmore was a big man, red-faced with red hair to match. He sported a full beard streaked with gray. Fannie Gilmore was short, round and dark. Cynthia could feel a loving warmth surround her as she was greeted by each.

". . . my newest bond servant," Elijah Jameison was saying. "Helen is her name. I thought she might be company for Elizabeth."

Cynthia detected a raised eyebrow from Fannie Gilmore. "Do come in, Helen. I'm sure Elijah would like to check on his supply wagon and he and Thomas will have man-talk to . . . to . . . well, to talk." She laughed easily at herself. "You and I can get acquainted."

"No need for ye to be fussin' over Helen, now,

Fannie. She'll be fine with some of your servants."

"Why, yes, Mrs. Gilmore, I . . ."

"Nonsense. Won't hear of it. Don't you think for one minute, Elijah Jameison, that I'd give up the chance for some woman-talk." She turned to Cynthia. "We don't often have visitors out in this neck of the woods, Helen." She took hold of Cynthia's elbow and steered her towards the house.

Thomas Gilmore slapped Jameison on the shoulder. "When Fannie's mind is made up, Eli, ain't no use arguin' with her. Come on, your wagon's this way."

Jameison opened his mouth to speak, then shrugged his shoulders as they turned and headed toward the out buildings. Children scattered as Shires slapped the reins and the coach moved forward.

Fannie Gilmore turned. "You children get outa the way of them horses. One o' you is gonna get killed one o' these days, I swear." She turned back to Cynthia as she opened the door. "Come on in, child. It ain't fancy, but you're welcome."

"Thank you, Mrs. Gilmore. I . . ."

"Just call me Fannie, dearie. Everyone does. I like it that way."

Cynthia stepped into an immaculately kept hallway. Stairs leading to the second floor were to one side, several doors opened off it and there was a door at the far end leading back outside. Fannie Gilmore rang a bell as Cynthia removed her wraps. A stately black girl entered silently from one of the doors.

"Sophie, take this young woman's things up to Miss Jane's room."

"Yes, ma'am."

"And, Sophie, have Willard bring us some tea."

"Yes, ma'am."

The girl disappeared upstairs. Fannie Gilmore led the way into a beautifully appointed sitting room. "Jane's my oldest daughter," she explained. "She's away to school just now. We expect her home for the holidays. Sit down, dearie, sit down. Willard will be here in a minute with tea."

"Are . . . are all the children I saw outside yours?"

Fannie laughed. "Lord, no. Only two or three — and of course, all the black ones. The others are children of our overseer. He has quite a large family."

Within minutes tea was set before them by an elderly black man. Fannie Gilmore looked the tray over as she poured the tea.

"Is anything wrong, ma'am?"

"Huh? Oh, no, Willard, everything's just fine, but I would like some of those little cakes Jenny does so well if there are any left."

"Of course. I'll be right back."

As she closed the door, Fannie Gilmore turned serious. "What's your name, child?"

"Why, Mrs. Gilmore, Mr. Jameison told you my name is Helen."

"Yes, I know, but I mean your real name. Elijah's not a bad sort, not really, but he does have his little peculiarities. Thomas and I know one of them is giving his servants high-sounding names he chooses for them."

"My name is Cynthia, Cynthia Fawley."

"How old are you, Cynthia? To look at you, I'd reckon you're not much older than my Jane."

"I'll soon be nineteen."

"Just as I thought. From London, eh?"

"Yes, ma'am, but how did you know?"

"I'm from London myself, though that was more

years ago than I care to think about."

Willard entered silently and set a dish of small cakes on the tray, then left just as quietly.

Soon Cynthia was feeling very much at ease with Fannie Gilmore. They talked about London. She was quite interested in the latest fashions.

"Not that my body is gorgeous, mind you, but I have a seamstress who does right well by me. She almost works wonders," she laughed, "considering all she has to work with."

Cynthia tried to describe as best she could what the fashions were when she left London almost four months earlier. "Of course," she added, "as quickly as fashions change . . ."

"Yes, yes, but I don't know of anyone else who's only two weeks off the ship. By the way, did you have a smooth voyage? I remember when Thomas and I came over, it was late in the year. Rough weather all the way. I was sick most o' the time. Thomas wasn't much better. Neither of us has ever wanted to set foot on a ship again."

"Then you and Mr. Gilmore were married when you came?"

Fannie smoothed her skirt, then folded her hands in her lap. "Well, not exactly. We were betrothed so to speak. We . . . uh . . . we . . ."

Cynthia hastily interrupted. "I'm sorry, Mrs. Gilmore. I didn't mean to pry. It's really none of my business."

" 'Course it ain't, dearie." Fannie reached over and patted her hand. " 'Course it ain't, but mos' ever'one else knows. My goodness, I must watch my language or Janie'll be so disappointed when she comes home."

Cynthia hid a smile as Fannie resumed. "It does beat all, Cynthia, when your children start telling you how to talk . . . and dress . . . and well, just about everything. I hope you're kinder to your mother."

"My mother died when I was twelve, Mrs. Gilmore."

"Oh, I am sorry to hear that, child. Every young girl needs her mother. Jane couldn't do without me, even though she likes to think she could. But now, where was I? Oh, yes. I was going to tell you about our voyage. Well, Thomas was young and romantic. Thought it would be fun to be wed on board ship. I was young and even more foolish than he. I agreed. 'Course, there were reasons for him wanting to get out of London as soon as possible—me, too, and we didn't have time for a ceremony, but that's another story." She paused for breath. "As it turned out, we didn't get married till after we'd set up housekeeping. With so many sick . . . the bad weather, there never seemed to be the time for even a simple ceremony—and after we landed here, we had to wait till the preacher came 'round. We had little money to splurge on separate lodgings, so it seemed the sensible thing to do at the time. 'Course, no one but us knew the difference, but over the years, seems like mos' ever'one knows now. Hasn't hurt us none, though. Only some looked down their noses at us, and them not worth knowin' anyway. Times was hard back then and I'm sure others found theirselves in the same situation." She took a deep breath. "My goodness, I didn't mean to rattle on so. I had asked about your voyage and here I'm doing all the talking. I'm afraid it's a bad habit most of us have being shut away from womenfolk the way we are—and poor Elizabeth, that's Mrs. Jameison, she has it even worse than me. So much further away from everything. Even a place like Birdsville is better than nothing. She'll welcome your company."

"I . . . I hope you're right."

"Take my word for it. She'll be thrilled that Elijah saw fit to buy your indenture. But . . ." Cynthia could see she was having trouble trying to decide whether or not she should say more. She waited. Finally, Fannie leaned closer and lowered her voice. ". . . Watch out for Elijah. He thinks he has a way with the ladies." She wrung her hands over some private thoughts. "Poor, poor Elizabeth."

Cynthia wished she would change the subject. She didn't want to hear about "poor, poor Elizabeth." She would come face to face with her new mistress soon enough and she wanted to make her own judgments, although her preconceived ideas about Elizabeth Jameison were anything but flattering. She envisioned a mealy-mouthed, pasty, whiney little bit of a girl who was afraid of her own shadow.

Fannie interrupted her thoughts. "You will be watchful of Elijah, won't you, dearie? I only mention it for your own good, mind you."

"Yes, Mrs. Gilmore. I'll do my best."

"Fannie. I told you to call me Fannie," she said as she poured more tea. "Now, tell me all about your voyage. This time of year it must be rather pleasant. Did you get seasick? They say some do regardless of the weather."

Briefly, Cynthia filled her in on the events which took place aboard ship. Omitting the worst, she concentrated on talking of the fever. She didn't know how much she could tell Fannie Gilmore. Captain Tarrillton had appeared to be a friend of Mr. Jameison's. Could he also be friends with the Gilmores? She decided it was best to keep things to herself until she learned more about these people.

"The fever," Fannie tsked when she had finished. "Aye, I've seen it more than once. It ain't discriminatin', it ain't."

They fell into silence and drank their tea. Finally, Fannie jumped to her feet. "Goodness, me, but it must be gettin' late. Thomas and Elijah will be wantin' supper soon. I must see to it. Would you care to freshen up a bit, dearie?"

Cynthia nodded.

"Good. I'll show you to Janie's room. I'm sure you'll find it quite comfortable."

Cynthia followed, but paused at the stairway. "But, Mrs. Gilmore, are you sure Mr. Jameison meant . . ."

"You let me worry about Elijah, child. You'll stay in Janie's room and no arguing."

"Yes, ma'am."

The evening meal was a harmonious affair. Cynthia was included at the family dining table as any guest would be and was treated accordingly. She sensed Elijah Jameison was disgruntled with the arrangement, though he said little. To make more than slight protestations would have been questioning the integrity of Thomas Gilmore as well as a flagrant insult to Fannie since it was she who insisted on Cynthia's place.

Cynthia tried to ignore Jameison's stares as much as possible during the meal and focused her attention on Fannie. Before they had finished, however, she discovered the Gilmores were only barely tolerant of Elijah. The insight surprised her. They were painfully polite toward him and asked the usual questions one might ask of a traveler, but much of their conversation centered around Elizabeth Jameison. Cynthia surmised the Gilmores were acquaintances of long-standing with Mrs. Jameison's family and had little use for her husband. Even though the barbs were slight and delivered with subtlety, she found it hard to believe he took no offense.

By the time the ladies had adjourned to the sitting room, Cynthia's regard for her hostess had increased and her interest in her new mistress had risen measurably. She now hoped she would have an opportunity to find out more about Elizabeth Jameison from Fannie.

"You and Mr. Gilmore, you know Mrs. Jameison's parents?" Cynthia asked as she sat down.

"Knew," Fannie corrected, "Knew. Lord, yes, we knew 'em. They been gone over ten years now, both of 'em. Smallpox. Somehow, Elizabeth managed to escape the disease, but the rest o' the family . . . except for one no-count brother. Lord knows where he is. He just up and took off 'bout the time she married Eli." She paused to collect her thoughts. "I sometimes feel I helped raise Elizabeth. Known her most o' her life." At the sound of a light rap on the door, Fannie stood. "If you'll excuse me, Cynthia, I must leave for a few minutes. I've got to say goodnight to the children. It's sort of tradition. Even Janie still expects it when she's home."

Cynthia nodded, settled into the chair she had chosen and watched Fannie disappear into the hallway. She leaned her head back and closed her eyes. The image came unbidden—dark hair, laughing blue eyes. In an attempt to control the threatening tears, she pushed herself from the chair and moved closer to the fire. An almost inaudible click brought her attention around to the door. Elijah Jameison rested easily against the closed portal.

"It would seem Fannie is quite taken with ye, Helen."

"I thought you were with Thomas Gilmore."

"Aye, that I was, but he and Fannie took

off—some silly ritual with their brats." He moved across the room until he stood in front of her. He reached up and entwined his fingers in her hair. "I'll come to ye tonight. In which room be ye?"

"Oh, you can't possibly, Mr. Jameison. . . ."

He pulled her head to one side. "Which room?"

"Miss Jane's room, upstairs, front of the house."

"Damn," he swore as he let go of her hair. "That's right by . . ."

The door swung open. Thomas Gilmore entered, followed by Fannie. "Ah, here you are, Elijah. I thought perhaps you'd like a game of backgammon before we turn in."

"Aye, that I would, Thomas, soon's I see to sleeping accommodations for Helen here."

"It's all taken care of," said Fannie. "She's to sleep in Janie's room. Chloe will sleep on a pallet by her, case she needs for anything in the night being as how she's in a strange house."

Jameison spread his hands. "But, Fannie, you surely don't want this . . ."

"No buts about it, Elijah Jameison." Cynthia looked from one to the other expecting an explosion. "You brought the girl here. I'll see to her comfort while she's in my house."

Cynthia saw Jameison stiffen but he held himself in check. Thomas Gilmore remained by the door, showing open admiration for Fannie. After a long pause, Jameison yielded with a slight bow. "Very well, Mrs. Gilmore. I leave her in your capable hands." When he raised his head, his smile belied the anger in his eyes. He moved toward the door. "Now, Thomas, you said something about backgammon?"

"I tell you, Garrett, this Patrick Henry caused quite a stir. I understand the meeting was in a real uproar after he spoke."

"Did he really say King George is a sick king?"

"It's all here in black and white." Thaddeus Overby tapped the paper with a plump finger. "Ever'one knows it, but no one wants to talk about it. Henry came right out and said it."

Garrett rubbed his chin thoughtfully. "Why isn't he in irons? Sounds to me like he threatened treason."

" 'Bout as close as he could come, but the vote was with him." Thad chuckled. "If it hadn't a been, I 'spect he'd a beat it back upcountry. Lives there, you know, and he does have his following. They're referred to as Henry and his High-blooded Colts. All young men, or so I hear."

"That's what it's gonna take, Thaddeus: strong-willed, young Americans."

Thaddeus nodded thoughtfully.

Garrett had awakened refreshed and ravenous. Thad brought food and drink and while Garrett dined on roast venison, washed down with tankards of ale, Thad had read him from the *Georgia Gazette* the speech Patrick Henry had given in the Virginia House of Burgesses the previous May.

"You mean you didn't hear about this in London?"

"Not a word, but it's possible the document hadn't reached London when I left."

"Probable—but even when it does, what's it going to mean? It's a known fact that Virginia sent resolutions of protest a year ago and they were ignored by the king." He tapped the paper again. "This pertains only to Virginia, and I understand the last two resolves were omitted from the final draft."

"It's a beginning, though, Thad. It's a beginning. What we need is a meeting of representatives from all the colonies—bring this Stamp Act business out in the open. It does no good to keep complaining about these Proclamations from the Crown behind closed doors separately. We need to unite on this."

"Lordy, Garrett, haven't you heard? There's just such a meeting going on right now. Started about three weeks ago. Calling it the Stamp Act Congress, they are, but Governor Wright wouldn't approve sending delegates. He wouldn't even call the assembly into session. Afraid that they'd approve such an action. It's being held in . . . oh, let me see." He quickly rummaged through the papers before him. "Ah, yes, here it is . . . New York. Now, listen to this." He scanned the newsprint, then began to read: "Alexander Wylly wrote to Massachusetts.' " He looked at Garrett. "The meeting was initiated by Massachusetts. Anyway—'Wylly wrote saying that no delegates would be sent to Congress.' " He paused as he perused the item, " '. . . and that Georgia is concerned with the welfare of the colonies and will support any action the congress takes.' " He laid the paper down. "Word is that Wright sent an observer, but no one seems to know who."

"That sounds like Wright," said Garrett. "Interested, but cautious. I really think Governor Wright . . ."

They were interrupted by sounds of a catchy tune from the next room.

>With the beasts of the wood
>We will ramble for food

"What's that?" asked Garrett.
"Sh-h-h. Just listen."

And lodge in wild deserts and caves
And live poor as Job
On the skirts of the globe
Before we'll submit to be slaves.

The last voice died away.

"That," said Thaddeus, "is what's come to be known as the 'Stamp Act Song.' Been goin' 'round the taverns for weeks now. I suspect it'll be with us for some time to come."

"Interesting."

"Uh-huh—and it seems to express the rising sentiment."

Garrett stood and stretched. "You say this Stamp Act Congress has been in session for three weeks?"

"Yup, but I'd think they'd be adjourning soon, what with the festivities comin' up next week."

"You're probably right. I'm planning a trip to Savannah in a week or so. Perhaps I'll know more when I come back. Something's got to happen, Thad, something's got to. That damned law goes into effect next week."

Thad chuckled. "Maybe on paper, but not in fact. The stamps ain't here yet. Says so in the *Gazette* that just come in yesterday."

"Maybe the ship sank," Garrett said thoughtfully as he pulled on his shirt.

Thaddeus shook with laughter. "Could be. Ever'one's wishin' it would." He paused and grew serious. "Lordy, Garrett, wouldn't that be a godsend?"

"Only a temporary one, Thad. We need a permanent understanding with Parliament. Things can't go on the way they have been with the Americans lining the Crown's pockets."

Garrett donned his coat and started for the door.

"Any card games in the other room, Thad?"

"A couple. Not very big stakes. Just some o' the boys havin' a good time. Oh, by the way, I missed Jameison. He'd left before I got a messenger over there."

"That's all right, Thad. If he knew anything he probably wouldn't have given you a straight story. I've never known the little weasel to be straight with anyone. He's a real popinjay if I ever saw one. Should be livin' in London. Saw a lot of his kind there."

"I hear his ambition is to go to court if he ever accumulates enough wealth. He may make it, too. Understand he's doin' right well off his wife's holdin's. She's the one I feel sorry for. Never could see why she married him. She's a real lady. Pretty, too."

"So I've heard, though I've never had the pleasure," said Garrett as he opened the door and entered the common room.

Eighteen hours later, under gray, drizzly skies, Garrett and Ben came into view of Garidas. Though he was wet and shivering from cold and exhaustion, he was pleased with his success at having made the trip to Birdsville. After a good rest he would make plans to leave for Savannah within the fortnight. He could delay no longer. He patted his side pocket. He had brought all the latest news for Jacob and at the last minute he had remembered Munsy's needles and thread.

Twenty-Six

It was a hasty farewell to the Gilmores under gray, threatening skies. Cynthia hated to leave the warm, loving home, but knew she had no choice. Fannie hugged her, at the same time extending an invitation to Jameison over her shoulder for him and Elizabeth to return ten days hence to join them in celebrating Guy Fawkes Day.

"Better yet," she said as she released Cynthia, "come next week. We'll celebrate The King's Day then you can stay over till Guy Fawkes Day. It's been so long since we've seen Elizabeth and that way we can have a good visit . . . and please do bring Cyn . . . uh, Helen back with you."

As he handed Cynthia into the coach, Jameison smiled, promising to speak to Elizabeth.

The coach lumbered forward. Jameison settled back into the seat opposite her. Though he leaned out the window to wave a final farewell before pulling the oilskins, Cynthia knew he was in a bad temper. He had been drinking most of the morning and she shuddered to think what condition he would be in by the time they arrived at Mountview.

"Never shoulda stopped," he mumbled. "Never shoulda." He raised the now-familiar flask to his mouth.

"Then why did you?" Cynthia asked, wishing the minute she had said it she could have taken it back.

He glared at her momentarily, as though he'd forgotten her presence until she spoke and resented her intrusion into his private thoughts, then he smiled. "Ah, sweet Helen, you are a bright spot this bleak day."

Cynthia braced herself, then seeing how drunk he really was, decided on a different approach. She smiled and reached to touch his hand still holding the flask. "Yes, Eli, but why *did* you stop if the Gilmores are so . . . so hostile towards you?"

" 'Sat noticeable, huh?"

"Well, not exactly noticeable. More of a feeling I got."

"It's that Fannie," he said, "That's what it is." He looked at the flask as though trying to judge its fullness. "How a mon . . ." He jerked his head up abruptly. "What's she say to ye?"

"Nothing, Eli, nothing."

"Nothing? The two of ye seemed cozy enough last night."

Cynthia wrung her hands in feigned distress. "But, Eli, what was I to do? I thought the Gilmores were close friends of yours. I certainly had no desire, nor was I in a position to insult them."

He nodded, seeming to see the logic in what she said. Cynthia waited. He spoke slowly. "Aye, girl, what were you to do? I never shoulda stopped." He raised the flask, drained its contents, then capped it and, failing to find its place in his pocket, flung it to the corner of the seat. He laid his head back against the smooth leather.

Cynthia could hear the light patter of rain on the roof of the coach. She hoped the soothing sound coupled with the motion of the coach and the effects of alcohol would lull him to sleep. She had no desire for a confrontation in the close confines of a coach.

He cleared his throat, then spoke so softly she had to strain to hear. "Elizabeth," he said. "She made me promise."

Within minutes he was snoring, his head lolling forward on his chest. Cynthia sighed her relief.

She knew they hadn't far to go before arriving at Mountview. "Less than half a day by coach," Fannie had told her. She was lulled to drowsiness herself, but fought sleep, wanting to keep an eye on Jameison. Eventually the rain ceased. Cynthia raised the oilskin and breathed deeply of the invigorating air. She pushed the furs away and leaned out the window momentarily, viewing the wildness surrounding them. Even a man afoot would have difficulty traversing the forest, she thought, as her eyes scanned the tangled underbrush. Droplets of water hit her face as they cascaded from overhanging branches in a sudden breeze. She retreated inside the coach, revitalized by the coolness. She again breathed deeply, enjoying the fresh scent of rain on earth and forest.

Jameison moved as though waking. She hastily dropped the flap, eyeing him cautiously. He slowly slipped sideways until his head rested in the corner. Cynthia breathed easier as he slumbered on.

Seeking the warmth of the furs, she again heard light rain on the roof. She leaned back in a corner and was soon fast asleep.

She awoke with a start. Jameison was beside her, his hand fumbling beneath her skirts.

"Mr. Jameison? Here?"

"The place is not of my choosin', lass. We're within an hour of Mountview. 'Twill be our last chance . . . but only for a few days, mind ye."

Thank God, she thought.

Few minutes had passed before he was spent and

struggling with his trousers. Cynthia sat up, pulled the furs around her, closed her eyes and ran her hands across her abdomen. She searched her mind for some kind of alternative, but found none.

Breathless, but having regained his composure, Jameison looked at her. "Put yerself together, girl," he ordered. "We're almost there."

It had stopped raining and the sun was flirting with dark clouds scudding across the sky when the coach turned off the road and followed a long, narrow drive before pulling up in front of a house not unlike the Gilmores'. A young black boy ran to hold the horses as an older man raced to open the coach door. His black, fuzzy head bobbed in greeting.

"Massa Jameison, Massa Jameison, so good to . . ." he eyed Cynthia and halted in midsentence, then caught himself and continued. "So good to have you home, sir."

"Hadley, this is Helen. See that she's taken care of, will you? House her with Naomi."

The black bobbed his head again. Just as Cynthia descended from the coach, a small, dark-haired woman, obviously the mistress of the house, appeared on the veranda. Cynthia stared in amazement. Why, she's lovely, she thought, I wonder why Jameison takes his pleasure elsewhere.

Busy giving orders to the one he called Roland at the supply wagon, Jameison had yet to see his wife when she called in a soft, yet commanding voice, "Elijah?"

He turned, swept off his hat and rushed up the stairs. "Lizzy!"

She shot a brief, dark scowl his way.

"Elizabeth, I . . . I've brought you something . . . er . . . someone from Savannah."

286

"Yes, Elijah. I can see you have." The loudness of her voice rose only slightly. "Hadley, bring her here."

Cynthia gathered her skirts and, feeling a bit nervous, ascended the stairs with Hadley at her elbow until she stood before Elizabeth Jameison. She curtsied low.

"Mrs. Jameison."

Elizabeth Jameison eyed her critically as she dismissed the servants gathered around. All retreated to the shadows, but stayed well within hearing distance.

She has a kind face, thought Cynthia.

"What's your name, girl?"

Cynthia cast a glance toward Jameison, then realizing Elizabeth was the one in charge here, straightened her shoulders and looked her mistress squarely in the face. "Cynthia, ma'am. Cynthia Fawley."

"But she prefers to be called Helen," said Jameison, twisting his hat brim.

Elizabeth Jameison raised an eyebrow. "Is that true, Mistress Fawley?"

"Mrs. Fawley, ma'am," Cynthia corrected her, "but it really doesn't matter what I'm called."

"A young widow," Jameison hurried to explain, "left penniless. I bought her indenture from a ship's captain, feelin' sorry for her, as I was."

Elizabeth turned to her husband. "Did you now, Elijah?"

Jameison studied the toes of his boots as his hands continued to torture his hat brim, reminding Cynthia of a naughty schoolboy. She stifled an impulse to laugh. He raised his head, meeting his wife's eyes.

"Aye, that I did, Elizabeth, and . . . and I thought she would be good company for ye."

"Why, how thoughtful of you, Elijah." She smiled, her tone of voice belying her words. "Shall we house her with Naomi for the time being?"

"Y-y-yes, Elizabeth. That was my way o' thinkin'."

"Very well." She turned toward the door of the house. "Hadley?"

Hadley appeared instantly. "Yes, mistress."

"Hadley, show Cynthia to Naomi's cabin."

"Yes, mistress."

Cynthia started to descend the stairs when Elizabeth Jameison stopped her.

"Mrs. Fawley?"

The turned, shading her eyes from the sun. "Yes, ma'am?"

"I'll send for you later. We'll discuss your duties. Until then, feel free to get acquainted. I'm sure Naomi will be most helpful."

"Thank you, ma'am."

Elizabeth gave a slight nod of her head, signifying Cynthia's dismissal, then turned toward the house.

As she descended the steps, Cynthia heard Jameison. "She and Fannie got on famously. I'm sure you'll find her to yer likin', Elizabeth."

"Thank you, Elijah. Come. We have matters to discuss."

Poor, poor Elizabeth, Cynthia thought, recalling Fannie Gilmore's words with a smile, has matters well in hand.

Naomi was old enough to be Cynthia's mother and stood a full head taller than her white counterpart. Obviously disliking the new arrangements that had just been explained to her, she folded her arms across her breasts and tapped her foot on the dirt floor as Hadley backed out the door, closing it behind him. Her brown eyes bore into Cynthia's for long seconds before moving over her from head to toe, then she moved around Cynthia in as wide a circle as the small interior would allow. She shook her kerchiefed head and finally sat down in the only chair in the room, a scowl on her black face.

Cynthia drew herself to her full height and took a deep breath before speaking. "I don't like this a bit better than you do. I shouldn't even be here. I . . . I wouldn't be, either, if it weren't for certain . . . certain turns of events."

Naomi smiled, showing even white teeth, then looked around the room. "We'll have to share the bed. Ain't no way 'round that . . . lessens you'd lak to sleep on the floor."

"Well, I . . . sharing the bed will be fine, if you're sure you don't mind."

The black woman stood erect, pride evident in her carriage. "Wouldna said it if'n *I'da* minded." She chuckled. "Guess ya knows the black don' rub off."

Cynthia smiled. "We . . . uh, we'll have to find another chair," she suggested.

"Easy 'nuf," said Naomi as she motioned for Cynthia to sit on the bed. She backed up and perched on the edge of the chair she had just vacated. "What's yer name, girl?"

"Cynthia Fawley."

"How long ya here for?"

"Five years, I think, but I . . . I don't know. Mr. Jameison never told me."

"How much he pay fo' ya?"

"I . . . I don't know that, either. Why?"

"Lawsy, girl, them's things ya should know. He could say he paid top price fo' ya and keeps ya here 'bout 's long as he wanted to, I reckon. Maybe 's long as ten years or more."

"Cynthia's mouth fell open in disbelief. "Ten?"

289

"I's sorry to scare ya, gal. Axuly, I don't think ya needs to worry none. The missus is fair-minded. She'll see yer done right by."

Cynthia watched as the black woman rose, walked to the fireplace and stirred the contents of a small black pot. "Reckon we can share this come supper. Startin' tomorrow we'll be gettin' double portions." She paused, then continued as though talking to herself. "Could be I'd be able to get somethin' extry from the big house for tonight if'n I asked." She moved to a corner of the room and removed a shawl from a peg, drew it around her shoulder, then turned to Cynthia. "We'll hafta have a peg put up fer yer clothes."

"Oh, I haven't many. Only what Mr. Jameison bought me in Savannah."

Naomi's eyebrows shot up. "Massa buyed ya clothes?"

Cynthia nodded, then reddened as Naomi's look told her everything.

"Shoulda knowed," Naomi said as she moved back to the fire. "Shoulda knowed. He never did hanker after black flesh like other massas."

Shocked by her bluntness, Cynthia tried to explain her state of fortunes when purchased from the captain.

"Don't matter none, girl. Had massa bought ya for anythin' but that, he woulda left ya in boys' rags till ya got here."

Cynthia felt the blood rush to her face a second time and was thankful for the growing darkness. She hesitated to tell Naomi too much. It had to be her secret for a while.

Silence prevailed in the small cabin until suppertime. Naomi left with a kettle for a few short minutes and returned with foodstuffs from the big house, then the two women moved the crude table to the side of the bed, so both could sit, and began their first meal together. Not having eaten since breakfast, Cynthia ate with relish the bits of wild turkey and biscuits from the big house and, though foreign to her, generously sampled the greens and blackeyed peas with pork fat from Naomi's hearth.

"Ya always eat that way, girl?"

"Oh, no," Cynthia said hurriedly, afraid Naomi might suspect something. "I just haven't eaten since breakfast."

The silence broken, Naomi continued, "Where ya gonna work?"

"I don't know. Mrs. Jameison said she'd send for me later and we'd talk about it."

"Probably after supper," Naomi said. "The missus ain't one to waste time. Puny as ya are, there won't be no field work fer ya. Probably in the laundry or sewin' room. If'n yer lucky, maybe even in the big house."

"I can sew," offered Cynthia.

" 'Course," Naomi continued as though Cynthia hadn't spoken, "bein' the only white woman at Mountview, 'ceptin' o' course the missus, could work fer ya or agin' ya. 'Pends on how the missus feels 'bout it, I guess."

Over coffee, the two women exchanged histories, or as much as each would tell.

Cynthia's surprise at learning Naomi had mothered several children turned to horror when she asked of their whereabouts.

Naomi had shrugged. "Sold, run off." She brushed tears from her eyes. "Babies. They was just babies. Thank the Lord I cain't have no more."

Dazed, Cynthia patted Naomi's hand, then left her to her grief. She began to clear the table when there was a light rap on the door.

Naomi didn't stir, so Cynthia opened the door. A small, wide-eyed girl stood before her.

"The missus says you's to come now."

Cynthia hesitated just a moment, then knocked on the door to which she had been directed. It appeared to lead to a room built under the stairs leading to the upper story of the house. Beckoned to enter from the other side of the door, she opened it quietly and entered a small, well-kept office. Elizabeth Jameison sat before a tall desk transferring figures from papers in her hand to a ledger. She motioned for Cynthia to sit, then laid the papers aside and turned toward her. She smiled.

"Mrs. Fawley, Cynthia, I'll not mince words with you. I'm not entirely happy with the transaction my husband made acquiring you. I do not feel you are suited to plantation work. You're too small for the heavy work and judging from your manners and the way you carry yourself, you have few domestic abilities. Am I right?"

"I . . . I can sew a little."

Elizabeth nodded. "Embroidery, collars, cuffs, hems?"

Cynthia nodded.

"Then you are of class. If that's true, how did you happen to come to America under indenture? Did your husband leave you penniless as Mr. Jameison said?"

Cynthia bit her lip. "Well, not exactly, ma'am." She raised her head and looked at Elizabeth. "He was going to sell me. I ran away. I . . . I had help from . . . from a friend. After some time, I struck a bargain with the captain of a ship to bring me here. I decided at least here I would have some say over my life even if I did have to work for someone else for a few years."

"Couldn't your parents have helped?"

"They're both dead, ma'am. And I had to tell the ship's captain I was a widow or he wouldn't have taken me on, so your husband didn't lie to you, ma'am. He . . . he didn't know."

"Whether or not Elijah lied to me, Cynthia, is the least of my worries. Right now, I'm worried about what we're going to do with you. Everyone here works, so we'll have to find a place for you." She stood up and paced back and forth in the small area. After a few moments, she paused. "By the way, Elijah tells me you got on well with Fannie Gilmore."

"Yes, ma'am. She was very kind to me. I liked her a great deal—Mr. Gilmore, too."

"Yes, so do I. Tell me, are you good with hair? I've never had a personal maid, but perhaps that would be something you could do until we find something you're better suited to."

"No, ma'am. I wish I were, but as you can see, I can hardly do my own, let alone someone else's."

"Well, then, we will have to stick with the sewing since you do have basic skills in that area. You can work with my seamstress, Josie. She's getting on in years and her eyesight isn't as good as it once was. She could use a helper for the more delicate work. Is that satisfactory with you?"

"Yes, ma'am, anything."

Elizabeth sat back down at the desk. "Very well, you come see me in the morning after breakfast. I should warn you that Josie may be opposed to the idea at first, but she'll get used to it."

Cynthia stood. "Thank you, ma'am."

Elizabeth turned back to her bookwork. Cynthia opened the door to leave.

"Oh, Cynthia?"

"Yes, ma'am?"

"Are you getting on all right with Naomi?"

"I . . . I think so, ma'am. We talked some over supper. She's had a hard life."

"Yes, I know. Most of our slaves have. I try to make it easier on them."

Garrett would have liked you, Elizabeth Jameison, Cynthia thought.

"I believe Naomi can help you adjust to life here if you'll let her, Cynthia. It's not going to be easy on you, either. I'd like to be your friend, but I can't bend the rules for you. It wouldn't be fair to the other indentures we have here."

"I understand, ma'am. May I go now?"

"Yes. Goodnight."

"Goodnight, ma'am."

Over the next few days, Cynthia settled into a routine. After breakfast with Naomi, she made her way to the big house where she spent most of the day making small, delicate stitches on family clothing or linens. Her fingers were sore at first but soon became calloused. She enjoyed the work and after the initial confrontation with Josie, they became friends. She ate the noon meal in the kitchen with the other house servants and occasionally, Nathan Tolliver would stop by for coffee on the pretext of having to talk to Mr. Jameison, which he never seemed to get around to. Daphne, the cook, told Cynthia that Roland had never made a practice of coming to the big house so often before her arrival.

The evenings were spent with Naomi, or in one of the other cabins. Cynthia discovered, for all their hardships, the people around her were of a happy nature and she and the other white indentures were accepted into the black circle.

Each night as she crawled into bed beside Naomi, she prayed that Jameison had forgotten she was alive. She fully expected him to corner her anytime and make demands. She had only seen him from a distance, but whenever she had she went out of her way to avoid him.

Twenty-Seven

Riding into Savannah from the west along River Road, Garrett emerged from the forest, letting Temple set her own pace. They had both spent a long two days on the trail. He was thankful it hadn't rained. The wind was at his back and even though he gathered his cloak close, it chilled him. The river lying far below to his left flowed dark and gray, the sound of it muffled by the wind in the trees. The fields on his right for the most part lay fallow, dotted here and there by small plots of harvested cotton plants waiting to be plowed under. He wondered if these planters had been as successful with the cotton as he had.

He pulled his hat low and gazed ahead. The western palisades were just visible and against the late-day skyline he could see the masts of ships lying at anchor in the river. He wondered if the *Providence* were still here and decided to check into the possibility after a good night's sleep. He would very much like to hear Tarrillton's story of Cynthia's death, if the man were alive.

Bay Street bustled with end of day activity. Garrett scanned the river below the bluff and was surprised at the number of ships of varying sizes riding anchor. He recognized a smaller ship anchored close to shore as one of those which plied the coastal trade routes, but in the failing light could not determine if the

Providence was among the larger ships further down river.

He paused momentarily and watched a group of soldiers who were positioning cannons on the bluff in readiness for the following day's festivities, then he turned Temple south onto Bull Street, bypassing MacHenry's Tavern. Since it was the eve of celebration for George III's ascension to the throne five years earlier, he hoped he wasn't making a mistake by wanting to exchange the noisy, boisterous tavern taproom for the solitude of Alex McDaniel's home and perhaps even a hot bath.

Temple, sensing the journey's end close at hand, perked up and began to fidget beneath him. He leaned forward and patted her alongside the neck.

"That's right, girl. We're almost there."

Beyond the business district, Bull Street was virtually empty. Here and there lighted lamps began to appear in windows. Garrett knew there would be a round of balls in the city tonight but felt Alex would remain home. He had severely curtailed social activities since the loss of Eva McDaniel two years earlier.

"You're still a young man, Alex, you should take another wife. Eva would have wanted you to," Garrett had argued good-naturedly with his friend just before leaving for London.

"And what of yerself, Garrett Carver? Don't ye fancy the warm touch of a woman at night?"

Garrett had smiled. "You know I have no trouble finding warm, willing women, Alex, but as for a wife . . . well, maybe soon. Life has been good to me lately and now that Garidas is completed . . ."

"It needs a woman's touch, Garrett, and the laughter of children," Alex had finished for him.

"Perhaps you're right, Alex. We'll see."

The remembered conversation brought Cynthia to mind. Garrett pushed her away, wanting only to remember her when there was time to savor the memories.

He had ridden the full length of Bull Street and reined Temple before a modest, white clapboard house. Lamps twinkled from within. He was glad there was no coach by the gate which would signify an intended departure. He eased from the saddle, stiff-legged. He had not yet become reaccustomed to such long hours astride a horse. Tying Temple to the hitching post, he kicked the cramps from his legs as he made his way to the door.

Before he could knock, the door was thrown open. "Jesus, Garrett, I thought maybe ye'd crawled off in them woods of yers and died."

Alex McDaniel was shorter and stockier than Garrett, but no less dominating.

"I'm sorry I didn't send a message, Alex. I didn't think it wise. I wanted to come myself."

"And right you were, Garrett. Right you were. Come on in. You must be starving." He glanced past Garrett's shoulder. "I'll have Ezra tend your mount." He peered closer though the descending darkness. "Is that Temple?"

Garrett nodded.

"God, what a magnificent piece of horseflesh!"

"You knew that when you let me purchase her, Alex. I'll always be indebted."

"Any foals yet?" Alex asked as he closed the door against the cold.

"Two. The latest last spring after I'd left. He's a beauty, Alex. Going to be a fine stud."

"I get first bid on his first foal."

"Done."

Alex led Garrett into his study, a warm, wood-paneled room which looked out onto the street.

"Help yourself to the brandy, Garrett. I'm going to see what Rheba has in the kitchen and instruct Ezra."

Garrett nodded his thanks as he sank into an overstuffed chair and stretched his legs toward the fire.

Alex closed the door then immediately re-opened it and stuck his head around the corner. "Would you like a bath?"

"I thought you'd never ask."

"Good. I'll have Ezra bring it in here. This is the warmest room in the house tonight."

Garrett poured a generous amount of brandy into a glass from the decanter beside his chair, leaned back, letting the warmth and relaxation ooze into his tired muscles, and awaited Alex's return.

Much later, after Garrett had eaten and bathed, he and Alex sat before the fire nourishing brandy and coffee.

"Have you seen Wright since the Congress?" asked Garrett.

"Not yet. Maybe you can get in to see him in the next few days. He's practically holed up in his house, what with the sentiment runnin' so high over this Stamp Act business."

"How'd the Congress vote?"

"Officially, I don't know, but word is every colony present agreed to a protest to the Crown. Most folks hereabouts are riled because Wright wouldn't send a delegation to cast a vote for Georgia."

"I understand he sent an observer, though. Who went?"

"No one knows or even if he sent one for sure, but that has been the gossip."

"Before I left for London he implied to me that he

was against this taxing business, but being governor, felt he had to enforce the law."

"I think he feels that way, Garrett. It's a shame more people can't understand his position. All he wants is what's best for the colony. He knows all these taxes are a hardship on the people." He paused. "Did you hear about the buffoonery Patrick Henry got away with in the Virginia House of Burgesses?"

"I read his speech in the *Gazette*."

Alex chuckled. "But the *Gazette* didn't carry the whole story. Guess he did some real play-actin' before he got to his speech. Paraded down one of the aisles pretendin' to be a young groom, bride to be on his arm. When he got to the preacher and handed him the papers, the preacher asked where was his official stamp. He then ran back up the aisles, horrified that he had forgotten the stamp and couldn't be married."

Garrett chuckled politely, trying to visualize the scene. Alex laughed heartily.

"Well, I suppose it loses somethin' in the retellin', but I guess after that, no one expected his speech to carry such fire."

"I'd never heard of him until Thaddeus Overby let me read copies of the *Gazette* he had saved."

"Neither had anyone else—not even in Virginia—but I doubt he'll be silenced now. Has quite a following, so I hear. A good head on his shoulders, too."

A long silence ensued, each man lost in his own thoughts. Finally, Alex cleared his throat.

"This Captain Tarrillton? You think he can be trusted?"

So Tarrillton is alive, Garrett thought. To Alex he said, "Only to the extent of his own greediness and he's been well-paid. He's on no one's side but his own—and he can only suspect my activities. All he knows is that I brought some arms in and that's not against the law."

Alex nodded. "They're safe. I've already gotten word that some of the smaller farmers are interested, but we don't want too many showin' up too soon. I did get one over to Jonas Mielke. Given time, he says he can outfit an army."

"I hope we don't have to."

"Me, too. Those that are interested seem to be the poorer farmers who have nothing more than the old firearms that have been passed down in their families. I think they're loyal enough, they're just looking for a good hunting weapon. 'Course, no one knows they're here yet except a few, but word has gotten around in the organization that some modern firearms have been ordered."

"Speaking of organization, there's not a lot of that out where I am, though there is a lot of interest."

"I was going to discuss that with you later after you'd rested, but now's as good a time as any. As you know, we're well organized here in Savannah, or at least we hope we are. You've been to our meetings and you're known. The general consensus as of last week was that you should be the one to head up the organizing of the country people in your area. Are you agreeable?"

Garrett nodded thoughtfully, then smiled. "I expected as much. I'd have been disappointed if I hadn't been asked, but no less loyal."

"I know that. I know, too, that you realize you were asked to go to England because of your relative anonymity, coming from the country as you do—and you did a fine job. Franklin's endorsement couldn't have come at a better time."

"Is there any set method I should employ going about this?"

Alex shook his head. "Once you have a meeting place, word of mouth will usually suffice. But the key word is caution. I cannot stress that enough. Our membership has to be guarded."

Garrett nodded. As much as he liked Alex, he hated being made to feel like a schoolboy.

Alex sighed and leaned forward. "I'm sorry, Garrett. I know you realize this, but there is a man in your area who some of us feel could be potentially dangerous. Do you know of an Elijah Jameison?"

"I know the man. I can't, however, say I'm friendly with him."

"That will make it easier for you, at least. Beware of him. Watch his activities solicitously. He's power hungry and, we believe, dangerous. On the other hand, there is an acquaintance of his, or to be more exact, of his wife's, whose friendship you might do well to harvest. If you don't already know him, seek out Thomas Gilmore."

"I've heard the name, but don't know the man. Jameison, on the other hand, I've never trusted. If you say he takes watching, I'll see to it."

Alex stood and walked to the fire, kicking an ember bark into it from the hearth. "More brandy?"

Garrett also stood and stretched. "No thanks, if you don't mind, I think I'll retire. It's been a long day."

"Right, and tomorrow we'll start early enough. Cannons are to be fired at dawn."

Garrett rolled his eyes heavenward, started toward door, then paused. "By the way, Alex, is the *Providence* still here?"

"Can't say that I know for sure. Probably not.

Most ships have been trying to clear port before the Stamp Act goes into effect. There's been some controversy over whether or not they'll be able to without the stamps once it does, and the stamps aren't even here yet. I suppose that decision will be left up to Wright."

Garrett nodded.

"I can send someone to find out first thing in the morning if you want me to."

"Thanks, Alex, but it's something I need to tend to myself. Personal."

"About the girl?" Garrett nodded. He had told Alex about Cynthia earlier in the evening.

"Very well, friend. Sleep well."

"Good night, Alex."

Garrett forced his way to consciousness through seemingly endless layers of blackness. He lay still, quite disoriented. Then it came again, a succession of loud booms, making the bed quiver. He had never felt the earth shake, but he had heard of the phenomenon. Still he had never heard of such loud noises associated with it. Several thoughts raced through his mind until he remembered the firing of the cannon at dawn. Of course, it was the beginning of the celebration of King George's Day. He rubbed his hands across his eyes, then looked around. The room was bathed in a faint orangish glow, chasing the grayness of predawn to the far corners. In the following stillness, he heard more familiar sounds in the house below and realized Rheba was beginning the preparations for breakfast. He knew Ezra would be in shortly to light the fire.

He heard a door open, then close in the hallway and knew Alex was already up and dressed. The thought made him feel a bit guilty, yet he knew Alex would excuse him because of his recent illness and the long ride from Garidas. He was anxious to be up and about, but when he moved to kick the covers away, he was painfully reminded of the two days he had spent astride Temple. He lay back and decided to wait for Ezra and the welcome warmth of a fire. There was a light rap at the door.

"Come in, Ezra."

The elderly black shuffled into the room, closing the door behind him. "Sorry I didn't do this earlier, Mr. Carver, but Master McDaniel said not to disturb you till after the cannon."

"That's all right, Ezra. I was just thinking how nice it is to have a holiday."

"Yassir. Rheba's got some hot water in the kitchen. I'll bring some up if'n you'd lak." The old man stood up as the fire took hold.

"I'd like that, Ezra. Maybe by the time you get back the room will be warm enough to get up."

"Yassir. Sure seems like we done had one cold October, even frost on the ground this morning." He shuffled toward the door.

"I noticed a lot of ships at anchor in the river when I came in last night, Ezra."

"Yassir. Lots of 'em stayin' for the celebrations today, I guess. Ol' Mose, the harbormaster's nigger, tol' me lots are leavin' with the evenin' tide, though. Don't want to be caught here with no stamp."

Of course, thought Garrett. That's why there were so many ships. He wondered if Tarrillton had stayed for the celebration and feasting.

"I'll be right back with that water, sir."

"Yes, thank you, Ezra."

Cynthia had been at Mountview exactly one week when she was summoned to the main house long before daybreak. She hurriedly dressed and rushed from the cabin, leaving Naomi half-asleep and mumbling. When she returned a scant twenty minutes later she found Naomi dressed, the bed made and coffee brewing beside the fire. She slumped onto the chair by the table.

"Yer goin' with 'em, ain't ya?"

Cynthia nodded. "How did you know?"

"Figures, that's all. No other reason for 'em wantin' to see ya this mornin'."

"It wasn't them. It was Mrs. Jameison. She said I was to go as her personal maid. I don't know why. She knows I'm no good at those things."

Naomi shook her head. "The missus ain't one to be wantin' to show off, not like the massa. Could be he has sumpin' to do with it."

A chill ran through Cynthia when she thought of Elijah Jameison. She had seen him only from a distance since her arrival and she was beginning to feel a sense of security.

"I don't want to go, Naomi," she blurted. "I want to stay here where I know I'll be safe with him gone."

Naomi stood beside the chair and cradled Cynthia's head to her breast. "Hush now, child. No use carryin' on. We ain't got no right to be sayin' what we wants."

Cynthia stifled her sobs. She knew crying was of no use, but it did relieve the tension. She had cried a lot the last few days, mostly in private, and felt certain it was related to her pregnancy. Every time she thought of Garrett tears welled inside her, for herself, for him and for their baby who would never know his father. Funny, she thought, but I've come to think of the baby as "him." I wonder . . .

Naomi interrupted her thoughts. "I asked, when ya leavin', girl?"

Cynthia shook her head back to the present and looked at her cabinmate. "I'm sorry, Naomi, what did you say?"

Naomi rolled her large brown eyes. "I said, when ya got to go?"

"Oh, in about an hour. I think Mrs. Jameison said something about an hour."

The prospect of traveling to the Gilmores' for a visit had already taken on a dreamlike quality. One part of her was anxious to go. She knew she was lucky to have been chosen and she liked the Gilmores. Another part of her dreaded the trip—the close contact with Jameison, the closeness of the coach. Contrary to her nature she had become terribly squeamish the last few days. She hoped she wouldn't become ill during the journey.

Once again Naomi shook her from her reverie. "Drink some coffee, girl. Breakfast'll be ready in a minute. You gonna have to stop all this daydreamin'. Gonna get yo' in a passle o' trouble."

Breakfast smells suddenly assailed her. "I . . . I'm not very hungry this morning, Naomi. I . . . need a moment alone. Some fresh air. I . . . I'll be right back."

Outside in the chill morning air, she fought the sickness rising inside her. When several gulps of air didn't help, she ran to the edge of the woods behind the cabin and clung to a tree. This was the first time she had been unable to control the sick feeling.

If I could just avoid food in the mornings, she thought, as she hurried back to the cabin, shivering. That's when I'm bothered most. Getting up sounds were coming from the other cabins as she entered her own, welcoming the warmth. Naomi didn't look up from her breakfast.

"I made you some tea," she said. "It'll help settle

your stomach."

Cynthia smiled weakly and sat down opposite Naomi. She knew their meager supply of tea was to be saved for Sunday dinners or special occasions. She felt guilty.

After a few minutes silence in which Cynthia gratefully sipped the hot tea, Naomi pushed her dish away.

"How far gone are ya?"

The bluntness of the question very nearly panicked Cynthia. She kept her eyes focused on her cup and fought for control. "I . . . uh . . . I . . . n-not-not far I don't think." She looked at Naomi, her eyes brimming with tears. "I've never been pregnant before. I don't know much about it."

"Who's the father?"

Cynthia lowered her gaze and shook her head.

"Ya don't know or ya won't tell me?"

"I . . . uh . . . I . . ."

"Is it Massa Jameison?"

Keeping her eyes averted, Cynthia nodded. She couldn't look Naomi directly in the face and lie to her.

"The no-count . . ." Naomi began, then sighed. "Well, like father, like son, I reckon."

Cynthia looked up. "You know his father?"

"Knew. Old man's been gone for years. Yes, I knew him. He was my daddy, too."

Cynthia felt her breath suck in. "Your . . . your? Then you and Elijah Jameison are . . ."

"Brother and sister," Naomi finished for her. "Halfways, anyway. There was another brother, older 'n me, but he and his ma was sold off when I was jes' little. Ol' Massa Jameison, he laked my ma. She was younger and prettier, or so she said. He kept us and I'm sure there musta been sumpin' in his will 'bout Elijah not bein' able to sell us. Lord knows if there hadn'ta been, he woulda got shed of me long ago. I know I always been a thorn in his side. Makes me feel jes' a little good at times." Naomi was smiling, looking off into space. "Yessir, that alone sometimes makes life worth livin'."

Cynthia thought about Jacob and what he'd said about his parentage. Somehow she didn't feel so badly about Jacob anymore. Naomi was in a worse position than Jacob had ever been—a slave to her own brother! Cynthia found it hard to comprehend.

" 'Course," Naomi went on, "no one here'bouts knows 'cept maybe for ol' Jess. He's so old he knows ever'thin' and me and him is the last of the ol' massa's slaves. Elijah done got rid of the rest o' them 'fore he married Miss Elizabeth. Jes' dumped 'em off at a slave market. That's what killed my ma. Sold her slave husband and children right away from her."

"But haven't you told anyone?"

Naomi's eyes slid back to Cynthia's face. "What for, girl? Wouldn't make no difference. And ol' Jess, he ain't tellin' no one, deaf and dumb as he is. Guess that's why Elijah kept him. He always was a good worker, too."

"But . . . but you're telling me."

"Well, that's different. Kind o' like it's in the family," Naomi giggled.

A wave of guilt washed over Cynthia. She felt as though she were intruding.

"Yassir, this will likely do it with Miss Elizabeth, too. Don't know why she ever did marry him. They ain't never got got along."

"You mean she'll leave him?"

Naomi began to laugh. "Lord no, girl. She'll jes' make life miserable for him is all. Why, ever'thin' you see 'round here is mostly hers."

Naomi walked to the one small window and raised the flap. "Lawdy, girl, it's gettin' nigh onto sunrise. That's when they'll be leavin', sunrise. We better be gettin' you put together."

Cynthia leaned her head back and observed the Jameisons through half-closed eyelids. She didn't know how to relate to Elizabeth Jameison. They had chatted amiably throughout most of the trip, Elizabeth treating her as though they were equals. She knew they were close to the Gilmores' now and wondered what her station would be once they arrived. She looked forward to seeing Fannie again but was apprehensive about the planned ten-day visit. She envisioned an unpleasant, tense situation between the Gilmores and Elijah Jameison.

She turned her head and looked out the window. It had turned out warmer than it had been since her arrival and droplets of dew, which had earlier been frost, glistened everywhere. It was pleasant enough in the coach with the breeze coming in through the open windows. The only discomfort she had felt had been oblique stares from Jameison. She hadn't been so close to him in over a week, but had learned this morning that he was quite docile in Elizabeth's company.

She stared at him hard for a moment before he turned her way. She closed her eyes. Yes, there was a certain resemblance between him and Naomi. She wondered if Naomi had been telling the truth, but then there was no reason for her to lie, and now that she knew, she could see with her own eyes, couldn't she? She still felt guilty for having become involved in something that was none of her business—but anything for this baby, she thought. He must have a decent beginning in life.

She thought back to Naomi's words as they were gathering her few belongings for the trip. "Don't worry none, girl. Elijah'll take care of you one way or another. Ain't the first time a massa got a servant with child and won't be no disgrace to him. Here 'bouts it happens all too often. Mostly black girls, though. Seems to me . . . well, it don't matter none. We can talk about it when you get back."

Cynthia wondered what it was Naomi hadn't told her, but dismissed it from her mind. They would talk about it when she returned.

Twenty-Eight

At breakfast Garrett and Alex discussed their plans for the day. Most business and all official offices would be closed, so it would be useless to try to see Wright in any official capacity.

"Well, I haven't seen him since I got back," said Garrett. "Perhaps I could stop by for a friendly visit."

"Good idea," said Alex. "Maybe you can find out who he sent to the Congress."

Garrett looked up from his plate and caught a twinkle in Alex's eye. "Do you really want to know?"

"It's not necessary, though it would be interesting to know which side of the fence the observer was on. Would tell us for sure where Wright stands."

Garrett finished his coffee, then stood and stretched. "Well, I'm off for a visit with the harbormaster. That shouldn't take long if the *Providence* has sailed, then I'll call on Governor Wright if I have time."

"Don't forget we're meeting at MacHenry's at eleven o'clock."

"I'll be there."

"Should be some feast."

"I'm looking forward to it."

Garrett walked out into the bright October sunlight. Temple stood pawing the earth just outside the stable, saddled and ready to go. Garrett mounted her slowly, wishing it were more fashionable for a gentleman to walk, but realizing he could not make his appointed morning rounds if he walked. As it was, if Tarrillton were still here, he might have to put off seeing James Wright until afternoon.

Half an hour later he stood leaning against the hitching post in front of the harbormaster's office. The *Providence* had sailed two days before and yes, Captain Tarrillton was alive and well. Garrett gritted his teeth in anger at himself for delaying the trip to Savannah for so long. Yet he realized it couldn't be helped. He had needed the time to regain his strength.

He mounted Temple and headed toward St. James Square and the governor's mansion. He hoped his call on James Wright would be more profitable.

Garrett waited in an anteroom while his arrival was announced to the governor. For lack of anything else to do, he inspected the portraits of the preceding governors of Georgia and wondered why they were here. A door opened behind him. He turned and Sir James Wright clasped his hand firmly in greeting.

"Garrett, it's good to see you."

"Governor."

"You're wondering about the portraits, eh?"

"Yes. That last time I saw them, I believe they were in Government House.

"They were, Garrett, they were. Times being what they are, though, I thought they would be safer here. But come on in, come on in. We can have some tea . . . er, coffee for you, isn't it? . . . and you can tell me about your trip to England."

Garrett followed James Wright into his study where a servant was ready to serve tea. Wright dismissed him with a wave of his hand. "And bring Mr. Carver some coffee."

"Yessir."

Wright indicated for Garrett to sit, then moved to a chair facing him on the opposite side of the fire. Garrett noticed he looked tired.

"How long have you been in town, Garrett?"

"Just last night. I'm staying with Alex McDaniel."

The governor nodded. Garrett saw traces of gray in his once dark hair. "You look as though you need some rest, Governor."

"It's this devilish Stamp Act business, Garrett. There's bound to be trouble the next few days. My aides are even advising I sleep with my clothes on, just in case."

The servant entered and set a steaming pot of coffee on the table between them, next to the governor's tea, then left.

"You expect it to be that bad?"

"Who knows? With so many people in town for the celebration, these Liberty Boys, as they call themselves, might try to stir up some trouble."

"Liberty Boys?"

"Of course, you probably haven't heard, living in the country as you do—and you have been gone most of the year, but there's a secret organization calling themselves the Liberty Boys and it seems to me their whole purpose is to stir up people. Mind you, we don't know who any of them are, not yet, we just know of them. Hell, we don't even know where they hold their meetings, but the time will come."

"And you say they're troublemakers?"

"Well, not yet they haven't caused any trouble, but we look for it in the days to come."

"And how do you feel about it, as governor?"

"To tell you the truth, Garrett, and this is just between you and me, I'm not sure. Basically, I agree with their ideology—but not their methods, if their methods turn out to be what we think they are. I'm as much against this Stamp Act as anyone else. The taxes already invoked are bad enough. This last is just an unnecessary hardship on us—on all the colonies. Being governor, though, I'm obliged to uphold the law."

"What if it gets too bad?"

"We've made plans for evacuation of the mansion and Government House, but I hope it won't come to that. The law goes into effect tomorrow. We have no stamp officer yet and no stamps. Perhaps any violence can be avoided, for a time, at least."

"I heard there was a Stamp Act Congress."

"Yes. Very successful, too, I hear. I know some are upset because I didn't send representatives, but I didn't think it prudent at this time."

Garrett waited. The governor offered no further enlightenment. Instead, he set his teacup down and leaned his head back in the chair. "Now, tell me of your trip to England. I understand you came back sick—fever on board ship, wasn't it?"

"Yessir. Several died."

"Yes, I know. I've seen the official report sent here by the captain."

Garrett spent a few minutes talking of his visit with his sister and the business pertaining to the plantation he had taken care of in London.

"Your sister? She has no desire to come to the colonies?"

"No, sir. She's quite satisfied with her life in London. She has a good husband and a fine family. They get by."

The governor sat up. "Get by? Get by? Good Lord, man, did you tell them of the opportunities here in Georgia? Of course you did, of course you did. All they had to do was see you and they would have known."

"Some people are set in their ways, sir."

He nodded. "And Oglethorpe? Did you see him?"

"Only briefly, sir. Just long enough to give him your regards. He was only recently commissioned a general and was very busy."

"Well, I appreciate your doing that for me, Garrett. You know, the old boy is still very much interested in Georgia."

"Yessir. He said as much to me."

Garrett noticed the hour was getting late and rose to leave. "I really must be going, Governor. I hadn't meant to stay so long."

James Wright stood, stretching as though he had just woken from a long rest. "Well, if you must, but I've enjoyed your visit. It's the most peaceful morning I've spent in weeks," he chuckled, "and will probably be the last for a while. I'm glad you're doing so well. I understood you were quite ill."

"Yessir, thank you, sir."

It wasn't yet eleven and since he was closer to Alexis's house than to MacHenry's Tavern, Garrett turned Temple in that direction. He had felt under a strain at the governor's house. He hoped it hadn't shown. Now he would like to refresh himself and perhaps take a short nap before the festivities at MacHenry's began.

When he did arrive an hour later, MacHenry's Tavern was noisy, hosting a jovial, boisterous crowd. The place reeked of alcoholic spirits and cooking meat. Numerous other food smells mingled with unwashed bodies and heavy perfume scents. A side board had been set up along one wall and was heavily laden with foods of all varieties. Comely girls, wearing low-cut dresses, passed among the revelers with beer mugs sloshing to the brim. The bar seemed to be the most popular spot in the dimly lit room so Garrett bypassed it for the time being to make his way toward a corner table where he spied Alex McDaniel in conversation with three gentlemen, two of whom he had seen before. All were oblivious to their raucous surroundings. He was slapped on the back many times in friendly fashion and mugs were raised to his health by total strangers. He smiled, acknowledging the courtesy, then pressed his way through to Alex's table.

"I've never seen MacHenry's so lively," he shouted when he finally reached his destination.

Alex, red faced from his efforts at trying to carry on a conversation in the din, indicated a chair behind and tipped against the table. "Sit down, Garrett. Sit down. We've been waiting for you."

Garrett nodded to Alex's companions as he made his way around the table.

"We'll save the introductions until later," Alex shouted as he raised an arm and tried to catch the eye of one of the serving girls. "First, a drink, then we'll retire to a back room MacHenry is holding for us."

Some minutes later the five of them entered the relative quiet of a private room. Garrett had been here on other occasions and knew it was but one of many rooms MacHenry had built onto the original building and now reserved for private parties. There were other rooms designated for more intimate privacy and Garrett had also, on occasion, visited those.

This room, large enough to accommodate a dozen

or more, was the least used because of its closeness to the kitchen, in summer months the heat being barely tolerable, thus it served the purposes of the Liberty Boys to a tee.

The five dispersed themselves around a table as though to play cards. A small, shapely black girl busied herself over a smaller buffet than the one in the taproom, though no less impressive in its variety. To one side was a small table holding all manner of drink.

As the girl passed them in leaving, the youngest of the group, a man Garrett knew, but whose name escaped him, patted her playfully on the behind. She turned and smiled, recognition in her eyes. The young man winked and Garrett knew they would later meet upstairs.

As the girl closed the door behind her, an older gentleman to Garrett's left burst into laughter. "Best be careful, Josiah, lest Emily should hear."

The young man reddened slightly. "Hell, we ain't married yet and her pa says we have to wait at least a year. What's a man to do to . . . ah . . . for . . . ah . . ."

The group burst into laughter. Josiah, embarrassed at first, finally joined in good-naturedly. As the laughter subsided, Alex stood.

"Now, this isn't a formal meeting, today being a day of celebration, and neither is it a closed meeting. Others will be in and out as the festivities of the day continue, but I do want to tell you that my friend here, Garrett Carver, has agreed to organize those in his neck of the woods who are in agreement with us. You've all seen him at our meetings before. Garrett lives up country close to Birdsville and, as you know, has just recently returned from England with the arms and information we wanted. Now, I believe introductions are in order around the table and then we can be on with the business at hand." He raised his half-full glass, should his meaning be lost on anyone present.

Those seated around the table were Josiah Bennett, the young man to Garrett's right, Thomas Wilkins to his left and Ephraim Jones directly across from him.

"Mr. Jones," Garrett said when the last man introduced himself. "Are you any relation to the Joneses at Birdsville?"

"Cousins."

"And do you know where his sympathies lie?"

"Why, I'm not sure I've ever discussed it with him. Francis and I usually don't see eye to eye on things, so I guess I just supposed . . ."

"Well, I shall contact him. May I use your name as introduction?"

Jones chuckled. "You may if you wish, but as I said, Francis and I are not always on the best of terms. Depending on his humor at the time, it may not even get you across the threshold."

The word "hanging" turned both their heads. Alex and Thomas Wilkins were talking to young Josiah.

"I tell you, Mr. McDaniel, I don't know."

"What is it, Alex?" asked Garrett.

"Bad business, I fear. Word had gotten back to us that some of our young hotheads are planning to hang a dummy of a stamp officer. I hate to see it start—give us a bad name."

"I saw Wright this morning," said Garrett. All heads turned his way. "He's expecting some sort of trouble."

"Being of the younger generation, I thought perhaps Josiah here would have privy to the goings on, but apparently they're keeping it pretty secret." He chuckled. "I can't say that it's a bad idea—just don't know what good it will do beyond causing harsh feelings."

"Does anyone know when it's supposed to happen or where?" asked Garrett.

"Not when, but supposedly it's going to take place in front of the governor's mansion."

"Well, if we can't stop it," said Wilkins, "perhaps the next best thing is to enlist some help and at least try to keep it under control."

Everyone nodded in agreement. "How about as soon as we eat?" spoke up Jones, patting his portly stomach. "We might have better luck encountering our members by staying here anyway. All know we were to meet here today if we could."

By the time everyone had eaten, a goodly group had gathered in the little room and all were in agreement that they should at least try to control the situation which threatened. They decided to disperse in pairs and patrol the town. The idea was not to stop the hanging of the dummy, but to see there was no violence and, if necessary, to protect their younger members. All, especially the older men, realized their strength lay in the young. They could ill-afford to curtail their wild, youthful activities. At the same time, perhaps the general populace would not view the hanging as an act of their organization if only the young men were involved.

Garrett teamed up with Alex. Both agreed it would look more natural since Garrett was a relative stranger to Savannah and was staying with Alex.

Much celebrating was going on in the streets. Alex and Garrett more than once had to side-step parties of drunken young men and even some women.

"Odd, isn't it," Garrett commented, "no one

likes the king, but all will celebrate his ascension to the throne simply because he is the king."

"Odd?" asked Alex. "Not at all. Power has always had its privileges. Being celebrated is one of them. To the comman man, the king is God. He rules our every move. I venture to say that even you and I would be awestruck were we in his presence, simply because he is the king."

Garrett mulled the words over in his mind, finally concluding that Alex was right. "I think I feel some semblance of that when I'm with James Wright, though I never before thought about it in exactly those terms."

"I'm sure you do. It's because we're taught to respect and revere authority. And speaking of Wright, did you have a good visit this morning?"

"Pleasant enough. He spoke harshly of the Liberty Boys—and I suppose he is within his rights as governor. I have to admit I was a bit nervous when he started talking about the organization. I was afraid he might know something, but after talking with him, I don't think so. On the other hand, he said he agreed with our politics but not our tactics."

"Ah, then he's grouping us all together with what's been happening in the northern colonies."

"I believe so, yes. I also believe that regardless of his personal feelings, he will enforce the law to the best of his ability."

"I'm sure he will. That's another aspect of having power—and not one of the better ones."

By sunset, having stopped now and again for a grog or a chat with friends, Garrett and Alex had made their third tour of Savannah without noticing anything of a suspicious nature. Garrett felt he now knew every street intimately. They stood in St. James Square opposite the governor's mansion, having agreed this would be their last stop before heading to Alex's for supper. People milled about the square in anticipation, some wanting a view of the governor, others waiting for the bonfire, which would be kindled at darkness, and the street dancing to follow.

As they conversed, small children ran to and fro, placing twigs and small branches on the growing pile of debris that would shortly be ignited in the final tribute of the day to King George. They noticed other members of their organization had also gathered in small groups about the square.

Suddenly a tow-headed boy, Garrett judged him to be no more than fifteen, ran from a side street and torched the pile in the center of the square. Was this the plan? wondered Garrett, but decided not. For one thing, it was too early, and he was sure James Wright was supposed to make an appearance before the lighting of the bonfire.

Next, three young men carried a makeshift gallows into the square and set it up directly in front of the governor's gate. They were quickly joined by another group carrying a hangman's rope, the noose of which was already around the neck of a dummy sporting a sign designating it as a "stamp official." With great ceremony, they passed judgment and proceeded to hang the dummy, all the while chanting, "Down with the stamp act, hanging for officials."

Ephraim Jones stepped out of the gathering crowd momentarily, but a look and a shake of the head from Alex propelled him back into obscurity.

Alex leaned toward Garrett. "The tall boy in the brown coat is Jones's son."

Garrett nodded.

The crowd was beginning to take up the chant with the boys, who were now parading around the bonfire, being joined by friends old and young. Within a matter of minutes, few knew for sure which young men had been involved in the hanging of the dummy.

A glance at the governor's mansion told Garrett there would be no appearance by James Wright tonight. A curtain parted slightly then fell back into place.

As darkness fell and the air grew chill, more and more people gathered about the fire. A wagonload of logs to feed the fire was pulled into the square and musicians assembled for the dancing.

Tired, Alex and Garrett circled the square and headed homeward. A pause and a look back. The effigy was silhouetted against the bonfire. In the darkness it appeared a gruesome reality. Garrett could only assume the silhouetted figure was what James Wright saw from his study where the light had just gone out.

Twenty-Nine

Time sped by faster than expected. There was only tomorrow then they would return to Mountview. Cynthia would love to have stayed at the Gilmores' forever. She hadn't felt so pampered, so secure since her childhood. She had had a minimum of chores to perform the last few days, her only duty being to keep Elizabeth Jameison's toilet articles and clothing in readiness. As neat and orderly as Elizabeth was, it had really been no duty at all.

With Elizabeth's permission she had whiled away her idle hours reading and taking long walks. She realized how fortunate her position was. Often visiting servants were given extra duties in the household, but both Fannie and Elizabeth insisted her time was her own. Cynthia realized why when she overheard Fannie and Elizabeth talking one day. Having just returned from a walk, she was passing beneath one of the sitting room windows which had been opened a crack. Hearing the voices she stopped to listen.

"Honestly, Fannie, I don't know why Elijah bought the girl's indenture."

"Come now, Beth, be honest with yourself."

"No, I thought of that, first thing. She is attractive . . . but it's been over two weeks and I know Elijah has made no move in that direction."

Cynthia felt her face redden even though she knew

her presence went undetected.

"Well, it must be difficult," Fannie continued, "having the only white indentured female in the area."

Elizabeth laughed. "I really don't know, Fannie. It hasn't been long enough to tell. My real problem is I'm not sure how to relate to the girl."

"It doesn't seem to me that you have any problem in that area. You get on fine with her."

"But it's different here. At home it's . . . well, I just don't feel right treating her like one of the blacks. They've never known another kind of life. When many of them came to Mountview it was to a better life than they had ever known, but Cynthia has known better. I know she has. I feel it. Why, I wouldn't be surprised if in London she was a rank above us."

"Oh, Beth, you're talking nonsense. Surely no one who was anyone would sell their wife."

"You know better than I would, Fannie. You lived in London."

"Of course I heard of such auctions. It was hard not to, but never having been a wife until I came here, I never thought about it. I guess I just assumed . . . well, I never associated such goings-on with the upper classes."

"Well, she's definitely class. I'm sure of it. But why would a husband want to sell her? She's a lovely girl. Never makes any demands, a good worker . . ."

"Who knows what a man thinks? Even my Thomas. I sometimes wonder about him . . . and Elijah, the way he treats you. I tell you, Beth, there's no understanding men. Why Elijah ought to be proud to have a wife . . ."

Cynthia hurried from the window. She could listen to no more. She didn't want to hear about Elijah and Elizabeth.

Unable to sleep, she lay mulling over the events of the past nine days in her mind. The overhead conversation had taken place the second day. She thought she could understand Elizabeth's position and her dilemma over how to treat a white indentured female. Given a like situation she felt certain she would also have reservations.

She thanked her lucky stars that Elijah had spent most of the time in Birdsville. No one seemed to know or much care what he did. He always left early, often even before breakfast, but he was never late for supper. Cynthia knew he spent most of his time drinking. It was quite evident each day when he returned. At least, she thought, it had made for pleasant evening meals—meals at which she had been included much, she thought, to Elijah's consternation. Each night he had retired shortly after eating, so her fears of having to spend time in close contact with him had been unfounded. She had seen very little more of him here than she had at Mountview.

Yet she was concerned. She dreaded the thought of being with him, but knew it was imperative if they were to build a relationship, however false on her part, that would ensure her baby a decent life. What Naomi had said about Elizabeth holding the strings to the pocketbook bothered her as well. If that was true, how would she and the baby be treated? Would Elizabeth run them all off, or would she feel some sense of responsibility since Cynthia was a servant?

Cynthia had seen like situations on more than one occasion in London. The girl involved would most often be paid off and disappear long before her condition was even noticeable, the mistress of the house usually oblivious to the circumstances of the girl's departure. Cynthia realized, however, that her predicament was worlds apart from London. The

Jameisons were responsible for her welfare until her indenture was worked off. That much she had learned from Nathan Tolliver. She knew they could sell her indenture—it had happened to Garrett—or, she thought, they could suggest she marry one of their male indentures or one of their blacks.

She hugged the covers to her for a moment then lay back down. It'll never happen, she told herself. None of it. Elijah won't let it. His ego wouldn't permit him. He must have some hold over Elizabeth. If the property and money are hers, there's no other reason for her to stay married to him, so if I can convince him this is his child, we'll be all right. I know we will.

She decided not to worry about it for the present and turned her thoughts, instead, to the planned festivities for the following day. Had she been in London she would know what to expect, but she wondered how these Americans went about celebrating Guy Fawkes Day. Surely, she thought, it'll not be as exciting as the celebrations I recall. As long as she could remember, she had taken part in the street dancing, was warmed by the bonfires, impressed by the fireworks over the Thames, and left a bit sad by the burning of the Guy Fawkes effigy. As a child she had been frightened by tales of Guy Fawkes, but as she grew older she had come to realize that in certain circles he was hailed as a hero. How hard it must be, she thought, for those of the Roman Catholic persuasion to face each November fifth. Cynthia Fawley, she told herself, the last few months have given you wisdom beyond your years.

She then thought of Garrett. She remembered thanking her lucky stars earlier and knew the idea would have amused him. Her latest revelation concerning the oppressed would have brought a proud light to his eyes. She hugged her pillow and drifted into sleep with his image in her mind.

She woke early. She almost always did of late. She lay quietly for a few minutes listening for the birds before she realized the sound outside the window was that of light rain falling. She stretched luxuriously then crept out into the cold to relieve herself in the chamber pot kept under the bed. Once again beneath the covers, she gathered them about her shoulders and snuggled down into their warmth. A fine day to sleep, she thought, Guy Fawkes or no Guy Fawkes.

Almost asleep, she heard the door open. She rolled over fully expecting to receive a cheerful greeting from Sophie who had come each morning to make sure she was up and dressed before Elizabeth required her. Poised on the threshold was Elijah Jameison wearing no more than a nightshirt, a finger raised to his pursed lips to signify silence. He peered over his shoulder into the hallway then closed the door as quietly as he had opened it. He moved swiftly to the bed and sat on it, forcing Cynthia to the far side.

"You can't stay here," she whispered. "Sophie will be here any minute to waken me."

"Don't worry about Sophie." He crawled beneath the covers and pulled her to him. "No one will be up this early except the cooks. It's a holiday. But just in case, I left word with Willard last night that you were not to be disturbed this morning. I told him you weren't feeling well."

"But you went to your room last night right after supper. When did you speak with Willard?"

"When he came to bank the fire."

"And you're sure it's all right?"

"Perfectly sure."

"Mrs. Jameison?"

327

"Sleeping like a babe. I think she and the Gilmores must have started celebrating last night. I could smell it when she came to bed."

Feigning enthusiasm, Cynthia snuggled against his shoulder. "I'm glad you planned this, Eli. I've missed you."

"Ah, sweet Helen." He was kissing her hair. "I was thinkin' that you might." He chuckled. "When one is accustomed to the finest things in life, they are missed when one is deprived of them."

You pompous pig, Cynthia thought, as she cooed softly in his ear.

He began to caress her. The nightgown slipped easily over her head. His nightshirt was discarded. Within minutes he was ready. Cynthia invited him to her with as much ardor as she could muster. Her enthusiasm fading fast, she clung to him as though in throes of passion so that he might not see her face.

She was barely able to smile as he slipped from the bed and retrieved his nightshirt. Ready to leave, he bent to kiss her. She forced her arms up around his neck and returned his kiss, trying to pretend the part of a lover.

"I must go now, dear, Helen, but I'll come to you again soon. Something will be worked out when we return to Mountview."

"Yes, soon." It was all she could manage as a feeling of sickness rose inside her. She pushed him away playfully, smiled wanly and waved him off.

He checked the hallway cautiously, blew her a kiss and was gone. Cynthia made a dive for the chamber pot. She would have to empty her own today lest someone notice. No, she thought, Elijah told them I was ill.

Guy Fawkes Day. Though not as exciting as those she had spent in the past, it was nevertheless festive.

There was good food galore. Much more than could ever be eaten by those in the big house. Cynthia was to fully enjoy her first holiday on a Georgian plantation. She was also to witness her first glimpse of kindness and generosity on the part of slaveholders since being with Garrett.

After her early morning encounter with Elijah Jameison, Cynthia was amazed to find that she was left alone for several hours. Elizabeth finally peeked in about ten o'clock to inqure about her well-being. Cynthia assured her she was fine, it was nothing more than an upset stomach. Elizabeth swept into the room and began tying the draperies back.

"Oh, my dear, I'm so glad. Fannie and I have been very concerned about you ever since Elijah told us."

"How did Mr. Jameison know?" she asked what she thought to be the expected question.

"Oh . . . well, I assume Sophie told him." By now Elizabeth was standing by the side of the bed. "Now, are you sure you're all right. Is there anything I can get for you?"

"No, ma'am. I'm fine—really. I see it's stopped raining."

"You were up earlier?"

"No ma'am, just awake. I was sick very early this morning. I feel fine now. I must have gotten rid of whatever it was upsetting my stomach. I'm ready to get up and enjoy the festivities."

"Are you sure? You look wan. Perhaps you should spend the day in bed. We could delay our return to Mountview for a day or two."

"Oh, no, ma'am. I wouldn't dream of delaying your return home. I'm fine. I really am." She pushed the covers back and sat on the edge of the bed. "See, fit as a fiddle. I think a short walk might do me good. Put some color back into my cheeks."

Elizabeth reached out and felt her forehead. "Well, if you're sure. You don't seem to have a fever. That's what Fannie and I were most concerned about, a return of that awful fever you had on board ship."

"No, ma'am, just an upset stomach."

"Very well," Elizabeth said, then called over her shoulder as she went out the door, "wear your finest. It is a holiday, you know."

When Cynthia descended the stairway a few minutes later she learned that early in the day everyone at the Gilmores', including the slaves, had donned their finest. The weather had miraculously cleared. It was a beautiful day. After a short walk, she caught a glimpse of herself in the hallway mirror and knew she looked the picture of health. To help it along, however, she gave each cheek a pinch before joining the Gilmores and Jameisons for dinner.

Everyone commented on her health and she assured them she was fine. Even Elijah seemed genial toward her, which was a switch for him when anyone was around. She could tell he was well on his way to being drunk, but didn't care. She chatted easily with Elizabeth and Fannie as she ate ravenously and forgot for a little while what her position really was.

The afternoon was spent relaxing. Strains of music came from the cabins behind the house and sounds of singing and dancing wore on till dark. Supper was light and Cynthia learned that the excess food had been parceled out to the slave quarters during the course of the afternoon.

The children seemed to be anticipating something and Fannie finally told them, "Soon now. They'll come soon."

"Who'll come?" Cynthia spoke without considering her place.

Fannie turned to her. "The blacks, my dear. They always come to serenade us on holidays. Guy Fawkes Day is always special for the children, though. After the serenade, we always have a fireworks display. Elijah brought the fireworks when he returned from Savannah. Later, he and Thomas will give us a real show."

"I'll look forward to it," Cynthia replied. She eyed Elijah Jameison and decided it was very possible he was in no shape to give anyone a show.

A serving girl set a cup of coffee before him. He pushed it aside, sloshing some over onto the white linen cloth. He stood. "I wanta dance. Can't your blacks play some music for us to dance?"

Fannie and Thomas exchanged a glance. "Well, I suppose they could . . ." Thomas began.

Elizabeth reached for Elijah's arm. He grabbed her hand. "Whatta ya say, Lizzie? Shall we? We haven't danced in years."

Elizabeth pulled her hand away. "Elijah, please. We're guests."

"So we are. If someone wanted to dance at my house, I'd let 'em. Whatta ya say, Tom, can we arrange it?"

"Well, yes, if that's what pleases you. . . ."

"It does." He turned to Cynthia. "And you, Mistress Fawley, would you care to dance with me?"

"I . . . uh . . . I . . ." Cynthia stammered.

"Yes," said one of the older children. "Let's have a dance. We never had on Guy Fawkes Day before. Only for birthdays and weddings."

By now the idea was beginning to appeal to everyone. Elizabeth began to laugh. "Go ahead, Cynthia. Dance with him if you like. When he's in a mood like this, nothing will dissuade him until he's had his

331

own way."

"It might be fun at that," Fannie said, rising and clapping her hands. "Thomas, you go get Mac and the other boys with their instruments. Elizabeth and I will get Willard and Elijah to help us move some of the furniture in the sitting room."

It was very late when Cynthia finally called it a night, yet she felt very little tiredness. She felt young and gay and carefree again. During the course of the evening she thought she had begun to see why Elizabeth had married Elijah Jameison. He could be fun and very much the gentleman. He seemed to enliven everyone present. Even Cynthia felt a bit of the doxy when she danced with him.

The serenading and fireworks had been splendid. Much more impressive than Cynthia had imagined. A buffet had been set up on a sideboard in the sitting room and the dancing had continued long into the night. Even the blacks who were playing seemed to enjoy themselves though they had been playing most of the day—and others stood in the doorways and at windows to watch their "white folk." Once, Cynthia had looked out a window on the side lawn, and was fascinated to find another party, completely black, taking place even though she knew it must be getting cold.

Though the hour was late, she was one of the first to retire, having been preceded only by the children. She hadn't really wanted to, but felt it prudent remembering her position—and her condition.

She lay in bed and listened as the music finally faded and the house became quiet. It's been a very, very long time since I've had so much fun, she thought. I wish Garrett were here.

Thirty

Garrett looked out on a gray, dismal day, then returned to the washbasin to shave. Rain, he thought, almost always rain on Guy Fawkes Day. He held his nose aside with one finger while he carefully scraped the lather and stubble from his upper lip. Finished, he wrung a towel in the warm water and washed the excess lather from his face. I hope it clears, he thought. Too much going on today to enjoy it in nasty weather.

He wished he were home. He could enjoy the quiet festivities they held each year at Garidas. He was glad he had thought to send fireworks the week before. At least the children wouldn't be disappointed. Should have gone home myself, he thought, but Alex had insisted on his staying.

"You've never spent Guy Fawkes Day in Savannah before, have you, Garrett?"

"No, never."

"Well, then, you should stay. A lot of fun. Much like the fairs in London."

Garrett recalled the fairs to which Alex referred, but only from the standpoint of a child who didn't have the price of admission. He remembered trying to sneak in once and having gotten caught, cuffed on the ear and booted on the behind none too gently for his trouble. So, he had stood on the outskirts looking in at the finely dressed ladies and gentlemen and all the glitter, wishing to be a part of the noisy crowd he was separated from by only a rope.

He smiled at himself in the mirror. Guess I stayed just to see what I've been missing out on all these years.

The Stamp Act had gone into effect just four days earlier on the first of the month, but as yet no stamps had been delivered into the colony. The land office was closed, courts had been suspended, but by special order from James Wright, ships were allowed to clear port. There was clearly nothing that could be done to enforce the act until the stamps arrived from London. No one knew when that would be, so the day was perfect for celebrating. Everyone in Savannah had been slightly jubilant the last few days over the failure of the Crown to implement its latest order. Even Governor Wright didn't seem overly concerned at the absence of the stamps. The eventual outcome was inevitable, but as long as there were no stamps available, there was always hope that something could happen to change the Crown's mind. The grievances that had come out of the Stamp Act Congress were now being prepared to be sent to Parliament. It was hoped the Crown would listen to her colonies.

By noon the weather had cleared. Garrett and Alex had decided to take dinner at MacHenry's Tavern so as not to miss any of the excitement. When they walked in the place was noisy, smoky, and reeking of spirits. It was overrun by sailors from the ships. They all seemed to be anticipating something. Garrett and Alex shrugged to each other and made their way to a back table.

As usual, the food was plain, but superb. They

had hardly finished their meal when the din surrounding them took on an air of suppressed activity. It reminded Garrett of an ant hill that had just been stepped on. Within minutes everyone was streaming out into the street. Not wanting to miss anything, Garrett and Alex followed. The crowd, composed mostly of sailors from the ships in the river, began to make its way toward the river. As it moved, more and more people joined in. Those in front were quite drunk and loud. It appeared they had decided to perform for the Savannahans. All they required was someone to play the part of a stamp agent, and it seemed as though they had someone in mind.

Almost to the waterfront, the leaders stopped in front of Tamminy's Tavern. They huddled together for a closed conference, hanging onto one another for support. Their decision made, the largest of the burly sailors broke away and entered the tavern. The rest shared some private joke. Within moments, the large man returned followed by a youngster who Garrett decided must be all-unsuspecting. Another conference, then two of the men broke away from the group and began to move the crowd that had gathered into a circle. Two sailors Garrett hadn't seen in the group before came running from the direction of the river carrying ropes and an assortment of padded sticks.

The stage was set. The mood was light and playful. The leader of the sailors stepped forward.

"Laydies and Laddies. We"—he gestured toward his friends—"we of the ships *Good Hope* and *Salvation* bein', o' course, the best crews in this 'ere 'arbor"—his friends cheered—"an' bein' in complete agreement with the plight o' you Georgians *and* the rest o' the colonies, we's gonna do a bit o' play-actin' fer yer pleasure and to show yous that we support yer position." He moved back to the group and pulled forth the young man who had been recruited from Tamminy's.

"Now, this 'ere is Billy Tallow. Billy, bein' almost as drunk as the rest o' us, has agreed to play the part of the stamp agent, causin', as we all know, the real agent ain't showed up yet."

The crowd cheered and guffawed, elbowing one another. The speaker held up his hand.

"Now you nice laydies and gentlemen cheer the boys on, just lak you would if Billy here was the real thing. Later maybe some of you can get in a lick or two, but remember, we're only play-actin'. Cap'n Blumson wouldn't take it kindly if Billy here was to be hurt. Agreed?"

The crowd joined in enthusiastically.

"Okay, boys, let's spread out."

The sailors formed two lines facing each other. Billy Tallow was placed at one end of the gauntlet. With much encouragement from the sailors and the crowd, he looked around, hiked up his pants, then ran forward. He pretended to ward off the blows of his friends, begging for mercy—saying he would henceforth refuse to further the Crown's cause by distributing stamps to the colonists. A part of the crowd cheered the sailors on. Another part cheered for Billy, saying he had mended his ways. The sailors gave no quarter. They pounced on him like a pack of hungry wolves, sticks flying. Garrett was sure more than just a few bruises would come from the melee.

Finally a cry went up from the crowd. "Hang the blackguard. Let's show King George and Parliament we mean business."

"Cut off his ears and send 'em to London," shouted someone.

The crowd roared encouragement. It was the cue the sailors had been waiting for. They lifted Billy to his feet. He was dirty, but for the most part, looked unhurt. He was smiling. Held on either side by two of his friends, he bowed. The crowd applauded.

"Thank you, one and all. 'Tis best I be put out of me misery. I can no longer live with meself knowing I've been in cahoots with the likes o' Parliament." He bowed again and as he raised his head, a noose was slipped around his neck. His hands were tied behind his back and he was pushed up the street. It was obvious they were heading back to MacHenry's which sported a large sign hanging out over the street. Billy Tallow fairly danced. He knew he was the star attraction.

By the time they reached MacHenry's, Garrett thought all of Savannah must by now be present. He nudged Alex and nodded when he saw one of the more foresighted sailors slip a second rope around Billy's chest and tie it. A horse was brought and Billy was helped into the saddle. Both ropes were thrown over the post holding MacHenry's sign. The leader once again stepped forward and quieted the crowd with an uplifted hand, then he turned to Billy.

"Now, Billy Tallow, self-admitted agent for the Crown who has been harrassin' these poor people here in the colony of Georgia, have you any last words or requests before we carry out this here hangin'?"

"Aye, that I do. I'd like a partin' kiss from that comely wench over there." He nodded in the direction of a very pretty, dark-headed young lady.

She blushed, then at the beckoning of the crowd,

stepped forward shyly. The leader whispered something in her ear and she shook her head, then peered over her shoulder into the crowd afraid, perhaps, someone might object. The mood of those surrounding the poor sailor on the horse hadn't changed. It was festive and jocular. Garrett surmised that if her father was present, he would make no protest. She stepped up beside the horse and with the help of the other sailors was raised so she might reach the lips of the "condemned" Billy Tallow.

Billy raised his head from the kiss and beamed. The girl rushed back into the cheering crowd. The sailor in charge turned to Billy.

"Now, Billy, you are condemned to die. Be ye ready to meet yer Maker?"

"Aye."

"Very well, then, on with the hangin'."

The crowd roared. Garrett wondered how they would end the parody—simply by untying the ropes and letting Billy down?—or perhaps by raising Billy by the rope around his chest, then lowering him? Or had the sailors ingeniously come up with a way to carry it further?

Billy leaned over to speak with one of his friends. He was fidgety and obviously becoming concerned over just how far the farce was to be carried. His friend patted him on the knee reassuringly.

Suddenly a small boy broke from the crowd and whacked the horse a resounding blow on the rump. It bolted from beneath Billy. He was left hanging in mid-air, saved only by the rope around his chest. The rope around his neck hung limply as he swung in an arc by the other. He, as well as the other sailors, were visibly shaken. They moved quickly to cut him down. The crowd, unaware of the near-tragedy, roared its approval. All but a few were obviously of the impression it had been planned to happen just as it had. Only those nearest were conscious of the ashen pallor on the faces of the sailors.

The crowd began to disperse. The sailors wandered off to the various taverns. Alex and Garrett headed homeward. They no longer cared to be a part of the festivities.

It was almost dusk. After the near-disastrous mock beating and hanging, Garrett had decided to return to Garidas earlier than originally planned. He had ridden Temple hard, hoping to make Birdsville by nightfall. He still had at least three leagues to go and never would have attempted it past dark with a wagon or coach, but knew Temple was sure-footed enough to get him there safely. He would take supper with Thaddeus Overby and relate to him all the happenings in Savannah. Thaddeus would be a big help in organizing a branch of Liberty Boys in the area. He already knew most of the people and where their sympathies lay. Though there were new people coming in almost weekly now, they all passed through Birdsville since it was one of the last centers of civilization west of Savannah, second in size only to Fort Augusta.

As darkness descended, he thought of Mourning Overby. Maybe I should marry her, he thought. Thad wouldn't object even though she is young. Pretty, too. I need a wife—and Mourning would make a good one. Knows what life here is like, a hard worker. Not a lot of frills to Mourning. A bit young and flighty yet, but as open and honest as the day is long. The more he thought about the idea, the more it appealed to him. He knew he was ready to settle down and raise a family. He had never even considered marriage before meeting Cynthia, but now it seemed the logical thing to do. How she had changed him. A part of him yearned for her—told him not to jump into anything for a while, not to betray the love they had shared.

"Hell," he said aloud. "She's gone. All the waiting in the world won't bring her back."

Mourning's a good choice, he thought. I don't love her, but I could learn to—and perhaps we would have a son to carry on the work I've started with the blacks. Jacob and I won't live forever.

It being unusual for someone to ride in so late, Thaddeus was at the door of the stable to greet him as he dismounted. He had made his decision. He removed the saddle and threw it over one side of a stall, then turned to his friend.

"Thaddeus, I want to marry Mourning."

Confused by this statement, Thaddeus began to sputter. Finally, he found his tongue. "Garrett, I don't know what to say. I . . . Mourning's just a child. Our . . . our only daughter."

"I know, Thad. I'll be good to her or I wouldn't ask. You know I'll be good to her."

"Have you talked to her?"

Garrett shook his head. He removed the bridle and tethered Temple in an empty stall. "Not yet. Wanted to talk to you first."

Thaddeus sat down heavily on a nearby bench. He looked all of his forty-eight years and more. Garrett hadn't expected it to be such a shock to him.

"Do you love her?"

"Nope. Did you love Clara when you married her?"

Thaddeus shook his head and began to smile. "No. No, I didn't, but don't you think you should wait a while? Aren't you just looking for something because of the girl who died?"

"Sure I'm looking for something. Must have been when I met Cynthia. I never entertained the idea of marriage before, but, hell, Thad, I'm thirty-three years old. If I want a family, someone to carry on my name, I have to think about it now. I can't live forever and even if I could, waiting won't bring back the dead."

"But why Mourning?"

"Well, I know here and I haven't met anyone I like any better. Given time, I believe we could have a good marriage and a good life and . . . I can give her that honeymoon she wants in England."

Thad stood up and slapped him on the back. "Well, at least you're honest, Garrett. I think you'll find Mourning easy to love. I believe she already has some feelings for you. She's been doing a lot of moonin' since you were last here. I'll be proud to have you in the family, Garrett. Proud."

Garrett smiled sheepishly. He didn't know why he felt so like a schoolboy.

"Do you want to see Mourning now? I think she's asleep, but I can wake her."

"No, tomorrow is soon enough. I know this is an important event in a girl's life. I want to say all the right words—not just spring it on her. Promise you won't tell her, Thad, not till I've had a chance to talk to her. I want her to be in complete agreement. I don't want her to feel like she's being pressured into anything."

"I promise. Now, let's go have a drink. I'll get Tony out to curry Temple. We need to celebrate, boy."

"And I need to eat something."

Thaddeus jabbed him in the ribs playfully and began to chuckle as they walked from the stable.

Thirty-One

The Guy Fawkes Day celebration at the Gilmores was an almost forgotten memory. Christmas was approaching with the speed of a runaway freight wagon. Cynthia, wanting to feel a part of the holidays, had asked Elizabeth for some fabric scraps. So, besides her regular sewing duties, she was busily making Christmas presents for those she knew best and felt closest to. A small scrap of linen had been laboriously embroidered over and over again with the initials EJ then cut into squares, made into little sachet pillows and awaited filling with perfumy herbs and spices for Elizabeth. A long border scrap had been retrieved from the rag pile and had been hemmed and embroidered with the same EJ and made into an ascot for Elijah. Even smaller scraps, some she had retrieved from beneath Josie's feet, were pieced together and quilted. These quilted pieces would be made into footwarmers for Naomi. She still wanted to do something for Josie and for Daphne and Hadley and if there was time, Nathan Tolliver. Next to Naomi, he had become her closest friend at Mountview, but she was afraid a gift to a single man would not be quite proper, so he was last on her list until she decided for sure.

Jameison had come to her frequently since their return to Mountview. Naomi always grumbled, but left when he appeared. Cynthia knew she had no other choice even though the two were brother and sister.

She sat in the sewing room working on new Christmas linens for the dining table. She raised her head to stretch her back and shoulders and peered out toward the cabins. When they had returned from the Gilmores', Naomi had met her at their door excitedly. She had done some checking around, she told Cynthia, and Elijah Jameison could be prosecuted for adultery if Cynthia would only go to the authorities. A slave would have no recourse, but a white indentured woman....

"And what would happen to me if I reported this to the authorities, Naomi?"

"Well, if Elijah is convicted, your indenture would be sold to another master."

"And what if he wasn't found guilty? Where would that leave me?"

"Yer condition will speak for itself, girl. All you got to do is testify."

"After that, what if I got a worse master? It's really not so bad here, Naomi. I'm treated well and Elijah, at least, isn't the animal Walter was. I can tolerate his attentions. I have to."

Naomi looked hurt. "I was only tryin' to help."

"I know, Naomi. I know, but I can't fight your battles for you. What's between you and Elijah you'll have to work out some other way. I have to think about the baby. You know as well as I do Elijah's the only chance in the world this baby has."

"Have you told him yet?"

"No, but I will soon. I have to. It won't be long before I'm showing."

She returned her attention to the hemming of the

large tablecloth. I'll tell him the next time he comes, she thought. She never knew when he was coming. He just showed up, usually late at night after the big house was quiet. Another week or two and I won't have to tell him, she thought. He'll know just by feeling me—if he doesn't already.

Naomi hadn't mentioned her going to the authorities for some time, but every now and then she still brought it up. Cynthia knew she would continue to slip it into their conversations. Naomi wanted Jameison punished for the hurt he had caused her over the years, and she didn't care if it were at Cynthia's hand. In fact, Naomi had no other way of getting back at Elijah. So far, Cynthia had refrained from telling Naomi the truth about the baby, but it suddenly occurred to her that Naomi would be almost as happy if she knew the truth as if Jameison were prosecuted. Cynthia smiled. She could almost see Naomi chortling over that one. The next time she brings up the possibility of my going to the authorities, I'll tell her, she thought. She knew Naomi would never tell another soul. She prided herself on her refusal to gossip and often refused to listen to it from others.

That evening Cynthia kept hoping Naomi would mention her prosecuting Elijah. Now that her decision was made, she could hardly wait to tell her secret, but she wanted to get into the telling of it in a natural sort of way. She didn't want to just blurt it out. But the hour grew late and after much talk about everyday activities, they decided to go to bed. Naomi banked the fire while Cynthia changed into her nightclothes and turned back the bed. Naomi was just putting on her nightgown and Cynthia was already in bed when they heard a soft knock on the door. They both knew who it was. Naomi scowled at Cynthia as she pulled a blanket around her shoulders and moved toward the door.

"I tell ya, girl . . ."

"Later, Naomi, please. We'll talk later. He might hear you now."

Naomi shrugged as she let Jameison in, raised her head in disgust at the two of them and left. Cynthia knew she would be back the minute Jameison left. She wondered briefly how Naomi always knew when he was leaving, but dismissed it from her mind for now. She would have to ask Naomi.

Jameison fairly swooped down on the bed. "You look fetching sitting there like that, my dear."

"Another few minutes and I'm afraid you would have found us asleep."

"You're up late as it is." He was removing his clothing.

"Naomi was in a mood to talk. I wasn't terribly tired so I obliged her." She could tell he had been drinking, but was far from drunk. He seemed to be in an uncommonly good mood. I have to tell him, she thought. It's best to do it while he's in good humor with me.

He slipped into the bed beside her and pulled her to him.

"Can we talk, Eli? We never talk."

"Of course we can talk, Helen, but first. . ."

"Please, couldn't we talk first?"

"If you wish." He pulled away and propped himself up on Naomi's pillow. "I have something to tell you, anyway."

"You have?"

"Elizabeth and I are going to Savannah next week. We go every year about this time. Sort of a holiday.

Elizabeth shops for Christmas trinkets. Would you like to come?"

Cynthia brightened, then slowly shook her head. "I . . . I don't think so, Eli. I don't think I should be traveling right now."

He began to chuckle. "Some sort of superstition?"

"You might say that." Cynthia took a deep breath then plunged ahead. "I'm going to have a baby."

In the dim candlelight she could see the muscles in his jaw working back and forth. He took a deep breath and let the air whistle out between his teeth. "I see."

"I didn't mean to just blurt it out like that. I wanted to tell you in a special way, but you can see why I can't make the trip, can't you?"

He nodded. She watched him closely, knowing the impact of what she told him hadn't yet struck home. Please believe me, she begged silently.

"I . . . uh . . . I thought surely you would have noticed by now. I've known for some time. Are you angry, Eli? Tell me you aren't angry."

He turned and looked at her. "Angry? Of course not. As a matter of fact, I'm rather pleased." He smiled one of his more winning smiles. "You know, Lizzie and I never . . . well, I was beginning to think maybe it was my . . . but now I know different. It's Lizzie, not me at all. I almost love you for this, Cynthia."

It was the first time he had ever called her anything but Helen or Mistress Fawley since the first two weeks they had been together. She let him pull her to him. He kissed her gently.

"Of course you can't make the trip to Savannah. You must take care of yourself and the wee one. The problem is how to tell Elizabeth."

Cynthia knew. She was glad she wouldn't have to face Elizabeth with the news. She had been through her own private hell over how Elizabeth would react ever since they had met. She had come to like and respect her so much.

"I'll have to tell her, though," he continued. "Soon, everyone will know, won't they?"

Cynthia nodded. "Are you really pleased, Eli? I was so fearful you would be angry."

"Quite the contrary, my dear. I couldn't be more delighted. We'll give the little scalawag a good home here at Mountview and I'll treat it as though it were my own."

"But it is your own."

"Yes, but we can't let on like it is, now can we? At least not for a while. Later, we can slowly move it into the big house. Elizabeth loves children. I'm sure she will have no objection to taking it under her wing while you go about your duties, but for the time being, we must keep the secret. Only Elizabeth must know, because for one thing she can always tell when I'm lying and for another, she thinks highly of you and would never believe you promiscuous. On the other hand, she knows I am and always have been."

"But Naomi will know."

"I'll speak to Naomi. She won't tell anyway. With her, it's a matter of family pride."

"Family pride?"

"Yes, Naomi's my half-sister. She hates me in the worst way, but she does have her pride. She won't talk."

"But why should it matter who knows, as long as you're going to tell Elizabeth?"

He took her hand in his. "Because, my dear, I

could be sent to prison for being with you and you . . . you could be sold away from us."

"But won't Elizabeth? . . ."

"She can't and she won't."

"How can you be so sure?"

"Just trust me, my dear. I'm sure. Don't let Elizabeth frighten you."

So he does have some kind of hold over Elizabeth, Cynthia thought.

"Now that we've talked," he said smiling lasciviously, "we can get on with the business at hand."

Cynthia smiled. He was making it all so easy, but hadn't she known he would? If only it had been Garrett she was telling . . .

Later he sat on the edge of the bed. "You didn't seem surprised to hear that Naomi is my half-sister."

"She told me weeks ago."

He turned, a scowl on his face. "What else did she tell you?"

"Not much, but she did tell me about her family members being sold away. You shouldn't have done that, Eli."

He turned so she couldn't see his face. "I know. It's the biggest mistake I've ever made. She has good cause to hate me. I can hardly stand having her around, though. She looks so much like my father, it's a constant reminder of what a weak person he was, lusting after black flesh like he did—and I . . . I loved my father, Cynthia. I idolized him. I never knew until he died the number of bastards he had fathered. Naomi was his favorite, though, even ahead of me, I think. She and her mother were the only ones he stipulated I couldn't sell."

"Then why don't you give her her freedom?"

"Can't. Even if I did, it wouldn't matter. I have to take care of her for all her natural life."

"But why did you sell her brothers and sisters and her children?"

"I had to. Even if I hadn't needed the money, I had to." He laughed softly. "Trouble is, he'll never know."

"And what about our baby? How will it be treated if you and Elizabeth should have one of . . ."

"We won't. It's been too many years. I assure you, this baby will have everything I can give it. I will not betray it. I promise you that."

"And Elizabeth?"

"She'll accept it. She'll have no choice. I'll see to that." He turned, smiling, his mood entirely changed. "Now, don't you worry your pretty head about Elizabeth or anything else. Everything will be fine. It's not all that uncommon for a man to sire children by someone other than his wife. In her own way, I think Elizabeth will be pleased. At least this child will be white and will one day be free and acceptable into society—if the whole thing is handled properly."

He got up to leave. "Elizabeth will probably want to talk to you after I've told her. Don't let her frighten you."

"She has never frightened me. I . . . I like Elizabeth."

"Yes, well, she has her moments." He bent to kiss her on the forehead and was gone.

Within minutes, the door opened and Naomi sidled in. She blew out the candle and crawled in beside Cynthia.

"Did you tell him?"

"Yes."

"How'd he take it?"

"Very well as a matter of fact. He seems pleased."

"The bastard. I hope the missus gives him what-for."

"He seemed very sure of her, said there was nothing she could do to either of us."

"He has somethin' on her all right. I've known for years. Wish I knew what it was. You're the one who coulda done somethin'—then we coulda all been shed o' him, Miss Elizabeth, too."

"I can't, Naomi."

"Ya could if'n ya wanted to."

"No, Naomi, I can't. The child isn't his."

There was silence from the other side of the bed. Finally, Naomi rose and carried the candle to the fireplace to light it. Back by the bed, she peered intently at Cynthia for long moments. Cynthia held her gaze evenly.

"You ain't lyin'."

Cynthia shook her head.

"But you tol' me..."

"I know what I told you, Naomi, but the child isn't his."

A smile spread slowly over Naomi's face. "But he thinks it is?"

"He does. Chances are good he'll be none the wiser, but I'm telling you now that this baby will be born ahead of schedule."

Naomi's laughter started as a chuckle and grew until it shook her whole body. She put the candle down lest she drop it, sat on the bed and hugged Cynthia.

"This is almost better'n seein' him in jail," she said, finally catching her breath.

"I'm sorry for lying to you in the beginning,

Naomi, but then I didn't know . . ."

"That's all right, child, that's all right." She was still chuckling. "But Lordy, if'n he ever finds out, there'll be hell to pay."

"He mustn't find out, not ever. It's the only chance my baby has."

"It ain't the only chance, girl, but right now, it would seem to be the best. Who *is* the father?"

Cynthia had known Naomi would want to know the particulars. She had gone over in her mind everything that had happened since the day at the cattle market. Somehow it was important to her that Naomi understand and accept the circumstances that had brought her halfway around the world to a new life, carrying a new life.

They talked long into the night.

It was a little past noon. Cynthia squared her shoulders and knocked on the door of the little office. After what seemed an interminable wait, she was bade to enter. She held her head a little higher as she opened the door.

Elizabeth sat at the desk, intent upon the book before her. She motioned for Cynthia to sit down. After some minutes, she turned.

"Well, let me look at you." She looked Cynthia over carefully from head to foot. "I should have known. Being a woman, I should have known."

Cynthia found her voice. "You're . . . you're not angry?"

"At you? No. Elijah is another matter. Anger is hardly a word I would use to describe my feelings for him."

Cynthia heaved a sigh. "I'm so relieved, ma'am. I was so afraid you'd be . . . well, I mean . . . I didn't want to hurt you."

Elizabeth leaned forward and patted her hand. "Let me assure you, you have in no way hurt me." She stood. Cynthia could see the tension in her shoulders. "I'm sure that no-good bastard I'm married to sold you a bill of goods about how it would be so much easier for you. . . ."

"Yes, ma'am, he did."

"Cynthia, do you know you could have him prosecuted for adultery?"

"Yes, ma'am. Naomi told me."

"Of course. Naomi would have found out about things like that. She has always sought restitution from Elijah. Not that I blame her. He deserves anything she can do to him and more." There was a long pause. Cynthia looked at her tightly clasped hands in her lap. What did Elizabeth want from her?

Elizabeth turned. "And have you thought about it?"

"There was nothing to think about, Miss Elizabeth. There's nothing I can do to Mr. Jameison."

"Oh?"

Cynthia could feel the tears stinging her eyelids. She raised her head and looked Elizabeth in the face. "The child I carry is not your husband's."

Elizabeth gathered Cynthia into her arms. "Thank you, Cynthia. I already knew, but thank you for telling me."

Cynthia took an offered handkerchief. She dabbed at her eyes. "You . . . you already knew?"

"Yes, I knew. That's why I never worried too much about his philandering. I knew there would be no bastards."

"But how?" A fear gripped Cynthia. "Does he know?"

Elizabeth sat down and faced Cynthia. "No, he doesn't know and I'll not tell him. I could have this morning, but it may serve my purposes better this way."

"Serve your purposes?"

Elizabeth took Cynthia's hand in hers. "There's not another living soul who knows everything I'm about to tell you, Cynthia, but I feel you deserve to know because you are now a part of it. Very innocently, you may have solved a problem for both of us. My problem, of course, is Elijah and how to be rid of him. Yours is the babe and its welfare."

Cynthia nodded, waiting for Elizabeth to collect her thoughts.

After a few moments, Elizabeth took a deep breath and began. She told a story of horror—of repeated rapings by her older brother after the death of their parents, of murder, of Elijah Jameison coming on the scene shortly after she had shot her brother in self-defense and helping her dispose of the body. Elijah had then proposed, knowing full well Elizabeth could not refuse. He knew too much. The one thing he didn't know, however, was that his virgin bride was pregnant by her own brother. Elizabeth never told him of the relationship between her and her brother—only that her brother beat her. This, he could see for himself.

"Fortunately," Elizabeth concluded, "the baby was never born. I miscarried in the second month. Elijah never knew. Had it worked out the other way, I'm sure he would have thought it his own."

"And he has held this over you all these years?"

"Yes. It won't be long now until I inherit all my family's land and fortune. My brother would have inherited . . . everyone thinks he just took off . . .

there's never been a trace of him found in all these years."

"But what if someone should find. . ."

"It wouldn't matter now. There would be no more than bones, and likely as not, his death would be attributed to Indians if the skeleton were found intact. By now, the bones have most probably been scattered by animals."

Cynthia could visualize the grisly scene. Elizabeth showed no emotion whatever.

On her way to the cabin for supper, she thought over the bargain she had made with Elizabeth. Neither would tell Elijah he was not the father of the unborn child, but should he discover it for himself, Elizabeth would guarantee Cynthia the care for her and the child as long as needed if Cynthia would back her in an adultery suit in the courts if necessary. Elizabeth definitely had plans to be rid of Elijah before her inheritance came and this was just the way to do it. Before Cynthia happened on the scene, she had no leverage, but now when he threatened to turn her in for murder, she could counter-threat with adultery and his part in disposing of the body.

She felt certain he would leave. With the absence of a body, murder was hard to prove and it would be his word against hers. On the other hand, with Cynthia's testimony, adultery would be easy to prove.

Within the fortnight, she and Cynthia were to take a trip to her brother's shallow grave to make sure there was no evidence.

Thirty-Two

In a few minutes it would be Christmas Day, 1765. Garrett sat in his bedroom in a large overstuffed chair staring into the fire. The house was quiet. Jacob and Munsy had left hours ago and he had heard strains of Christmas songs and solemn hymns coming from the blacks' quarters ever since supper. He knew he was welcome among his people and in years past they had rejoiced as one, but tonight he felt a need to be separate. Memories of Cynthia filled his mind. He could almost see her in the dancing flames. Suddenly he had an urge to visit the cabin. He wanted to be entirely alone with his thoughts for at least a few hours. He quickly dressed and left the house, picking up a bottle of brandy from the dining room sideboard on his way out.

Temple pranced with excitement as he saddled her and led her from the stable. She shivered slightly in the bitter cold. He returned to the stable for a blanket. There was little protection for Temple at the cabin should the wind come up. It must be Christmas, he thought, as he settled into the saddle. He knew the prayers and songs of worship concluded at midnight and the last song his mind could register was of a lighter vein. The blacks were now boisterously launching into one of his favorites, "The Boar's Head Carol." He listened a moment then turned Temple toward the drive.

It was a clear, moonlit night. He gave Temple her head and she covered the distance in record time. He tied her close to the cabin and spread the blanket over her. There was no wind. Everything was perfectly still and peaceful. He stood momentarily at the doorway looking up at the stars before entering.

Standing back as the fire began to crackle, he reached for a mug from the cupboard built against one wall. He sloshed some brandy around in it then threw the dark liquid onto the fire. The flames flared briefly. He spread a fur before the hearth and stretched out on it, the bottle of brandy within easy reach. As he sat nursing the small mugful, he thought of Mourning Overby and the conversation he had overheard between her and Thaddeus that morning some six weeks ago.

"But Papa, I don't want to marry Mr. Carver!"

Garrett had just stepped from the small back room and was partially hidden by the jutting-out of the bar. He remained in the shadows. Thad and Mourning were across the room and could not see him even if they turned his way. He was surprised Thad had already spoken to the girl after promising he wouldn't.

"I'm sorry, Mourning. I thought you liked Garrett."

"I like him fine, Papa. I think he's a most handsome man, but he's so old. I don't want to marry an old man."

"But what about the way you was makin' eyes at him the last time he was here?"

"I was just practicin', Papa. Every girl practices. Ask Mama."

"Your mama thinks this would be a good match for you, Mourning. Garrett will be good to you. He can give you all life's comforts."

"But he's too old, Papa. When I marry, I want a young man."

"Young man, old man—listen to me, Mourning Overby, most girls would jump at the chance to marry Garrett Carver. Besides, I already told him we would be delighted to have him in the family."

"Without even talking to me?"

"I gave it my hand on it, Mourning. That's the way it will be."

"If you say so, Papa, but I don't have to like it."

Garrett quickly backed up then opened the door and entered the common room with a great flourish. He didn't want Mourning forced into a marriage she didn't want.

"Ah, Thad, Mourning."

Mourning turned, eyed him up and down for a moment then placed her hands on her hips. "Mr. Carver, Papa told me about your proposal and I'm right flattered. I like you fine, sir, but I don't love you and I don't believe you love me. . . ."

"Now, Mourning. . ."

"No, let me finish, Papa. I'll marry you, Mr. Carver, if that's what you want, because Papa says he already gave his word. Now . . . that's all I got to say. When you want to be doin' it?"

Garrett, taken aback by the outspokenness of the girl, smiled briefly then moved to stand in front of her. He glanced at Thaddeus who looked shocked, ashamed, and miserable. He put his hands on Mourning's shoulders and felt the girl's warmth through the thin shawl.

"You're right, Mourning. I don't love you, but I do hold you in high regard. Perhaps that isn't enough for a young girl with her whole life ahead of her. Perhaps I'm just being a foolish old man."

Mourning eyed him closely, the color rising in her cheeks. Garrett knew she was trying to decide whether or not he had overheard the conversation between her and her father.

"How about I release your father from his promise? I don't want to force you into anything. That's no way to start a life together."

Mourning's face beamed into a smile. "Thank you, Mr. Carver." She turned to her father. " 'Course, it has to be okay with Papa, too."

Thaddeus nodded. Garrett knew he had no wish to sadden his only daughter. Later, Thad apologized for Mourning's outspokenness and for having broken his promise. Garrett shrugged it off, telling Thad nothing had changed between them. It was an awkward moment.

He thought about it now and realized it had actually been for the better. Mourning had shown more sense than had either he or Thad. He would always have a special place in his heart for her for having spoken her mind. Marriage at this time would have been a disaster. He still thought of Cynthia constantly. Everything he did or said brought memories of her in one way or another.

He quaffed the brandy in the mug, poured another and repeated the process, all the while questioning the fairness of having found her at all only to lose her so soon. A wave of grief threatened but he had no more tears to shed and knew it. The pain remained deep within, only slightly eased by the effects of the alcohol.

He stood, at once angry with the God he only half believed in, the world, and his place in it. Hadn't he tried to do the right thing in his life? Wasn't he trying to help the down-trodden? Wasn't he a good and decent person? All the things he had come to believe in—were they for naught? He strode to the door and jerked it open. The storm within abated some, confronted as it was by the beauty and peace of the night. He walked to where the drive met the road and searched the heavens for his answers. There were none. A lonely, unintelligible cry escaped his lips as he sank to his knees.

He sat leaning against his heels, looking skyward, until the cold began to penetrate his heavy winter clothing. Pushing himself to a standing position once more, he allowed that the peacefulness of the night and perhaps even the sacredness of this holiest of holy nights had somehow quelled the raging anger within him. Christmas, he thought. Tomorrow I'll make a new beginning. Heavy-footed, but lighter in heart, he returned to the cabin.

Some hours later, Garrett awoke with a start. The fire had died down. He was getting cold. What time was it? He peered toward the oilskin-covered window, but no light penetrated. He knew he must return to the house before dawn. Some of the heartier souls would have sung and partied all night just to be the first to shout Christmas greetings to him at cock's-crow. He couldn't disappoint them, especially the children.

As he sat up, his head pounded, but he knew some of Munsy's strong, hot coffee would help that. He latched the door as he went out and breathed deeply of the early morning air. He scanned the eastern sky and guessed he just might have time for a hot bath before the Christmas festivities officially began at Garidas.

Cynthia stood by the small fireplace fingering the greenery she and Naomi had gathered to make the cabin more festive. Naomi would be coming in a few minutes then they would go to old Jess's cabin where, Naomi had explained, they would begin the "singin' and the worshipin' for the Chris' chile."

They had all gathered earlier at the big house for the ritual bringing in and lighting of the yule log. Cynthia had, at first, been surprised that the old customs were being preserved in this wilderness. The whole place had been in a festive uproar since the feast of Thanksgiving. Daphne and her kitchen help had cooked for days, first making and storing the traditional Christmas cakes. After that, it had been a glorious round of doing, from killing and butchering the pigs for roasting to putting the final touches on the delicious puddings and dressings just today. The men had picked out the yule log weeks ago and this afternoon had dragged it to the front door of the mansion with much ceremony. The boys had collected holly, mistletoe and evergreen boughs for decorating. Everything was polished to perfection in readiness. Cynthia felt an excitement she hadn't felt in years.

She had thought to surprise Naomi with her Christmas gift but when she had lain hers on the table this morning at breakfast, Naomi had immediately retrieved a gaily wrapped package from beneath the mattress and lain it beside Cynthia's. They had smiled, hugged each other and agreed to wait until the following morning to open them.

Cynthia jumped with a start when she heard the ringing of the cowbell. She knew this was to summon them to old Jess's. She wondered what kept Naomi.

The door flew open with a rush and Naomi came in breathless. "The cowbell's already rung."

"I know. I was waiting for you."

"Ya ready?"

"I guess so." Cynthia pulled her shawl about her shoulders and bent to blow out the candle.

As the two women walked between the rows of cabins, they could see others hurrying to the last cabin on the north side. Naomi had told Cynthia they always gathered at the cabin of the oldest slaves. There were three who vied for the honor, so they had come to taking turns.

The little room was crowded. Cynthia and Naomi sidled in and found room to stand along one wall. She spotted Nathan Tolliver across the room and flashed him a smile. He slowly began to make his way around the room to stand beside her. He had a blanket slung over one arm, but transferred it to the other and squeezed her elbow as he came up to her.

"A happy Christmas to you, Miss Cynthia. You sure look pretty tonight."

"Why, thank you, Nathan. You . . . you look nice, too." Her nose wrinkled at the clean smell of soap. She looked up at him. His blond hair had been brushed and pulled back at the nape of his neck with some kind of tie. His gray eyes twinkled when he caught her looking at him. He flushed slightly and looked down, a smile showing even, white teeth.

Cynthia glanced quickly around the room, greeting those she felt she knew well, nodding to those she didn't. Never before had she realized there were so many people at Mountview. As more late-comers arrived, everyone crowded together to make room. Nathan moved to stand behind Cynthia. His body shielded her from the cold coming through the cracks in the wall. She looked up and smiled her appreciation.

What meager furniture old Jess had was pushed back against the walls. Bundled babies were laid side by side on the bunk, the young mothers positioning themselves close by. The table was to one side of the fireplace and was laden with all varieties of festive treats. Cynthia knew most had been sent from the main house, but those who could had each provided something. She and Naomi had made rice cakes and sent them over earlier. They had also given most of their supply of tea for the occasion. Others had done the same.

"Do you like to sing, Miss Cynthia?" It was Nathan Tolliver at her shoulder.

"Oh, yes. As a child, I would go carol-singing with my parents and our neighbors. When I got older, I got to go mumming once, but that was before my mother died."

"Did you now? I went mumming as a lad in Coventry. Great fun. They don't do that here. Everything is too spread out. Mayhap it's done in Savannah. I don't know."

Everyone hushed as old Jess stood. His black face beamed as he made signs of welcome before reclaiming his seat by the fire between Darlan and Mable, the other two "elders." The Christmas celebration was begun when he bobbed his gray, fuzzy head toward one of the older girls who stepped forward and began to recite "Joseph Was an Old Man." Cynthia knew the legend well. It told of Joseph, as an old man, walking with his young bride, Mary, to Bethlehem. When they come to a garden where cherries are growing, Mary tells Joseph of the visits of the angel. Joseph is filled with doubts and jealousy. He refuses to pick the cherries for Mary, but the tree hears Mary's request and bends over so she might pick the fruit herself. Seeing this, Joseph knows he should have not refused to pick the cherries and falls on his knees and begs forgiveness for his unfounded suspicions.

The legend went on to tell of the birth of the Christ child. Cynthia was most impressed that the girl knew the entire poem. Even she had never learned the whole thing.

" 'Tis the closest thing they have to a bible, to my way of thinkin'," Nathan whispered into her ear.

Cynthia nodded, but wondered where they had learned the legend.

The girl sat down and almost immediately the entire gathering began to sing "Lullay, Thou Little Tiny Child." Cynthia and Nathan joined in. They sang one Christmas song after another and when solemnity turned to merriment, Cynthia and Nathan pushed their way out the door for some fresh air.

Nathan shook out the blanket he held over his arm and threw it around his broad shoulders. Cynthia could see it had been stitched into a crude cloak. She gathered her shawl close. She now wished she had worn the cloak Elijah had bought her in Savannah.

"I'm sorry," Nathan apologized. "You're cold. Here, take my cloak."

"No, no. I'm not cold yet, but I do need some fresh air. It's so close inside."

"Aye. Come, let's stand between the cabins. It's likely warmer there."

Cynthia let him take her elbow and steer her between the cabins. He leaned against the outside wall of Jess's and watched her.

"The . . . uh . . . the moonlight shines off your hair."

Cynthia looked up at the cloudless sky. There was a hazy ring around the moon. "It's a beautiful night, isn't it? So still . . . so peaceful."

"Aye, and so cold."

"Yes," Cynthia agreed as she pulled her shawl closer. "I should have worn a cloak."

"Please, take mine."

"Thank you, Sir Galahad, but I'll not have you freeze just because I'm a dolt. We can go back in a minute."

He leaned against the wall once more. "I'll be a free man six months from tonight."

"Why, Nathan, how nice. You must be excited."

"Aye. Master Jameison—or actually, 'twas the missus—gave me a choice of land parcels. The one I like is on the northernmost boundary of Mountview, at the bend in the river. It's never been worked. It's good, rich land."

Cynthia's teeth were beginning to chatter. "I . . . I'm happy for you, Nathan."

"A man could support a family on land like that. 'Course, not right away. 'Twould take time."

"Yes." Cynthia was beginning to realize where the conversation was leading. It gave her an uncomfortable feeling. Besides, she was cold. "Could . . . could we go in now? I'm getting cold."

"Of course. I'm sorry . . . I . . ." Their eyes met briefly. Cynthia could see the longing in his. In an instant he had thrown his cloak about her and she was in his arms. He pulled her close and kissed her with passion. As she closed her eyes she imagined it was Garrett who was holding her. When she opened her eyes she was frightened by the heady feeling his closeness gave her. She pushed away from him. "Nathan, please don't . . . I . . ."

He pulled her back within the warmth of the cloak. His voice was husky with emotion. "I love you, Cynthia. I want you to be my wife."

"But Nathan, I . . . I . . ."

He put a finger to her lips. "Hush. Don't say anything now. Think about it. There's lots of time. It can't be for a while." He bent to kiss her again. She didn't refuse. His hands roamed awkwardly over her back and came to rest on her waist. Suddenly he pushed her away, his brow creased with confusion.

"My God, you're with child!"

Cynthia bit her lower lip. She didn't know whether to act offended and leave or try to bluff her way through. She decided on the latter.

"That's a terrible thing to say, Nathan Tolliver. Why only yesterday. . ."

"I could feel a fullness in your waist just now when I held you. It wasn't there six weeks ago when you went to the Gilmores'. A man notices those things. I helped you into the carriage, remember?"

She hadn't remembered or she would have been more careful where she let him touch her. "As I told Naomi, I . . . I've just put on a couple of pounds, that's all."

"There are some things I'm not completely ignorant of, Cynthia. I was married once. My wife died in childbirth, the babe with her. I can tell the difference."

Cynthia choked back the threatening tears. It had been bound to happen. She raised her chin and looked Nathan in the eyes. "You're right, Nathan." Her voice came out almost a whisper. "You're absolutely right. I am with child. Soon everyone will know, won't they?" She tried to laugh but could hold the tears no longer.

He pulled her to him. She welcomed his warmth and the strong arms that held her. "But when? Who?" He held her away a little so he could see her face. "It's Jameison, isn't it? He . . . he. . ." But he couldn't finish.

Cynthia, unable to speak, only shook her head. Nathan took it as a sign that she was too overcome to talk about it. He turned her, still holding her close and led her away from the festive sounds toward his own cabin. Neither spoke until he opened the door. "Come. We'll have some tea and talk."

Cynthia sat perched on his only chair, a million thoughts racing through her mind, as he lit a candle, built up the fire, and put water on to boil. What was she going to tell him if he insisted on knowing who the father was? Did she want to lie to this man who claimed to love her?

He came and sat on the foot of the bed, less than two feet from her. In a few minutes, he reached out and took her hand. "I think we should be married right away . . . if that bas . . . if the Jameisons will let us."

Cynthia drew her hand away. "I can't marry you, Nathan. Not you or anyone else."

"I do love you, Cynthia. Just because he . . . he forced himself on you doesn't mean I can't love you."

"You don't even know me. There hasn't been time."

"I know enough. I had thought two or three years from now with luck I might be some ahead to pay off your indenture. We could be married then, but now . . . now, I think it should be right away."

Cynthia felt a shudder run through her. She looked at him, blinking back the tears. "You're very kind, Nathan. I thank you for your offer, but I can't marry you. I can't marry anyone. I . . . not even if the Jameisons would allow it."

"Lord, girl, you've got to give the babe a proper name—even if it is . . . his." The last word was spit out angrily. "I'd be good to it, I swear."

The water began to boil over, making hissing sounds. Nathan went to move the pot from the fire. As he made tea, Cynthia rehearsed in her mind what she would tell him. He moved the crude little table to a spot between her and the bed, set a mug of tea in front of her, then resumed his seat.

"Sorry, I have no milk."

"That's all right. It tastes good without it. It's hot. That's what matters tonight."

Nathan nodded. Cynthia hoped he wouldn't question her further.

After a few moments silence, he spoke. "Can I speak to the Jameisons?"

Cynthia shook her head. "It won't do any good. I can't marry you."

"But why? Why won't you marry me?"

"I didn't say I won't, Nathan. I said I can't."

He shook his head slightly, the subtle difference in her wording finally dawning on him. He sat in thoughtful silence for a few moments sipping his tea. "Very well, why can't you marry me?"

Cynthia studied her tea leaves for a long time, then took a deep breath before speaking. "I have a husband in England."

Nathan's mug slipped from his hand and thudded to the dirt floor.

Cynthia continued, "I can't marry you. I can't marry anyone until . . . until . . . until forever, I guess, because I'll never know when he dies."

She looked at him. She could understand the bewildered look on his face. "He was going to sell me, Nathan. He was going to sell me to the highest bidder at an auction. I ran away. I . . . I sold myself, but at least this isn't forever."

Nathan stood and walked to the fire. He looked at the flames without seeing them. Cynthia waited, watching his back. Finally, he turned.

"Who besides me knows you have a husband?"

"Mrs. Jameison knows and Naomi."

"He doesn't know?"

"He thinks I'm a widow, but he knows about the baby."

Nathan came and sat across from her again. He rested clenched hands on the table. "You know you could prosecute him for this."

"I know. Naomi told me, but where would that leave me and the baby?"

Nathan nodded, then spoke slowly. "Do you think he would agree to a false marriage ceremony to protect his child?"

"A what?"

"A false marriage. You and me. Someone has to claim the child and I could be the father as easily as Jameison. I was with him in Savannah. It would protect your name in years to come and it would also protect him, though I wouldn't mind seeing him go to prison."

Cynthia felt a great admiration, not unlike love, for Nathan. Tears sprang to her eyes. "You . . . you'd do that for me?"

He nodded.

"I . . . I think you'd better think about this more carefully, Nathan. There's nothing for you in an arrangement like that."

He grinned. "I, my love, would have the companionship of a lovely lady day and night, which is more than I dared dream in my present position."

She brushed away her tears. "You know, Nathan Tolliver, you're very much like a man I used to know. I loved him dearly."

"Then you'll think about it?"

"I . . . I don't know. It's all so complicated and confusing. I'll have to talk to Mrs. Jameison first."

"A good idea. She's the logical one to go to. Does she know of your condition?"

"Yes. She knows everything. She's been very supportive."

"A great lady, that one."

Cynthia agreed as she made a mental note to discuss Nathan's idea with Elizabeth. They had some time ago made their trek to the shallow grave in the woods and found nothing. Since then, Elizabeth had shown more confidence and deliberation in her treatment of Jameison. Cynthia wanted to ask why she hadn't as yet confronted Elijah, but had not had the opportunity.

It was close to dawn when Nathan walked Cynthia back to her own cabin. They had spent the hours getting acquainted. He hadn't pressed her for a decision, but had extracted the promise that she would think about it just before kissing her lightly and departing.

There were still muted sounds of singing coming from Jess's as she slipped in beside the sleeping Naomi. She knew that within a short time they were all expected to congregate at the big house with Christmas wishes for the master and mistress.

It's Christmas, she thought, and it will very soon be a new year. It can only be a better one for me. She drifted in and out of sleep for several minutes, experiencing bits of dreams first of Garrett and then of Nathan before they finally merged into one who was somehow her son.

Thirty-Three

Munsy was in the midst of spring housecleaning. She had been at it for days now, even having some of the rooms repainted. All the winter curtains and rugs were being cleaned and stored, replaced with the lighter, airier summer things. Floors were being stripped of old polish and newly applied. Heavy winter quilts and counterpanes were being beaten and folded with paper between the folds for storage. The bedding that could be was washed and hung to dry. All of Garidas was in a state of disarray. Outside, much the same process was going on. The cured tobacco had all been prized into hogsheads which stood in the barns awaiting shipment. Daniel had crews working daily on the grounds, cutting the recently-turned-green grass to an even height, clearing out and burning the new spring forest growth that threatened to encroach, both around the lawns and along the drive. He had set others to work clearing that part of the river road which ran through Garidas. Fields had been turned and harrowed and were ready for planting. The young, tender tobacco shoots were faring well and would now thrive when placed in warm soil.

Garrett and Jacob had taken refuge in the library, insisting Munsy leave them one place in all the confusion where they might conduct the necessary business of Garidas. They had been poring over accounts most of the morning.

"Late spring," Jacob commented as he turned from the window where he stood stretching.

Garrett looked up from the ledger into which he had been transferring figures of his latest purchases for Munsy. He laid his quill to one side, corked the ink bottle, and slammed the book shut.

"There, that's done." He rose and moved to the window beside Jacob. "It does seem to have finally turned spring. We should be able to plant the cottonseed next week and set out the tobacco shoots by the end of the month."

"You think cotton's worth all the trouble, Garrett?"

"I'm sure. Daniel's worked hard to clear the field for it. We'll plant all the seed we have."

Jacob moved to the liquor closet and poured them both a snifter of brandy.

"We haven't a thing to lose on the cotton, Jacob. Remember, our London agent said he'd buy all we could produce."

"I know, I know," Jacob settled into a chair beside the fire. Even though the days were warmer now, a fire was still necessary every morning. "It's just . . . well, I always have trouble adjusting to new things, I guess. Change ain't easy at my age, you know."

Garrett chuckled and leaned against the window sill. "No, I don't know. I don't even know how old you are."

"Pert' near old enough to be your pappy, I'd say."

Garrett looked incredulous. "You're joshin'!"

Jacob shook his head.

"Why, you're no more'n eight, maybe ten years older than me."

"Sixteen, near as I can figure. I think I'm fifty."

"You can't be. You don't look. . ."

"Hell, Garrett, you know it ain't years what make

a man old. It's thinkin' and feelin' . . . and lately I been thinkin' and feelin' old. The fever tuck a lot outa me . . . and us losin' Miss Cynthia like we done . . . it's been a long, cold and nasty winter. Just feelin' old, I am."

Garrett took a close look at his friend. It was true, the fever had taken its toll. His hair was now salt and pepper when only a few months ago it had been charcoal black. The lines in his face had deepened. New ones had been etched. "But fifty ain't old, Jacob."

"Oh yes, it is, Garrett, oh yes, it is. Jes' you wait and see how you feel when you're fifty."

Jacob seemed to be looking beyond him at something out the window. "I think company's comin'. Believe I just saw a flash of color through the trees."

Garrett turned to look, but could see nothing. "It's probably one of the hands is all." He turned back to face Jacob. He wanted to cheer his friend. The sadness in Jacob's voice and the sound of defeat frightened him.

"No, it's company. I see 'em now, just comin' into the clearing."

Garrett turned. "It's Alex McDaniel." He set down his brandy and both he and Jacob rushed from the room. They greeted Alex on the front walk.

"Alex, old friend." Garrett thumped him on the back. "I never, ever would have thought to see you in this part of the country."

Alex stretched his back and rubbed his posterior as he nodded acknowledgment to both of them. "Garrett, Jacob. Thought I'd take you up on your long-standing invitation. However, I'm not too sure but what I'll be wishin' I hadn't made the trip. My old bones won't take the jostlin' like they used to."

Garrett looked towards the drive. "Did you come alone?"

"And who'd be comin' with me? Ezra? He ain't straddled a horse in years, 'ceptin' for errands around town. Yes, I came alone. The roads seem safe enough and I met several travelers. Quite a bustle on the roads this time of year."

"Yes, everyone's getting ready for spring planting. But come on in, come on in. Can you stay long?"

"I was figuring on about a week. Have to get back to tend to my own plantin'." Alex stopped at the foot of the steps. "You have a beautiful place here, Garrett. A beautiful place. I can see why you're always so anxious to get back home."

"We like it, Alex. It wouldn't have been possible without Jacob. We've come a long way in the last sixteen years." Garrett put an arm around both men's shoulders and the three of them entered the main hall.

Alex's mouth fell open. "My God, Garrett. It's a real castle. Your ideas or Jacob's?"

"Actually, some of both."

"That ain't true, Alex," Jacob interrupted. "I tried to argue Garrett out of all these ideas. Houses just ain't built like this, you know."

"I know, I know. Jesus, Garrett, you shoulda been an architect."

Garrett laughed, a bit embarrassed. "Well, time will tell, Alex. One of these days, the whole thing may come falling down around our ears, then we'll know Jacob was right after all."

"I have to see the whole place, Garrett. The whole place. It's absolutely amazing."

"Well, I'm afraid it's a little torn up right now. Munsy's in the throes of spring housecleaning. Speaking of Munsy, she ought to have dinner about ready."

"I'll check," offered Jacob. "She's probably

already got an extra place set."

"Good. I'll show Alex to his room so he can freshen up."

After dinner, the three of them retired to the library. Garrett poured brandy all around and they settled into chairs around the fire.

"Now, tell us, Alex, what's happening in Savannah?"

Alex lit his pipe before answering. "Not much lately. You missed all the excitement. Around the first of the year there were what coulda been explosive situations."

"What happened to that group of country hotheads that was gonna meet there about three months ago?"

"I'll get to that, Jacob. To begin with, the first stamps arrived in Georgia about a month after you left, Garrett, on December fifth, brought by the ship *Speedwell*. At that time, there were over sixty ships anchored in the river, most of them ready to sail."

Garrett nodded. There had been near that many the day he left Savannah.

"However," Alex continued, "no one wanted to act as stamp distributor. I mean absolutely no one wanted the job."

"Can't say I blame 'em," Jacob spoke. "I sure wouldn't want the job, tempers bein' what they are."

Alex and Garrett nodded agreement. "Well, everything stayed pretty much the same till after the holidays. Then, on January second, over two hundred of our people assembled in front of Wright's. Rumors were flying that he was going to appoint a temporary stamp agent—we decided to confront him."

"Why weren't we informed of that assembly?"

"I tried to get word to you, Garrett, but the weather was bad that week after Christmas and our messenger had to turn back. We made a good showing, though, mostly from the coastal areas. Some messengers we sent into the back country couldn't get through, so don't feel too badly."

"It's probably just as well. That time of year, only a handful of us would have tried to go anyhow."

"That's how we figured it and with swollen creeks and rivers, you were safer here, I'm sure."

"But what happened?" Jacob was leaning forward eagerly.

"Wright met us at his gate, musket in hand. When we asked if he intended to appoint a temporary stamp distributor, he said—and these are his exact words—'Your action is hardly the manner in which to wait upon a governor. However, I will do my duty to the king, and if asked to temporarily appoint a stamp distributor, I will do so.' "

"Feisty little fellow, ain't he?"

"That he is, Jacob. We think it scared him pretty good, though. We dispersed, but vowed to reassemble if he took any action. Later we heard the only action he took was to move the stamps from Fort Halifax to the guard house in the center of town. Had them placed under heavy guard. The rumor was that Governor Wright spent several nights full clothed, ready for action." Alex chuckled at the last thought.

" 'Course, I can't say I wouldn't have done the same thing in his shoes, 'cause the very next day the stamp distributor, an Englishman name of George Angus, arrived at Tybee Island. He was brought to Wright's house where he began to distribute stamped papers."

"So now all papers have to have stamps." Defeat

sounded in Garrett's statement.

"Not at all. Everyone cooperated for a few days till the port was opened and the ships were cleared. Since then there's been a general agreement to buy no more stamps."

"But how do you conduct your business?"

"We manage. There's more'n one way to skin a cat, you know."

Garrett smiled. "You mean no one's bought stamps since the first of the year?"

Alex shook his head. "No one." He rose and walked to the fireplace, tapped the ashes from his pipe and placed it in his pocket before turning back to them. "What's more, there are no longer stamps to buy."

Garrett and Jacob both showed surprise. This they hadn't heard about. Over the months an occasional messenger had brought Garrett word of what was happening in the organization—but no stamps?

Alex continued. "You remember those hotheads you asked about earlier, Jacob?"

He nodded.

"Well, apparently when they were planning their trip to Savannah the rumor reached Wright that several hundred back country people were marching on the city. Elijah Jameison was in town about that time. We think he carried the rumor. Have you been keeping tabs on him, Garrett?"

"Not personally, but the friend of his wife's, Thomas Gilmore, that you suggested I contact, has been. I haven't heard anything from him, though, so I just assumed Jameison hadn't made any moves."

"He probably hasn't, and the information we believe he gave to Wright was at best misinformation. But about those purported hundreds of country people—as a precaution, when he heard they were coming, Wright had the stamps moved to Fort George on Cockspur Island, below town. 'Course, we know the threatened invasion of Savannah never took place, but it made Wright uneasy. The *Speedwell* was sailing on February second and, duty to the king be hanged, Wright had the stamps put on the ship and hauled out of Georgia.''

"Wright did that?"

"Yep. Guess he decided the damned stamps were too much trouble."

"But what happened to those who went to Savannah?" Jacob asked. "We only know of a couple who were in the group and they been close-mouthed about the whole thing."

"And no wonder." Alex sat back down. "With the stamps being gone, it kind of took the wind out of their sails. They were two days too late. Oh, they made a big show. Marched in with guns, flags, and drums just like they was ready to start a war, but nothing came of it. We kept a close eye on 'em, but the governor handled it all right. Expecting real trouble from the show of arms, he had them met by about a hundred rangers, sailors and armed citizens. There was only about a handful of 'em and when they found out the stamps were gone, they milled around for a while trying to think of what to do. Most finally wandered off into one tavern or another."

Garrett leaned back in his chair. "I'm glad the majority of our boys elected not to go. I just wish we had a better system of getting the news out here."

"Now that the weather is more settled, we could set up a courier system."

"Good idea, Alex."

"However, that may not be necessary at this time."

"What do you mean? It's important we have the news so we can decide on our actions."

"You're right, Garrett, but here, take a look at this." Alex reached into his breast pocket and handed Garrett a copy of the *Gazette*. "I thought I'd save the best till last."

Garrett sat up in surprise. "I understood Johnston had discontinued publication in December. Couldn't afford the stamps, so I heard."

"You heard right. This is the first issue he's printed in all these months."

Garrett scanned the paper, then smiling, handed it to Jacob. "It's true?"

"It's right there in black and white. Parliament is considering repeal of the Stamp Act. Now, fill our glasses and I'll tell you about the celebration Savannah had when that news came out."

Garrett moved to the liquor closet. "Do you really think it will happen, Alex?"

"Yes, Garrett, I do. And you know why? Because this is the first time all the colonies have united together against a foolish law passed by Parliament and imposed upon us. I think it's shown London that we're a force to be reckoned with, that we're not going to sit back and let them tax us into the poorhouse. At least, that's what I hope it shows 'em."

Garrett handed him his glass. "Well, let's pray you're right."

"Shall we drink to the Crown, gentlemen?"

"No, I think not," said Garrett. "Let's drink to the abolition of tyranny, instead."

"Amen," Jacob said as he stood and raised his glass.

Thirty-Four

Cynthia listened to Nathan's even, deep breathing for a moment before pressing her aching back against his warmth. She felt a contentment that was very closely related to happiness. The void Garrett's death had left in her life was beginning to fill and she often fantasized herself actually married to Nathan. They had been living as husband and wife since the first of the year. Only Elizabeth knew the truth.

Elizabeth was in full agreement with Nathan's plan when Cynthia presented it to her. Elijah had been more difficult to persuade. Cynthia was with Elizabeth at the time. They plied Elijah with drink before presenting him with the idea of a marriage between Cynthia and Nathan. His only real objection was he wanted Cynthia's child to bear his name. Choosing her words with great care, Elizabeth pointed out to him that all their slaves bore the name Jameison and any child born to a mother in bondage was, by law, also in bondage. Cynthia's child could, therefore, carry his name until Cynthia had fulfilled her obligation, at which time, the child might take the name of Cynthia's dead husband, so what difference did it make if she married Nathan Tolliver?

Jameison had smiled wickedly, sending chills up Cynthia's spine. She felt sure he had no intention of ever releasing her from bondage if he could avoid it. She looked at Elizabeth who sat serenely waiting for an answer and was glad she had her for an ally. Elijah finally gave the answer they wanted with the snide comment, "She's no good to me for a while, anyway. She won't be doin' him any good, either.'' Cynthia watched as Elizabeth struggled to mask her hatred for the man. Moments later his laughter rolled over her own taut nerves as they closed the door to his study behind them.

Elizabeth took Cynthia's hand and squeezed it. "Don't let him scare you. We'll take care of him in time."

"Why not now?"

"It wouldn't do any good now. There's no way to get to Savannah. The roads are nearly impassable this time of year. If we threatened him with an adultery suit, he'd know we could do nothing till spring, but he could do a lot of damage before the roads can be traveled. Soon as the planting is done, I promise. He can be useful then and it will give me time to look for an overseer. I really don't think we can handle this place without the help of a man."

"We?"

"Of course, dear. I was hoping you'd stay on with me. You have no place to go."

"Then why not ask Nathan to be your overseer? He told me he'd be a free man in June. It'd work out just right, wouldn't it?"

"We'll see, we'll see. It might at that if Nathan is agreeable. I've had the impression these past months, though, that he's anxious to have a place of his own. But we'll see. Right now, we have a wedding to plan."

Elizabeth had taken great joy in planning the wedding. It had been simple, but impressive. No one, not even Elijah, suspected that the "preacher" Elizabeth sent for was really a childhood friend of hers who was with the military at Fort Augusta, so convincing was he as the stern, solemn, man of the cloth.

"His father really was a minister," Elizabeth confided to Cynthia and Nathan, "and after the death of his parents, Benjamin received the remainder of his education under the Reverend Whitefield at Bethesda Orphanage. He knows how to act and what to say."

Cynthia moved closer to Nathan. Though she didn't love him like she had Garrett, she knew it would be easy. They had formed a workable bond and she had not been unhappy playing the role of his wife these past months. He was a good man, kind and soft-spoken, but Cynthia refused to let herself love him. She also refused to think about the kind of relationship they would have once the baby arrived. Except for sharing the same bed, and that out of necessity, they were more like brother and sister. She knew Nathan loved her. She could see it in his eyes, but so far he had kept a respectable distance between them, the only affection shown being an occasional kiss on the cheek. But what about after the baby? she wondered. *How will he react once I've returned to my normal shape?*

She turned over, trying to relieve the pain in her back. It had ached off and on for the last few days but tonight even the heat from Nathan's body would not give her relief.

She had never told Nathan the truth about the baby's father. She knew he deserved to know that much, but the time had never seemed suitable. *I have to tell him,* she thought. *It's not fair to keep that from him.* A light pressure rippled through her abdomen. She waited a few minutes, trying to contain her excitement and breathe normally. After the second sensation of pressure which gave her more pain in her back, she turned and shook Nathan awake.

"It's the baby. Go get Naomi."

Nathan looked at her groggily. "It can't be. It isn't time yet, is it?"

"Yes. Now, please hurry."

Nathan, fully awakened by the tone of her voice, jumped from the bed, pulled on his pants and went rushing from the cabin. In a few minutes he was back with Naomi.

"You think it's time, girl?"

Cynthia nodded. "I wasn't sure at first, but . . . but my water just broke."

"Now, don't get panicky, girl. You're built for it." She turned to Nathan. "Get me some water and some clean towels, then get out of here." She smiled when she saw the worried look on his face. "This won't take long and you'd just be in the way."

Cynthia moaned as the first real wave of pain shuddered through her body. Nathan moved to her side and took her hand. She squeezed it and tried to smile.

"You're a good man," she managed.

"Water and towels," Naomi ordered. "Then get out. This ain't no place for a man." She pushed him aside and began to strip the soaking bed, leaving one thin coverlet over Cynthia. When Nathan brought the towels, she spread one beneath Cynthia's hips and laid the others to one side. She straightened and placed her hands on her hips. "Go over to my cabin, Nathan. In a box under the bed you'll find some old rags of towels. Bring them. Sure be a shame to mess up all your pretty weddin' towels."

"It's all right," Nathan assured her. "It's for Cynthia . . . and the baby."

"Just ain't no sense in it, though. Go get my old ones. They don't look like much, but they're clean. Now move it afore this youngin gets here. And where's that water?" she asked as Nathan turned to leave.

He stopped at the door and rubbed his hands nervously on the sides of his pants. "I put some on to boil."

Naomi began to laugh. "Don't need no boiled water yet, boy. Won't need no hot water till we're ready to bathe 'em."

"But I thought . . . I mean, when my wife . . . my first wife. . ."

Naomi laughed harder as she pushed him out the door. "That's just to keep husbands busy and from underfoot. Now go get those old towels and bring back some cool well water. I'll be needin' it to bathe this girl's brow."

As soon as he was gone, Naomi had Cynthia turn on her side and began massaging her back where it hurt. "This won't take long, girl. Not long at all."

The early morning sun cast a rosy glow in the small room. Cynthia sat propped up with pillows looking at her son, his hair still damp from the washing Naomi had given him. Tears came to her eyes. All these months she had been so fearful the baby might have somehow been injured by her fall on board ship or the fever, but he was perfect, absolutely perfect. She could see so much of Garrett in him.

"He don't look nothin' like you." Nathan's voice startled her in the stillness of the room. He had stayed with her through it all. She looked up at him. He was standing at the head of the bed looking over her shoulder at the bundle she held. Naomi had left only minutes before. "He don't look nothin' like Jameison, neither."

Now's the time, she thought. She took a deep breath and, looking at the sleeping infant, spoke slowly and deliberately. "That's because Elijah Jameison is not the father of this child." She closed her eyes and waited. Nathan had never been really angry with her.

There was a long silence, then she felt the pressure of him sitting down beside her. She opened her eyes and looked into the soft gray of his.

He spoke quietly. "I knew that. It was too early." He paused a moment, searching the depths of her green eyes. "Who is?"

"Do you remember when I told you Christmas Eve that you reminded me of a man I once loved?"

Nathan's eyes took on a faraway look for an instant before he shook his head. "I'm afraid not. I think I was too shocked to remember much of that night, except I knew I loved you and I wanted you for my wife." He reached out and laid his hand over hers. "I still do."

"Oh, Nathan, don't make this any harder than it already is. If . . . if you would put the baby in his cradle and make some tea, we could talk."

Cynthia watched as he carefully took the child and laid him in the cradle he had built, covered him, then moved across to the fire to make tea. He's better than I deserve, she thought. Perhaps when we're both free, we could move away and have a real life. We could even marry if that's what he wants. No one need know I left a husband in England. Or we could live like Thomas and Fannie Gilmore did. No one would be the wiser, if we moved some place else.

When the tea was steeped, Nathan poured them both some then sat on the edge of the bed, waiting.

"His name was Garrett Carver," Cynthia began. "He helped me escape from London—from the wife auction. I fell in love with him and would have followed him to the ends of the earth. He . . . he died of the fever just days before our ship dropped anchor at Savannah."

"Carver . . . I've heard the name. A big planter, isn't he?"

"Yes . . . he was."

"So he was bringing you to America with him?"

"No. He didn't want me to come to America. I don't think he loved me until later, not really, anyway. He told me some real horror stories about women alone here, most of which I've found were true, but I was hopelessly in love by then and I was determined not to scare. I also thought it a good idea to put an ocean between Walter and myself. I knew what ship Garrett was sailing on but I had no money to pay my passage. I struck a bargain with the captain to travel as an indenture. Garrett didn't even know I was on board for some weeks because the captain kept . . . kept me prisoner."

"Prisoner?"

Tears came to her eyes. "Hush, Nathan. Let me finish. I . . . I need to tell this. He . . . the captain . . . he . . . he drugged me and . . . and he tried to rape me but there was a fire on board ship and he was summoned. After that he didn't . . . I don't know what happened . . . but he didn't try to rape me again. Instead, he beat me, tore my clothes to shreds and . . . and kept me prisoner. When I must have looked like the filthiest, lowest kind of slattern, he turned me over to some of his men to . . . to . . ." She couldn't go on. She buried her face in her hands. She finally looked up. "Fortunately, and I don't know why because one of them knocked me unconscious, they were unsuccessful in their assault."

Nathan set both their cups on the floor then gathered Cynthia into his arms. "Why didn't you tell me this before?"

"I . . . I've never told anyone all of it." She gulped for air. "I . . . I couldn't. It's . . . too painful to remember. Naomi knows most of it. Elizabeth some. No one else." She sat quietly for a moment, then continued. "Garrett found me after . . . afterward and took me to his cabin. By then the fever was running wild. Garrett and Jacob spent most of their time tending the sick. Almost everyone was sick, even the captain . . . or, or. . ." She sighed. "I don't know what would have happened if Captain Tarrillton hadn't gotten sick. Unfortunately, he recuperated. One of the men who . . . who tried to rape me came down with it. It wasn't long after that I got sick, and then Garrett. The last I knew, Jacob got it. I was well by then and was trying to collect supplies so we wouldn't have to leave the cabin. I'd heard the captain was up and about and I didn't want to be in his hands again. I was going after water when he surprised me. I remember falling. I guess I must have hit my head. After we dropped anchor in Savannah, he told me Garrett had died. He . . . he seemed rather pleased about it." Tears began to fill her eyes. She swallowed hard. "You know the rest. He sold me to Jameison."

"You believed this . . . this Captain Tarrillton when he told you Garrett was dead?"

"Yes. I . . . he was very sick, Nathan, and with no one to care for him . . . yes, I believed it."

"But didn't you ever think he might have lied?"

"I thought about it later, but no, I'm sure it's true. If Garrett were alive, he would have found me by now. We were going to be married. We were going to return to England. He planned to pay whatever Walter wanted for my freedom. I . . . I'm sure that's the one thing Captain Tarrillton told me that was true."

Nathan sat for a moment just looking at her. "I wish I had known. You can't imagine the torture I've gone through thinking you carried Jameison's child. Why did you let everyone believe it was his?"

"I didn't know what else to do. I knew I was with child before we left Savannah. I didn't plan it, Nathan. You must believe that. Not in the beginning. But after he threatened me and . . . and violated me the night we spent at Bent Tree, I decided I could claim he was the father and perhaps ensure the child a decent life." She sat very still for a moment staring off into space, then said quietly, "I just didn't know what else to do."

Nathan stood and walked away from her, then turned. "But why did you let me go on believing it? Surely you know how I feel about you. I would have protected you."

"Against Jameison?"

"You could have brought him up on adultery charges. A man doesn't have to get a woman with child to be an adulterer."

"At first I was afraid. I . . . I didn't know how it was here. Later, there was more to it than that. It has to do with Elizabeth. That's why I had to talk to her first about a wedding for us."

"Mrs. Jameison? What's she to do with it?"

"She knew from the beginning the child wasn't her husband's. I can't tell you how. She swore me to secrecy, but she wants to be the one to bring adultery charges against him or at least threaten him with it. She wants to get rid of Jameison. Something about an inheritance she doesn't want him to get his hands on."

"When's she going to do this?"

"Soon now. She said when the planting was done. She wanted time to find an overseer and if you agree to take the position, I think it will be soon."

"She spoke to me of the overseer position. I wasn't sure she was serious, Cynthia. If I'd only known, I'd already have given my answer. Why didn't you tell me earlier?" He paused. "That was it. I couldn't figure out why she would need an overseer and why me? Why she asked me and not him. It was more like she was just mentioning it. I thought little more about it. She's never said another word."

"But you'll do it?"

"Of course I will. At least for a while, if it will help you and her." He came and sat back down beside her, took both her hands, kissed them, then looked into her eyes. "I think you're two of the finest ladies I know."

Cynthia cast her eyes downward for a moment, then looked back at him. Pulling her hands free from his, she reached up, drew him to her and kissed him. He encircled her with his arms as she lay her head against his chest.

"I think I could learn to love you, Nathan."

He tightened his hold on her. "I had hoped you could."

They sat that way until the baby began to squirm and fuss in his cradle. Nathan stood and brought him to Cynthia.

"Have you chosen a name?"

"Yes, I have." She looked at him. "If you're agreeable, I'd like to name our son Nathan Garrett Carver. . ."—she paused and smiled—"Tolliver."

"I like it," Nathan said quietly. "I like it very much."

Moments later, Nathan was pacing the small room while Cynthia cooed to the baby. He stopped and looked out the window then moved to her bedside in quick strides.

"You know, when Jameison gets back from Savannah, there's going to be hell to pay. When he hears, he'll know it's not his child."

Cynthia looked up, her face glowing. "I know, but I refuse to think about it now. I'm too happy. I'm just glad he wasn't here to spoil today." She began to rock the baby in her arms and hum to him. "We'll call him Nate," she said. "It would be too confusing to have two Nathans."

Nathan sat beside her. "Cynthia, we have to think of Jameison. There's no telling what he will do to you. We're going to have to get you out of here—you and the baby."

"There's plenty of time, Nathan. He's only just left. He's not due back for two weeks. By the time he gets back we can lie about the date of birth and maybe he'll believe it's his. It would only be a little early then."

"You want him to go on believing it's his?"

"Only for a short time . . . until Elizabeth can confront him."

Nathan brushed a hand through his blond hair. "He'll learn the truth, Cynthia. Someone will tell him."

"Then Elizabeth will help us. I know she will."

"Very well, we'll consult Elizabeth. You'll need a few days rest, anyway, before you can travel." He sat watching her for a few minutes, then reached out and took hold of the baby's hand. "I'll try to be a good father to you, Nate," he whispered. "A very good father."

Gray eyes swimming with love and devotion met green aglow with happiness and contentment.

"I think I would have liked your Garrett," he said. "Look at all he's given me."

Thirty-Five

A late rain delayed the planting at Garidas for a few days so the day Alex left, Garrett rode with him as far as Birdsville. After a parting drink at Thaddeus Overby's, Alex took the stage road and headed downriver to Savannah. Garrett turned Temple northward. During his visit, Alex had renewed Garrett's interest in Elijah Jameison's activities and Garrett decided it was time to find out what the man was doing and perhaps pay him a visit. Before doing so, however, he felt he should consult Thomas Gilmore. Following the directions given him by Thad, he had no trouble locating the Gilmore house.

There was a flurry of activity as he rode into the yard. Children, both black and white vied for the honor of holding his horse. He dismounted and handed the reins to the nearest who was unmistakably one of Thomas Gilmore's sons. Garrett guessed him to be no more than eight years old. He squatted in front of the boy.

"Is your father home?"

Confronted by such individual attention from a stranger, the boy backed up shyly.

Garrett heard a door slam and stood. A dark-headed, round, little woman stood on the porch, wiping her hands on a towel.

"You children go on, now," she called not unkindly. "You, Peter, you may stay and hold the gentleman's horse."

Out of the corner of his eye Garrett saw the lad puff out his chest proudly. The other children moved to one side to let Garrett pass. He removed his hat, mounted the stairs, and greeted the cheerful-faced little woman.

"Mrs. Gilmore?"

"How may I help you, sir?"

"I'm Garrett Carver. Is your husband about? I'd like to speak with him."

"Oh, Mr. Carver," Fannie brushed loose hair back from her face, a bit embarrassed. "I've heard so much about you from Thomas." She turned and headed into the house. "I feel I should know you. Please do come in. I'll send someone after Thomas."

"Mrs. Gilmore, please. I . . . I don't want to be any trouble. I only want to talk with your husband. If you'll tell me where he is . . ."

Fannie turned. "No trouble at all, Mr. Carver, and most folks call me Fannie. I insist on that. And I also insist on you coming in. I'm not sure where Thomas is—in one of the outbuildings, I expect. I'll send someone to find him."

Garrett spread his hands in defeat and smiled. "Very well, Fannie. And I'm Garrett. On that, I insist."

"Good," Fannie said as she opened the door. She paused and turned to the little boy in the yard. "Peter, take Mr. Carver's horse down to the stable and tell Donny to tend her. Mr. Carver's goin' to be stayin' for supper."

"Fannie, I can't impose," Garrett protested as they entered the house.

"No imposition, I assure you. I know you must be tired from your long ride. Thomas told me you live someplace west of here. Really out in the wilderness, aren't you?"

"You might say we're a bit out of the way."

"I should say. Now, if you'll excuse me, I'll go

send for Thomas." She waved her hand toward one of the doors off to their left. "Go on into the sitting room. I'll be right back with some tea. Thomas will be glad to see you, I'm sure he . . ." She stopped in midsentence. "Would you prefer coffee?"

"If it's not too much trouble."

"No trouble at all. Always keep some warm for Thomas. He's gotten to be a real colonist, you know. Me? I still prefer my tea." She laughed.

Garrett entered the sitting room as Fannie disappeared through another door. While he waited, he admired the tastefulness with which the vivacious little woman had decorated her home. She had surrounded herself with lovely things, none of which, however, would make a man feel uncomfortable. The room exuded warmth, as did its mistress.

Fannie entered in a whirl of skirts, carrying a tray. Garrett noticed that in the few minutes she had been gone she had caught up the stray hair, removed her apron and added a touch of color to her cheeks. Of course, he admitted as he watched her, he could be wrong about the cheek color. It was probably natural coloring caused by her heightened activity. Garrett couldn't imagine anything about Fannie being unnatural.

"Thomas will be here shortly," she announced as she set the tray down and began to pour his coffee. "Please sit down, Garrett."

"Thank you, Fannie, but I've been sitting in the saddle most of the day. Would you think me too ungracious if I drink my coffee standing?"

Fannie laughed. "Not at all, but I'm going to sit."

"Please do." Garrett knew she had probably been on her feet since long before dawn.

"This is a lovely room, Fannie," he said as he accepted the mug she held out to him. "It's so warm, so comfortable."

"Yes, it is, isn't it?" she said as she looked around. "I'm glad you find it pleasing. Oh, by the way, I hope you don't mind a mug. Thomas always likes to drink his coffee from a mug."

"So do I, Fannie, so do I."

Thomas Gilmore walked into the room, wiping his hands with his handkercheif. "Garrett Carver!" his voice thundered with pleasure as he pocketed the handkerchief and extended his right hand toward Garrett. "By God, it's good to see you again."

Garrett had met Thomas Gilmore only twice before, but felt as though he had known him most of his life.

"Good to see you, Thomas," Garrett said as the burly red-head pumped his arm in greeting.

Thomas turned to Fannie who handed him a mug of coffee.

"I was just telling Fannie how much I like this room. It's so warm and friendly."

Thomas Gilmore flushed, a bit embarrassed. "Yes, I suppose it is."

"And tell me," Garrett continued. "Where did you find a treasure like Fannie?"

"That, Garrett, is a long story. Maybe some day I'll tell you."

Fannie stood to leave. "Thank you for the compliment, Garrett. Now, I know you men have things to discuss, so if you'll excuse me, I'll be seein' to supper. You are staying, aren't you, Garrett?"

"Of course, Fannie. I'd love to."

"Have you seen the latest *Gazette?*" Thomas asked as Fannie left.

"Yes, Alex McDaniel brought me a copy. He's been visiting at Garidas the last few days."

"It's good news, isn't it, Garrett?"

"That it is, Thomas. That it is."

Thomas Gilmore sat down. "Well, what brings you clear over here, Garrett? I know you didn't just come for the visit."

Garrett set his empty mug on the tray. "Alex brought me some disturbing news, Thomas."

"Oh?" Gilmore sat a little straighter.

"Yes. He thinks that possibly, just possibly your friend Elijah Jameison has been carrying rumors to Savannah. There's a possibility that Wright has him spying on the organization out here."

Thomas Gilmore burst into laughter. "To begin with, Garrett, Jameison is no friend of mine. He just happens to be married to a girl Fannie and I care a great deal about. As for him carrying rumors and spying, I don't know. The rumors, probably. The spying, doubtful. The man's a drunkard, Garrett. Any information he might be able to glean from some unsuspecting soul would be so twisted and out of proportion by the time Wright got it, it would be of no use to him. You know Wright far better than I do. Do you think he would rely on such a person?"

Garrett shrugged. "He might if he were desperate for information. Are you sure Jameison isn't just play-actin'? Using the guise of a drunkard as a way to get information?"

"Hadn't thought about it, but hell, Garrett, I've known Jameison for nearly eight years now. I've rarely seen him completely sober. I don't know why Elizabeth puts up with him." He shook his head. "Don't know how she's kept their place going—and made a profit, too."

"Thaddeus speaks highly of Mrs. Jameison. Says she's a real lady."

"Aye, that she is. She's been almost like another daughter to Fannie and me ever since her folks died, then a few years later her no-count brother just up

395

and disappeared. Shortly after that, she married Jameison. We knew nothing about it till it was done. We never could understand why. It wasn't like Elizabeth to jump into something like that."

"Well, perhaps I'll have the opportunity to meet her. I wanted to talk to you first to get your impressions of the man, but I do believe it's time I talked with Elijah Jameison."

"You know him?"

"Only slightly. I'm afraid we sort of locked horns the last time our paths crossed. He was very indignant about the way I run my business with the blacks."

"That's Elijah, all right. Finds it hard to keep from meddling in other folks business, be he drunk or sober."

"Well, I'm going to do a bit of meddling myself. I plan to head on up his way first thing in the morning and feel him out on this spying business. Thaddeus tells me he has a plantation up close to Fort Augusta."

"Elizabeth owns the land. Left to her by her family . . . but won't do you no good to head that way. Elijah left here about noon today—on his way to Savannah, so he said. He only stops by here to please Elizabeth and take her news of the Gilmores. He was gonna try to make Bent Tree by nightfall."

"Damn," Garrett said. "I won't have another opportunity for a while, either."

"You might go ahead and visit Mountview. Elizabeth would love the company and she might be more open with information about Elijah's activities than he would."

"That's a thought."

"Besides that, they have a new indenture on the place, a woman. She's a real pretty little thing. Might appeal to you, you being a bachelor. Fannie and I were quite taken with her. Feel sorry for her, though, the way Elijah treats his servants. When they passed through here, he wouldn't even call her by her real name. He's strange that way—wants his servants to have high . . ."

They were interrupted by a soft knock on the door. Fannie opened it a crack and peeked in. "Sorry to disturb you, Thomas, but Elijah just returned. His horse went lame the other side of Birdsville. He's walked back. I told him to stable the horse. I thought you'd want to know."

"Thank you, Fannie. Yes, I'm glad you told us."

"Good," said Garrett. "It will save me a trip up north and I can be on my way home tomorrow. I really hated to leave for so long anyway this time of year, but felt I had to."

At the supper table it was obvious to all present that Elijah Jameison had made a previous stop in Birdsville. When Garrett brushed by him to hold Fannie's chair, the man reeked of alcohol.

Once they were seated, Thomas Gilmore spoke. "We were talking about you just as you came in, Elijah."

Jameison glanced at Thomas sideways. "Oh?"

"Yes, I was just telling Garrett about your newest indenture. Being a bachelor, I thought he might be interested in meeting her."

"I think not, Thomas. No decent mon"—he stressed the decent, giving it an entirely different meaning—"would want any part of the little hussy."

Fannie gasped. "Elijah, I will not tolerate you speaking of . . . of that poor girl like that in my house."

"Please let me finish, Fannie. The girl went and got herself with child. No tellin' who the father is."

Garrett detected a note of sarcasm in his voice. "Anyway, Elizabeth thought it prudent to marry her off. She and Tolliver been married since just after the first o' the year."

"Well, at least Elizabeth is looking out for her." Fannie sounded somewhat relieved.

"That's Lizzie for ya," Jameison said. "Champion of the down-trodden. Think that's why she married me, Fannie?" He laughed.

Fannie folded her hands and placed them in her lap. "I'm sure Elizabeth had her reasons for marrying you, Elijah, none of which I know—but I do know Elizabeth and I'm sure they were good ones."

Jameison laughed again. "If only you knew, Fannie. If only you knew."

After supper the children were dismissed to their rooms. The men adjourned to Thomas's office while Fannie disappeared into the kitchen.

A few minutes later, brandy in hand, Thomas Gilmore excused himself, leaving Garrett alone with Elijah Jameison.

Jameison laughed as Thomas closed the door. "It's a goddamn ritual around here, Carver. Their little brats are more important to them than their guests. It never fails to irritate me when they go off like that. Do it every night, I guess—at least every night I'm here."

Garrett twirled the brandy in his glass. "Have you children, Jameison?"

"No, not yet, but soon now." He downed his drink and stood to pour another.

"Oh? Mrs. Jameison's expecting?"

"Elizabeth?" He laughed drunkenly. "Hardly. It's the little she-bitch Thomas and Fannie spoke of. She's a real piece if I do say so. Can't let Thomas know, though." He put his finger to pursed lips.

"He's the real true sort. Probably never humped anyone but little, fat Fannie in all his life. He wouldn't approve. Neither would Fannie. Lizzie knows, though. She's been very understandin' 'bout it all." He laughed—at some private joke, Garrett decided.

Feeling a bit embarrassed and wanting to change the subject, Garrett stood and walked to the fire as Jameison resumed his seat. He had often heard men speak of their servants as Jameison did. It always made him angry.

"Thomas tells me you were on your way to Savannah when your horse went lame."

"Aye. Just goin' for a wee bit o' pleasure afore the plantin' starts. You know how it is—with one what likes it but is out to here," he said, holding his hand in front of him to indicate a pregnant woman, "and another what don't—a man has to take his pleasure elsewhere. Some o' course, find it on their own doorstep, but not me. I never hankered after black flesh."

Garrett cleared his throat and struggled to control his anger. "Are you implying that I do, sir?"

Jameison waved his hand. "Course not, mon, course not—but even if I was, there ain't no shame in it. More'n one planter has stocked his slave quarters by plantin' his own seed." He chuckled at his own wit. "There's plenty o' talk, though, 'bout how you love your blacks—even givin' 'em freedom. Makes it hard on us honest, hard-workin' planters. Makes our blacks restless when they hear o' such goin's on."

Garrett fought for control. "It might interest you to know, Mr. Jameison, that my blacks would work to the death for me because I treat them decently. They have helped make me a wealthy man and with no ill feelings because they know freedom is in their future. Can you say the same for yours?"

"Can't say as I'd want to. It ain't normal to treat 'em like anything other than the animals they are. Some I got not even knowin' how to talk. I keep a tight rein on 'em and treat 'em good long as they behave. They know the punishment if they don't. Lizzie and I have done all right treatin 'em like most ever'one else does."

"So I hear. It's a lucky man who can marry into such holdings—and get a pretty wife to boot."

Jameison glared at him, but Garrett could see he couldn't decide if he had been insulted or not.

After a few minutes silence, during which Jameison poured himself still another brandy, Garrett spoke again. "Are you going to see Governor Wright in Savannah?"

Jameison's interest perked up. "The Governor? Why should I?"

"Oh, I just wondered. If you were, you could carry a message to him for me." Garrett paused to choose his words carefully. "We . . . we backcountry people have to do all we can to help during these trying times, don't we?"

"Not me. I help no one but meself."

"But surely now you'd want to help the governor if not before."

"Only if it helps me."

Garrett glanced toward the door furtively, using a bit of play-acting to convince Jameison they shared a conspiracy. He lowered his voice.

"Then you're also one of his spies?"

Jameison cocked his head to one side as though trying to understand the implication of Garrett's question. Failing to do so, he shrugged.

"Let's just say I try to stay on friendly terms

with him, that's all. I have passed on certain bits of information to him if I thought it would benefit both our causes. But what about you, Carver? Are you for or against the Crown?" He peered at Garrett closely, then laughed. "For it, o' course. You don't want to upset any apple carts."

Garrett nodded, as though he were in agreement with Jameison. "Well . . ."

" 'Cause if you did," Jameison continued, "someone just might pass a law making it illegal to free slaves like they done up in Virginia." He pushed himself out of the chair and bowed a bit unsteadily, but most ceremoniously. "I humbly apologize, Mr. Carver. I fear I have unjustly maligned you. For all your strange ways, I do believe you're on the right side. Somehow, I can see that now." He raised his glass in salute and drained it.

Garrett acknowledged his apology. "As for Governor Wright, though, will you or won't you take a message to him for me?"

They heard Thomas Gilmore outside the office door.

"Sssh," Jameison cautioned in a whisper. "We'd best not discuss this in front of Thomas. I 'spect he's got leanin's toward those sons of licentiousness."

Garrett nodded as Thomas entered the room.

"Gentlemen. Please forgive me, Garrett. It's a nightly ritual with the children. Elijah has become accustomed to it."

"Yes, so he told me."

Jameison poured himself another drink and, weaving from side to side, headed for the door. "I believe, gentlemen, I shall call it an evening. That walk back was quite tiring. Shall I see you in the morning, Mr. Carver?"

"I'm afraid not, sir. I shall be heading home at first light."

"Oh, too bad."

"I wish you a safe journey to Savannah."

Jameison turned. "Oh, I meant to tell you, I fear I'll not be going to Savannah at this time, after all. I'm going to rest my horse for a couple of days then return to Mountview. I know Thomas has no mount to spare, and even if he had, I've already lost a day and the plantin' won't keep forever." He directed his next remarks toward Thomas Gilmore. "Of course, Thomas, if I can once again rely upon your hospitality."

Gilmore inclined his head. "You're welcome, Elijah. You know that."

Jameison weaved through the doorway. When they were sure he was gone, Gilmore turned to Garrett, his face a question.

"Alex is right, Thomas. He's a dangerous man."

"Then he is spying for Wright?"

"Worse than that. He's an opportunist." Garrett paused a moment, thinking. "Maybe, Thomas, just maybe we can put his greed to work for us."

Thirty-Six

Cynthia could stand it no longer. She hated being ordered to stay in bed when she felt fine. There had been a constant parade through their cabin the last three days and she had enjoyed all the attention lavished on her and the baby, but today was different. It was lonely. Nathan had agreed to act as overser of Mountview once he was a free man so Elizabeth, wanting desperately to confront Elijah upon his return from Savannah, had decided that with Nathan's help she would undertake the planting. Everyone had been ordered to the fields before dawn.

Cynthia was surrounded by almost total silence, the only sounds reaching her was the twittering of birds in the trees behind the cabin. She knew the only activity would be at the big house and that's where she decided to go. It took her hardly any time at all to dress and straighten the bed. She felt good being on her feet again. She laid little Nate on her bed and fussed over him until she thought he looked just right.

"We're going visiting, little man," she said as she picked him up and cuddled him close to her.

She stepped out into the warm May sunshine and inhaled deeply of the fresh spring air. Life is glorious, she thought as she slowly made her way to the big house. She hadn't been on the front porch since the day of her arrival, but since she felt so good and a bit devilish, she decided to go to the front door like a real visitor. She was sure Elizabeth wouldn't mind.

She knocked and waited. Lettie, one of the young housemaids opened the door.

"Why, Miss Cynthia, what you doin' comin' ta this door?"

Cynthia swept through like the grand lady she felt. "I have come to visit Miss Elizabeth, Lettie. Will you tell her I'm here?"

Lettie's eyes widened in amazement. "Lawdy, Miss Cynthia. Miss Elizabeth ain't gonna like this. She powerful busy today."

"Oh, Lettie, please just go tell her I'm here."

"Yes, ma'am, but she ain't gonna like it none. None at all . . ." Lettie mumbled as she disappeared up the stairs.

Cynthia felt a twinge of guilt as she watched Lettie go. She had no right to give orders to Lettie or any of the other servants, yet she instinctively felt that because of the color of her skin, none of the blacks, save perhaps Naomi, would ever seriously question an order she gave.

She sat on the little bench to one side of the hall to wait and she was dumbfounded that she hadn't realized before the power she could wield at Mountview if she so chose. At the same time she realized she was caught somewhere between those with the real power and those without. She instantly knew that her alliance with Elijah counted for nothing. The color of her skin had little more influence. It was Elizabeth's silent acceptance and endorsement of her as the only other white woman on the plantation that assured her position.

I must leave, she thought. Lettie's right. Elizabeth will very likely be angry about this. She stood to go and was almost to the door when she heard Elizabeth behind her.

"I'm glad you came, Cynthia. I was ready for a break."

"We ... uh ... we"—she nodded toward the sleeping infant in her arms—"we felt like going visiting."

"Well, I'm glad you did." Elizabeth laughed. "Come on into the parlor and let me look at him. I didn't get much of a chance the other day. There were so many who wanted to pay their respects. Are you feeling well enough to be up and around?"

They entered the parlor and sat side by side on the divan.

"I'm a bit stiff and sore," Cynthia admitted. "But otherwise I feel just fine. Too good to be cooped up in that cabin any longer." She removed little Nate's outer blankets and handed him to Elizabeth.

"Oh, he is a lovely baby, Cynthia. Is he good?"

"Nathan and I think he's just about perfect. He sleeps constantly. I ... I worried about him sleeping so much at first because I took a nasty spill before I knew I was carrying him, but Naomi told me all babies sleep a great deal."

"Well, he is beautiful and I'm glad you came to visit." Elizabeth fussed over the baby for a few minutes, then handed him back to Cynthia. "If you'll take him, I'll go have Daphne fix us some tea and cakes." She rose to leave, then paused at the door. "I really am glad you came to visit this way. It's almost like having a real visitor, you know?"

Elizabeth had been gone only a matter of minutes

when Cynthia heard the sound of hoofbeats. She laid little Nate on the divan, folded a blanket in front of him and moved to the window to see if she knew the approaching rider. She pulled the curtain a little to one side and peeked out. She was horrified to see Elijah Jameison dismounting. Panic-stricken, she was rooted to the spot. She tried to think what to do as she watched him mount the stairs and cross the porch to the door. She heard him enter and finally, moved to action by the slamming of the front door, she bolted across the room and gathered the baby to her bosom, her eyes fastened on the closed door that separated them.

"Lizzie," he called. "Lizzie!"

Oh, dear God, don't let him come in here, Cynthia prayed. She knew she would have to face him eventually, but not now . . . not yet. She heard the click of the latch and it seemed an eternity before the door was swung open and she stood facing him.

Little Nate began to squirm in her arms. She knew she was holding him much too tightly. She tried to hold him even closer.

Cynthia thought they must have stood there like that for hours just looking at one another before Jameison finally walked into the room, leaving the door open.

"Well, well, what have we here? May I see?"

Cynthia shook her head and backed away. She could smell liquor on his breath.

He turned abruptly and walked to the liquor cabinet, his back to her. "A man's gone four days and all manner of things can happen."

Cynthia struggled to find her voice. "Why . . . why are you back so soon, Eli?"

He turned to face her. "My horse took lame just outside Birdsville. I laid over at the Gilmores' a couple of days, then decided I'd come on back and start the plantin'. Savannah can wait. It was strictly a pleasure trip anyway." He paused. Cynthia watched him. "Guess it's a good thing I did, or I might never have known, eh?"

Cynthia waited for the storm she knew was brewing beneath the calm exterior. She must think of a way to escape. Oh, Elizabeth, where are you, she pleaded silently.

He quaffed his drink and poured another. "You'll have to pay for this, you know . . . this deception." He paused. Cynthia took another step backward.

"I think twenty lashes given in front of everyone should help salve my ego, eh?" He chuckled. "It might be delicious to see the flesh ripped from your lovely body."

Cynthia sucked in her breath.

Jameison laughed. "Not too much, though. I'll be wanting it again real soon."

He downed the drink and pointed at her, glass still in hand. "You know, I think you're just what I figured you was." His whole expression suddenly changed. "A filthy little trollop!" he shouted. "Probably bedded every sailor on the *Providence*, eh? You and Tarrillton, you planned this, didn't you? Fever! Bah! And me tryin' to be so kind and gentle—givin' ya time to recover. Ha! The laugh's on me, ain't it?" He threw his glass down. "Damn it, woman, did ye think me stupid? Dinna ye know I'd be findin' out?" He began to move toward her.

Cynthia backed away, slowly. "It's not true, Eli," she said, trying to keep her voice calm. "None of it.

The baby's not yours. That much is true, but I had to . . . to tell you something. I didn't know what you would do if you knew I was with child when you bought my indenture." She managed to maneuver him around the room, all the while talking until she was between him and the door. She turned to run through the open portal just as Jameison lunged for her and the baby. He managed to grasp the blankets around little Nate.

"No!" Cynthia screamed. "No!" She let go of the blankets and holding the now-screaming infant to her breast, she turned once again toward the door. She was met by Elizabeth Jameison. White as a linen shirt, but steady with determination, Elizabeth leveled a pistol on Jameison from the folds of her skirt.

"Try to touch her or the baby again, Elijah," Elizabeth spoke slowly, "and I'll kill you."

"Get out of here, Elizabeth. This is none of your affair."

"You're wrong, Elijah. It is my affair. Everything here is my affair. Do you hear me? Everything. You will be out of this house and off my land within the hour or I will see you behind bars for adultery."

"Adultery?" Jameison began to laugh. "The little bastard's not even mine, Lizzie."

"I know that, Elijah. I've known it all along. The paternity of the child is not the issue. You *are* an adulterer and Cynthia is willing to testify to that fact."

Jameison sat down on the divan. "Go ahead, Lizzie. Try to get rid of me and I'll see you swingin' from a scaffold in Savannah. I swear I will."

"It won't work, Elijah. It won't work any longer. There's nothing left at William's grave. Cynthia and

I went to make sure of that late last fall. Animals completed his destruction years ago. I no longer have to be afraid of you."

The color drained from Jameison's face as he stood, the baby's blankets still in his hand. "I'll swear to it, Lizzie. I'll swear I saw you kill him."

"With no evidence, it will be your word against mine. Besides, you didn't see me kill him. You only helped dispose of the body and that for your own gain. You're just as guilty as I am, Elijah. Don't you think the magistrate will see it that way? And you know they're more lenient with helpless women."

Jameison laughed nervously as he moved forward. "Helpless? You've never been helpless in your life, have you, Lizzie?"

"Not hardly. Now get out of here and never come back or I will have you prosecuted."

Jameison bowed his head in defeat. "I guess I know when I'm beaten. It'll take me awhile to collect my things, though."

"You'll leave this house the same way you entered it, Elijah, with the few paltry pounds you have on your person."

"And Naomi. She's my property."

"Naomi stays. She's suffered enough at your hands."

"Very well, Lizzie—and glad to be rid of her I am."

Neither woman had noticed him twisting the baby's blankets into a whip-like affair until he swung it. As it coiled around Elizabeth's outstretched arms, the pistol discharged with a loud report, filling the room with heavy, gray smoke.

Dark red blood spread slowly across the front of Elijah's white linen shirt. He looked from the wound to them incredulously, then slumped forward and fell at their feet, red foam bubbling from his mouth and nose.

Elizabeth dropped the pistol and buried her face in her hands. "Oh, no, not again. Not again. It can't be. What have I done? What have I done?"

Cynthia, somehow, clear-headed, transferred the squealing infant to her left arm and knelt beside Elijah's inert body. "He's still breathing, but just barely." She looked up at Elizabeth who was white as a sheet. She could hear running footsteps of servants. She stood and grabbed Elizabeth by the shoulder. "Get hold of yourself, Elizabeth. The servants are coming. It was an accident, remember that, an accident. You didn't do it on purpose."

Elizabeth looked at her with a blank stare.

"An accident," Cynthia persisted. "An accident."

Elizabeth nodded numbly.

Cynthia retrieved the baby's blankets, shook them out and wrapped them around him, rocking him gently. She looked at Elizabeth as she stepped through the door and met Hadley, Lettie and Daphne just coming into the entryway. She closed the door behind her. Hadley was the logical one to send, but they would need his strength. She looked from one to the other of them.

"Hadley, Master has had an accident. Miss Elizabeth is with him. Go to her. She'll need your help."

Hadley nodded and disappeared into the parlor.

She turned to Lettie. "Can you ride a horse?"

The girl nodded.

"Good. We need Mr. Nathan right away. Do you think you can find him?"

The girl nodded again.

"Master's horse is tethered out front. Take it. Tell Mr. Nathan that Master had an accident and to come right away."

The girl nodded, but made no move to leave.

Cynthia stamped her foot impatiently. "Then get going, damn it!"

The girl turned and ran out the door. Cynthia watched her leave then turned back to Daphne. "Where is everyone?"

"Only ones here at the house is ol' Josie and some of the kitchen help. Miss 'Lizabeth sent the rest o' them to the fields to help Mr. Nathan."

"Here." Cynthia placed little Nate in Daphne's care. "Send one of the kitchen girls to turn back Master's bed. We should try to get him upstairs and make him comfortable."

Daphne nodded and left. Cynthia took a deep breath before opening the door to the parlor.

Hadley had removed a scarf from one of the tables and stuffed it inside Elijah's shirt to slow the bleeding. Cynthia knelt beside Hadley. Elijah was struggling for air, his face ash gray.

"He gonna die, sure, Miss Cynthia."

"Yes, I know." Cynthia bit her lower lip. "Do you think we can get him upstairs?"

"No, ma'am. Better to leave him here." Hadley sounded very sure of himself.

"Do you know anything about medicine, Hadley?"

The servant shook his black head. "No, ma'am. Mabel use to be the one what done the fixin' up o' things like this, but she done gone near blind now. Only other one ever done any people nursin' round here is Miss Elizabeth." He nodded in the direction of the divan and for the first time, Cynthia noticed Elizabeth. She was drawn up at one end of the divan, rocking back and forth, her arms folded across her stomach. Her eyes stared out into space, seeing nothing.

Cynthia turned her attention back to Elijah. "Is there nothing we can do, Hadley?"

The elderly black shook his head. "Jes' stay with him till it's over, Miss Cynthia, that's all."

A scant half-hour later, Cynthia had Elizabeth in her own room resting. She and Hadley had persuaded her to drink enough brandy mixed with water to allow her to relax. Elizabeth had complied much as a child might, but hadn't spoken a word to either of them.

When it was finished, they covered Elijah's still form with a sheet and both of them were sitting on the top porch step when Nathan came into view astride Jameison's mount. Cynthia met him halfway across the clearing and quickly told him what had happened. She felt a great weight being lifted from her shoulders as Nathan took charge.

He told the other servants the pistol had discharged accidentally when Master Jameison was showing Miss Elizabeth and Miss Cynthia how to use it should they ever need it for protection. No one questioned the story.

They buried Elijah the next morning.

"He always wanted to go to court," Elizabeth told them wryly. "Bury him on the east side of the house. That's as close as he'll ever come to getting there."

She hadn't spoken another word. She was absent from the graveside.

Thirty-Seven

July, like the end of harvest, was an easier, almost lazy time of year for planters, both large and small. Crops had been planted weeks before and aside from the never-ending hoeing of weeds, a task assigned to field hands, it was now up to nature to reward them for their labors. It was a time when animals needed minimal care, having been herded onto some of the seemingly endless lush pastureland for the summer, when carefully tended gardens began to show signs of producing the fresh fruits and vegetables so sorely missed during the long winter months. July was a time for socializing with one's neighbors and friends, for traveling to visit distant relatives. Houses were opened late in the day to facilitate ventilation and many a warm evening was spent enjoying idle, relaxed conversation in yards or on porches waiting for a cooling breeze.

Garrett most particularly enjoyed this time of year. It gave him and Jacob an opportunity to spend time together as they had years before. Unlike those first years, however, when all their could-be lazy days were spent clearing new land, they could now go fishing if they chose or ride over the land they both loved. Or, as today, they could be returning from a trip to Savannah which had been planned strictly for pleasure, an unthought of luxury during their early years together.

The sun was just touching the western horizon. They could see Birdsville in the distance. Both men rode easily, shirt sleeves rolled up, collars open. It had been a warm day. They had shed their coats early and tied them on behind their saddles. Neither had spoken much throughout the day, but then there was little need for conversation between the two. Each seemed to anticipate the thoughts of the other when a stop or change in pace was needed.

Garrett smiled to himself. He was glad he had suggested the trip. It had been just what Jacob needed. He seemed more himself now, having been pulled from the depression he had let get hold of him these past weeks. It couldn't have come at a better time, Garrett thought.

"Sure were lucky," Jacob muttered for what must have been the twentieth time since they left Savannah the day before.

"You're reading my thoughts again, Jacob."

Jacob turned slightly in the saddle and smiled. "I never dreamed I'd see such a celebration as there was in Savannah the other day."

"I'm just glad to see you smiling again, friend."

"What's not to smile about? I was beginnin' to wonder if I'd live to see the repeal of the Stamp Act."

"And why not?"

"Oh, I don't know. Just seemed last year was a bad one. Guess I needed a change. This trip did the trick. I feel ten years younger."

"Couldn't have anything to do with the little wench I saw you dancing in the streets with, could it?" Garrett teased.

"It might," Jacob conceded. "It just might at

that. Cute little thing, wasn't she?"

They rode in silence for a few minutes.

"Yessir, we sure were lucky to be in Savannah when we were," Jacob muttered.

The long awaited repeal of the Stamp Act had been handed down in Parliament on March eighteenth. Most were in agreement that the colonies' boycott of British trade was what finally convinced the Crown of the serious consequences of the act. When word had reached Georgia only two days ago, Garrett and Jacob had decided to cut their Savannah trip short and return to Birdsville with the good news. They had waited only long enough for James Johnston to put out a special edition of the *Gazette,* several copies of which they carried with them. Their time had not been spent idly because all of Savannah turned out the night the proclamation was read publicly to partake in the celebrations. Garrett had been pleased to see that even James Wright looked happy and relieved that this burden had been lifted from his shoulders.

It was almost dark. Less than a mile from Birdsville they spurred their horses into a gallop and rode into the little settlement whooping like a couple of wild Indians. Within minutes, a small gathering was collected around them. Garrett dismounted and, untying the small bundle behind his saddle, began to distribute copies of the *Gazette*. Jacob did likewise.

"It's been repealed!" they kept shouting over and over.

The crowd joined them in their reveling, some stopping long enough to carry one of the papers to lamplight to see for themselves that what they were told was true.

Thaddeus Overby was one of the last to join the crowd. When Garrett spied him, he pulled him to one side.

"We need to send messengers, Thad. We need to spread the news and those in the organization deserve a real celebration. We'll call a meeting."

By daybreak the next day, riders had been sent out in all directions to inform the populace of the repeal of the Stamp Act. Jacob had left for Garidas, telling Garrett he wanted to be the one to carry the good news home. Garrett and Thaddeus spent the day going over plans for a celebration for their Liberty Boys, as they had privately come to call them, and late in the afternoon, Garrett mounted Temple and rode out to Thomas Gilmore's to carry them the good news. He knew they had probably already been informed, but he had missed a home environment while in Savannah and he knew he would find one with Thomas and Fannie. He was also anxious to see if more had been heard from Elijah Jameison.

Thomas and Fannie greeted him warmly and insisted he stay for supper, which he had known they would do. Their oldest daughter, Jane, was home after completing her education and Garrett found himself charmed with her company. He also found himself comparing Jane with Cynthia and realized with a wrenching of his heart how much he still missed her.

After supper, while Thomas and Fannie were upstairs with the younger children, Garrett and Jane wandered out onto the porch.

"A terrible tragedy for Mrs. Jameison," Garrett said. He had asked Thomas earlier about

Jameison's activities and had been informed of his death.

"Yes," Jane said softly. "I feel so sorry for her. She's almost like a sister to me. She's had so much tragedy in her life. Mama has sent countless invitations for her to visit since it happened but they've all gone unanswered. That's why we're going there next week. Mama and Papa didn't want to intrude on her grief any sooner."

"How did it happen? Do you know?"

"Papa said, according to the message they received, it was an accident. Elijah was showing Elizabeth and Mrs. Tolliver how to handle a pistol and it discharged. Mrs. Tolliver—that's the bond servant Elijah bought last year. I haven't met her but Papa says she's a real beauty. I guess Nathan is a very lucky man." Garrett could detect a hint of bitterness in her soft voice. "Seems odd," she continued. "I know Elizabeth could handle weapons. She showed me once when we were little more than children. Her father taught her because of the trips they made out here when it was more wilderness than it is now." Garrett could see the shrug of her shoulders in the dim light filtering through the gauzy curtains of the dining room where servants were busily clearing the dinner table. "Oh, well, I suppose it was probably more for Mrs. Tolliver's benefit. I'm sure Elijah knew Elizabeth needed no instruction."

A slight breeze caressed them and Garrett could detect the faint scent of flowers and knew it came from Jane. He had noticed it earlier when he held her chair. He shifted from one foot to the other a bit uneasily. He glanced toward the open doorway.

"I hope your parents come soon. I really must be

heading back to Birdsville."

Garrett could sense she knew of his discomfiture. He felt she was totally aware of the effect she was having on him in the soft summer darkness. She did not, however, betray a thing.

"In that case, Mr. Carver, I shall send for your horse. You know, of course, Mama and Papa both made it clear that you're more than welcome to spend the night."

"Yes, I know . . . and I thank you and your parents, but the road is good, the moon is out and I promised Thad I would return tonight. Many will have already gathered by now and he may need some help keeping the celebrating within limits."

"If you'll excuse me, then, I'll see what's keeping Mama and Papa." She disappeared through the door in a rustle of skirts.

Garrett relaxed when she left. It's still too soon, he told himself. She's a lovely girl but you're still comparing every girl you meet with Cynthia. Besides, it would seem she also has a bit of a broken heart to mend, he thought, as he recalled the sound of her voice when she spoke of Nathan Tolliver.

Within minutes he had said his goodbyes and was so deep in thought as Temple carried him away from the Gilmores' that he hardly noticed the coach he passed at the end of their drive.

Naomi sat beside Elizabeth Jameison and held her hand. Darkness had descended but she knew they were close to the end of their journey. She hoped the Gilmores wouldn't mind their arriving unannounced. They had sent so many invitations which had gone unheeded, no one at Mountview being sure Elizabeth even understood. She was, for the most part, lost and silent in her own world. Nathan had decided only this morning that perhaps a change was what she needed. Naomi, who had become Elizabeth's constant companion, agreed and they had set out late in the day, Naomi and Nathan both knowing full well they would arrive at their destination after dark. Nathan had wanted to see them safely to the Gilmores' himself, but had, at the last moment, delegated the responsibility to Shires, the Jameison's usual driver, telling Naomi he feared the loss of hands if he left. Naomi had nodded in understanding as he handed them into the coach.

Nathan Tolliver had taken complete control of Mountview after the accident. Someone had to and all agreed Nathan was the logical choice since the mistress had already promised him the overseer's job when his indenture was up in a few weeks. During the week following Jameison's death, some of the younger, more willful blacks disappeared and Nathan had to let them go, knowing he had no authority with which to stop them. He told Naomi he considered sending for Thomas Gilmore, but hesitated when he realized Gilmore had no more authority over Elizabeth's affairs than he himself had. Then they were all relieved when Elizabeth seemed to be totally herself once again. It only lasted for a few days, but during that time, she signed documents giving freedom to both Nathan and Naomi and giving Nathan full authority as overseer of Mountview to conduct necessary business. Cynthia was hurt because Elizabeth had not also signed her papers of release, but both Nathan and Naomi had convinced her it was most likely an oversight on Elizabeth's part, and one that would probably be rectified once Elizabeth was in full control. After all, they reasoned, how long could one grieve over a no-good like Jameison. Only Cynthia knew there was more to it than that.

It was a warm summer night and Naomi had left the curtains open. She took only cursory notice of the rider departing the Gilmores' as they turned into the drive, wondering briefly what someone else was doing out this time of night.

When the coach pulled up in front of the house, they were greeted enthusiastically by the elder Gilmores and Jane, all of whom Naomi knew well from past visits. She smiled with some satisfaction as Elizabeth seemed to come back to their world long enough to greet their host and hostess before the invisible veil was once again dropped.

Fannie looked to Naomi for an explanation.

Naomi shook her head. "Could we see her to bed first, Miz Gilmore? I'm sure she's tired after the long, hot ride."

"Of course. How stupid of me." Fannie nodded to Jane who rushed ahead of them to ready a bed for Elizabeth.

Naomi took Elizabeth's arm and spoke to her as she would a child. "Come along, now, Miss Elizabeth. Miz Gilmore and I's gonna help you to bed."

Elizabeth looked at her and smiled as they led her into the house.

Later, Naomi sat at the kitchen table with Thomas and Fannie Gilmore. She told them of all that had transpired at Mountview since Jameison's death.

"Mr. Nathan is doin' right well," she concluded. "He wants desperately to hold ever'thin' together for Miss Elizabeth. We know she can't go on grievin' forever."

Fannie shook her head. "I think it's more than grief, Naomi, if what you say is true."

"Every word of it, Miz Gilmore. Every last word, I swear."

Fannie turned to her husband. "What do you think, Thomas?"

Gilmore stood, jamming his hands into his pockets. "I think, Mrs. Gilmore, this is something we should discuss privately."

Having been reminded of her position, Naomi stood to leave. She could see the fire smoldering in Fannie Gilmore's eyes and was glad she wasn't Thomas.

Fannie stood and Naomi knew she was trying to ease an awkward situation when she spoke cheerfully. "I trust you will sleep well, Naomi. I'm glad you and Mr. Tolliver decided to bring Elizabeth to us, even unannounced. My, it's been almost like a party around here tonight. First Mr. Carver and now Elizabeth."

Naomi turned at the door. "Mr. Carver? That must be the gentleman I saw riding out."

"Yes, it must have been. Garrett brought us good news, the repeal of the Stamp Act."

Naomi nodded and smiled then left, closing the door behind her. She could hear the beginnings of an argument as she made her way through the unfamiliar house.

"Thomas Gilmore, if you ever—"

"Jesus, Fannie, she's only a servant."

"That's right, Thomas, a servant, not a slave and I believe her. If Elizabeth saw fit . . ."

Naomi could well imagine Thomas Gilmore being

defeated by the fiery little woman he loved.

She lay awake on her pallet beside Elizabeth's bed long into the night wondering where she had heard the name Garrett Carver before this evening. She finally remembered and was sure she was right. But how could it be? Cynthia said he died on board ship. She turned over to sleep knowing it would be no problem to find out from the Gilmores' house blacks.

Early the next morning, while the house still slept, Naomi searched out Sophie. After a few minutes conversation, she questioned Sophie about the rider she had noticed the night before when she arrived. Sophie confirmed her suspicions and Naomi wandered back into Elizabeth's room thinking how to solve this new dilemma. She cared for both Nathan and Cynthia. She had seen a bond growing between them these past months and did not like to be the one to sever it. She knew, however, that regardless of her actions, one or the other would eventually be deeply hurt.

Thirty-Eight

The private celebration Garrett and Thad had planned for their Liberty Boys became almost a full-fledged festival, rivaled only, in Garrett's mind, by Guy Fawkes Day in Savannah. It seemed as though everyone in the countryside had wanted to attend and most brought their families. The awareness of the long harvesting days ahead seemed to produce a boisterous, festive atmosphere with prizes being put up by first one planter and then another for the hastily organized races and contests of marksmanship. One could dance in the center of town almost any hour of the day or night and gambling was heated around the ever-present cockpits. Several young men organized a game of football and none walked away from the rough-and-tumble scrimmage without at least a bloody nose or black eye to show for his participation.

The reveling had drawn to a conclusion after two long days and nights and Garrett had returned to Garidas where the clear, warm summer days coupled with the late spring rains had precipitated an early harvest. Daniel made it quite evident that even though he was willing when necessary, he was glad this year's harvest was not totally in his hands.

For the past few weeks now Garrett had been up every day long before dawn and was more often than not in the saddle by four-thirty. Jacob rode with him some days, Daniel others, but usually he spent the days alone going in one direction while Jacob went another, riding from field to field lending a hand here, offering advice someplace else. A new barn was being built to store the cotton crop and the existing ones were beginning to fill. Already the oats, barley and flax had been harvested and stored. The last of the corn was being shelled and milled and most of the people had moved on to the large wheat fields. The tobacco plants stood over six feet tall and would be ready to cut within a fortnight. Jacob still scoffed at Garrett's belief in cotton but even he was impressed by the healthy green growth that promised an abundant crop.

Garrett welcomed the long, hard days which left him little time to think, when he could do little more than fall into an exhausted stupor shortly after the evening meal, occasionally while still at the table. Munsy clucked over him daily and even with all her duties during this busy season found the time to lecture him regularly. He knew she was right, that he was still being affected by his bout with the fever and that he should take it easier and delegate more of the work to Daniel, but he found he couldn't—partially out of guilt over having been absent the year before and partially because he simply needed to be occupied, to have no time to think. He found it difficult to put his feelings into words, but one day he did make an attempt to explain to Munsy, after which she watched him closely, but said little.

It had been almost a year. He still found himself thinking of Cynthia. It seemed to him as though each season brought new and varying thoughts about her. He couldn't help but wonder and speculate on the different phases of life she would have enjoyed as mistress of Garidas—and those she would have found tedious and tiresome. He often found himself in a dream world where he could visualize her finding joy in the smallest wonders of nature. He occasionally thought he felt her presence in the house and he could imagine her going about the tasks that Munsy so capably handled.

To his surprise he discovered that each time he thought of her it was a little less painful and he knew that someday the brief time they had together would be in proper perspective for him—a bittersweet memory to be treasured forever.

One morning late in August, he caught Munsy eyeing him critically as he downed a snack of beer and cold ham to tide him over until breakfast. He smiled in her direction.

"You lookin' some better here lately, Mr. Garrett. Not like you was so lost."

"I am better, Munsy. The hard work has been good for me. I feel strong as an ox." Garrett ignored her reference to Cynthia.

"An eatin' like one, too." Munsy paused as she poured him more beer. "Better drink up. Gonna be a scorcher today."

Garrett nodded agreement as he looked out the open doorway. He wiped his hands on a napkin and stood. Munsy reached out a hand and placed it on his forearm. She looked long and hard into his eyes.

"You ain't so lost anymore, are you, son?"

Touched by her concern, Garrett bent and kissed her weathered, black cheek. "I'm fine, Munsy. Really fine. I'm looking forward to things again. Why, by Muster Day . . ."

Munsy pushed him away playfully. "Muster Day! Good Lord, Garrett Carver, ain't you gettin' too old for them boys games?"

Garrett threw his head back and laughed. "Never,

Munsy, never. Besides, I've been made a captain this year, so I have to go."

She made a motion toward the door. "Well, you'd best be off to work then so's you can play when the time comes."

Garrett stepped outside and found the morning air still close. It promised to be a hot, muggy day. He was smiling to himself as he walked toward the stable. It was true. He was looking forward to things again. The next big event in this part of the country would be Muster Day which was held in Birdsville each year at the end of harvest. Having missed last year and having been appointed a captain even in his absence, he was looking forward to it with some eagerness this year.

It was almost the end of the work day and the field Naomi had been working was finished. She and the other women had helped load the last sheaves of wheat onto the cart. The other women had headed toward their quarters to fix the evening meal for their families, but Naomi, pretending to want a drink of water, had accompanied the cart to the barn, then when no one was paying any heed she had slipped out the far door. She and Elizabeth had been back at Mountview for over a week now and since Elizabeth seemed in complete control again, she had not had an opportunity to speak to Nathan. That was what she had decided she would do, and leave the telling of it to Cynthia up to him.

She found him in the tobacco field where she knew they had started cutting and spearing the bright green leaves earlier in the day. Nathan looked up briefly. He was showing one of the younger boys how to correctly spear the broad leaves close to where they had been cut through the thick stem. Satisfied that the boy understood, he handed over the long thin stick and walked toward Naomi, mopping his brow on the sleeve of his shirt.

"Is something wrong, Naomi? Someone been hurt?"

" 'Course not. Do I look in a panic?"

"What are you doing here, then?"

"We finished up the field we was workin'. I need to talk to you and I thought maybe we could walk in together tonight."

Nathan nodded. "I'll be with you in a minute, Naomi. My mount's tethered up by the barn."

"I'll start on ahead then."

Within minutes Nathan had caught up with her. He dismounted and, reins in hand, walked beside her. Once again, he ran his arm across his forehead.

"Sure a hot one today."

Naomi nodded in agreement. "Feels like it might cool some tonight, though."

"You said you wanted to talk to me, Naomi. Is it about Mrs. Jameison? I know we haven't had a chance to speak since you returned from the Gilmores', but she seems to be herself again and I didn't think it necessary."

"It's not. I think Elizabeth is herself again. I hope forever, but only the Lord knows." She had practiced over and over what she would say to Nathan, but now she hesitated. "No, it ain't about Elizabeth."

Nathan waited patiently while they walked a few more paces. Finally, Naomi stopped in the shade of a tree, took a deep breath and looked him in the face. Her dark eyes bored into his light ones.

"Tell me, Nathan Tolliver, are you and Cynthia living like husband and wife in every way?"

Nathan was so surprised he actually took a step backward. In a moment he regained his composure. "I . . . I . . . what kind of question is that, Naomi?"

"I know ya wasn't afore the babe came and I know you ain't married—at least, I figure you ain't and I know for sure the babe ain't yourn or Jameison's."

Nathan peered at her closely. "How do you know all this?"

"I knew most of it long before anyone else around here. Remember, I lived with her. She told me some about her life before and I know now she's told you, too."

Nathan nodded. "Go on."

Naomi took a deep breath and tried to calm her hands for which she could find no place. She finally clasped them behind her.

"Well, I know she left a husband in England. That's why I figure ya ain't married for real. I also know the father of the babe was a man who sailed on the same ship and now Cynthia thinks he's dead. I ain't told another soul. I don't aim to, though I figure Elizabeth knows some of it or she wouldn't have helped you two pull this thing off. . . ."

Suddenly Nathan grabbed her by the shoulders. It shocked Naomi into silence.

"Tell another soul what, Naomi? What is it you're trying to say?"

"I . . . I . . . he ain't, Nathan. I know I've done this poorly, but he ain't dead. I heard about him at the Gilmores'. I might have even seen him though it was dark and I couldn't say for sure."

Nathan stared at her, not believing.

"I . . . the night we arrived, Mrs. Gilmore said a Mr. Garrett Carver had just left. I'm sure we passed him at the end of their drive."

Nathan shook her. "Are you sure that was the name, Naomi? Are you sure?"

She nodded. "Much as I hate it, I'm sure."

Nathan dropped his hands to his sides. His shoulders slumped visibly. Naomi wanted to reach out and comfort him, but knew comforting would only make it worse. She knew he wasn't seeing her or anything else, but unable to stand the pain in his eyes, she turned away.

After a few minutes silence, she spoke, her back to him. "I'm sorry, Nathan. I really am, but I thought you ought to know. I've spoken to no one else about this. I won't. If Cynthia is to know, I feel it's your place to tell her. I . . . I wouldn't have told you, either, but you had to know. If I could run into him or the hearing of him, so could she." Brushing tears from her cheeks, she walked toward her quarters without looking back.

Several minutes passed before Nathan realized Naomi had left. He turned and found his horse waiting patiently where he had dropped the reins. He leaned his head against the side of her neck and stroked her. She neighed softly.

"If it's true," he said, "I have to tell her."

He gathered the reins and turned toward home, the horse plodding along behind him. He was not in his usual hurry to greet Cynthia and little Nate tonight.

Cynthia noticed a difference as soon as he walked in the door. He looked more than tired. She had come to know Nathan's moods well and something was troubling him.

She approached him cautiously. "You're back early today. Little Nate's still sleeping. Has . . . has something happened? Has someone been hurt?" She knew accidents in the field were an ever-present danger during harvest season.

"No, no one's been hurt." He sat down heavily and leaned on the table.

Cynthia automatically moved to pour him a cup of hot coffee. She placed it in front of him.

"But something's troubling you. I can tell."

Nathan looked up into her face which had taken on a worried look. "Do you really know me that well?"

Cynthia blushed and turned away. "Well . . . I . . . there are some things I notice more than others." She chose not to tell him how her thoughts had been running the last few weeks. She had decided it would come in time and would be better for the waiting until they were both ready.

"Sit down, Cynthia. Please. There's something I have to tell you."

She sat opposite him and a shiver ran through her as she looked into his eyes for the first time since he entered. She reached out her hands for his. He pulled away.

"What is it, Nathan? What's happened?"

He set the coffee aside and ran a hand over his face. "I learned something today that's going to change things between us, Cynthia. It's going to change everything."

Fear gripped her for an instant as she thought back over the last year. Then she realized she had nothing to fear. She had told Nathan everything about herself. There was nothing he could have found out about her to change his feelings.

"But, Nathan, I told you everything. If you've heard something, it has to be a lie."

"I know, Cynthia. I appreciate your honesty, but it wasn't anything about you."

She rested her hands in her lap and waited. Nathan

stood and walked to the open door, leaned against it for a moment then silently closed it. He turned back.

"I wish I didn't have to tell you this, but Naomi's right. You should know."

"Naomi? I've hardly seen her since she and Elizabeth returned from the Gilmores.' "

"Yes, I know. I believe that was planned on Naomi's part."

"What was planned? Nathan, what's going on?" If it weren't for the look in his eyes, she could almost believe he and Naomi were planning some sort of surprise, but no, whatever it was, it wasn't pleasant.

Nathan walked back to the table and leaned on it, directly opposite her, hands spread wide. He looked at her for a long time.

"Cynthia, you know I love you."

She nodded.

"I would never do anything to hurt you."

She nodded again.

He took a deep breath, then cast his eyes downward. "Garrett Carver is alive."

Cynthia was stunned. She couldn't believe she had heard right. She looked at Nathan's strong brown hands for a long time before they came into focus.

"What . . . what did you say?" Her voice was barely above a whisper.

Nathan pushed himself away from the table. "He's alive, Cynthia. Garrett Carver. Little Nate's father. He's alive."

"Why are you telling me this when I know . . . Who told you such a thing?"

"Naomi. She heard about him at the Gilmores'. She thinks she may have even seen him, though she said she can't be sure. I don't doubt her, Cynthia. I'm sure she wouldn't have told me such a thing if she weren't sure."

"But it can't be. It just can't be. If he was alive, he would have come looking for me. I'm sure he would have."

"I don't know, Cynthia, I just don't know. You thought he was dead all this time. Perhaps he thought the same of you."

She stopped to consider the possibility for a moment before speaking, then more to herself than Nathan, she said, "That has to be it. Captain Tarrillton told us both the same thing, but why? He had nothing to gain." She stopped and looked closely at Nathan. She had forgotten the pained look in his eyes. "Oh, Nathan, what are we going to do?"

"Not we, Cynthia, you. This is a decision you'll have to make. You know I love you. I won't pressure you, but you have to decide what you're going to do. All our lives are involved. Yours, mine, little Nate's, and . . . and his. You'll make the decision for all of us. I'll abide by whatever it is."

"I'll need time, Nathan, time. I . . . I think I should go talk to Naomi myself."

Later that evening Cynthia took little Nate and moved back in with Naomi. Nathan was in full agreement. It was best they not be forced to be together until Cynthia had made her choice. He hated thinking of it in those terms, but there was no other.

Thirty-Nine

Birdsville looked very much like he would expect a military encampment to look when Garrett rode in the evening before Muster Day. An occasional tent or lean-to could be seen, however, it was still warm enough so that most had brought no more than a bedroll. Horses had been picketed nearby where grazing was plentiful and groups of men were gathered around smoldering cook fires drinking coffee or brandy while they exchanged news. Garrett knew most of those present hadn't seen one another since the previous year. There were many acquaintances to be renewed. Here and there a shout of recognition turned his head. He would raise an arm in acknowledgment and ride on. No one pressed him for conversation. For that he was glad. He was tired and hungry but knew Thaddeus would have a warm meal and a bed that was at least passable.

He heard the boisterousness of Thad's clientele as he dismounted before the low log building that served as a stable and almost immediately wished he'd taken Thomas Gilmore up on his invitation of a place to sleep. He chuckled to himself as he unsaddled Temple. Maybe Munsy's right, he thought. When I consider a good night's sleep over the festivities, perhaps I am getting too old for these games.

By the time he entered the common room, however, he decided that he was in the mood for a drink and perhaps a bit of joviality after all. Thad greeted him warmly as usual and as soon as he could free himself, made his way to Garrett's side.

"Room's ready, Garrett. I knew you'd be wantin' it," he shouted above the din.

Garrett nodded his thanks.

"Why don't you wash up from your ride while I have Clara fix ya some supper?"

"Good idea, Thad, and I want a large brandy to take with me."

His bulk more of an asset than a hindrance, Thad moved through the crowd to the bar, poured Garrett a drink and held it to within his reach. Garrett shouted his thanks, then turned toward the back room sipping from the mug.

He closed the door behind him. The noise was only a little less noticeable in here. He set the drink on the table and began to remove his dusty outer clothing. A good brushing is in order here, he thought. As he poured water into the wash bowl there was a knock on the door, then the door opened. It was Thad.

"Couldn't have heard you even if you yelled," he said to excuse his entrance as he closed the door. "I almost forgot to tell you, Garrett. There was someone here asking for you. Yesterday, it was."

Garrett paused, interested. "Oh?"

"Yes, and from what I hear, she's asked all over town."

"She?"

"Yes, a woman. I didn't see her. I was working out back at the time. Clara says she's a pretty little thing—but she didn't know who she was. Said she'd be stayin' at Bird's till tomorrow if you come in."

"She didn't leave a name?"

"She did, but Clara couldn't remember it. She was occupied at the time with so many comin' in and all. She did say it had a foreign sound to it, though." A loud noise in the outer room distracted Thad for an instant. He wiped his hands across his rotund belly and turned to open the door. "Anyway, the girl said she'd be at Bird's."

"Thanks, Thad. I'll look into it," Garrett said as he turned back to the wash bowl. A foreign sounding name, he thought as he splashed water over his face and neck, then he chuckled—haven't we all foreign sounding names here in Georgia? But he knew what Thad meant—a name that sounded a bit different. He searched his mind and could think of no one he knew, especially a woman, who would have a foreign sounding name and be looking for him. He knew there was a Salzberger settlement down toward Savannah, and they certainly had such names, but he knew few of them and only men. Perhaps it was a French name, he thought, as he lathered his face to shave. He immediately thought of Cynthia and halted his actions. As he caught his reflection in the small mirror, he leaned forward and spoke.

"Well, perhaps some of her relations may have traced her to the colonies after all."

Cynthia paced back and forth in the small room. This was the hardest, she decided, this waiting. She knew now without doubt that Garrett lived. He was fairly well known in Birdsville and she had been assured that he was seen here several times within the last year. She left the only name he knew her by, Faucieau, with several of the townspeople. If he did show up for Muster Day, he could hardly miss hearing about her, of that she was sure, but where was he? Why didn't he come?

She had been here almost two days now and had seen other men drift in singly or in groups, but so far, no Garrett. She knew they had to leave tomorrow or Elizabeth would send someone after them.

"Sit down, girl. All the pacin' in the world ain't gonna make it happen no faster."

"I can't, Naomi. I just can't. I get too nervous when I sit and the time seems to go so much slower."

"Can't make it go no faster, not even if ya wanted to."

Cynthia turned angrily. "I don't want it to go faster, Naomi. I don't want it to go faster. We have to leave tomorrow and . . . and what if he doesn't come?"

"He will. He will." Naomi sounded so confident.

"But how can you be sure?"

"Lak I tol' ya before, girl, if'n he don't come, he'll be fined by whatever law there is here. 'Sides that, it'd be a mark agin' him. All the big planters show up for Muster Day, even if they's too old to hold a gun. It's jes' that way. Nobody wants to miss it 'lessin' they have to. It's like a big party. Come mornin', you'll see what I mean. Now, sit down and relax. Frettin' over it ain't gonna help none."

Cynthia sat on the bed. She missed little Nate sorely and hoped he was being well taken care of. She was glad he was as old as he was and that he had taken to Eulie's breast so readily. She was thankful Eulie had delivered a few weeks ago. Otherwise, her plan to come to Birdsville might not have taken shape. As it was, she had asked Eulie to act as wetnurse for little Nate and she had Naomi bind her own breasts off and on for the last few weeks. It had been like weaning little Nate slowly and she was now in no discomfort.

She thought back over the last few weeks. When Elizabeth discovered the move across to Naomi's cabin, she had insisted Cynthia and the baby join her in the big house for their mutual companionship. Cynthia had been reluctant at first, but Elizabeth appeared so lonely, she finally acquiesced. She and little Nate had been given a room of their own and she was allowed the run of the house except for Elizabeth's office. She soon found she was expected to do little more than be available when Elizabeth wished her company.

Almost immediately they once again became confidantes with Cynthia telling Elizabeth what she knew of Garrett from Naomi, and Elizabeth disavowing having heard about him from the Gilmores. She added that she could recall no visitors during her stay but that wasn't so unusual during harvest season. On the surface Elizabeth appeared to be happy for Cynthia, but there was an undercurrent of feeling that Cynthia couldn't quite put her finger on. Elizabeth dissuaded her from looking for Garrett by reasoning that if she couldn't find him or if he no longer wanted her the trouble they had gone to protect her name and the baby's would be for naught. Each time the subject came up Elizabeth knew how to squelch any new arguments Cynthia presented. Her ploy was to prey on the guilt feelings Cynthia had about Nathan. Cynthia recognized she was being maneuvered and each time she approached the subject with new resolve. It was to Elizabeth's advantage, however, that she was often able to bring Cynthia close to tears when she spoke of Nathan.

It was so complicated, Cynthia tried to push it from her mind. She knew Elizabeth was being purposely malicious but she could find no reason for it. She suspected Elizabeth was bordering on insanity. Then Naomi had told her about Muster Day and she was more determined than ever to at least seek news of Garrett if all efforts to actually find him failed. She felt she could make no rational decision about her life until she had seen and talked to Garrett.

Elizabeth had flown into a fury when she asked if she might go to Birdsville to seek news of Garrett. She accused Cynthia of being an ungrateful wretch. After all, she and the baby were being well taken care of and had the best of possible lives at Mountview. She couldn't understand why Cynthia wanted to go running after some man. They were all alike—couldn't be trusted, wanted a woman for only one thing unless she was rich. The rich ones were negotiated for and the poor ones . . . well, they were used and discarded.

Just short of threatening to run away if Elizabeth wouldn't give her permission for a trip to Birdsville, Cynthia stormed from the room and sought Nathan. It hadn't been an easy task but she had told Nathan of her plan and the reasoning behind it. In the end, Nathan was the one who convinced Elizabeth to let Cynthia go. It was done with the understanding she would be accompanied by Naomi. The baby must stay behind to discourage her entertaining thoughts of running away and they had to be back at Mountview by sunset of the third day or Cynthia would be listed as a runaway and face the possibility of being returned in shackles. Cynthia had gladly agreed to everything and since that day her emotions had wavered between elation one moment to despair the next. What if Garrett didn't want her? What if he had married within the last year? What if she couldn't even find him? So many questions and, so far, no answers.

She jumped up and began to pace again. She caught Naomi's exasperated look out of the corner of her eye but ignored it. She had spent most of the day in the common room occupying the table where she and Jameison had sat over a year ago. She felt certain now that the horseman she had seen that day had been Garrett. She hoped he would enter Birdsville by the same route and she would catch a glimpse of him. She had relinquished the table only at Mr. Bird's insistence of needing it. She and Naomi had returned to their room and eaten their supper in relative silence.

Cynthia stopped at the window for a moment and tapped her foot impatiently before she turned. "I can't stand this any longer, Naomi. Let's go for a walk."

Naomi said nothing but rose and walked to the door. Any meaningful activity was better than this.

After eating, Garrett brushed his coat as best he could before leaving Overby's. He had thought to have a word with Clara on his way out, but when he saw how busy she was, he abandoned the idea. Once outside he decided to walk the short distance to Bird's Inn. It was almost dark. As he walked, he puzzled over why a woman by the name of Faucieau—if that was the name—would be seeking him. He finally concluded the woman, whoever she was, just might be a decoy for Cynthia's husband and he had best be on guard.

As he neared the combination inn and post office, he could hear laughter and loud voices filtering out into the night. The partying had started in earnest now and would continue throughout the next day. As he reached the door he stood aside to let two women pass. The light behind them threw their faces into darkness and he was so preoccupied he paid little attention except to note that the larger of the two was a stately Negress. In the next instant, his head was reeling. It couldn't be, but it was. She was standing close enough he could feel her warmth. He didn't know if he should touch her or not. Her lips were moving. She was speaking. Had he heard right over the buzzing in his ears?

"What . . . what did you say?" Did he dare even speak her name?

"You *are* alive. You really are."

Garrett shook his head to clear it. Cynthia reached out a hand and laid it on his arm.

"Oh, Garrett, I didn't stop to think what a shock I would be to you. I . . . I've at least had time to get used to the idea of seeing you again."

"This . . . this isn't a dream? You're real?"

Cynthia nodded.

He threw his head back and laughed the way she remembered so well. She had forgotten how much his laughter meant to her. He picked her up and swung her around, then moved deeper into the shadows and they were in each other's arms. He was kissing her—first on the mouth then the eyes, the cheeks, the neck and finally on the mouth again, deep and claiming. Breathless and trembling, she finally pushed away from him. She noticed Naomi had moved a discreet distance from them but even at that, she was thankful for the darkness.

"Garrett, please," she spoke only for his ears. "We . . . we have to go someplace."

His voice was husky with emotion when he spoke. "You're right," he agreed. "The street is no place for our re—union."

She knew he paused purposely as he spoke the last

word and tried to stifle her giggling with a hand over her mouth.

He took her hand and whispered close to her ear, "Your room or mine?"

"Yours," she spoke without hesitation. "Naomi must be left someplace to go."

He tilted his head in the direction of the black woman standing off to one side. "Yours?" he asked, although he could not imagine Cynthia owning another person.

She shook her head. "My friend. My very dear friend, I might add. If it weren't for Naomi, I might never have known you were still alive. Captain Tarrillton told me you died of the fever."

"I heard you died from a fall—a broken neck to be more precise."

Cynthia could detect the anger and hatred in his voice. She moved close and put her arms around him. He held her and kissed the top of her head.

"Let's not talk about that now, Garrett. There'll be time later. Let's . . . let's not even think about it."

"As you wish, my love."

"Good. Now, come and meet Naomi, then take me to your room."

Thad's business was so brisk Garrett whisked Cynthia into his room without notice. She stood still in the darkness, as directed, until Garrett could reach the candle and light it. He turned, held the candle high and inspected her for a moment before setting it back on the table. When he held his arms wide, she rushed to him. Tears were streaming down both their cheeks. He held her close and moved his hands over her back.

"My love, my love, it's so hard to believe. I never thought I'd hold you again."

She turned her tear-stained face up to his. Blue eyes met green briefly before his mouth came down on hers passionately. The blood surged through her veins warming her, exciting her. She had almost forgotten the effect his kisses could produce.

When he finally lifted his head, Cynthia was breathless with anticipation and the wanting of him. Her whole being ached for him.

Garrett was in physical agony. It had been so long, could he please her tonight? He struggled to control the fire raging within his loins that only her nearness could cause.

When he slowly began unbuttoning her dress, she did likewise with his shirt. They were both deliberate in their movements, feasting on one another with their eyes as the clothing fell away.

They lay very close for a while just holding each other, savoring each touch, each small caress, enjoying the sensation of flesh against flesh. Ever so slowly Garrett began to run one hand up and down her side from breast to hip, lightly, softly. Cynthia's pulse quickened. Her emotions soared as his mouth tenderly claimed hers, tongue probing, exploring. She returned his kiss with all the ardor, all the passion, all the love she felt.

Prolonging the moment when they would join in ecstasy, they openly admired one another's body in the candlelight, each showering the other with kisses, tender caresses, warm gentle touches.

When their bodies could no longer accept being separated, Garrett entered Cynthia, gently, slowly. She welcomed him warmly, running her fingers through his dark hair as they began to move. She arched up to meet each thrust joyfully, the fire they kindled soon became all-consuming and they were lost in passionate perfection. They reached the peak together then lay still to let the feelings subside. Each felt the other's tears of happiness warm against his cheeks.

Later, much later, still aglow from their lovemaking, Cynthia snuggled close against Garrett's shoulder.

"Garrett?"

"Ummmmm?"

She could tell he was close to sleep. "I know we haven't spoken of the past year so as not to spoil anything, but there is one thing you should know."

He encircled her with his arms and kissed her lightly. "I know all I need to know," he said. "You're alive. That's all I need."

Cynthia smiled in the dark. "But this you really should know."

"Is that the only way I'm going to get any sleep?" he teased.

"The only way." She was practically bursting with the news.

"Very well, then, tell me. I'm ready, whatever it is."

"I don't really think you're ready for this."

"I'm ready for anything," he assured her.

"Very well," she paused for effect. "Garrett Carver, you are a father."

Garrett took a deep breath and exhaled very slowly. He felt as though he had been hit in the stomach. "Did . . . did I hear you correctly? I'm a father?"

"Yes, a son. Almost . . . almost six months old now. Oh, Garrett, he looks just like you. Why, if it hadn't been for . . ."

Garrett interrupted her by getting out of bed. He moved to the table, lit a candle and brought it back with him. He looked at Cynthia for what seemed like a long time to her.

"You're serious, aren't you?"

"You . . . you're not happy about the baby." It was a statement rather than a question. She hadn't expected this.

He turned around and pulled a stool over to set the candle on. He sat on the edge of the bed and ran his hands through his thick hair, more as a delay for time than for anything else. She had told him what she thought would be exciting news for him, for any man. He had reacted badly.

"Happy?" he finally said. "Happy is hardly the word. I'm stunned."

He turned to her and smiled. She was up on her elbows now peering at him closely.

"Then you're not unhappy about it?"

Garrett reached out and covered her left hand with his. "My God, Cynthia, I was ecstatic when I found you tonight . . . and now, to learn I have a son, I'm just . . . well, I'm stunned. There's no other word for how I feel at this moment."

Cynthia scrambled to sit up. "He's a beautiful baby, Garrett. Dark hair, dark blue eyes . . ."

"We'll be married right away," he interjected, thinking of his own miserable childhood. "He may have been born a bastard. He'll not stay one."

Cynthia seemed to shrink from him. "We can't be married, Garrett. There's still Walter."

Garrett stood and flung his arms downward. "Hang Walter," he said as he began to storm about the room. "That can be remedied in time. Until then, no one will know but you and me."

Suddenly Cynthia started laughing. He turned.

"What do you find so damned funny?"

"You're not very convincing, Mr. Carver, without your pants."

Seeing the ridiculousness of the situation, Garrett began to laugh, too. He moved to blow out the candle, then joined her on the bed and took her into his arms. He kissed her deeply, passionately. When she began to move against him once again, all thought of anything but the present was lost to either of them.

When Cynthia awoke, Garrett was gone. She hurriedly dressed and left. She saw no one on the way out. She squinted her eyes against the bright sunlight and her mouth dropped open in amazement. Every way she turned she saw men drilling. She wondered how she had slept so well with all the commotion. From the shadows cast by the sun, she guessed it to be almost noon. How was she ever going to find Garrett? She couldn't, that was all and she knew it. She lifted her skirts and ran toward Bird's Inn. Naomi would be fit to be tied.

Garrett, though he hadn't been conscious of watching for her, saw her from the edge of the meadow where he was drilling with his company of militia. He watched as she glanced around then lifted her skirts and ran toward the inn. He would call for her there once the games started. He turned his attention back to the business at hand.

Cynthia and Naomi were well out of town before she realized she should have left a note. Garrett had no idea they were leaving at noon or why. She begged Naomi to turn back. Naomi refused.

"It's for your own good, girl. You don't want to be labeled a runaway. 'Sides, you can write him a letter and someone'll be passin' by to take it to him."

"Naomi, you don't understand. We talked. We talked about a lot of things, but we never got around to really talking. I don't even know where he lives."

Suddenly she burst into tears. "He doesn't know where I am, either. All he knows is I'm indentured, but he doesn't know to whom." Suddenly she grabbed Naomi's hands holding the reins. "We have to go back. We just have to. He doesn't even know my real name. When he comes looking for me he'll never be able to find me. Please, Naomi, please?"

Naomi pulled on the reins and halted the small wagon Elizabeth had let them use. She turned to Cynthia.

"Listen, girl, if'n we ain't back by sundown you know Miz Jameison gonna send someone for you. If'n she has to do that, it could lengthen your indenture if'n she chooses."

"But, Naomi . . ." Tears were streaming down Cynthia's face.

"Hush up and lissen to me, girl. Just stop and think. If'n we's back when we's supposed to be, Miz Jameison is most likely to trust you again, and you can plan another meeting with him to do the talkin' you shoulda done this time. If'n we ain't, she likely won't ever let you leave again. You hear what I'm sayin?"

Cynthia nodded. She knew Naomi was right. Elizabeth *had* become very strange and most difficult. What Cynthia hadn't known until now was how astute Naomi was.

"You write your man a letter. Send it to Birdsville. Someone'll see it gets to him."

Cynthia nodded again.

"It won't be more'n a few days till he gets it and from what I saw last night, it'll be some of the worst days of his life, but he'll survive." She slapped the reins against the horse's rump and clucked at it to move.

Cynthia sat in misery for several minutes until

446

Naomi began to chuckle.

"If'n I had me a man like that, not so sure I'd wanta do much talkin', neither."

Cynthia smiled. Having Naomi's approval meant a lot—especially since Naomi was so fond of Nathan.

"That's better," Naomi said when she saw the smile. "You've made your decision, too."

"Yes, I have. I'm going to marry Garrett."

"I knowed it. No mistakin' the love between you two."

"I love Nathan, too, Naomi, a great deal and I think . . . no, I'm sure we could have been happy if Garrett really were dead or if I'd never known any different."

She saw Naomi grimace.

"Please don't feel guilty for telling us, Naomi. You were right. If you could hear about Garrett, so could have Nathan and I. Had it come sometime in the future, we can only imagine the amount of misery it would have caused all of us."

"I don't feel too guilty, girl, not after seein' you with Mr. Carver. Mostly, I just feel sad for Nathan."

Cynthia nodded and they lapsed into silence.

Forty

Garrett was beside himself when he found Cynthia gone. He asked about town but no one knew any more than what Thaddeus had told him—that her name was Faucieau and she was looking for him. He sent word to Jacob that he was going to be delayed and why, stocked up on supplies and was saddling Temple when Thad came into the stable.

"This is crazy. You know that, don't you, Garrett?"

"I have to find her, Thad. She's my whole life."

"But where you gonna start? You don't even know what direction to take."

"It doesn't matter. I'll find her."

"But she could be anyplace—even across the river in the Carolinas."

Garrett turned angrily. "I'll find her, Thad. That's all there is to it. Don't try to stop me."

"I'm not trying to stop you, son, but you're not thinkin' straight. Give it more thought before you head out. Weather'll be closin' in soon. Not likely you'll find her before then."

Garrett led Temple out into the bright sunlight and swung into the saddle. Thad laid a hand on his leg.

"How you gonna go about it, Garrett? Someone

oughta know."

"I'm going to make an ever-widening circle around Birdsville. That seems the only logical way."

"Well, good luck. There's lots of trails and little-known roads leading into even lesser-known farms—but good luck just the same."

"Thanks, Thad." He turned Temple and headed south. It was mid-afternoon.

Within a fortnight the roads had become muddy, treacherous bogs. He was low on supplies and it was near freezing every night. Knowing it was senseless to continue, Garrett turned Temple homeward. He was hoping there would be word from Cynthia when he arrived.

The rain had let up to no more than a light drizzle when Garidas came into view three days later. The early evening lights were a welcome sight. Temple perked up her ears when she realized this was home. They were both tired and covered with mud when he dismounted at the stable door. Through an exhausted haze he saw Daniel, Munsy and Jacob coming toward him. The next two days were lost to him as he slept twice around the clock.

"Jacob! . . . Jacob!" he bellowed.

Jacob came hurrying into the main hall through the kitchen doorway. Garrett was standing on the balcony just outside his room leaning against the railing. He felt refreshed, but groggy-headed.

"Any word?"

"From her?"

"Who else would I be asking about? Of course from her."

Jacob hung his head and shook it.

Garrett raised his eyes heavenward. "God, where is she? Where is she?" He pounded a hand against the railing. "I've got to find her, Jacob. You've got to help me."

Jacob nodded and crossed the room. Garrett turned and entered his own room, leaving the door open.

"How long have I been sleeping, Jacob?" he shouted as he pulled open his closet door to select clothing. "What time is it? Hell, what day is it?"

When he got no reply, he stepped back out onto the balcony which encompassed the main hall. There was no sign of Jacob. He had assumed he was coming up. He shrugged his shoulders and resumed dressing. He was just pulling on his pants when Jacob appeared in the doorway.

"Where you been? I thought you were coming right up."

"Went into the library," Jacob said as he held an envelope toward him. "This came yesterday from Alex McDaniel. I think it's important."

Garrett took the envelope and turned it over. It bore Alex's seal. "Why do you say that?" he asked as he tossed it onto the bed and sat to pull on his boots.

"There was a messenger here the day you left for Birdsville. Said he had a message for you from Alex. Nothing written and he wouldn't tell me what the message was. I thought he had probably caught up with you in Birdsville until that came."

"How long have I been sleeping?" Garrett asked as he stood to shake his pants legs down over his boots. "What time is it?"

"You been sleepin' two days and it's almost suppertime."

"Good, I'm starving." He picked up the letter from Alex and left the room, closing the door behind them. They traversed the balcony to the stairway.

"Has the weather cleared?"

Jacob nodded. "I'd say we're in for a cold, dry spell. Gettin' close to hog-killin' time, you know."

"Daniel will have to handle it. You and me are setting out first thing in the morning."

"Not me," Jacob said.

Garrett stopped halfway down the stairs and looked at his friend. "I'm sorry, Jacob. I didn't mean for it to sound like an order. You will go with me, won't you? I need your help."

"Not me," Jacob repeated as he moved on down the stairs, "and it ain't got nothin' to do with the way you said it. Hell, Garrett, I'm gettin' too old to go bouncin' 'round in the saddle and sleepin' on the ground in the cold. Daniel's the one to take."

"Daniel doesn't know what she looks like, Jacob. You have to go."

"Then wait till warmer weather. It's foolhardy to set out now, anyhow, and take a chance on more storms."

Garrett seemed to consider it for a moment when he paused by the kitchen door, then he shook his head. "No, I have to find her, Jacob. Her and the baby."

"Baby? Your message didn't say nothin' 'bout no baby."

Garrett smiled sheepishly.

"Well, whatta ya know about that? Jes' what you need, too—with her still havin' a husband and all."

"I know. That's why I have to find her. We've got to get this mess righted before he gets too old."

"And a boy?"

Garrett smiled again as he pushed open the

kitchen door. "I'll tell you about it while we eat."

While they were waiting for Munsy to serve supper, Garrett opened the letter from Alex. The message was short and to the point:

> Imperative I speak with you at your earliest convenience about plans made to sail to England. Time is of the essence, since I understand you hold passage on the *Faith and Charity* due to set sail 6 December next.
>
> A.

Garrett crumpled the paper then smoothed it out and handed it to Jacob who read it quickly.

"Same as two years ago," he said as he handed it back.

Garrett nodded. "You'll have to go to Savannah, Jacob," he said quietly, "and explain to Alex why I can't go."

"You gotta go and you know it. It's your duty. 'Sides, seems to me it'd work out perfect. You could clear up your husband problems and worry about findin' her when you return."

Garrett shook his head, then turned to look out the windows as he tapped his fingers nervously on the tabletop.

Having a dislike for the sea, as he did, he spent a miserable ten weeks about the *Faith and Charity*, made even more so by his constant thoughts of Cynthia. His accommodations were comfortable and the crew congenial, but nothing could stop his constant worrying. He knew Alex and Jacob were right. This was not the time of year to be wandering about the countryside trying to find her and that, coupled with the prospect of being able to settle with her husband, was what persuaded him to make the voyage. He feared Cynthia would be distraught when he didn't come for her—and he felt that was what she expected—but he hoped this delay in their being together would enable them to be married all the sooner.

He spent little time chastising himself for not having gotten more information the night in Birdsville. He had done all that during the two weeks he spent searching. Instead, his hours were filled with planning ways to continue the search when he returned. When the weather permitted him a stroll on deck, he would stand by the railing and remember his last voyage and the time they spent together. His nights were restless and filled with dreams of golden hair and green eyes.

He vowed this would be his last voyage on behalf of the Liberty Boys and made a mental note to tell Alex. Aside from the fact that once he found Cynthia he never wanted to leave her again, he suspected that his usefulness to the organization in this capacity was coming to an end. He was becoming too well-known and too many voyages of this nature could become suspicious.

He spent only a week in London before booking passage for the return voyage. He had, without trouble, gathered the information Alex wanted. It had all happened before his arrival and, furious as he was, there was little he could do except sail back to Georgia with the bad news. The ailing William Pitt, always a friend to the colonies, had retired and Parliament was now in the control of Charles Townshend, the powerful chancellor of the exchequer. Townshend dominated the government and this was what Alex and the others had feared. Garrett now knew why. It was reported that certain measures had been introduced in Parliament and would soon be passed which would have dire effects upon the colonies. They were touted as the Townshend Acts and from what Garrett had heard, they not only penalized New York for not complying with the law requiring the colonies to provide quarters for British troops, but they also imposed customs duties on colonial imports of glass, lead, paints, paper and tea. His report to Alex also stated that those in the know suspected that subsequent legislative acts would establish commissioners in the colonies to enforce the customs services and to make sure the duties were collected.

The *William and Mary* sailed in three days. During all his spare time this past week he had combed London looking for Walter Faucieau. He had asked wherever he went. No one knew the name. Someone had, however, suggested he inquire of Madam Lucinda Devers. She or her girls, it was said, knew every gentleman of means in and around London. As a last resort, Garrett had done just that. Madam Devers was most kind and gracious, but no, she knew of no one named Faucieau. A woman of indeterminate age—Garrett guessed her to be about sixty—she said she had known an elderly gentleman named Faucieau when she was much younger, but she was sure he was dead now and he had had no sons, only a daughter whose name eluded her after so many years.

Garrett thanked her and left the well-appointed house to walk the streets. Only three days and not an idea of where to start looking. He could, of course, delay his departure but thought better of that when he realized it would be well into spring when he landed in Savannah—just the time when he wanted to resume his search.

He walked for some time, thinking and trying to reach a suitable solution. He soon realized he was in the vicinity of the docks. Fog was settling in and it was beginning to get cold. A noisy pub caught his attention and he decided to go in for a grog and warm up a bit before returning to his rooms.

The room was dim and hazy with smoke. He selected a table near the door but out of its draft and sat down to wait for one of the serving girls. He had hardly gotten settled, however, when he heard a familiar voice from the direction of the bar. He couldn't place the voice, though he knew it from his past. He turned slightly and saw it came from a short, stocky man whose back was to him. Recognition came swiftly and he stood so fast he knocked over his bench. All attention in the room focused on him, but for an instant Garrett saw only one face. Then he noticed that Tarrillton was not alone.

He glared at first one and then the other of the two men flanking Tarrillton and they backed away. Keeping an eye on them, he motioned with his hand.

"Outside, Captain. It seems we have some unfinished business."

Resting his hand close to the butt of a pistol in his sash, Tarrillton cast a sideways glance at his companions. "Eh, and what might that be, Carver?"

"I said outside. I'll not dirty her name by even mentioning it in this foul dung hole."

Tarrillton laughed nervously, his hand inching toward the pistol. "So, that's what yer here fer, is it? Well, let's have a drink, Carver. You don't want to go dyin' over a pretty little whore. . . ."

Garrett was on him in two strides. Tarrillton only had time to draw the uncocked pistol. Garrett knocked it aside with his left hand as he sank his right into the flab of Captain Tarrillton just below the juncture of the ribs. The blow lifted the corpulent man off his feet. Garrett felt the weight of him in his shoulder and back. Tarrillton landed but did not fall. Garrett had him by the front of the jacket and shirt and was slowly cutting off his air supply. As his face began to turn red, Garrett released him and shoved him toward the door. A look over his shoulder revealed that no one was going to get involved on the captain's behalf.

Garrett pushed him through the door and pinned him against the outside wall. Fog swirled around them, but Garrett could clearly see the grotesque face in the glow emitted from the windows.

"Carver . . . Carver," the captain began. "I'm not a well man . . . I . . ."

Garrett braced an arm under his chin. "You'll be even less well if you don't tell me everything you know."

"She . . . she died. The Fawley girl died. Fell and broke her neck."

Garrett pushed his arm tighter against the man's throat. "What did you say?"

"She . . . she died. She . . ."

"No. About her name. What was the name she gave you?"

"F-F-Fawley. Mistress Fawley. A widow." Sensing Garrett's confusion, Tarrillton continued,

"She was a strumpet, Carver. A piece of baggage . . . not fit for . . . for a gentleman."

Garrett tightened his hold. "Hold your tongue, you lying bastard. I saw her only three months ago. I know she lives. Where is she? Who bought her indenture?"

Tarrillton felt the anger and hatred coming from the man who held him so powerless. Let Jameison fight his own battles, he thought. "Ja-Ja-Jameison. Elijah Jameison. An old friend of mine. I . . . I sold her head rights to him."

Garrett struggled with a strong desire to slowly wrench the life from the man. Finally, he flung him aside. "You're stupid, Tarrillton. A stupid man. I'd have paid anything for her freedom." He turned and walked into the fog.

It all fit—or almost—Garrett thought as he retraced his steps to Madam Devers. The Gilmores had mentioned a female indenture at Jameison's, but she had gotten married. Jameison had said so himself and Janie Gilmore had been visibly shaken by the news. Could Jameison have had more than one? Indentures of either sex were rare nowadays. Could the Gilmores have been mistaken? Garrett didn't know. The problem at hand was to find Walter Fawley.

He knew it to be late when he once again asked to see the madam. He was ushered into a small sitting room where she joined him shortly.

"I'm sorry to trouble you again," he said as he stood to greet the stately, elegant lady.

"No trouble, I assure you," she said as she motioned for him to sit down. "You're good for my reputation," she added with a twinkle in her eye. "And twice in one night."

Garrett smiled. "Well, it would seem I was mistaken about the man's name I am looking for when I was here earlier. It's not Faucieau. It's Fawley, Walter Fawley. Do you know of a man named Fawley?"

"This is very important?"

"Very, or I wouldn't go to such lengths to find him."

"It has to do with a girl. His wife perhaps?"

"Yes. Then you do know him."

"Everyone knows him or of him," she said. "At least everyone in my business, that is. He's a sorry little man. A not too honest merchant. Treated the girls badly. After one incident, I finally had to forbid him entrance. I heard later he had married. I felt sorry for the girl. I heard she was young and lovely."

"Yes, yes, she is."

"And you love her. And you've come to rescue her. I'm sure she needs it by now unless the weasel mended his ways with women."

"Well, in a sense you're right," Garrett said. Then he went on to tell Lucinda Devers briefly of all that had happened. "I've come to buy her," he concluded. "He wanted to sell her at the cattle market. I hope to convince him to sell her to me."

"I wish you luck," she said as she handed him a slip of paper. "Here's his address."

Garrett stood and bent to kiss her hand as he took the paper. "If you were thirty years younger," he said teasingly, "I might be tempted to stay with you awhile."

Lucinda Devers chuckled with delight. "If I were thirty years younger, Mr. Carver, I'm sure you would stay."

Garrett was up early the next morning and ordered a coach. After giving the driver the address, it seemed only moments before he was deposited in front of a modest brick house which spoke of an easy life. He gave the coachman instructions to wait, mounted the stairs and rapped on the door. A servant opened it.

"I'd like to see Mister Walter Fawley, please."

The girl's eyes opened in amazement. She turned and disappeared. Within seconds, a portly, balding man with squinting eyes came to the door.

"May I help you?"

"Are you Walter Fawley, sir?"

"No. No, I'm his brother Samuel. Who, may I ask, are you?"

"My name is Garrett Carver. I'm an American colonist, a Georgian. I have business with your brother."

"Won't you come in? Mr. Carver, is it?"

Garrett nodded as he stepped over the threshold. Samuel Fawley closed the door and Garrett stood facing him in the dim hallway.

"My brother is dead, Mr. Carver. Has been for over a year. What kind of business did you have with him? I've been over all his accounts. I don't recall seeing your name."

Garrett was stunned by the news, but managed to answer. "No, you wouldn't find my name in his accounts. It was business of a personal nature."

"Then I'm afraid I can't help you, sir. I'm only looking after his business affairs."

"I have news of his wife, Mr. Fawley. He did have a wife?"

Garrett could see the sudden interest in the man's face.

"Why, yes, yes he did. She disappeared the same night Walter was killed. There's been no trace of her found. I think, Mr. Carver, you'd best come into the study where we can discuss this at greater lengths."

He poured them each a glass of port, motioned Garrett to a chair then took his place behind a large oak desk.

"Now, tell me, sir, what do you know of my sister-in-law?"

Garrett proceeded cautiously. "Her name is Cynthia, correct?"

Fawley nodded, a slightly puzzled look on his face.

"She's small and blonde?"

"Yes, yes, that's Cynthia. A lovely young thing. My brother idolized her."

"I was coming to tell your brother that she is in Georgia and is alive and well," Garrett only half lied. He would have told Walter Fawley that, he reasoned.

"Georgia! But how . . ."

"Did your brother die at a cattle market?" Garrett interrupted.

Fawley nodded, still obviously puzzled. "He . . . he received several blows on the head. One, probably here"—he pointed to his temple—"the doctor surmised was what caused his death. But how did you know?"

"I've spoken with Cynthia. She was also struck that night and carried off. She knew nothing of her husband's fate, I'm sure. Later she was sold into bondage to a ship's captain. She lives in bondage now in Georgia as an indentured servant."

"So that's what happened." Samuel Fawley nodded slowly as though it were all beginning to make sense. "I always felt there was more to it than we heard."

"More to it?" Garrett asked.

"Yes, their driver came back with some cock-and-bull story about Walter going to sell Cynthia, but we all knew he was lying. I dismissed him immediately. As I said, Walter adored her. Besides, I knew he would never be party to a wife auction. They would only have attended for the sport, I'm sure."

Garrett nodded as though in agreement. Let the man draw his own conclusions. He had no wish to malign the dead. He rose as though to leave, thrilled that Cynthia was free to be his.

Fawley stopped him. "Does she wish to remain there, Carver? In Georgia, I mean? She's a wealthy woman. She can pay her way out of bondage and do whatever she wants."

Garrett paused. "Wealthy?"

"Yes, she was Walter's only heir aside from me. She has a sizable inheritance. Since no trace of her was found, it's been held. Even this house belongs to her. I only stay here when I'm in town on business."

"I shall see that she gets word," Garrett said. "She can correspond with you as to her wishes."

The little man rose and walked around the desk. "Good," he said. "It was most kind of you to bring us word of her. If you'll come round tomorrow, I'll have documents you can carry to her. Are you returning soon?"

"Yes, I sail day after tomorrow on the *William and Mary*."

"Then I shall look forward to hearing from her." He paused at the door. "By the way, Carver?

Have you an interest in Cynthia?"

Garrett had been expecting this. "Only in so much as I abhor slavery of any kind," he said, "and a bond servant is little more than a slave. Her plight was brought to my attention by an associate—a Thomas Gilmore and his wife who are friends to the family that bought her head rights. I spoke to her myself only three months ago. At the time I didn't know I would be coming to London on business, but I felt she would want her family here to know what happened to her."

Samuel Fawley nodded, seemingly accepting it as truth.

"Until tomorrow," he said as he opened the door and extended his hand.

"Since you don't know me, sir, would you feel more comfortable if I sent my agent around?"

"Not at all, Carver, not at all, but do what's most convenient for you."

When Garrett boarded the *William and Mary* two days later, he had not only the documents proving Cynthia's inheritance, but also a small fortune that Samuel Fawley had insisted he take to her so she might buy her freedom and keep herself until she decided what to do.

Forty-One

It was near planting time. He not only had Mountview's fields to worry about, but also his own few acres he had been clearing when time permitted. Still, Nathan knew this was his only opportunity to spare a few days until after harvest. Thaddeus Overby's directions had been exact and Nathan was impressed as he rode into Garidas. Garrett Carver was obviously wealthy, but what kind of man was he really? How could he use Cynthia as he had, promise her marriage, then never come looking for her?

Nathan intended to find out. Cynthia hadn't asked for his help. He had taken this upon himself. He suspected she was pregnant again and he guessed about five months along, though she wasn't showing as early as she had with Nate. He smiled when he thought of the youngster who seemed so much a part of himself. Little Nate was almost a year old now and toddling everywhere. He followed Nathan about the grounds close to the house whenever Cynthia permitted and Nathan took great pride in his accomplishments as though he were his own. As hurt as he had been when Cynthia told him her decision, he hadn't found himself able to reject the child.

Neither had he been able to stop loving Cynthia. He doubted he ever would, and the pain and despair he had seen on her face these past few weeks when

Garrett didn't come for her was more than he could tolerate. He also detected something in her eyes that reminded him of a frightened animal. After giving it some thought, he concluded she was afraid of Elizabeth discovering her condition. Naomi finally told him Cynthia had written several letters to Garrett but had received no answer. Nathan suspected these had been destroyed by Elizabeth. Though he had no proof of this, he did know Elizabeth had changed a great deal since Elijah's death. She had become unpredictable, malicious in small ways, and very protective of Cynthia. Even if Elizabeth had destroyed Cynthia's messages, Nathan reasoned, there were other ways Garrett Carver could trace her if he really loved her. Whatever the reason for Carver not coming, Nathan intended to confront the man and settle this once and for all, for Cynthia and for himself. The waiting was no good.

He dismounted in the center of the long, curved drive and handed his reins to one of the small boys vying for the honor. He climbed the two stairs to the lawn and stood for a moment to admire the columned structure before him. If he worked all his life he could never hope to give Cynthia half as much as Garrett Carver had to offer. He let out a low whistle of admiration as he crossed the lawn and stepped up onto the porch. He raised his hand to knock but the door was thrown open by a cheery-faced, round, little black woman.

"Mr. Garrett Carver, please. I'd like to see him."

"He ain't here," Munsy said with a smile as she took in his rough clothing, "but Jacob is. Wanna see him?"

"Jacob? Who's Jacob?"

"Jacob Townsley. He and Massa Carver are sorta partners."

"Sorta partners?"

" 'Peers to me you don't Massa Carver too well. What you want, anyhow?"

"I don't know your Master Carver at all, Miss? . . ."

"Munsy," she finally offered, a frown creeping onto her brow.

"I've never even met Garrett Carver, Munsy. I came to speak to him about Cynthia Fawley."

Her eyes widened as she raised her hands to her cheeks. "Oh, Lawdy," she said before she whirled around. "Jacob, Jacob!" she screamed. "Come quick. There's some fella here says he knows somethin' 'bout Mister Garrett's gal."

Jacob had seen the rider through the library window, determined he didn't know the man and since he was busy, elected to let Munsy answer the door. He turned back to the bookwork at hand and heard nothing until Munsy screamed. Even though he had left the library door open, he couldn't believe what he heard. He rose, dropped his quill and was in the main hall in a few quick strides. He stood eyeing the tall, fair young man at the door for a several seconds.

Nathan, totally unprepared to be greeted by a black man cleared his throat to hide his surprise.

"You're . . . you're Garrett Carver's partner?"

Jacob cast a sideways glance at Munsy, raising one eyebrow. "Well, sorta. Who are you?"

"My name is Nathan Tolliver. I'm overseer of Mountview, the Jameison plantation which is north of Birdsville, close to Fort Augusta."

"And you have word of Miss Cynthia?"

Nathan nodded.

"Well, come on in, son. Come on in. This is good news."

Nathan was awed as he followed Jacob across the main hall and into the library. He had never before seen a house built like this one. The only word that came to mind to describe what he saw was luxurious.

Once in the library, Jacob paused long enough to pour them each a glass of brandy. Again surprised, Nathan began to feel a bit uncomfortable. He knew it was against all convention for a black man to take such liberties in the main house.

Sensing the young man's uneasiness, Jacob proceeded to reassure him as he handed him the brandy. "It's perfectly all right, Mr. Tolliver, it really is. Garrett Carver and I are partners and have been for many years, in every sense but one. It's against the law for me to own property. Therefore, all you see is his. He shares it with me, including the profits."

Nathan opened his mouth to speak, but Jacob continued.

"I can only surmise that the reason you didn't speak out in indignation is because you either are or have been a bond servant. A gentleman planter would have spoken right up. Some have. Am I right?"

Nathan nodded. "I'm a free man less than a year, but I am overseer of Mountview."

Jacob studied the gray eyes for a moment. "I believe you. No reason not to. And Miss Cynthia, she's at Mountview?"

"Yes, she is. Actually, Mr. Townsley . . ."

"Call me Jacob," he said. "Everyone does."

Nathan sipped the brandy, then began again. "Actually, Jacob, I came to ask Garrett Carver why he hasn't come for Cynthia. She can't just leave to look for him. She's an indenture. It's been months now since she saw him in Birdsville. She's growing desperate. I also believe she's pregnant."

Jacob watched the young man across the desk for several minutes. How like Garrett he was, only younger. He set his glass down, rose and walked to the window. With his back to Nathan, he spoke.

"You're in love with her, aren't you?"

"Yes."

"And you believe she's pregnant for a second time?"

Nathan was relieved that Jacob knew about the first baby. He wasn't sure Cynthia had told Carver, but she apparently had, so there was nothing he could inadvertently reveal that might be injurious to her.

"Yes, I do. And I believe she's frightened that Missus Jameison will find out before Carver comes for her. She's written several letters to him. Surely by now . . ."

Jacob turned suddenly. "There's been no correspondence from Miss Cynthia."

"But even if he hasn't received word from her, he could have traced her by now."

Jacob smiled knowingly. "You came to confront Garrett and have it out with him, didn't you?"

"I did. I can't stand to see the agony she's been going through continue."

"I'll tell you something, Nathan. He hasn't come because he isn't here. He's in England." Jacob moved and sat in a chair close to Nathan. "Oh, he searched for her all right till the weather closed in last fall, then he was called to England on business. Alex—that's a friend of Garrett's in Savannah—Alex and I had one hard time convincing him he should go ahead and make the voyage. He was dead set on searching until he found her."

"But surely he could have checked on her papers of indenture in Savannah."

"He did. There was no record of a Cynthia Faucieau."

"Faucieau? But her name's Fawley."

Jacob's eyes widened in amazement then he smiled. "Well, that's explained. Anyhow, Alex and I finally convinced him that he could not only tend to his business while in London, but he could also . . . ." He paused. "You know she left a husband over there?"

Nathan nodded.

"Well, we convinced Garrett he could also look up this husband and settle matters on that end. Being a logical man, he agreed that was the best course. After all, it wasn't the time of year to go searching about the colony."

Nathan sat very still for a time, his eyes studying the landscape out the window. He knew he had to ask, but he wasn't sure he was ready to hear the answer. He finally took a deep breath and spoke.

"Then he does love her? He wants her?"

"More than life itself. He grieved for over a year when he thought her dead, then when he found her and lost her again all in one day at Birdsville, he was frantic. The only thing that persuaded him to abandon his search and go was the prospect of settling her affairs in England so they could be married as soon as he found her. But, since you believe she's in trouble, perhaps we should help her on his behalf."

"What do you mean?"

"I have complete control of Garidas in his absence. Finances, too. I believe you're who you say you are and I believe your main interest is in helping Miss Cynthia. Therefore, I'm going to advance you the money to buy her indenture on one condition."

"What's that?"

"You're to tell no one, except, of course, Miss Cynthia, where you got the money. You can make up some sort of story, I'm sure. I don't think either Garrett or Miss Cynthia would want it bantered about that he had to pay for his wife."

Nathan nodded his agreement, though he winced at the word "wife." She had been so close to being his.

"Once you've done that, you're to bring her here immediately. If there is some possibility that the discovery of her condition would put her in danger as you have implied, time is of the essence."

"I'm not sure it would put her in danger, but Missus Jameison lost her husband about a year ago. Since then, it's been hard to determine how she will react to certain situations. She's become very protective of Cynthia. Hardly allows her any freedom, even on Mountview. I only suspect that is what Cynthia is afraid of. I could be wrong."

"Right or wrong," Jacob said, "if anything should happen to that gal now that I know where she is, Garrett would have my head—partner or no. I think it best we get her entirely out of the reach of Mrs. Jameison if we can."

"Very well," Nathan said. He could think of nothing else.

Jacob rose. "Good. It's almost supper time. I hope you'll spend the night and get a fresh start in the morning."

Cynthia saw Nathan when he rode into the clearing. He had been gone four days and no one seemed to know where. Even Elizabeth was at a loss. She said he had asked for some time off for personal business and she assumed he had gone to Savannah to file claim on the fifty acres she had given him. Cynthia felt there was something more. Nathan had been watching her closely these past few weeks and Cynthia suspected he knew she was again with child. She only hoped Elizabeth would be the last to discover it. She had presented Cynthia with more and more tirades on the faults of men these past months and Cynthia was genuinely afraid of what would happen when her condition could no longer be hidden.

She was glad Nathan was back. She wanted to run to him, tell him everything and ask for his protection, but held herself in check as she had for so long. Surely Garrett would be here before it was too late. She returned her attention to the table covers she was stitching intricately. She had long ago resumed her sewing duties for lack of any other activity. She still did the fine handwork Josie could no longer manage, only this time she had elected to work in the main sewing building away from the house. Elizabeth made it plain it wasn't necessary, but with little Nate playing at her feet, she enjoyed the work. It made her feel useful and she liked being away from Elizabeth's ever-watchful eyes even for a few hours each day.

It seemed only a matter of minutes when she heard someone enter the room. She turned and found

Nathan looking a little ill-at-ease in a woman's domain. He immediately swept off his hat and strode across the room to her side.

"Where's Elizabeth?" he asked in a hushed tone.

"In her room. She's been there for two days and won't allow anyone in except Naomi. I haven't seen her but Naomi says it's worse this time. Says she just lies there and stares at the ceiling for hours, then for no reason lashes out in anger and hatred. Naomi's worried about her, but surely it'll be like the other times. Why?"

"I have some urgent business to take care of, that's all, but maybe it's better this way."

"Better?"

"Never mind. I'll be back in a few minutes." Cynthia opened her mouth to speak but Nathan turned and left the room, closing the door softly behind him.

She cocked her head to one side for a moment, then shrugged her shoulders and returned to her stitching. She looked down at little Nate who had fallen asleep on a pallet by the wall. A warm feeling of love swept over her as it always did when she saw him in slumber. She hoped this next baby would be a little sister for him.

Nathan went straight to Elizabeth's room and rapped lightly on the door. Naomi opened it and stepped into the hall.

"You're back, huh?"

"Yes. I thought I should let Elizabeth know. Is she? . . ."

"Just lying there staring at the ceilin'. It's been two days now, though it's different this time."

"I know. Cynthia told me."

"I don't think you should go in. She's had fits

anytime anyone but me was in the room."

"Whatever you say. I have some business to take care of. I'll be back later to check with you."

Nathan turned and descended the stairs. In a moment he was opening the door to Elizabeth's office. He had only been in here once before when she had given him his free man's papers and shown him the document she had drawn up giving him the power to transact business for Mountview during her absences. He hoped she hadn't revoked or destroyed the latter. He closed the door behind him and stepped across to the desk. He reached for the box where she said the paper would stay. With trembling hands, he picked it up and walked to the window for better light. He hesitated only a moment, then lifted the lid and began to rifle through the papers. The document was third from the top. It was still intact and he had seen nothing so far to indicate it had been revoked. He kept digging. The very last paper in the box was Cynthia's indenture. He withdrew it, carefully replacing the others, then walked back to the desk. He set the box in its place then taking paper and quill, hastily wrote a new indenture paper showing Jacob Townsley as owner. Satisfied that it was in order, he dusted the paper, rolled the two together and stuffed them inside his shirt. He recorked the ink bottle, then stood and placed the money Jacob had given him in the box.

He was perspiring from tenseness as he stepped back into the hallway. Taking a deep breath, he bounded out of the main house returning to the sewing cabin. He found Cynthia just as he had left her. He walked across the room and crouched by her side.

"I want you to get your things together. I'm taking you away from here, you and little Nate."

Startled, Cynthia dropped her sewing to the floor. "You're what?"

Nathan stood. "Come outside where we can talk."

Cynthia followed, asking one of the girls busy stitching clothing to keep an eye on the baby. Outside, she shielded her eyes from the bright sunlight momentarily. Nathan led her to the shade of a large oak tree away from the buildings.

"Nathan, what's this all about? You know I can't leave. Elizabeth will have me posted as a runaway. She's threatened before."

"You can and will. I've sold your indenture."

"You've what?"

"I've sold your indenture to Jacob Townsley. That's where I've been the past four days. I went to find out why Carver hadn't come for you . . ."

"Nathan, you had no right. It's . . . it's none of your affair."

Embarrassed and angry, Cynthia turned away. Nathan grabbed her by the shoulders and turned her to face him.

"Will you just listen to me?"

She made no reply. Fighting desperately not to cry, she finally nodded.

"I couldn't stand to see you in such misery. Naomi told me about the letters you had written and that you got no reply. Someone had to do something before you start showing and Elizabeth finds out." He stopped abruptly, a red flush showing beneath his golden tan.

"Then you do know."

"I've suspected. The important thing is to get you out of here. I believe you have good reason to be afraid of Elizabeth, especially the way she's acting now."

"But how did you manage to get her to agree to selling my indenture?"

"I didn't. Right after Elijah died she drew up a document giving me the power to transact business for Mountview. It hasn't been revoked or destroyed. I found it in her papers along with your indenture. I drew up a similar paper transferring your indenture to Jacob Townsley. No one would argue that Elizabeth is in no condition to conduct business arrangements at this time."

"But Garrett—why didn't he? . . ."

"He's in England on business. He's not expected back for another six weeks." Seeing her look of desolation, he quickly added, "He looked for you, Cynthia. Jacob said he looked until the weather forced him home and the only thing that persuaded him to make the voyage to England was so he could confront your husband and settle things with him." He paused a moment to let her grasp the situation, then he continued. "Jacob gave me the money and I put the sale in his name. I know it's illegal for him to own property, so he'll have to make some arrangement about that. But by putting it in his name, Elizabeth won't be able to trace you. She'll never know but what he's a white man, I promise you that."

Convinced he was serious, she finally smiled. "You know you're putting your own position in jeopardy, don't you?"

Nathan lowered his eyes. "It doesn't matter, Cynthia. I love you. I want you to be happy."

She reached out. "Oh, Nathan."

He pulled away. "Don't, Cynthia. It's hard enough as it is."

There was a long silence between them. Finally, he spoke.

"You . . . you go get your things together. I'll see to little Nate and get a wagon of some sort ready. There's no use taking chances. I want the two of you out of here within the hour. And Cynthia," he called as she headed for the main house, "don't say a word to anyone about this. I'll explain to them later."

In the room Elizabeth had let her and little Nate use, Cynthia quickly gathered their belongings and tied them into a bundle. Just as she reached the head of the stairs, Elizabeth came out of her room. Cynthia was surprised at the change in her. Her usual well-kept hair was stringing about her face. There were large circles under her eyes and she was wearing an old dressing gown partially open, almost exposing her breasts.

"I thought I heard someone out here. Where's Naomi?"

"I . . . I don't know. Perhaps she's in the kitchen or . . . or. . ."

Eyes narrowing, Elizabeth walked toward her. "What's in the bundle?"

Cynthia felt a knot of fear just below her heart. "Laundry. I . . . I was taking it to the wash house," she stammered.

"Liar!" Elizabeth screamed, her face twisted in rage. "You're running away! You ungrateful whore! Can't stand to be without a man, can you? Well, there's men here. Black ones, white ones. Take your pick. Lower yourself, dirty yourself, spread your legs for any of 'em. That's all they want from a woman, anyway, and if that's what it takes to keep you happy, you have my permission!"

"Elizabeth, you're not well. I'll go find Naomi."

"I'm fine!" she snapped. "And you'll go no

place. You're my property, you understand, my property. Take that bundle and get back to your room."

Cynthia backed up slightly, clutching the bundle tighter.

Her anger heightened by Cynthia's hesitation, Elizabeth grabbed for the bundle with one hand and slapped Cynthia with the other. The last thing Cynthia remembered was hearing her own screams as she fell.

Nathan, wondering at Cynthia's delay, left the baby in the care of one of the stable boys and went to find her. He heard the scream just as he reached the porch stairs. He took them in three strides and was unprepared for what he saw when he opened the door.

Cynthia lay in the hallway unconscious, her golden hair spread over her face. He went to her quickly. She was still breathing and he swiftly felt her limbs for broken bones. There were none, but there was a nasty gash on her forehead. Hearing a moan, he looked up. Elizabeth was crouched on her knees at the top of the stairs swaying back and forth moaning unintelligibly. He ignored her and bent to pick up Cynthia. As his right hand slid beneath her slight frame it was met by a warm, moist stickiness. Realization of how seriously hurt she was swept over him, sickening him. He stood with his burden and looked up at Elizabeth again.

"You may have killed her baby, but you haven't killed her." He turned and walked out of the house, yelling at the top of his voice for Naomi.

"Baby?" Elizabeth asked in a child-like voice. "Baby?"

Cynthia had lost a lot of blood by the time Nathan laid her down in Naomi's cabin which was the closest to the main house. Though they know nothing short of a miracle would save the baby, they worked feverishly trying to check the flow. Cynthia came to and drew her legs up sharply in pain when the fetus was expelled. She passed out again almost immediately. It was a girl, tiny, but perfectly formed. Naomi wrapped the little body in an old blanket and Nathan took it outside to bury it. Better Cynthia never see, they decided, without speaking a word.

When the bleeding was finally brought under control and Naomi said everything appeared to be about normal, they turned their attention to the gash on her forehead. It wasn't deep but had turned a nasty purple around the dried blood and a good-sized knot had formed. They cleansed the wound and bandaged it, then Naomi shooed Nathan outside while she undressed and bathed Cynthia.

It was near sundown. After changing his own blood-stained clothing, Nathan went to the stable to unhitch the horses, then retrieved little Nate and, leaving him in Daphne's large, capable hands, went to check on Elizabeth. He found her in her room, curled up tightly on the bed, her back to him. She was rocking back and forth ever so slightly.

"Mrs. Jameison, I'd like to speak with you, if I may."

There was no response.

"Mrs. Jameison?"

Still nothing. Nathan walked around to the far side of the bed. Elizabeth's face was devoid of expression. Her eyes blank. He turned and left.

Three days later, against strong protests from Naomi, Nathan bundled Cynthia as comfortably as he could in the back of a wagon, placed little Nate beside her and set out for Garidas. Though Naomi told him of all the dangers involved, he felt all

Cynthia needed now was time. He promised Naomi he would travel slowly and by way of the main roads. It would take them longer to reach Garidas that way but he knew it would be safer for Cynthia.

Within the week, they were turning into the long drive leading to Garidas. Cynthia was feeling well enough that she insisted on sitting beside Nathan. He didn't object. They placed little Nate between them. As soon as the wagon came into view of the house, Cynthia's mouth opened in astonishment.

"Why, it's . . . it's . . ." Words failed her.

"It's even more awesome inside," Nathan offered.

Just then, Jacob came running out to greet them followed by an assortment of other blacks.

"Miss Cynthia, Lordy, you're a sight for these old eyes."

Jacob helped her down and embraced her in a bear hug, then somewhat surprised, turned to Nathan.

"I thought. . ."

Cynthia, noticing the exchange, took Jacob by the arm. "I lost the baby several days ago, Jacob. An accident. That's why we weren't here sooner."

"Oh, I . . . I . . . but you're all right now?"

Cynthia was sure she saw a blush on his dark face. "Yes, I'm fine, Jacob. Just tired."

Nathan came around the end of the wagon holding little Nate. Cynthia turned.

"Jacob, I'd like you to meet Nathan Garrett Carver Tolliver. We call him Nate for short."

"I should hope so." Jacob took the boy and held him up at arm's length. "By golly if he don't look just like his daddy."

Cynthia saw Nathan wince and turn away to get their things out of the wagon. She went to him and laid a hand on his arm. Jacob shooed everyone back toward the house.

478

"Nathan, I . . . I'm at a loss for words. My . . . my gratitude is too deep for . . . for expression. How will I ever thank you?"

Her green eyes were swimming with tears as they met the soft gray of his. "Just be happy, Cynthia. That's all I ask. Just be happy."

"Won't you stay awhile?" she asked as he motioned to one of the blacks and handed their meager belongings over.

"I can't. I've dreaded this moment for a long time. Now that it's come, I don't care to prolong it."

"Will . . . will I ever see you again?"

He smiled. "Of course you will. We're practically neighbors. Just . . . just don't invite me to the wedding. I don't think I could stand that."

Cynthia forced a smile. "Of course. I'll remember."

Nathan climbed into the wagon. "Take good care of my namesake. I'll come see him sometime."

"Please do, Nathan. Anytime. Anytime at all."

He slapped the reins against the horses' rumps and the wagon lumbered away. He turned to wave and Cynthia raised her arm in response. She watched until he was out of sight.

Forty-Two

Hindered by spring storms, the *William and Mary* dropped anchor in the Savannah River days later than expected. Garrett was among the first to go ashore. He went immediately to Alex's house where he stayed only long enough to give Alex his report, collect some supplies, and saddle Temple, who had been left in Alex's care for over six months. Alex agreed to see that his belongings were claimed and sent to Garidas. Impatient as he was, he let Temple set the pace. His destination was the Jameison plantation. He had only to stop in Birdsville to ask directions from either Thad or the Gilmores. He leaned more towards Thad who he knew would ask fewer questions. He had Cynthia's papers in his pocket, and the money Samuel Fawley had sent him through the London agent was tucked safely in his saddle bags.

Two days later, tired and hungry, he rode into confusion. As he came in sight of the house at Mountview, a young man about his size, though fairer, was sprinting across the clearing toward the slave quarters. A movement on the porch of the main house caught his eye and it was immediately evident why the young man was in haste. The woman standing on the porch was wielding a large pistol. Instantly, the pistol was trained on him.

"Get off my land!" she screamed. "I don't need a man—any man. Now get!"

Garrett raised himself in the stirrups to announce

his business and that was the last thing he remembered.

"Get him out of here, Nathan Tolliver, and yourself with him!" she screamed as the smoke cleared. "Go grub on your measly little acreage. See how far you get without my help. If you ever again set foot on any part of Mountview, I'll kill you. Do you understand? So help me, I'll kill you." Elizabeth Jameison turned, walked into the house and closed the door.

Nathan hurried to the side of the unfortunate intruder. Thank God you aren't hurt badly, he thought as he examined the crease on the man's forehead. Nathan had never seen him before, and apparently, neither had Elizabeth. He felt sure she wouldn't try to scare off an acquaintance, though he had to admit that lately it was difficult to ascertain what Elizabeth would do. Only hours before she had regained her senses and found out he had sold Cynthia's indenture. He had expected her to be angry and perhaps even let him go as overseer, but he hadn't expected such outrage as this or her threat to kill him. He brought the stranger's horse close and with the help of one of the blacks, loaded the inert body across the saddle.

"Nathan." It was Naomi just coming out of the house. "Nathan, you need help?"

"No, he ain't hurt bad. Just knocked out. I can handle it. I'm taking him to my place."

"Who is it?"

"Don't know. Never saw him before."

"Well, if you need help, come get me."

Nathan waved his acknowledgment as he led the horse toward the road. Naomi paused slightly as she opened the door. Even from this distance and angle she had a feeling there was something familiar about the man on the horse.

It was almost dark when they reached the crude lean-to Nathan had built. He now wished he had more substantial lodgings, but had had no need before tonight. Logs lay nearby and were ready to be split and erected into a cabin, but there had been no time with the clearing of the land this past year. Nathan eased the man to the ground in front of the lean-to, took him beneath the arms and dragged him to the back of the shelter, covering him with his own blanket which he untied from behind the saddle. Then, taking the bucket he had left on his last visit, he mounted the horse and headed to the river for water. He was back within minutes. His patient hadn't moved. After staking and unsaddling the horse, he quickly laid kindling, struck a flint to it then began to peruse the man's saddle bags for supplies.

Garrett opened his eyes to firelight. He blinked several times to bring his surroundings into focus. The young man he had seen running across the clearing was going through his things. He tried to find his voice, but his mouth felt dry and pasty. What if Cynthia's money was discovered?

"Leave it alone," he finally croaked. "Leave it alone or I'll kill you."

Nathan turned, startled. "Now that's the second threat I've had in little over an hour, and it appears to me that you're hardly in a position to be making one."

Garrett raised on one elbow. His head throbbed. He fell back.

"I'm not a thief," his companion said. "I was looking for supplies. Do you have any?"

Garrett nodded and motioned toward the small canvas sack partially hidden by the saddle bags. He closed his eyes and waited for the throbbing to subside, as he heard the young man rummaging through his meager supplies.

"Well, we won't dine royally tonight," Nathan said as he spread out the sack and laid the hardtack, dried meat and fruit on top of it. "But I can go hunting at first light for breakfast, or fishing if you prefer fish."

Garrett opened his eyes. "Water. Do you have any water?"

Nathan took the tin cup that had fallen out of the bag, rinsed it out, filled it and handed it to Garrett. "How are you feeling?"

Garrett sipped the water, rinsed his mouth and spat before he spoke. "Like a herd of horses are running around in my head. What happened?"

"She clipped you a good one. Knocked you out. Don't think she meant to, though. I think she only meant to scare you off."

"Who is *she?*" he asked as he dipped his handkerchief in the water and put it to his forehead.

"Mrs. Jameison, owner and mistress of Mountview," Nathan said as he reached for a piece of dried meat.

"Elizabeth Jameison?"

Nathan nodded, chewing.

"Whew! I heard she was such a lady—and pretty, too."

"She is, or rather was, on both counts till her husband's accident. Been real strange ever since. Kinda has spells where she don't know nothing."

"Who are you?"

"Nathan Tolliver. Up until a few hours ago, overseer of Mountview—now just a fifty-acre farmer."

"Well, Nathan Tolliver, I guess I owe you a debt

of gratitude." He paused. "I came to see Mrs. Jameison on business. Perhaps tomorrow will be a better day."

Nathan shook his head. "I doubt it. She's not so tolerant of men lately. She probably won't even see you. What kind of business?"

"She has an indenture I have business with, a Cynthia Fawley."

Nathan swallowed so fast he choked. "Cynthia?"

"Yes. Tell me, how is she?"

Nathan cleared his throat before speaking. "Don't know. Her indenture was sold 'bout two months ago. Who are you, anyway?"

"Sold! But it can't be. Not when I've just found her. Who to? Surely you know that much. Where can I find her?"

"Are you her husband?"

"Not yet. I'm Garrett Carver. Tell me where she is."

Nathan started laughing. "I should have known. I should have known without asking. You know, Mister Carver, I've had no real desire to meet you. I even told Cynthia don't invite me to the wedding."

"What are you talking about? Tell me where she is or I'll. . ." Garrett tried to stand and bumped his head on the low roof. He sat back down with a thud, his hand on the back of his head.

Nathan reached for a piece of hardtack. "She's at your place."

Garrett eyed him suspiciously. "My place? But you just said her indenture had been sold."

"It was. I sold it to your partner. She's there now, safe and sound. Jacob told me not to tell anyone, but I'm sure he didn't mean you." Nathan was grinning, showing even white teeth. "Sorry I didn't tell you right off. I thought you might be her husband come to find her."

"He's dead," Garrett said. "Has been all these months."

By the time they had finished the meager fare supplied from Garrett's bag, each had told the other of the recent events concerning Cynthia. The fire died down so they stretched out to sleep in the close confines of the lean-to, each with his own thoughts.

"I'll go with you in the morning, Garrett, just in case you're woozy from that crease in your brow," Nathan finally said as he looked up at the starry sky.

"I appreciate your concern, Nathan, but it's not necessary."

"I know. I'd just feel better knowing you got home safely. Wouldn't forgive myself if you didn't, not after Cynthia waited all this time."

"But you haven't a horse."

"Naomi will bring me one if I ask. Mrs. Jameison'll never know."

"If you're sure. I'd welcome the company."

Nathan turned on his side away from Garrett. "I wish I didn't like you so damned much. I didn't want to. I was prepared not to."

Unable to think of an answer that would soothe Nathan, Garrett remained silent, closed his eyes and thanked the heavens he had met Cynthia before Nathan had.

She had chosen the room next to Garrett's until his return and by now, Cynthia felt very much at home at Garidas. She saw and felt luxuriousness all about her, in the house, in its furnishings and was once again impressed with Garrett's impeccable taste and the richness with which he enjoyed life. Every aspect of the plantation seemed to run smoothly like a finely-tuned instrument and all her wants and needs were taken care of by everyone around her. Not enough could be done for her and little Nate. He had learned how to navigate the long stairways and ran freely about the house, never far from loving, helping hands. Jacob actually doted on the toddler and Cynthia was amused at the budding relationship. If she scolded the boy he would go looking for "Akup" to make things better. Though Jacob was never far away and had never directly interfered with her disciplining of little Nate, on the rare occasions when he needed it, she suspected he would undermine her authority in small ways much like a grandfather might.

Amid all this splendor, she was still not happy. She missed Garrett sorely and had been disappointed for many days now as she watched the long drive—ever since Jacob had told her they could expect him home any time. She willed the time to go faster. She knew she was becoming short with everyone and was especially curt with little Nate whenever he tried to interest her in something. She was worried and had seen the same look on Jacob's face at the breakfast table, though neither had spoken of their thoughts to the other.

Little Nate was napping. Jacob had suggested she do the same but she was restless. She wandered from room to room and finally out onto the porch, her eyes going automatically to the long curve of the drive. She sat down on the top step. Why did she feel so much like crying?

"This will never do," she chastised herself aloud. "I'm safe. I'm free and surely today he will come. He just has to. I can't stand this waiting much longer." If he doesn't, she thought, I'll ask Jacob about going to Savannah. Surely the waiting will be easier there.

Nathan reined in his mount by the cabin at the end

of the drive to Garidas. "This is as far as I go, Garrett. I think it's safe to let you go the rest of the way on your own."

Garrett halted Temple and turned in the saddle. "You won't stay for supper." It was a statement rather than a question.

Nathan smiled. "There are some things I don't care to be a party to."

Garrett nodded his understanding and held out his hand. Nathan took it.

"There's so much I owe you. Perhaps some day. . ."

"Perhaps," Nathan said as he withdrew his hand, turned and rode away.

Garrett sat watching him for a moment, then turned Temple into the drive. He urged her to a gallop as the house came into view through the trees. For a long time he hadn't been sure that was what he wanted, but when he saw Cynthia running toward him, even more beautiful than he remembered, he knew this as the fulfillment of all his dreams.

Epilogue

They reined in when they came to the drive leading to Mountview. She wanted a moment to prepare herself for what she would find beyond the grove of trees.

"You sure you want to go alone?" he asked.

Green eyes met blue with confidence. "I have to. This was a part of my life you didn't share. I refuse to involve you with it now. I have to find out. You do understand that, don't you?"

"I do." He looked around. "I'll wait for you by that fallen log over there."

She looked in the direction he indicated and nodded, then her eyes came back to his. "I love you," she whispered.

"And I, you."

She raised her arm and slapped the reins against the mare's rump. The horse broke into a trot and in the short distance from the road to the clearing where the drive ended she relived in her mind the time she had spent here.

Too much tragedy in that house, she thought, as she reined in and sat viewing the two lone black sentinels which was all that remained standing. It's good it's gone.

Movement in the rubble caught her eye. She knew even from where she sat it was Nathan. He saw her at almost the same instant and began to pick his way through the debris toward her. She urged the horse forward and met him where the front steps once stood. Soot streaked his blond hair and face, and covered his clothing and bare arms. He tethered the horse and moved to help her down, but noticing the grime on his hands and the finery of her clothing, backed away apologetically.

"It's all right, Nathan. I'm washable," she laughed nervously.

His gray eyes pierced hers. "I daren't touch you, Cynthia, for I'd never want to let you go."

"It wasn't meant to be, Nathan."

"No, I guess it wasn't." He half turned from her.

"Besides, I heard you were married to Janie Gilmore. Children, too." She saw him wince and wished she hadn't said it. He didn't deserve it.

"Aye," he said. "It's a good marriage. Fine kids." He turned to face her. "But I don't love her, not the way I love . . . loved you."

"Please don't, Nathan. Can't we be friends? We were when I left."

He just stood there a moment looking at her before he smiled. "Aye, Cynthia, we can and I'll be grateful for it. It's more than some have."

"Then lend me just one hand, friend," she spoke as she extended a gloved palm toward him, "so I can at least dismount in a ladylike manner."

Once she was on the ground he turned to survey the rubble. "I'm sorry, Cynthia. I thought I was over us years ago but . . . it's just . . . there's been so much remembering these past several weeks. I've been trying to get it cleaned up for you, though."

"For me? But you didn't even know I was coming."

"Figured you'd come soon as you could once you heard 'bout your new holdings."

"My what? Nathan, look at me. My what?"

He turned, his soft gray eyes puzzled. "You mean you don't know she left all this to you?"

"Me? But why?"

"She loved you, too. In a strange way maybe, but she loved you. Many's the time she said you were the closest thing to a sister she ever had. You shoulda come back to see her, Cynthia, you really shoulda."

Bewildered, Cynthia sat on the tethering block. "I couldn't Nathan. I just couldn't come back here. You know that. Not until now, that is."

"If you haven't heard, why *are* you here?"

"To see you. I heard about the fire and I had to find out what happened. I had to see for myself that it was really gone."

"It's really gone and her with it."

"Where . . . where is she?"

Nathan nodded eastward. "Over there. It seemed the logical place."

"Not beside him?"

"Not right beside him, but close. I couldn't bring myself to put her right beside him, knowin' how she hated him."

Cynthia smiled at his small final gesture to Elizabeth. "How did it happen, Nathan? An accident?"

"She set it deliberately. Naomi tried to stop her but Elizabeth locked her out."

"Where's Naomi now?"

"In her cabin. I just left her napping. Her health is failin' some these days. She's all that's left now, you know. Elizabeth sold off all those she could. The older ones died. She tried more'n once to chase Naomi off but Naomi stuck by her. She remembered Elizabeth like she used to be, before you left."

"It started back then, didn't it? After the accident."

Nathan nodded. "Over the years it just got worse. She did seem a bit like her old self for a spell after Jane and I got married, but it didn't last. There were too many ghosts for her here. She shoulda moved away."

Cynthia nodded, then spoke quietly. "And how are you, Nathan? You're looking well."

He smiled. "I am. We all are, 'ceptin' Naomi. She could use a change."

"I'll send a coach for her as soon as I return to Garidas," she promised. "If . . . if you think it's a good idea."

"You could take Jameison's coach. Won't be nobody around here needin' it."

"No . . . no, I can't. I want nothing to do with anything he was a part of."

"Then what are you gonna do with the property? I understand this isn't all of it, either."

"I . . . I'm not sure. I'll have to think about that and talk it over with Garrett."

"Where is Garrett? He didn't let you come alone."

"No, of course not. He's waiting for me. I . . . I wanted to do this alone," she added when she saw the look in his eyes.

"He's well?"

"Yes, he's well. Quite well, thank you."

"And the boy?"

"He has ways about him that remind me of you, Nathan. He's eight years old now, you know, and has a brother and a sister."

Nathan nodded. "Does he remember me at all, Cynthia?"

"I don't think so, not anymore. He did at first, of course."

"Maybe we'll come visit soon and I can see him

". . . just see him, that's all."

"Of course, Nathan. I wish you would. You're welcome any time. I . . . I'd better go now. Garrett will be worried."

"You won't get him and stay for dinner? Jane'll be disappointed."

"Please give her our apologies, but Garrett has business in Birdsville tomorrow. We have to get back."

He moved to help her mount. "Garrett's a lucky man," he spoke close to her ear.

"Thank you, Nathan," she said without turning, "but I'm the lucky one." Once she was settled in the saddle she looked down at him. "I know of no other woman so fortunate as to be loved by two of the finest men living." She reached out and touched his cheek. "Goodbye, Nathan."

She turned the horse and rode across the clearing, stopping at the drive to wave. Nathan raised his arm in return.

"I was about to send in a rescue team, Mrs. Carver," Garrett said when she rode up to him.

She laughed good-naturedly. "Why, Mr. Carver, were you worried?"

"Only about Nathan," he teased. "I know the effect you have on men."

Garrett mounted and they turned the horses south toward Birdsville.

"We have to go to Savannah before we return home, Garrett."

"Savannah? Why?"

"Nathan said Elizabeth left me all her property. I want to give Mountview to him. We have to go to Savannah to do something like that, don't we?"

"Yes, yes we do."

"Then we will. We can get the supplies we need in

Birdsville and oh, yes, we have to send a message to Jacob to send a coach for Naomi. She was napping and I didn't get to see her, but she's ailing and Nathan believes a change might help her. I . . . I guess she's mine, too. No, that couldn't be. Elizabeth gave her her freedom years ago. Well, maybe she'll want to live with us . . . maybe . . ."

"Wait . . . wait a minute." Garrett reined in his horse as he reached out and stopped hers. "Cynthia, do you realize what a constant amazement and joy you are to me?"

Her eyes sparkled with happiness. "Really?"

"Really," he said as he led her horse off the road into the dense forest.

"Garrett, here? Now?"

"Why not?"

Cynthia giggled with pure pleasure as she slid from the saddle into his arms.

EXCITING BESTSELLERS FROM ZEBRA

PLEASURE DOME (1134, $3.75)
by Judith Liederman
Though she posed as the perfect society wife, Laina Eastman was harboring a clandestine love. And within an empire of boundless opulence, throughout the decades following World War II, Laina's love would meet the challenges of fate . . .

HERITAGE (1100, $3.75)
by Lewis Orde
Beautiful innocent Leah and her two brothers were forced by the holocaust to flee their parents' home. A courageous immigrant family, each battled for love, power and their very lifeline—their HERITAGE.

FOUR SISTERS (1048, $3.75)
by James Fritzhand
From the ghettos of Moscow to the glamor and glitter of the Winter Palace, four elegant beauties are torn between love and sorrow, danger and desire—but will forever be bound together as FOUR SISTERS.

BYGONES (1030, $3.75)
by Frank Wilkinson
Once the extraordinary Gwyneth set eyes on the handsome aristocrat Benjamin Whisten, she was determined to foster the illicit love affair that would shape three generations—and win a remarkable woman an unforgettable dynasty!

THE LION'S WAY (900, $3.75)
by Lewis Orde
An all-consuming saga that spans four generations in the life of troubled and talented David, who struggles to rise above his immigrant heritage and rise to a world of glamour, fame and success!

Available wherever paperbacks are sold, or order direct from the Publisher. Send cover price plus 50¢ per copy for mailing and handling to Zebra Books, 475 Park Avenue South, New York, N.Y. 10016. DO NOT SEND CASH.

BESTSELLING ROMANCES BY JANELLE TAYLOR

SAVAGE ECSTASY (824, $3.50)
It was like lightning striking, the first time the Indian brave Gray Eagle looked into the eyes of the beautiful young settler Alisha. And from the moment he saw her, he knew that he must possess her—and make her his slave!

DEFIANT ECSTASY (931, $3.50)
When Gray Eagle returned to Fort Pierre's gates with his hundred warriors behind him, Alisha's heart skipped a beat: would Gray Eagle destroy her—or make his destiny her own?

FORBIDDEN ECSTASY (1014, $3.50)
Gray Eagle had promised Alisha his heart forever—nothing could keep him from her. But when Alisha woke to find her red-skinned lover gone, she felt abandoned and alone. Lost between two worlds, desperate and fearful of betrayal, Alisha hungered for the return of her FORBIDDEN ECSTASY.

BRAZEN ECSTASY (1133, $3.50)
When Alisha is swept down a raging river and out of her savage brave's life, Gray Eagle must rescue his love again. But Alisha has no memory of him at all. And as she fights to recall a past love, another white slave woman in their camp is fighting for Gray Eagle!

TENDER ECSTASY (1212, $3.75)
Bright Arrow is committed to kill every white he sees—until he sets his eyes on ravishing Rebecca. And fate demands that he capture her, torment her . . . and soar with her to the dizzying heights of TENDER ECSTASY!

Available wherever paperbacks are sold, or order direct from the Publisher. Send cover price plus 50¢ per copy for mailing and handling to Zebra Books, 475 Park Avenue South, New York, N.Y. 10016. DO NOT SEND CASH.